SPYDER
HOLE

SPYDER HOLE

BOB NESOFF

ARPress
45 Dan Road Suite 36
Canton MA 02021

Hotline: 1(800) 220-7660
Fax: 1(855) 752-6001

Ordering Information:
Quantity sales. Special discounts are available on quantity purchases by corporations, associations, and others. For details, contact the publisher at the address above.

Printed in the United States of America.

ISBN-13:   Softcover   979-8-89389-215-4
            eBook   979-8-89389-216-1

Library of Congress Control Number: 2024905937

CONTENTS

ACKNOWLEDGEMENT

Few undertakings are as solitary as writing. But even that can't be done entirely alone. To my good friend, Howie Cohn, thank you for undertaking a review of the copy to catch any typos I may have missed. To my Brothers in the Special Forces Motorcycle Club, Bill "Murph" Murray, Tom Brown, Pete Rebsch and Ben Vasquez for being an inspiration for what a Special Operator should be and truly always had my 6. Also, to Maj. Gen. Tom Needham for looking over the manuscript and his kind words that are on the back cover. Tom was a Green Beret and had a distinguished military career. While most of the character names in the book are fictitious, one is not. Col. Joe McCrane was my commanding officer in the 11th Special Forces Group and truly epitomized what a Special Forces operator should be. He left us way too soon. Mention must be made of the love of my life, my wife, Sandy, for putting up with night after night sitting alone while I hit the keys to complete this manuscript. In fact, the book would never have been completed had she not in sweet, dulcet tones said: "Either finish the damn thing or forget about it." My grandchildren, Amanda, Matt and Kyle wanted to be included. Checkout the characters of those names.

Spyder Hole is meant to not only tell a story of what is entirely possible in a world of political correctness, but of the brave military that protect us all. My hat is off to the Green Berets, CIA, SEALS, Marine Recon, MI-6, SAS, the Mossad and Sayaret Matkal for all they do to protect the entire world. And they do it with little to no fanfare. The end result is the important thing, not personal glory.

Got Your 6
Bob Nesoff

"For it is written that a son of Arabia would awaken a fearsome Eagle. The wrath of the Eagle would be felt throughout the lands of Allah and lo, while some of the people trembled in despair still more rejoiced; for the wrath of the Eagle cleansed the lands of Allah; and there was peace"
Qur'an (9:11)

"I fear we have woken a sleeping tiger"
Isoruku Yamamoto
Japanese Admiral
December 7, 1941

"If you slap me in the face, I'm not the type of person who'll turn the other cheek. You slap me in the face; I'm going to kick the shit out of you."
Anthony Imperiale
New Jersey State Senator
1970

I

BLOOD ON THE BEACH

July 1, 2001

Hesh Whitman tilted his head back, relaxing as the rays of the early morning sun warmed the muscles of his body. It had been a hell of a week and it was good to have a couple of days off. The penetrating heat of the rising sun sank deep into his neck as he moved his head from side to side, listening to the crackling of his joints.

A smile crept across his face as he stole a glance at the shapely body on the beach blanket alongside of him, the almost non-existent bikini bottom covering the most beautiful set of buns he had ever seen; the tie-string top casually draped, unbound on the blanket.

He looked around the beach as he leaned on an elbow. Weekday mornings were always quiet and there were no more than about two dozen other sun worshippers spread out across the length of the white sand beach. The granules looked as though they had been bleached by the sun as they glistened toward the edge of the rippled waters gently flowing in from the Red Sea where the waves darkened the moist sand.

The waters, lapping at the shore had a peaceful affect on him as he lay there watching the narrow, smoky contrails of a jet lazily streaking across the sky heading on a course for Europe and moving far ahead of the trailing sound of its engines.

The beach at the Gulf of Aqaba near Eilat and barely a stone's throw in from the Jordanian border was cove-shaped and ringed with high dunes, creating a natural barrier that seemed to keep the outside world and its troubles at bay. Hardly a wisp of wind found its way over the tops of the dunes and the water, out to the dual points of the pincer ends of the cove, was a series of gently rolling waves that showed no foam and didn't break until only yards from shore.

Even though Eilat was considered a strategic location, only a few kilometers east of the border with Jordan and near the Egyptian line, it had become a popular place for both Israeli and Arab sun worshippers, a sort of neutral zone where all could relax in peace without giving any thought to international politics. It was an unspoken rule that all were cut of the same cloth, equal to one another and any hint of political discussion was shunned.

Hesh and Shoshanna had been unable to take a proper honeymoon but belatedly had managed a week away at the hedonistically named "Herod's Forum," one of the more upscale hotels at Eilat and decided to stretch their budget a bit more by booking a corner suite overlooking the sea.

The night before they had spent hours dancing, pressing their bodies close to each other, in the Red Night Club at Herod's and then back to the suite for a continuation of the night's entertainment.

It was so relaxing that none of the beach goers had even stirred off their blankets to venture into the water, opting instead for the quiet time before the mid-morning buses arrived with hordes of vacationers and their little rug rats scampering across the beach kicking up sand.

Hesh smiled as his bride of less than a month shifted slightly and then moved her torso back and forth to create an indentation for the comfort of her plump breasts, jutting white from under her arms. She purred softly as Hesh slowly stroked the middle of her back with his index finger, pushing aside a few grains of the sugar white sand clinging together in the slight drops of perspiration beading up on her tanned skin.

Playfully, he moved his hand along her waist and down to the blanket, then under her stomach. His finger moved slowly between the blanket and the flatness of her stomach, even flatter from the pressure of her body. His finger crept toward the tiny triangular piece of cloth only slightly smaller than the one covering her buttocks.

She tilted her head slightly towards him and mouthed the words "I love you," just as he reached the top of the triangle. Hesh slid his fingers between the cloth and her stomach, then down and playfully yanked at the fine, curly pubic hairs.

Startled, Shoshanna sat bolt upright, letting out a sharp cry of pain. She reached across the blanket and shoved Hesh's face down into the sand, adding a dirty look to express her displeasure as he laughed at the topless beauty glaring down at him.

With a gasp, Shoshanna realized she had come up without the top to her bikini and was sitting there, breasts exposed. With her left hand covering as much as possible, she poked Hesh in the ribs with her right hand and then reached down for her top.

Hesh winced as her jab caught him off guard and then turned toward her, laughing as she sat with a scowl that turned to a half-smile on her face as she struggled to place the covering over her breasts. She looked around the beach and relaxed as she realized no one had been close enough to see what happened. Shoshanna's dignity was intact…almost. The others on the beach had yet to move; it was quiet, it was peaceful and it was a catharsis for all who were there.

He watched her face with fascination as she grimaced with the job at hand and then, suddenly, turned curious as a red splotch appeared on her forehead. There was a smacking sound and a splatter of skin and bone as her face jerked upward and her body sank slowly to the blanket. Shoshanna's legs, almost straight out, moved in short, jerking motions, her shoulders keeping the same beat as her body convulsed.

Blood poured from a hole in her forehead as her lifeless form stopped all movement.

A second shot cracked from atop the dunes and Hesh felt the searing pain as a bullet ripped into the fleshy part of his thigh. Still, he sat there, too stunned to move, staring first at the dunes and then to the bleeding, lifeless form that only seconds before had been his bride and then back to the dunes. He was frozen to the spot, a sudden welling of emotion in his stomach with bile creeping into his throat.

The quiet scene erupted into confusion and screaming as the other beachgoers came off their blankets, running, but not knowing where to run for safety on the open and exposed beach. The space between the blankets and the dunes was wide open with no cover or protection from the withering fire that now came their way. Some hopelessly tried to burrow their way into the sand while others simply panicked and ran, only to fall and stain the sand red as bullets ripped into them.

Snipers had set up positions on the southern end of the dune and separated themselves by a hundred yards, permitting them to cover the beach in a crossfire that allowed no escape. The concentrated fire took its toll as bodies, Israeli and Arab vacationers alike littered the white beach.

Hesh lay still, knowing that any movement would bring another bullet tearing into him and with the horrible realization that there was nothing at all he could do for Shoshanna or any of the others. All he could do was to try and save himself.

The cries of pain and agony from the women and small children were mixed with fear and bewilderment. Hesh watched in horror as a little girl, about four years old, stood over the body of her mother, holding the woman's lifeless hand and pleading for a response.

The girl stood there as the crackle of fire from the dune increased, kicking up spurts of sand and then her chest flew apart as a bullet tore into her. Her little body flipped up in the air and then came to rest on top of her mother.

Hesh dropped his head to the blanket and blinked as his eyes filled with sand. He waited, knowing that the killers on the crest of the sand dunes would soon work their way down to the beach to finish their job, eager for the coup d'grace, putting a final bullet in the head of any who showed even the slightest glimmer of life.

"Bastards!" he screamed, with no sound coming from his mouth. "How the hell did those assholes in security ever let these animals get through?"

The numbness and pain of what lay on the beach in front of him was overwhelming. Every muscle in his body felt as though they would burst and his heart pounded, trying to tear its way through his chest.

Tears ran down his face, mixing with the sand in his eyes as he looked at Shoshanna, the back of her skull ripped off and her face covered with blood. She lay partly on her back, her head tilted to one side, eyes wide open as if staring ahead in shock and disbelief, the gaping wound still pouring blood. Her bare breasts, pure white and outlined by the tan of the rest of her body, contrasted the red that now covered her.

It wasn't hard for him to play dead. He felt dead inside and Shoshanna, his life, was dead alongside of him.

The sounds of firing drew closer and Hesh knew that the killers were making their way toward the victims.

He'd have to make a move before they got to him…but what? There was no place to go; no cover.

Hesh heard repeated short bursts of fire and he knew the terrorists were making sure they left no survivors, putting another slug into each body as they passed, finishing off the wounded and adding another nail to those already dead. He knew his only chance was a dash for the water, but with a wounded leg, how fast could he run?

He tensed every muscle in his body and sprang to his feet, dashing with all the speed he could muster, to the water's edge. If he could catch them off guard for the few seconds it would take, he might make it.

Hesh felt the throb in his wounded thigh and knew he was still bleeding badly. He braced for the hot flash of pain that came with every movement. Bending into a low crouch, he sprinted for the water.

He could hear shouts of confusion and then shots whistling overhead as he prayed for the cold of the Red Sea only about thirty yards away, but what seemed to be a football field beyond him.

In mid-beach one of the gunmen stood, hesitated as he pushed back the black and white kaffiya from his eyes, took aim and squeezed off a shot at the low, sprinting figure racing for the water's edge.

Pain seared through Hesh as the slug tore into his buttocks, dragging him down into the sand. He rose and dragging his right leg, slowly tried to cover the remaining ten feet to the Red Sea.

The gunman raised his weapon and took slow, deliberate aim at the painfully staggering form. His right index finger began to tighten and slowly squeeze the trigger of the AK-47, a smile creasing his face… then suddenly relaxed and went limp as a shrill, piercing sound whistled overhead, punctuated by a staccato thump…thump…thump.

The man pushed the kaffiya, the towel-like head covering common to Arabs, from his head and looked skyward just in time to see the streaking jet coming in at him out of the sun. He couldn't see the blue Mogen Dovid, the Star of David, painted on the side of the fuselage, but he could see little orange bursts of flame spurting from the nose of the fighter.

The gunman watched in frozen fascination as a dual track of sand erupted in little puffs in a trail heading straight for him and then, involuntarily flinging his gun high in the air as the line of cannon fire struck him. It climbed his legs and chest and finally into his face, battering his body as he flew straight up and then slammed back down into the sand. He was dead before his feet left the ground.

At water's edge Hesh, oblivious to the burning of salt water in his wounds, turned, fully expecting another shot to finish him off…a prospect at that point he had little regret about. At least he'd be with Shoshanna.

Hesh saw the Arab gunman raise the Russian assault rifle and take aim. He moved slowly backwards into the cold water, the subconscious urge for survival taking dominance over his lethargic fatalism. He moved slowly, his eyes closed, waiting for the crack of the rifle and the slug that would take his life.

As he moved his injured leg gave out and he fell backwards into the sea.

An eternity of seconds passed and Hesh struggled to the surface, still expecting to collect a slug in the face. He blinked the saltwater from his eyes and looked toward the dunes. The shrieking sound overhead didn't register in his fogged mind, but he could see the terrorists racing at top speed for the cover of the dunes.

Then a second fighter streaked overhead, guns blazing away at the fleeing Fedayeen.

Hesh found himself screaming at the top of his lungs, encouraging the fighter pilots, cursing the fleeing terrorists, and crying. He sat down in the water and it was there that the rescue teams found him; the blood flow had turned to a trickle, but he was dangerously into a state of shock from both pain and loss of blood.

Slowly, the mist began to clear from his eyes and he looked up to see the face of a stranger staring back down at him.

Hesh moved to get up and out of the water and found himself covered with white sheets.

"He's coming around," the stranger's soft voice murmured.

"Capt. Whitman, can you hear me? Welcome back. For a while we weren't sure you'd be staying with us. Your wounds aren't too bad…

superficial for the most part, but you did lose a lot of blood and you didn't appear to be fighting."

"I suppose I should say something bright and original like 'Where am I? Who the hell are you? So, if you don't mind, why don't you just cut the crap and answer the questions?"

"The same smart ass. You never change, do you?" came a familiar voice from somewhere on the other side of the hospital room. "Just relax for a few minutes and we'll fill you in on everything."

With difficulty, Hesh lifted his head from the pillow to search out the speaker. The pain, reduced to a dull throb from the white hot and searing flashes through his body, was almost tolerable as he leaned on his side.

Turning his head, Hesh spotted the smiling face of Dan Halevi, his boss. He sank back on the bed and let his muscles relax for the first time since the shooting had begun.

"You had us worried for a while, pal. We expect casualties while you guys are working, but this business of getting your ass shot up on the beach is a bit unorthodox."

Dan's voice still carried more than a little trace of his New York City background. Unlike Hesh, who was a Sabra, native born to Israel, he had come to the embattled country less than half a dozen years before, drawn by the lure of a Jewish homeland and the need to do something to help it.

Hesh's eyes misted over as he looked toward Dan.

"Shoshanna…?"

"Kid, she's gone. That first bullet took her right out…she didn't feel a thing. But you knew that without asking."

Dan's voice dropped to a soft, almost whisper-like tone. It hadn't been too many weeks ago that he stood shoulder to shoulder with Hesh as best man at his friend's wedding, the two of them watching Shoshanna walk down the aisle on her father's arm.

Dan never knew Chava, Shoshanna's mother, but he had seen pictures of her; tall and wispy with an aura of strength that so many Israeli women exuded. The pictures showed Chava, a woman with long blond hair that cascaded down below her shoulders, ending midway toward her tiny waist; a body offset by full and firm breasts and such a resemblance to Shoshanna that they could have been twin sisters rather than mother and daughter.

Chava had met a similar fate while Shoshanna was only a child, barely beyond the suckling stage. She was at her job, caring for the small children of the kibbutz when the nursery suddenly disintegrated, the target of a PLO rocket attack, killing the beautiful young blond and almost thirty children.

Shoshanna was one of only six children who survived the attack and she spent more than two months in a hospital recuperating. She was too young to remember the horror or even her own mother, but the little jagged scar that ran down the inside of her leg was a lifelong reminder of what she had gone through.

"What about her…?" Hesh's voice trailed off. "She'll have to be…"

Dan looked at the pain-wracked young man, the words almost choking their way out of his mouth.

"Amanda and I made all the arrangements," he softly responded. "You've been here four days and we didn't know how long it would be before you came around…or if you would. The wounds weren't that serious, but you lost an awful lot of blood and were in a pretty deep state of shock."

"She's buried…and I wasn't even there?" The words hissed from between his lips with both remorse and unmitigated fury.

Hesh fell back on his pillow and lay there, staring at the ceiling, his eyes misting as he tried to control his anger.

"Look kid," Dan said, trying to break through the silent wall Hesh had suddenly put up around himself. "What can I say? Any words are going to be nothing more than a cliché, but at least you're still alive."

"Am I?"

Hesh grimaced in pain as he again pushed himself up on an elbow, aiming a cold stare that bored a laser-like hole through the doctor.

"How long before I can get out of here and get back to work?" he demanded.

"Well, aside from the major loss of blood, you seem to be healing fairly well. Your body has good recuperative powers because of your age and physical condition. I'd say that you should be out of here by the end of the week."

Hesh turned to Dan:

"Are we going after them?"

"Yes!" came Dan's abrupt reply and the tone of his voice ended any further discussion. It was something you simply didn't talk about in front of people who weren't involved.

Hesh opened his mouth to say something, but the look on Dan's face cut him off before he could speak.

The doctor motioned Dan toward the door as Hesh lay back on his pillow, his eyes closing from the strain and the effects of the sedative that was slowly dripping into his arm from the IV strung on a pole alongside the bed.

Dan reached for the doorknob to leave and, as he did, turned toward Hesh. An overwhelming sadness enveloped him, not only for the death of Shoshanna, but for the shambles that Hesh's life was in.

"Dan," came Hesh's voice, barely above a whisper. "I want in when it happens."

"Lay down and shut up. We'll talk about it when you get out of here."

Dan stepped out of the room, closed the door and walked with the brisk step that had always been his trademark, toward the elevator and out of the building.

He had wanted to talk with Hesh before the meeting in the Minister's office to see if there was any critical information he had to share. But it had taken only a moment to see that he could not lend anything of importance. Hesh was as much a victim as those who had died on the beach at Eilat… only perhaps more so; he was still alive and would suffer with the memory of it and the loss of his bride for the rest of his life.

The bright Israeli sun struck Dan as he exited the hospital and made his way toward the parking lot and the borrowed government car he had left there. In a few minutes he'd be at the airport for the quick flight back to Jerusalem.

He drove through the entrance of the small commercial airport outside the resort city and headed past the private planes, corporate jets and commuter aircraft that lined the edge of the narrow runway. He aimed for the military section that was separated from the rest of the facility by a nondescript chain link fence topped by a roll of razor wire with its sharp edges curled around the fence-top giving almost total protection from unwanted visitors.

He paused at the gate manned by a young, uniformed sentry with an Uzi sub-machinegun slung casually over his shoulder, his finger nervously wrapped around the trigger. Dan handed the soldier his ID card.

The young man stiffened as his eyes traveled from the thumbnail picture of Halevi to the inscription at the top of the card: "Institute For Intelligence and Special Assignment," in Hebrew, the official name for the Mossad, Israel's much improved version of the CIA.

The guard snapped to attention, his heels clicking loudly and smartly saluted as he bid Col. Halevi to pass.

Dan parked the car and walked to the waiting two-seater jet fighter at the ready for takeoff. He stepped into the flight suit offered by a ground crew member, pulled on a helmet and clambered up the short ladder to the second seat. Strapping himself in, he pulled the microphone to his lips and informed the pilot in a cold and matter-of-fact voice that he was ready.

The crew member didn't wait for instructions and had jumped to the nose wheel, pulling the aluminum chock that kept the sleek craft from rolling and then turned to the rear wheel chocks. He gathered their tie cords and hauled them away from the fighter.

The pilot, a 24-year-old "Yishuv," female fighter pilot, gave him a "thumbs up" sign, released the brakes and moved slowly to the taxi line. She turned onto the designated runway, revved the engine and released the brakes. As if catapulted off the deck of a carrier, the jet accelerated to full speed, raced down the runway and lifted into the air.

The pressure of the acceleration pressed him back into the soft seat, his cheeks tightened from the increasing G-force, distorting his face. The fighter lifted smoothly off the runway and climbed rapidly into the air, banking sharply to travel northward in the direction of Jerusalem.

Dan could feel his facial muscles relax for a brief second as the plane leveled off. He was suddenly slammed into the seatback as the pilot kicked in the afterburner, boosting the jet to near maximum performance and well beyond the speed of sound. He looked down as the fighter streaked through the sky and crossed over the beach that only days before had been the scene of hell and bloodshed, taking the lives of those who died as well as destroying those who lived. Today it was peaceful and vacationers had already returned to take in the pleasures of the sand and water, totally oblivious to the carnage of only a few days before.

The pilot aimed the nose skyward and began a climb through the cloud cover and into the bright, unhindered rays of the sun. Dan pulled the darkened sun visor over his face and closed his eyes. The flight would be the only small respite he would have or could expect in the coming week.

A scant two hours later Dan stood before the inner council of the Defense Ministry. Reuven Ben Chaim, Minister of Defense and Internal Security, himself no stranger to the violence of the area and in days gone by, somewhat prone to occasional tactics that might be described as terrorist by certain factions, sat back, fingers entwined across his chest and motioned for Col. Dan Halevi to make his report.

Dan looked toward "The Old Man," who was scarcely older than himself, but who had earned his reputation leading Israeli Special Forces against Arab marauders and racking up an impressive number of kills.

Ben-Chaim was a tall man, more than six feet, four inches, with graying hair and a small but widening bald spot working its way out from the middle of his head, belying his relative youth. He wore a moustache that ran down the side of his mouth, coming together to form a modified Van Dyke beard. His calm and almost cherubic face had caused more than one adversary to assume he was of little threat or consequence.

It never happened a second time.

Ben-Chaim was second in command to Jonathan Netanyahu, the brother of former Prime Minister Bibi Netanyahu, who was the only man killed in the operation to rescue the hostages in the famed operation at Entebbe Airport in Uganda.

The minister, clad in a tie-less, open necked sport shirt and sandals, sat back in his leather bound, high-backed swivel chair, his forefingers pointing away from his hands and touching at the tips. He tilted his chair back slightly and looked at Dan, barely moving his fingers in a silent order for the Mossad officer to take a seat at the table.

Ben-Chaim looked across at the half dozen men seated at the rectangular, dark conference table, leaning forward in anticipation.

The room was austere with few decorations. On the wall hung two portraits; one of Chaim Weitzman, Israel's first president and the second of David Ben-Gurion, the nation's first Prime Minister.

Across from the portraits was a picture of Orthodox Jews praying at the Western Wall, known to the Jews as the "Wailing Wall," the only remnant of King Solomon's temple and perhaps the holiest shrine to Jews worldwide; a site totally denied them during the many years of Arab control of Jerusalem.

The windowless room was designed for security to prevent external attack and for total privacy for the conversations held within its confines. Hidden behind the plaster were small tuning-fork devices that vibrated to thwart any bugs that might have escaped the frequent security checks.

"Minister, gentlemen, I am happy to report that Capt. Whitman will be out of the hospital before the end of the week once he's had an opportunity to recover from the massive blood loss he suffered. Unfortunately he was not able to add anything significant to what we already know. Once the bullets started flying and his wife was killed, there was nothing more he could do than try to save his own life.

"Our network has pieced together the raid at Eilat and the other two at the Tel Aviv marketplace and the tourist bus near Masada and there is no doubt but that they were a well coordinated effort under a single command. The main thrust was intended to cause economic injury with our tourist season beginning. But more than that, the Camp David meeting is to start soon and any disruption would have major international repercussions.

"If they can put a crimp in those talks and provoke a full scale retaliation, they've accomplished their objectives," Dan concluded.

"The Prime Minister wants us to respond immediately Col. Halevi," said Ben-Chaim in a voice that was surprising for its cold and almost emotionless tone. "He feels that if we mount a swift response, it will deter any more raids for a while."

"I disagree," came a voice from the opposite end of the table. "They always expect us to hit back and take that as the simple price they have to pay. But it gives them the opportunity to proclaim more martyrs and use it as an excuse to hit us again. They know the United Nations will ignore their provocation while it condemns our response." Shmuel Cohen, Minister of Culture, sat back and let his words bounce of the table, hoping his argument would penetrate to the hard-liners surrounding him.

"Well, we could always sit back this time and fool them by doing nothing," interjected Haym Silver, Deputy Defense Minister. "Maybe that will embarrass them into coming to the table at Camp David. They know, and you know," he said, focusing an icy glare at Cohen, "that if we do or if we don't, they will strike again. They hope it will either strengthen their position or our response will cause a backlash against us from the usual suspects and supporters. We have enough to deal with our brothers in 'Jews for Peace' and 'J-Street,' that would have us post "kick me" signs on our backs"

"Arafat has moved more to becoming a statesman than a terrorist," Cohen noted to the assembled officials. 'Even the world recognized that when he was given the Nobel Peace Prize."

"My dear Shmuel, pardon me for saying this, but that's pure bullshit," said Silver. "The man's whole life has been a lie. He claims to have been born in Jerusalem in 1924, but his birth certificate comes from Cairo. He claims to want peace, but his every action is the absolute contrary.

"He is a coward. After the so-called Six Day War he escaped Israel by dressing as a woman and carrying a baby. And he is a closet homosexual who tries to cover up with bluster and a sham marriage. So don't try to convince me that if we ignore him, he'll go away," Silver almost spat his words into Cohen's face.

Ben-Chaim moved to try and quell the rising tempers and motioned to Dan.

"Ministers, I agree that we have to do something, but I don't think it should be exactly what, where or when they expect us to respond.," Dan offered.

"What then, Colonel?"

"Our intel points pretty strongly at the Black Winter faction supported by Iraq."

"Go on."

""Salim Hassan heads that faction and our intel notes that he never sleeps in the same place for more than a night or two. That's why we've had so much trouble tracking him down. We have a source, fairly reliable, who may be able to give us a heads up on where he'll be laying his head in the next day or so."

The ministers moved closer to the table in a conspiratorial huddle. Not a word came from any of them as Halevi spoke.

"Many of our agents are non-Israelis and some of our sympathizers are not even Jewish. We've learned that Hassan has set up a station for planning and operations in Tyre. It's northern and southern sections are separated by both Israel and Syria, giving it an interesting disconnect. We're pretty sure that the plans for the recent series of raids were developed at this location. That means the top brass was present."

Dan pointed to the map attached to the rear wall of the conference room. He noted that Tyre, although it was located on the Mediterranean Sea in the northern portion of the country, gave the terrorists ample opportunity to follow an overland route through Syria and Southern Jordan to the far southern tip of Israel and Eilat. They could cross from Jordan into Israel in minutes and be at the beach, less than five kilometers from the border before they were even noticed.

"Our operative has learned that Faraq Medvi, Hassan's second in command and the architect of Black Winter's raids, will be in Tyre."

The ministers looked at Halevi with curiosity, not one of them showing any recognition of Medvi.

"His identity has been well-shielded to protect him. While Hassan seeks the publicity and notoriety for propaganda purposes, Medvi handles the day-to-day operations and may, in fact, be the actual top dog. Our information indicates that he planned these raids as well as other major operations.

"It is our recommendation that a ready team be sent into Tyre and that the Black Winter headquarters be destroyed. They would never expect such an action and it will throw them off guard. By hitting them at this location, we can put a crimp in their ability to plan raids for a long time to come."

Dan pointed to the map and noted the northern tip of Israel jutting up alongside the disputed Golan Heights to the east, separating Israel from Syria and then moving on to Jordan, bypassing the Sea of Galilee, at 209 meters below sea level.

"If we move our team through Golan, then cross through the tip of Israel we will be able to avoid detection and they would never expect an attack to come from the north. All of their resources will be aimed between Tyre and Israel. Lebanon is less than 50 kilometers wide at that point making it an easy in and easy out for our boys.

"At best we get Medvi; at the least we destroy their headquarters and send a message. If we kill him and his staff, we will have knocked out much of their high command…or at least the brains of their operation."

"Col. Halevi, thank you for your report and the paper you have drawn on the proposal for us. Please be available in the event we have any questions," Minister Ben Chaim said, leaving no doubt in Dan's mind that it was time for him to exit the conference room.

Dan turned and saluted the council with a half bow from the waist, nodding his head. He pivoted and walked rapidly from the room.

"Damn," he muttered, "put two Jews together and you could debate the placement of a dot over an "i" …put a council together and a thousand years from now they'll still be arguing over when the Exodus should begin."

He had little doubt that they would be discussing and arguing what, if any, action should be taken until the sun rose.

"Damn politicians!"

Dan left word with the Security Desk, telling them he could be reached at the King's Row Tavern on Ben Gurion Place, a short distance from the ministry. A cool drink and a bite to eat would be welcome. So would the relaxation in a cool room away from the politicians.

He walked at a quick-step down the street and through the colonnaded entrance to the tavern, squinting as his eyes adjusted to the dim light contrasting to the desert sun outside. The room was rather upscale, catering to the hordes of government workers in the area and was as secure a location as any in the city. Anyone seeking to become a martyr would have a difficult time penetrating the entrance.

From the exterior it looked similar to many other taverns throughout the city and appeared to be an easy entry. What anyone walking down the street did not see was the trained "profiler" sitting in a window overlooking the street.

Behind a door on ground level were four very burly men with forearms like the trunks of a Lebanon cedar. If they received a signal from the profiler they moved with the speed of a lightening storm into the street, grabbing the suspect, pinning arms to his side and gripping his hands to prevent the detonation of any device.

If there was a mistake, profuse apologies would follow and they would melt back into the building. If there was no mistake…and that was more often the case…the puzzled and frazzled would-be martyr was hustled out of sight and given the opportunity to spill his guts…or have them spilled on the floor.

Faced with a choice of dying slowly instead of becoming a martyr or holding a frank discussion with these ox-like men, the choice was more often than not a flow of information. Any thought of eternity with seventy-two virgins was quickly dispelled when the hopeful shaheed realized that he would be leaving this earth without the necessary equipment to make any use of heavenly female companionship.

Today Dan paid scant attention to any of this. He wanted a drink and he wanted to relax, knowing that if he was given the green light the next few days would be hellish.

Sitting at a corner table, his back against the wall, his eyes focused on the entrance, he could see everyone who entered the tavern. Dan ordered a rum and Coke, known in the Caribbean as a "Cuba Libre," a Free Cuba, a habit he had picked up on the boardwalk in New York's Rockaway peninsula at Schechter's Bar and Deli and then refined the taste in the Caribbean where rum was both plentiful and dirt cheap.

As he relaxed and slowly sipped the drink, memories began to flash back…his enlistment in the U.S. Army after graduating from C.W. Post College on Long Island; deciding to put his ROTC training to good use in the extreme by volunteered for Special Forces, the elite Green Berets. He could still feel the strain of the pre-breakfast five mile run followed by a brisk crawl through the Carolina swamps. Parachuting into Panamanian jungles was always a joy. Sure it was.

He smiled as he remembered the day he put the Green Beret on in place of the standard Army cap he had worn. Placing his unit flash onto the front of the Beret and his second lieutenant's gold bar onto the flash, made him feel as though he had just grown six inches.

The training was suddenly put to use when Saddam Hussein invaded Kuwait and President George Herbert Walker Bush ordered American troops into the fray. Dan found himself with his team alongside Navy SEALS swimming ashore under cover of darkness, to clear the beaches for a massive troop landing.

He never thought he'd take any pleasure in depriving another human being of life, but that changed after what he had witnessed the day he moved over a dune and slit the throat of an Iraqi in the process of raping a 14-year-old girl.

He always regretted the fact that they could not move fast enough to stop the Republican Guard from setting fire to the Kuwaiti oil fields and causing a major ecological disaster as the greasy smoke drifted worldwide.

Dan had never been a particularly observant Jew, but when he saw the SCUD missiles raining down on Israel and that little country sitting back and taking it because President George H.W. Bush had asked them not to retaliate and offend Arab sensibilities, it offended his sensibilities.

His anger rose watching the combined Arab nations waffle and even offer aid to Saddam Hussein and Arafat, but looked the other way at atrocities that were being committed by their kinsmen.

What Dan saw here was not an "exit strategy," but a blueprint for future disaster and the resurrection of Saddam Hussein. He saw the political "concern" over what would happen if Hussein was overthrown and the area destabilized as Colin Powell predicted.

"Shit, we took care of one little tin horn dictator and we could take care of another. You just need a pair of balls. A big pair of balls," he thought.

And that was sorely lacking in the American political establishment.

Dan returned to Fort Bragg and waited six months until his time was up, put his precious Green Beret and the uniform with a fruit salad of ribbons on the left breast, into a plastic bag, hung it in the closet and accepted early retirement. He took a job with a New York daily newspaper as a foreign correspondent and he and Amanda were off around the world.

Not long after they returned from an overseas assignment, he was approached by an old acquaintance from his Special Forces days, Matt Morton, who had gone over to the dark side of the Spook World…working for the CIA. He and Matt had gone through Special Forces training at Fort Bragg together and then, as assignments to various SF Groups were made, Matt disappeared into the dark void of intrigue.

These disappearances were not unusual and although most knew where they had gone, it was not a topic up for discussion. Every Green Beret was fodder for the clandestine world of spies. Some moved completely behind the dark curtain into that world while others maintained their military affiliation and worked with "The Company" on individual assignments. Still others maintained their role as the best Special Ops soldiers in the world.

Dan had even briefly stepped over the line and worked with them on a case involving military espionage and helped break up a cell of Marines working as Embassy security in overseas missions earning extra money selling classified documents to the Libyans. But the life didn't appeal to him and he cut it short, putting the Beret back on and rejoining the 11th Special Forces Group. They were stationed at Miller Army Airfield on Staten Island, only a stone's throw from family and friends on the Rockaway peninsula.

Matt made a cautious approach to Dan about reentering the world of Black Bag Operations. Dan's response was a slight smile creasing his face and an almost imperceptible sideways nod of his head, indicating "Thanks, but no thanks."

"If you change your mind, let me know. There's a guy in the Israeli embassy I think you might be interested in talking to."

Matt slid a piece of paper with a name jotted on it into Dan's hand and then changed the subject.

On a trip to Israel Dan and Amanda saw that except for the Ultra Orthodox, the Israelis weren't particularly religious. And the Orthodox reminded him of the Ayatollah Khomeini and his religious zealots. They too thought they were God's voice on earth and controlled much of what the government did.

Dan spent many hours fighting with himself about uprooting Amanda from the only life she had ever known, leaving her family, few in numbers that they might be, and moving half way around the world to start a new life. After weeks of inner turmoil he finally broached the subject to her.

The ever-understanding Amanda, who had been experiencing the same feelings, put up little resistance, bid her family and friends goodbye and they packed for the trip to Jerusalem. Dan contacted the Israeli consulate as Matt Morton had told him to and was put in touch with a military attaché. In short order the IDF welcomed him with a commission as a major in the Sayaret Matkal, Israel's Special Forces. He was an invaluable asset with his training in special operations and clandestine warfare.

Dan rose rapidly through the ranks to full colonel and it wasn't long before he was tapped for intelligence work, ultimately ending up assigned to the Mossad.

Dan looked up and saw the ministry clerk coming through the door, silhouetted by the bright sun streaming in behind him. He looked like some mythical creature, bathed in light, moving purposely toward Dan.

Halevi nodded, neither man speaking, got up and reached for his pocket to pay the bar bill. Dan's quick pace soon left the young man far behind as he strode across the busy street to the Ministry building for a decision he both wanted and yet, feared getting.

Less than an hour later, a broad smile creasing his face, Dan was on his way to Mossad headquarters to finalize plans for the operation. He was still dazzled by the speed and lack of red tape with which he was given permission to implement his proposal. He marveled even more when Minister Ben Chaim said the OK had come from the Prime Minister himself.

"The two old terrorists probably put their heads together and remembered what it was like a few years back," he thought to himself. "If they were still blowing up Arafat's Fatah, they damn well would have come up with something like this."

According to his plan it would take four days to get everyone in place without arousing suspicion and hoping that he would be given the go-ahead, Dan had ordered preparations to get underway.

"Easier to stop than to get a running start," he thought.

The terrorists had come to expect an Israeli response to their attacks within a week, so a diversion had to be set up. Dan ordered an easy in-easy out attack on a known Hamas training facility in Syria. The attack was to be limited to aircraft with fighter strikes only, risking no ground troops and with only minimal danger to the pilots.

"Hesh'll kill me," Dan thought. "But there's no way we can wait for him to get up to snuff."

It took two full days for his agents to work their way into place in the vicinity of the Black Winter Hamas Faction headquarters in Tyre. The building, located in the midst of a bustling marketplace, gave it a singularly inconspicuous look, but also left it vulnerable to the hordes of people passing the gate each day.

It also brought the terrorists what they believed to be a measure of greater security because the Israelis, like the Americans, went to great lengths to avoid civilian casualties in any attack. The terrorists had no such compunctions.

The air strike was slated for the morning before the planned raid in Tyre and went off smoothly with the Israelis sustaining no casualties, but with the terrorist wannabees suffering losses in men and equipment.

"Sonuvabitch!" mumbled team member Yaacov, a British expatriate Jew, as he scanned the headlines in the Jerusalem Post. "The fucking United Nations held an emergency meeting and condemned the raid against the base, but said nothing about Eilat."

The words spat from his lips in anger.

"They kill civilians, we go after terrorists and the world condemns us. Fuck them...fuck them all!!!" he said, raising the index and middle fingers of his right hand, palm facing inward, in the reverse of Winston Churchill's famed "Victory" salute. To the British this gesture was the same as an American "Middle Finger Salute."

The raid served a second purpose aside from the diversion. Agents were reporting that activity at the Tyre headquarters had picked up and several familiar faces were seen entering the walled compound.

If all went well there could be a bonus of having the hierarchy of Black Winter gathered at the compound to plan its "retaliation" against the Israelis for having the temerity to respond to a murderous attack against civilians.

"And, God willing, Medvi will be there as well."

The desert camp was a smoldering ruin and an entire contingent of terrorists lay dead in the sand. Now came the hard part...sitting and waiting until noon of the following day in order to allow as many of the Jihad leaders as possible time to gather at the compound.

And come they did with Halevi's spotters capturing pictures of several Palestinians on the Israeli "Hit Parade," entering the compound. The agents saw no one leaving, giving them confirmation that there was, indeed, a high level meeting in progress.

The hours ticked away slowly with no sign of Medvi, but a virtual Blue Book of Black Winter planners was seen gathering inside the walls.

At precisely 11:55 a.m. the first bomb exploded, producing more smoke and noise than damage. It had been planted the previous day by a Mossad agent around the corner from the entrance to the compound to draw attention away from the assault team.

With vendors scattering from their stalls, the confusion created a mob scene of Arabs running in all directions. No one paid any attention to any other activity in the area.

The first squad, dressed as marketplace vendors, hit the rear wall and scaled it in seconds. The lightweight, rapid firing Uzi sub-machineguns came out from under their Bedouin robes and before the astonished security guards could react, they were dead and the gates to Hell opened.

A scooter raced down the street to the front gates of the compound, it rider's robes flowing in the wind. He slowed at the gates and slammed a package against the wooden doors, then raced off into the confusion of the crowd. Seconds later the explosive package splintered the entrance, leaving it open to the world.

Dan led the second wave through the front gates before anyone in the street realized what was happening. A third unit remained outside to provide security, blending in with the panic surrounding the compound.

The stunned Arabs stood with their mouths agape as the Israelis stormed through the compound, racing up the stairs, firing as they went.

Precisely two minutes later another explosive device went off two streets away, drawing responding troops further away from the compound.

Dan heard the explosion as he raced at the head of his squad up the steps to the second floor of the building, firing at the now alerted guards. His rapid movement and 30-rounds-a-second Uzi cut down the first man who stepped in front of him. The man's AK-47 flew into the air as he slammed back into the wall behind him, leaving a trail of blood and bone to drip down the wall.

A second man appeared in a doorway atop the landing and then toppled over the railing and onto the floor below as Dan raked a trail of slugs across his chest, creating a dotted line of red spurts flowing down the front of his white robe.

One grenade took out the heavy door at the top of the steps and the second, a concussion flash-bang grenade, dropped everyone inside.

Leapfrogging each other, Dan and his men kept up a withering fire as they sprayed the room. They moved quickly inside, guns at the ready, only to find all those who had been at the meeting were dead. Blood and gore spattered the walls and the chairs they had been sitting on around the heavy wooden conference table, had been splintered into near toothpick-sized fragments.

It took only a fraction of a second for the attacking force to realize what they had stumbled into. Maps of the United States, Mid-East and several European countries lined the walls. Outlined in red marker were the sites of recent terror attacks while others were highlighted in yellow.

A bank of high powered radios sat in an alcove and a heavy steel safe was snuggled into a corner of the room. Two desks had been overturned, one of them falling atop three bodies lying in the middle of the floor.

Dan motioned for one of the men to help move the desk and then with the toe of his boot, began to turn the dead guerillas faces up. A smile creased his face as he looked down on the body of Faraq Medvi. He recognized the others as Medvi's top lieutenants and ranking members of the Mossad's "Most Wanted" list.

Dan reached into his pocket and removed a flat metal object the size of a credit card. The mini-camera was one of those modern techno advances that not too many years ago could only be found in the kit bag of Dick Tracey or James Bond, but today could be purchased over the counter at any Radio Shack. Dan had picked his up during his last visit home.

"I had a feeling this would come in handy," he said to no one in particular.

Motioning to one of his lieutenants, Dan nodded toward the safe and then pointed the flat, compact digital camera, snapping pictures of the bodies for later confirmed identification, as well as the maps and radio equipment. He took snippets of hair from Medvi and his lieutenants for DNA tests so there would no questions later.

His assistant began to carefully place strings of C-4 explosive on strategic sections of the safe. He looked at Dan for a sign that they were ready to go and moved through the doorway as his commanding officer replaced the little camera in his shirt pocket.

Seconds later a controlled explosion rocked the building and dust and debris blew through the doorway in a windstorm. Peering back into the room they could see the safe door ajar, hanging by one hinge.

"You're slipping," Dan said, smiling at his explosives master. "I remember when you would blow the door off and the papers would land in alphabetical order.

"Cut the shit SIR!" he replied in a mocking tone. "Let's get the crap and then get the hell out of here."

Dan pulled the little camera from his pocket again and began to take pictures of everything in the room. Then he stuffed the papers into a backpack and ordered the room to be doused with gasoline. A block of C-4, lightweight, malleable and devastating, was primed with a three minute fuse and set in the middle of the room.

"Let's move," he shouted as his strike force began to race back down the stairs, jumping over fallen guerillas and debris, noting also that miraculously none of their party had been injured.

The exterior team had been hard at work while they were inside and the entire structure had been packed with explosives as was the wall surrounding the compound.

At exactly 12:03 p.m. a series of explosions rocked the area surrounding the marketplace; mud and brick buildings tumbled down creating confusion as panic took the place of any semblance of order.

Halevi signaled his men and two minute timers were set for the charges in the building and the compound's walls. The two teams raced for the rear and the waiting Lebanese Army trucks that had just pulled up. They piled in and the trucks roared off, seemingly carrying troops being disbursed for security; or, as the local citizens had come to expect of the army, getting out of there for their own safety and to hell with anything else.

As the compound faded into the distance, the raiders could hear a roar and watched as the charges detonated and a plume of smoke rocketed skyward. In the melee at the marketplace the confused and disoriented Arabs stopped and stared as the walls and structures of the compound collapsed into a cloud of dust and a very big pile of rubble. The entire compound had imploded on itself. The double minarets and the dome of the Shia mosque that stood out so prominently as the city's lone skyscraper, was obscured by the rising cloud of concrete dust and smoke.

Dan turned to the men in the truck…"Well, Joshua, the walls came tumbling down…"

He clutched the stack of papers they had liberated from the blown safe and thought his evaluation team and intelligence experts would have a field day going over the information they contained.

Leaning back against the wooden slotted side rails of the canvas covered truck, Dan closed his eyes. He was tired…so tired. Dan peeked through his slitted eyelids at his watch. It was 12:10 p.m.

II

DEVASTATION

Classification: Utmost Secrecy

From: Director

Institute for Intelligence and Special Assignments

State of Israel

To: Director

Central Intelligence Agency

United States of America

Date: 7 August 2001

Information obtained by this agency indicates an attempt may be made by certain forces to assassinate a sovereign monarch while in New York City. Our information indicates the collaborators are high-level elements of the Black Winter Faction of Hamas and another organization as yet unidentified. Urgent that representatives of our agencies meet in neutral location to consult.

MEMORANDUM

Classification: TOP SECRET

From: Director

Central Intelligence Agency

United States of America

To: Director

Institute for Intelligence and Special Assignments

State of Israel

Date: 8 August 2001

Your message received. Suggestion for urgent meeting is agreed. Our agency recommends meeting be held two days from this date in London. Time and place to be fixed by our representative.

End….

MEMORANDUM

Classification: TOP SECRET

From: Director

Central Intelligence Agency

United States of America

To: Director

Institute for Intelligence and Special Assignments

State of Israel

Date: 8 August 2001

Additional information re London meeting. Our representative will arrive LHR (Heathrow) via Virgin Atlantic Airlines ex JFK/NY. He will transfer to the Sheraton Park Lane Hotel on Piccadilly in Mayfair and register as James Daily. Arrival at hotel timed for 1300 hours local time, 10 August 2001. Suggest your representative make contact in the Palm Court Lounge exactly one hour after arrival.

End....

MEMORANDUM

Classification: Utmost Secrecy

From: Director

        Institute for Intelligence and Special Assignments

To: Director

        Central Intelligence Agency

        United States of America

Date: 8 August 2001

Message received and agreed upon.

End….

III

DEAD MAN

"**H**e's a dead man! How long could he live even if we managed to free him,?" demanded the young man dressed in light, sand colored fatigues, a red and white kaffiyah folded neatly behind his ears.

"Sayyid, even if he lives for only one day after we have freed him, it will have served our purpose," the bearded older man replied, rising from his seat behind an ornate wooden desk. He moved slowly across the room and stood towering over his seated younger guest.

The old man stood more than six-feet tall with an upright frame that seemed to add height to his imposing figure. His young companion followed the speaker with his eyes as the grey haired elder moved easily, in spite of a pronounced limp, to the front of the desk and seated himself on its edge.

He wore the traditional flowing robe of a Bedouin chieftain that defied the heat of the Arabian Desert outside of the air-conditioned room. Overhead a fan added to the faint hum of the air-conditioner and brought a downdraft that riffed his salt and pepper beard.

The younger man, in his early twenties, was tall and well built, his hair cut short unlike the other youth of his day. He wore a black and white checkered kaffiyah head scarf and camouflage fatigues pressed with a crease sharp enough to cut a finger. He sat ramrod straight as the older man spoke.

"Sayyid," he said in a low, almost conspiratorial tone, "there are only a few of us and if we hesitate, we will all be gone. The heritage I promised your father will die with us. I know that what I am proposing may sound futile, but without it everything you have prepared for all your life will have been for nothing."

"Sir!"

"Wait, Sayyid, please. Let me finish." His voice came in a clipped, formal old school manner. "Each year our numbers dwindle; grow smaller before your eyes. But you know that without my saying so. The only way we can ever hope to gain any momentum is through a dramatic action.... an action such as we have been discussing here; one so audacious that it will set the world on fire and force them to take notice of us and impossible for them to ignore.

The old man paused long enough to permit Sayyid to absorb what was being said, but not so long that he would have an opportunity to voice an adverse opinion. It wasn't time yet.

"You have seen so many of your friends and associates, those whom you have grown up with and who have been schooled in our ways since birth, drift away. The rest of the world has only seen us on the run for half a century; they have seen our heroes kidnapped and executed by that bastard regime in Palestine...a regime that is a vilification of the human race, people we should have wiped off the face of the earth."

The old man's face had turned a bright red and spittle formed in the corner of his mouth. His voice and blood pressure seemed to be rising at the same rate, but he was on an emotional roll and seemed incapable of stopping.

"How many of us have had to run and hide like common criminals, including your own grandfather and father?" And for how many years have we had to contend with their infiltrators and agents dogging our every step?"

The old man's hands shook, more with emotion than the unsteadiness of old age, but his grip was still strong as he grasped Sayyid's shoulder.

"Your father named you for me, Sayyid, and it is my place that you will take as the head of our people, the true leader. You've been prepared for this all of your life and this is your destiny."

"Sheik, I'm sorry. I didn't mean to question what has to be done. There is no doubt in my mind that it will be done and will succeed. I am a soldier and I obey my orders."

A smile crept across the old man's face as he walked, pulling his game left leg and, once again, seating himself behind the imposing desk.

"Sayyid, I know you and your brothers will fare well. There can be no mistakes because the world will be watching every moment and every movement of this action, this drama as we play it out. What we are going to do is even more daring a plan than the taking of the Achille Lauro, or the bombing of the Marine barracks in Lebanon by our shock troops. It is far more audacious even than the raid by the interlopers in Entebbe that brought them so much cheer and respect around the world when they rescued the hostages and killed our troops. It will revitalize the spirit of our people to once again reassert themselves and take back the land that is rightfully theirs."

The sudden ring of the telephone snapped them out of their reverie and the old man reflexively reached for it. His greeting in English seemed out of place and the conversation quickly reverted to Arabic. The discussion was brief and in clipped phrases.

"Sayyid, the others are waiting for us."

Young Sayyid al Khalil Ibn Hassan rose and walked across the room, moving slowly so that the limping man could precede him without the appearance of any deference to his disability.

Twenty years before with Sayyid's father, on a raid into Israel, Hassan's knee had caught a bullet from an Israeli soldier as the men led a raid on a small farming kibbutz in northern Israel. They had just made their mark, killing fifteen men and women working in a field and nearly a dozen children attending class in the commune's nursery school.

They were running toward a fence line that acted as a demarcation between Israel and safe haven in the Arab world when they found themselves in the middle of crossfire from an army patrol. Hassan's career ended, his life ebbing into the desert sand as his friend, Sayyid, dragging his left leg, the knee shattered, crawled through an opening in the fence.

He managed to burrow into the sand and sanctuary from the vengeful eyes of the Israeli patrol.

Hours later a young goatherd bringing his flock out to search for errant blades of grass, found the unconscious man, near death, lying face down in the sand. Dehydrated and with serious sunburn. It was months before he was able to regain any mobility, but for the rest of his life the game leg was both a reminder of his hatred for the Zionists and a motivator to destroy them.

Fall 1948

At the onset of the United Nations ordered partition creating the State of Israel, the Grand Mufti of Jerusalem, the most influential Arab leader of the day, called for the total destruction of the Jews.

Leaders of the newly created state pleaded with their Arab neighbors to remain on their lands and work together to create an oasis in the desert. But most heeded the Mufti's words that promised the Jews would be destroyed and their lands divided amongst the Arab peoples.

The Grand Mufti, an ardent supporter of Hitler and the Nazi regime during the recently concluded war, carried his hatred for the Jews into his mosque and all of his preaching's.

The Grand Mufti idolized Hitler and his efficient machine for killing Jews and vowed they would never gain a foothold in the Holy Land.

June 5, 1968

Spring in Los Angeles was always a pleasure and the young couple passing the Ambassador Hotel was enjoying the weather. He held her close, his arm across her shoulders and she slipped hers around his waist.

As he leaned over to kiss her, an alley door to the hotel suddenly slammed open and a man and woman burst through it. They ran from the alley to the street yelling in delight:

"We've shot him! We've shot him!"

The young couple stepped back in shock as the man and woman approached.

"Who did you shoot?" demanded the young man.

"Bobby Kennedy," the woman declared and kept running. Her white dress with blue polka dots disappeared into the crowd walking past the hotel.

The young couple stood, frozen in their steps, watching the man and woman disappear into the early morning darkness of the street. Before they could continue walking, two rather large and burly men came rushing through the open door and up the alley toward them. These men carried guns and were shouting, demanding to know if they had seen anyone exit the building?

They related what they had seen and after providing identification, were permitted to go on their way. The next morning they were stunned to see the story in the newspaper of the assassination of Sen. Robert F. Kennedy, who had just won California's Democratic presidential primary election and the arrest of a Palestinian, Sirhan Sirhan for the shooting.

Sirhan was later convicted of murder and sentenced to death in the gas chamber. That was commuted to life imprison when the U.S. Supreme Court ended capital punishment. Despite pleas from several Arab governments for his release, Sirhan has been turned down for parole.

IV

REVENGE

"**Y**ou Goddamn sonuvabitch!" Hesh thundered at Dan.

"You gave me your word that you'd wait until I was out of the hospital before retaliating. You Goddamn promised!"

"Kid, there was no choice. You've been here almost two weeks and if we had waited, the opportunity would have been gone and wasted. As it is, we're onto something big. I promise, from this point on you are part of the entire operation. You're in it."

"Goddamn it Dan, Shoshanna was buried while I was still unconscious. Then you go after them while I'm on my back in the hospital. What the hell more is there for me to look forward to?"

"Easier to say than to do, but relax. We picked up information on the raid indicating the Rat Pack is up to a major operation. We think it's going to be in the United States, but we're not sure. It looks as though they are going to go after a prominent world figure in New York."

Hesh dropped his legs over the edge of the bed and slowly buttoned his shirt.

"Dan, she's dead. We weren't married a month and now she's gone. I was lying here while she was buried and I couldn't even say good bye. If we wiped those bastards off the map, it wouldn't be enough."

"Kid, no one ever said the world was fair. We live with the cards that are dealt to us and we either sit back or we draw to them and see if we can make that inside straight. Relax and you'll get some new cards from the top of the deck. We haven't begun to deal the hand yet."

Hesh's lip curled and his handsome dark eyes lowered. Water welled in their corners and he turned away from Dan.

"Finish getting dressed and I'll take you home and when I get back from London I'll fill you in on everything and we'll see about getting this operation underway.

Little more than two hours later Dan sat back, relaxed for the first time in days, as he looked out the porthole of the El Al 747 SP, watching the buildings breeze by as the craft lifted off the runway at Ben-Gurion for the non-stop flight to Heathrow.

The weather in London always seemed to be the same…dank, chilly and a sun that peeked out from the clouds as though it was ashamed to show its presence. Now it had fallen below the horizon of ancient homes and modern skyscrapers, casting a creeping shadow over the city's horizon.

It was dark as Dan exited the airport and climbed into one of the oversize black cabs for which the city is famous.

"Park Lane Hotel, Mayfair" he almost growled at the driver.

"Be there in a jiff, Guv," came back the cheery retort.

The ride went fast and Dan was settling down in the comfortable seat when the taxi came to a garishly lighted intersection, looking for the entire world like a miniature Times Square. Neon lights flashed on and off and on the sidewalk was a statue of the Greek god of love, Eros.

Dan looked at it sideways. It had been a while since he was here. At that time the statue was in the middle of a traffic circle, or "circus" as the Brits called it, the famed Piccadilly Circus. Now the statue was on the sidewalk in order to ease traffic at the congested intersection and the circus was out of town.

"What the hell," he thought, "my life's enough of a circus right now."

The Park Lane sat in the city's Mayfair District, not far from Oxford Street and its famed department stores. Shopping was a favorite haunt of both British and Continentals and for many Americans who crossed over to pay their dues at such iconic stores as Marks & Spencer and Harrod's.

The cab hung a right onto Piccadilly and headed away from the city center toward Green Park and Mayfair. London traffic is little different that that found in mid-town Manhattan in New York except that people drove on the other side of the road. It hardly ever lets up and this section of Piccadilly was no different.

Green Park came up on the left and Dan looked out the window to see if he could spot Buckingham Palace at the far end. The greenery was too full and the palace was no where in sight. On the right he spotted the white flag with red circle of Japan, hanging over the entrance to that country's embassy. A rather large man in a dark suit stood at the door and would effectively block any unwanted visitor from entering.

A block away he saw the distinctive "S" design of Sheraton Hotels and the Park Lane. Instead of pulling up at the Piccadilly entrance, the cabbie hooked a sharp right onto Brick Street, a narrow, cobblestoned alleyway. He moved left around the curved roadway and stopped with what actually was the main entrance to the hotel, hidden from the frantic pace of Piccadilly.

Dan peeled off several pound sterling notes, paid the drive and made an easy exit from the cab's ample door opening. Hauling his pullalong, he navigated the three steps down and walked over to the registration desk. The quick formalities done, Dan turned to the elevator behind him and rode it to his floor.

His room faced over Piccadilly, as was his preference. Rooms in the rear of the hotel faced over other buildings and offered any interloper interested in eavesdropping, a grand opportunity to do so without detection. This side, overlooking Green Park was less vulnerable, especially with the din of the traffic outside. Amazingly, as loud as the cars, trucks and buses were on the street, the noise never penetrated the serenity of his suite.

Moments later, having freshened up, Dan changed into a pressed suit and returned to the lobby.

"I'm meeting a friend," he informed the Maitre 'D., "A Mr. Morton."

"Certainly sir, please follow me."

Dan was led through the Palm Court lounge to a corner of the dining room and a table hidden from the view of the entrance, beyond the huge "groaning board," display of meats and side dishes set up in the middle of the room. The red, mid-backed chairs provided comfort and the glassed breakfront containing an immense collection of books gave the room a certain intellectual flair.

The man sitting at the table was strikingly handsome with the solid jaw of an athlete, dark hair and eyes that were as cold as a pool of ice water.

Dan knew the look. Agents who have spent any prolonged period of time "in the cold" develop it. And, as well, Dan knew the man. Frankly, just as Dan preferred to see airline pilots with gray hair indicating age and experience, he also preferred to deal with other agents "who had the look."

"Hello Matt, how are the wife and kids?" Dan intoned with warmth in his voice and a smile for a man he had not seen since his separation from the Green Berets.

Morton rose and grasped Dan with a firm handshake and then the two men grabbed each other in a tight and affectionate hug.

"It's good to see you again. How was the flight?"

Although they had served together in the American Special Forces, both played the game and went through their identification ritual. Then, with formalities accomplished, the two men had a casual dinner, savoring the thick British-style cuts of beef. Dan had a drawn look of severe disapproval and reprimand from the waiter when he ordered his steak well done "with no pink showing" and as close to cremation as possible.

The Brits do a great job on beef," he smiled at Morton. "But their style is to serve it as though it just came in on a gurney from a Red Cross blood drive. There isn't a Jewish mother in New York worth her salt who would ever serve a cut of meat that wasn't as tough as shoe leather. My mother would have done a great job with either a flame thrower or napalm."

Morton smiled and for a second the coldness of his eyes warmed up. There was an unspoken feeling between these two men, each recognizing the professionalism of the other. In their business, first and instant impressions were not only important, but frequently were a matter of life and death. They may have been soldiers together, but this was different. It was a world that Morton had lived in for much of his adult life and even with his experience Dan was not as tenured as his old friend.

Morton and Halevi had hit it off again. They knew instantly that they could work together and, more importantly, be able to safely turn their backs and be covered.

After dinner they departed the hotel and turned left, walking up the street. Traffic never seemed to ebb here and the noise it created drowned out the conversations of those passing by.

Dan spoke first.

"We can't figure out who they are going to hit, but the information we captured seems to indicate that they are going after royalty and that it'll be in the United States."

"I've checked with our State Department and the White House and neither has any information about a visiting monarch on either a state trip or informal agenda," Morton added. "We thought at first that it might be Prince Charles coming over for a polo match in Westhampton, but that was cancelled long enough ago that it can't be him."

Morton continued walking, looking at the ground as he made his way. Suddenly his head jerked up.

"Holy shit!" the words exited through his clenched teeth like escaping steam. "That's got to be it."

"What the hell are you talking about?"

"Dan, next week the United Nations is holding a major conference on aid to Third World Nations and there'll be top diplomats and government representatives from around the world. The opportunity to make a speech on that stage draws these politicians like flies on a pile of cow manure. There'll probably even be some minor royalty. Who the hell do we look for?"

"Let me add to your pleasure. Just before I left Jerusalem I was told that our crazy Rabbi and his bunch of militant juveniles, the ones who call themselves 'Response,' have announced that they'll disrupt the session if Arafat expects to speak.

"We have mishuggah Jews and mishuggah Arabs on our hands converging on the same spot at the same time. Maybe you and I ought to plan a fishing trip in the Guatemalan jungle."

Morton smiled at Dan's suggestion.

"Do you think that's far enough away so that they can't find us?"

"Nah! I guess not. It looks as though we're just going to have to see this thing through."

Morton flagged a cab and turned to shake Dan's hand.

"I'll see you in the morning. Why don't we meet at the embassy for breakfast? I want to go over this with the station chief and then talk to Washington on the scrambler to see if we can get any input from them or some updated intel.

"OK Matt. I've got to bring one of my men in from Jerusalem; one of my best agents, but he's got a lot on his mind. The Arabs wasted his wife a couple of weeks ago while they were at the seaside on their honeymoon. He collected some pretty bad wounds and wasn't able to even get out of the hospital for her funeral.

"Hesh and I have been in some pretty tight situations and I could always count on him. I just hope he can get beyond his personal grief when we deal with these bastards."

The CIA agent flagged a cab and climbed into the back seat, giving the driver instructions to Grosvenor Square and his hotel across from the American embassy.

Dan continued walking toward Oxford Street, needing some quiet, down time for himself. He smiled at the crowds waiting to get into the London Hard Rock Café and the young lovers wrapped up in each other. Pictures of Amanda and the peaceful interregnum he had between his service in the Green Berets and joining the Mossad, seemed to be two lifetimes ago.

His thoughts wandered to Hesh and then to the raid in Lebanon. He could see the PLO terrorists as bullets from the Uzi tore into their bodies. A chill ran through his back as the scenes of death and destruction ran graphically through his mind.

"When the hell does this ever stop? They kill us…we kill them…then they kill us again and we respond. Shit! There's got to be a better way."

He wandered along Oxford Street, oblivious to the famed stores lining its walk and the crowds of shoppers milling about. He passed Marks & Spencer and then turned toward Great Portland and the far end of Piccadilly, not even realizing the distance he had covered.

He hailed a cab and headed back to the Park Lane. He took the lift to his floor and walked to his room. Skirting the hotel operator, he opened his attaché case and took out a satellite phone and connected a small scrambling device to it, then placed a direct call to Jerusalem.

"Have the office cut tickets and be here by tomorrow morning. Fly in on El Al," he told an astonished Hesh Whitman. "Tell them I also want tickets for both of us from London to JFK, leaving tomorrow night on Virgin Atlantic. Have them book you First Class so that you'll be ready to roll as soon as you land. By coming in on Virgin, we'll have a separation that we wouldn't have had flying into the States by El Al. Tell them I want First Class tickets on Virgin, or 'Upper Class,' as they call it. We're going to need the comfort and rest. If anyone gives you a hard time, tell them to check with the Minister's office for approval.

"Do not discuss with anyone or say anything more than the fact that you are meeting me."

Dan replaced the receiver on its base, disconnected the little device and then picked up the room phone, leaving a wake-up call with the front desk. He lay back on the bed and was asleep before he could even dream.

V

TWIN MONARCHS

"**T**hank God that rank still has some privileges," Dan thought to himself, sinking into the comfortable wide, soft seat of the Virgin Atlantic wide bodied jet as it slowly moved from its suckling-like position at the gate, its umbilical cord disconnected and rolled toward the long, narrow strip of tarmac where it could pick up enough speed to get its ungainly tons of steel safely into the air.

The 757 slowly lifted off, becoming a swan instead of an ugly duckling, gracefully beginning an ascent over the London rooftops.

The looping North Atlantic route would take almost eight hours but the flight would be a bit more tolerable in the front of the plane rather than back in "cattle class."

Dan liked the wide seats and staggered, lateral conformation that provided absolute privacy. He and Hesh could sit across from each other, have a meal and discuss their business without danger of being overheard. Then, business accomplished, the seat rolled flat, the flight personnel provided a fitted sheet, pillow and covers and they could catch a couple of hours of comfortable sleep before deplaning at JFK. He needed his wits about him and as sharp as they could be at all times. This was one way of guaranteeing the rest and down time to accomplish that.

On this flight the plane was far from full and their seats, amidships, provided them even more privacy. The flight would land in New York early the next morning and this gave them an opportunity to relax and catch their breath for a few hours. Dan knew that once in New York the pace would become unrelenting.

The Stew came by and placed a copy of the New York Times on his tray. Dan glanced at the banner headline on the newspaper announcing the gathering of world leaders at the United Nations, then pushed it aside and closed his eyes.

September 10, 2001

The day in New York was in sharp contrast to London. The sun was shining and the air was warm and dry. The two Israeli agents collected their luggage and headed for the VIP lounge off the Customs and immigration section of the JFK's Terminal 4. Matt Morton was there with representatives of the State Department and his own agency and quietly and innocuously expedited Halevi and Whitman's official entry into the United States. From there they exited through a private portal and off to the side of the long building.

"I've got a car waiting and we'll take you to your hotel."

"Thanks Matt, but I'd rather not be seen arriving in a government car. Let's face it, they're unmarked but are so standardized that anyone can spot them from a mile away. Hesh and I will take a taxi and we'll get together with you tomorrow morning."

Morton raised his index in salute and then added his middle finger in a "peace" sign, clapped Dan on the shoulder and turned to his car. Dan and Hesh hauled their pullalongs to the taxi rank and took their place in line.

Dan gave the turbaned driver instructions to take them to the Park Central Hotel on Seventh Avenue, directly across the street from two famed New York landmarks, the musical nirvana of Carnegie Hall and its namesake eatery, the Carnegie Deli.

Dan loved New York and he especially liked the location of the Park Central, only blocks from Central Park and right in the heart of myriad activities. He always reserved a corner suite so that he could look down Seventh Avenue and into Times Square with its never ending hustle and bustle. The construction of the hotel muffled out the street noise below and gave him a silent window overlooking the "City that never sleeps."

"Do me a favor, would you please?," he said to the cabbie. "Swing up First Avenue and past the United Nations."

"You gentlemen are truly lucky," commented the driver. Dan had noted from the registration card posted on the dashboard that his name was Amit Patel; no doubt a Sikh, many of whom now seemed to be the majority of taxi and livery drivers in New York.

"How's that?"

"We should be sitting in solid traffic at this time of day. I don't know where all the cars are, but they certainly are not on the Van Wyck Expressway," he said in a clipped, formal and sing-song voice.

As the cab rumbled over the pock-marked Queensboro Bridge and onto 59th Street, Dan looked down at the murky East River below. The driver came off the bridge onto the FDR Drive and circled south to 42nd Street. He didn't mind the circuitous route because the meter was running.

He pulled off at 42nd Street and turned north on First Avenue.

"Look at the security," Dan nudged Hesh. They sure are putting on a big show."

"Sonuvabitch," moaned the cabbie in very unSikh-like language. "Here's all the traffic we didn't see before. All these cops really screw up a traffic flow."

NYPD patrol cars lined the east side of First Avenue along the curb at the United Nations building. Uniforms could be seen on both sides of the street and one Traffic Enforcement Agent, the "Brownies," despised by both cops and civilians, was valiantly attempting to make cars go the way he wanted them to instead of following the natural flow.

Hesh sat back and stared out of the cab's window as the flag lined gardens of the huge, slab-like United Nations international headquarters passed slowly. Although it sits in New York City, the U.N. has Vatican-type authority and sovereignty within its walks. NYPD and even the FBI could not enter without permission.

It took the taxi more than a few minutes to weave through the heavy traffic and then into the normally clogged Mid-Town Manhattan streets as it attempted to head uptown toward the Park Central.

"Well," Dan thought, "anyone who might even be thinking of hitting the U.N. had better be using a helicopter or a speedboat. There's just no other way to make a quick getaway in this traffic. I almost forgot what it was like and how little I've missed it."

"Holy shit!" yelled Hesh as he threw himself over Dan as he reached for his gun in one smooth motion.

"Don't do it," Dan screamed. "Wait!"

A man with a gun had suddenly appeared in front of the cab and the driver instinctively jammed his foot down on the accelerator. The car lurched forward and with no where to go in the traffic, the cabbie slammed the brake, flinging Dan and Hesh into the Plexiglas shield separating the passenger compartment from the driver. The shield had become common years back as cabbies suffered robberies and even murder for the few dollars they carried.

The man pointed his gun at the cabbie and then whirled around in the opposite direction and fired. A return shot from down the street caught him in the shoulder and spun him around in time for a second slug to shatter his spine. The man dropped the gun and slumped in a heap on the roadway.

Two uniformed cops came running up, guns drawn, and turned the body over. The gunman, who appeared to be Hispanic, was dead.

"You guys OK?" asked one of the uniforms.

"Dan struggled to get Hesh off and back into his seat.

"You know, we've got to stop meeting like this," he joked.

He inconspicuously pushed Hesh's Glock 40 under the front seat and out of view.

"What the hell happened?" he demanded.

"Can you believe this dumb shit?" the cop responded. "You got more security here than in the president's bedroom and this schmuck tries a snatch. "He grabbed some dame's pocketbook and then turned on us with a gun; but he does all of this in front of the United Nations and half of the NYPD standing around."

The cop quickly asked for and wrote down the information on their driver's licenses for his report and for them to be called as incident witnesses. Not that the information would do him any good because the Mossad Document Center provided the best forgeries in the world.

"It's a long walk to the Park Central," Dan ordered, "but it'll take them forever to sort out this traffic mess. Grab your suitcase and let's get the hell out of here."

Dan paid the cabbie, added a few extra dollars as a tip for the shortened ride and the two men began the cross-town trek. They made it to the hotel in about twenty minutes and entered the peace and quiet of the Park Central's lobby, sweat dripping from their faces.

The Park Central was ideal for his purposes; in the center of the City and yet separated from much of the frenetic activity just beyond it's doors.. It was frequented by upper class tourists, musicians because of its proximity to Carnegie Hall, and often by celebrities. But never by diplomats and intelligence agents hampered by government expense account restrictions. Because of his deep cover and position, Dan had no such restriction.

The doorman rushed to assist them, a quizzical look on his face. Not too many guests arrived sans vehicle, carrying their own luggage and soaked from sweat.

Dan had reserved a suite on an upper floor with a southern view toward Times Square and had a second, connecting bedroom for Hesh. He retrieved his MasterCard card from the clerk and headed to his left for the elevator bank.

As the doors slid shut, Hesh turned to Dan.

"Sheesh, when I saw that clown with the gun, I thought it was all over. All I could see was dark skin and his black moustache and I thought that one of Uncle Yassir's boys had tracked us down.

"It was close. All that had to happen was for the cop to have seen your gun and we'd be at headquarters right now explaining to some kid assistant D.A. why we had a piece in New York. Next time keep your hand the hell off your gun."

Goddamnit Dan, I thought that guy was going to take us out. What the hell was I supposed to do…just sit there and wait for him to shoot?"

"Under those circumstances, yes," he growled. "I don't want the State Department contacting our people to ask why two armed agents are running around in New York. The right people from their government know we are here, but we can't have political appointees asking questions. The CIA knows, but if word gets out beyond that, the whole thing will go up in smoke.

"Morton can cover some things for us, but a shooting…near the UN… impossible.

"So next time, if there is one, stay away from the gun."

Hesh's face had the look of a man hit with a sledge hammer, but he turned away from Dan and said nothing.

———•◦◦•◦◦————

"C'mon kid, I'm going to show you a sandwich the likes of which you've never seen before."

Hesh cocked his head and looked at Dan with puzzlement on his face. He turned to Morton and the CIA agent shrugged his shoulders. Obediently, the two men rose and followed Dan through the lobby and onto Seventh Avenue heading south with Carnegie Hall behind them. Two blocks later he turned into the Stage Deli as though he was simply following his nose. The three men walked in and asked for a corner table. The waiter, as brusque as would be expected from the senior wait staff of a New York deli, pointed to a table, flung the menus on the flat surface and walked away, returning moments later with three glasses of water.

"Are you ready to order?" he demanded.

"Hey, how about giving us a chance to open the menu," Dan retorted.

The man harrumphed and walked away. Hesh and Morton sat back, laughing at the scene that had just played out.

The lunch crowd had about petered out and they were almost alone in the corner of the restaurant, giving them the opportunity to talk without curious ears picking up on the conversation.

Morton spoke first:

"I have had our people going over the reports you provided and nothing seems to come together. We've gone over the list of dignitaries at the UN meeting and there are no twin monarchs expected there. We've gone over the list name by name, country by country to try and pair some of them up, but it's a zero."

Dan lowered his head and shook it from side to side.

"OK, we know that something is going to happen. But what and where? You don't need an assassination of a world figure in the United States any more than we need another suicide bomber in a Jerusalem marketplace. If we coordinate with UN Security the word will get back to the Arabs that we are on to them. Their security leaks like a colander.

If we don't and something happens, we're culpable and we'll have to live with that. Talk about being between a rock and a hard place."

"There was no specific date in your information, Dan. We'll coordinate with Secret Service and the FBI to provide some extra security while the meeting is going on. NYPD can kick in with some of their people and State Department Security will have a contingent here. We'll do all we can. The teams from these agencies have tremendous experience and are amongst the best in the world.

"My position is almost the same as yours. I'm an American intelligence agent, but my agency has no authority to operate within the United States. And there are enough slugs out there who would love nothing better than to find out that a Company agent is working on a case, especially if that slug was a congressman or senator, especially Sunday Chuck."

Dan looked at him quizzically.

"Sunday Chuck is one of our elected federal legislators who calls a press conference every Sunday and blathers about nothing of major importance," Matt said. "If he ever got wind of this we'd all be nailed to the wall of his publicity machine.

"So we all have to be rather circumspect in how we handle this. If we get anything, we turn it over to the FBI and then we take a step back."

"OK, let's narrow it down and see if we can get a handle on whom they are going to go after. We'll go over the list of attendees and see what we can come up with. I want to meet with our delegation and get some input. My thinking is that they'll go for a non-American or non-Israeli to try and create dissention. They might even try to blame us for the hit. Let's get together tomorrow for breakfast and coordinate."

September 11, 2001
8:30 a.m.

"Dan, when you were a Green Beret you also worked for the Company. You know how things are and how limited we are when it comes to operating within the United States."

"Matt, we're all up the creek if anything happens. We've got to get beyond the political bullshit. We know something's going to happen; we just don't know exactly what it is or the timetable."

Hesh sat back on his chair in the Park Central's restaurant, just off the lobby and facing out onto Seventh Avenue with throngs of people passing by on their way to work. The masses of humanity passing the window all had frozen faces, showing no emotion as they trekked their daily trek to offices.

Dan sat, quietly gazing at the rapidly increasing rush hour traffic as suburban commuters pushed into Manhattan, eager to pay exorbitant parking fees rather than join millions of other lemmings on buses and trains.

On the sidewalk the crowd noticeably increased in size; people passed others they had been passing for years with no sign of recognition, the ultimate in anonymity. It was a warm and perfectly clear day and people were lightly dressed. The hordes on the street moved with quick precision, always forging ahead with no emotion showing on their faces, the quintessential New Yorkers.

Hesh reached across the table for the coffee carafe and poured another cup for himself, nodding to Matt and Dan. Both men shook their heads negatively and Hesh replaced the pot, sprinkling artificial sweetener and a milk substitute into his cup. He sat back and sipped at the brimming cup, a feeling of relaxation pushing the tension into a corner of his mind for the moment.

The young Mossad agent glanced at his watch…8:45 am….and then looked to Dan.

"What are we going to do, Boss? I feel helpless just sitting here."

"We don't know what the hell we're going to do," Dan responded with more than a drop of impatience in his voice. "If we knew who these goddamn twins were, we could do something. Two of the best intelligence agencies in the world here and neither one of us can solve a riddle put out there by a terrorist group from a Third World country."

Halevi's voice had a tinge of anger toward his young partner.

Matt spoke in a quiet voice: "We don't have a lot of time and if we can work together instead of clawing at each other's throats, we might be able to…."

8:46.40 a.m.

His voice trailed off as one of the white jacketed waiters ran into the room and behind the bar, empty at this time of the morning. The waiter climbed on a bar stool and turned the television on.

Pictures of the World Trade Center's North Tower, smoke pouring from it, came onto the screen.

"A plane just crashed into the tower," he yelled.

All conversation stopped and every head in the restaurant turned toward the screen. Not a word was spoken, but the gasps of the patrons expressed more than spoken words.

"How the hell could that happen on a day as clear as this?" a man in a blue striped business suit mumbled.

Another, older man, said he remembered when he was a child and an Air Force bomber crashed into the Empire State Building.

Dan looked at Hesh and Matt.

"That happened in fog. This is a day without a cloud."

The agents sat, stunned, trying to gather their thoughts. Time passed without realization of its passage.

9:59 a.m.

As they looked at the screen a low flying jetliner could be seen racing toward the Twin Towers and suddenly the South Tower erupted in a ball of fire. The gasps of all those in the restaurant filled the room.

"Oh my God," one man gasped, "my wife works there. Oh my God!"

"Dan, this isn't an accident. This is an attack.," Matt gasped. "The Twin Towers, the Twin Kings of the New York Skyline!"

The sudden wail of sirens filled the air and the throngs on the street froze in their tracks, looking upward, curiosity on the faces of some, horror on others.

Dan's face was ashen.

"How the hell did we miss that? Oh Lord, how many people…? How the fuck did we miss that?"

September 15, 2001
Jerusalem

"Dan, I'm not going to accept your resignation." The Minister said. "You did your best. This isn't a perfect world and the work we do isn't perfect. Stop blaming yourself, take Amanda and get the hell out of here for a while. Come back when your head is clear and you're ready to start working on capturing the bastards who did this.

"The disinformation has already started with factions within the PLO spreading the libel that hundreds of Israeli citizens and Jews who worked at the Twin Towers were warned in advance not to go to their offices on Sept. 11. The same ones who believe the Holocaust never happened and is a figment of Jewish propaganda, are the only ones who believe that.

"I need you with a clear head and I will not accept your resignation."

"I should have known. I should have figured it out."

"Bullshit," the old man spat. "You and Hesh did the best you could and there is no blame that falls on your shoulders. You've both been through tremendous pressure lately with Hesh's wife murdered, the raid and then this horrible attack.

"You're two of my best men and I have no intention of letting you go and losing either one of you."

VI

2006 ASSASSINATION

Every major city in the world has its central spot where traffic jams seem to congeal. In Paris the Place de l'Etoile, originally named for the rough star the intersection forms as it circles the world famous Arc de Triomphe, the Napoleonic arch under which victorious French troops paraded and where Hitler's Nazi army rubbed salt into the Gallic wounds after France's collapse, by parading his legions through this holy spot.

In a fit of nationalism the government renamed it Place Charles DeGaulle for the tall general and later president, who led the troops of the French government in exile against Hitler. But they never reckoned with the fierce independent streak of the Parisians who refused to adopt the new name, although it was for their one true hero since Napoleon. The council finally relented and placed both names on street signs.

Traffic around the arch at all times was solid. So solid that it took on the look of Saturn's rings. Tourists stood in awe, wondering how cars, motorcycles and scooters managed to move in and out of the lanes as they rapidly circumnavigated the arch, some drifting off and down the Champs-Elysees, past the crowded sidewalk cafes that line both sides of the boulevard and toward the Place de la Concorde and its giant Egyptian obelisk at the far end of the wide thoroughfare. Pedestrian crossing was even more daunting.

People sat and sipped their drinks, totally oblivious to the din and bustle all around them, tuning out the raucous noise and surrounding themselves with an invisible bubble of tranquillity.

In the center of the Etoile stood a blue-caped gendarme, his rounded pillbox hat perched arrogantly atop his head, his arms waving incomprehensibly at the passing vehicles. Amazingly, the drivers seemed to be able to comprehend his silent directions and the flow moved smoothly.

The sidewalks were filled with people, mostly tourists come to see the famed arch, watching the drama and waiting their turn to cross over and view the Tomb of the Unknown Soldier in the center of the landmark.

The gendarme crooked a finger at one car, moving more slowly than the rest and indicated that he wanted the driver to speed up and move on. The driver, his woman passenger and a small child were involved in animated conversation and seemed not to notice the orders.

As the vehicle came abreast of the policeman it suddenly erupted in a ball of flame, disintegrating into tiny shards of steel that spewed across the intersection like a swarm of angry fireflies, biting into the faces and bodies of those standing on the sidelines.

The Place de l'Etoile filled with a black, acrid smoke as chunks of steel began to rain down. The car that had exploded was gone, as were its passengers. So was the gendarme who had been standing only a millisecond before in the intersection. Both had disintegrated from the force of the powerful explosion and the heat it generated.

Spectators dodged and ran as vehicles that had been adjacent to the explosion, came tumbling and rolling across the street toward them. A driver ran from his car, clothes and flesh burning from gasoline that had sprayed him.

Bodies lined the l'Etoile and the streets were awash in blood and body parts from those who had been close to the ignition zone. The sounds of onrushing police and emergency vehicles shattered the air while many of those injured, too stunned to realize what had happened, simply began to walk away from the scene.

Asuncion, the capital of Paraguay, was always hot. It didn't seem to matter what the season was, the sun was ubiquitous and singed everything it touched.

Natives mingled with tourists and a city that didn't seem to know what century it was in let itself sleepwalk through the day. Men in business suits carrying attaché cases walked the street alongside peasants in ponchos and wide brimmed straw hats looking, and smelling as though they had just come in from the pasture. In many cases they had.

The Hotel Imperial was one of the few in the city that was able to cater to foreign visitors and tourists without giving them the amenities generally demanded. It was from an earlier era, before air-conditioning, before central international reservations and before the turmoil of the modern world. Guests could register and not be concerned that anyone would look too closely at their identity papers. It suited certain visitors perfectly.

In a room facing out from the rear of the building, a location rarely requested even by the regular clientele of the Imperial, sat a dark skinned man with hair curled in small ringlets that looked like coiled springs. On the table in front of him was a map of the city and four black and white photographs. The map had been pushed to the far end of the table, but the man held one of the photos in his hand, fingering it and slowly, unconsciously folding the edges.

He jumped involuntarily as he heard a sharp knock at the door. Reaching to the bed behind him, the dark man hefted a compact submachine gun and moved quickly and lightly to the right hand side of the door.

"¿Si? ¿Quien es?" he asked, nervously fingering the trigger of the fully automatic weapon. He stood to the side of the door so that any shot that might punch through the wood did not catch him.

"Rueven," came the response from the hallway.

The dark man twisted the doorknob and let the door swing in, stepping aside as it did so that he was able to cover the entryway with the muzzle of his weapon.

The door slowly inched open and a short, stocky man stepped in, hands held open, palms up and extended in front of him.

"Put the damn gun down before you blow my head off," Rueven grumbled.

"Bullshit!" responded the dark man. "How the hell did I know it was you until I could see you? I take no chances."

"Save the gunplay for Frey. Have you gotten the material put together yet?"

The dark man moved a packet of papers across the table and Rueven spread them out. He sat and studied the documents for about five minutes and then turned to his companion.

"Tell me, Jake, have you gotten his movements timed yet?"

"Yes. He was easy. Unlike his compatriots he has become a creature of habit. They do everything possible not to set a pattern. He goes about his day as though he couldn't care less who knew what he was doing."

"Then we go today," said Rueven, a grim look with no hint of any human warmth spread across his face.

Two hours later at the busy marketplace in the ancient section of Asuncion, an old man made his way through the crowded aisles of stalls filled with meats and produce, clothing and hardware items. A few of the items on sale were obviously there should a tourist happen to stumble in, but the bulk of the marketplace was for the residents of Asuncion who did their everyday food and necessities shopping in this open air supermarket.

The old man carried a woven straw basket with a fixed handle over this left arm and moved slowly, picking and choosing vegetables with great care. The basket filled with considerable weight, but he never seemed to notice; a chicken, its neck draped over the side of the basket, swayed with the rhythm of his movement.

The vendors nodded and smiled at him as he passed their stalls and he had a personal greeting for each of them. He had been coming here since early in 1946 after making his way across Europe, the Continent still devastated by the ravages of the recent war.

Although he seemed to belong among the stalls and with the people who manned them, he was different. His carriage was more erect, he was taller than the short, dark haired Indians who populated the market and even though his skin had been darkened by the South American sun, he was still considerably fairer than that of any man around him and the few hairs left on his head still held a hint of the blond they once were. The vendors had the look of their Indian ancestors and he had the look of his Teutonic fore bearers.

With his basket filled, the old man began moving toward the street, politely greeting in flawless Spanish, those he passed. It was nearing siesta hour and the streets had begun to empty. Within minutes the heavy rolling doors of the marketplace and every other store in the city, would slide shut for the mandatory two hour siesta

The old man walked out into the bright day and turned left to head towards his modest apartment on a block of balconied row houses only a short distance away. His wife would be waiting for him, looking out the window of the small living room and through the wrought iron bars of the balcony.

Together they would retire to the bedroom for their traditional mittagsschläfchen, afternoon nap. He still could not bring himself to call it a "siesta." It was all so peaceful and he seemed to be a man of mild composure who had done little more in his life than quietly pass through, known only to family and a very small circle of friends, leaving barely a ripple behind for history to note that he had ever existed.

As he moved slowly down the sidewalk, an old car pulled abreast of him and Rueven stuck his head out of the window.

"Guten tag," he called to the old man. "Wie geht es Inhen?" "Where are you going, sir?"

The old man's head suddenly came up and he looked directly into Rueven's eyes.

"Lo siento senior, I am sorry" the old man replied. "No lo conozco." He said. "I do not understand."

"Achtung, Herr Frey," Rueven said, his eyes turning to ice. "You don't know me, but I know you."

The old man watched in frozen fascination as Rueven slowly raised the muzzle of his compact Uzi machinegun flush with the car window and saw the flashes of flame spurting from the dark opening of the muzzle.

His basket flew from his hands, vegetables, bread and the swaying chicken scattered across the sidewalk as the slugs ripped into him.

Blood poured from the holes in his chest, running down, staining his starched white shirt and pooling on the sidewalk as his body crashed to the ground.

Jake pushed his foot down on the accelerator and the ancient car leapt forward, crashing through a pushcart filled with fresh flowers and sending its vendor scampering for his life. The car sped around the corner and disappeared into the narrow, winding streets of Asuncion. It would be found later by the National Police, abandoned and with no leads as to who had been driving.

—ooo⟨◉⟩ooo—

Martin Kazic walked to his car in the crowded parking lot of the Paterson, New Jersey City Hall. A man in his mid eighties, Kazic was a powerful and influential leader in the Croatian community in this northern New Jersey town.

Politics was the key to almost anything in Passaic County and especially in this city so dominated by its diverse European and African nationalities, although they were rapidly losing sway to the surging numbers of Hispanics and Palestinians. .

If you could produce votes from your own ethnic community, you could command power from the city's politicians. If you had a draw in another ethnic group, you were revered by those power brokers.

Martin Kazic, to the amazement of all, was not only able to bring in solid voting blocs from the East Europeans in the city, but the Palestinians, who rarely trusted anyone beyond their mosque or madrassa, followed Kazic's lead. He could produce votes and that was the coin of the realm in Passaic County.

Kazic's family had been a local power in Europe and Martin had carried on the tradition even into the dark days of World War II. There had been some questions about his activities and which side he may have really been on, but those doubts were never expressed out loud; not if you wanted to remain healthy.

When he left his beautiful walled city of Dubrovnik on the Adriatic Sea and moved to Passaic County after the conflict with the Serbians, he resumed his position as leader of the Croatian community.

Croatia was virulently anti-Semitic during the dark days of World War II and had repressed the more moderate Serbian community. In the 1980s it reversed itself and the Serbs went on a rampage throughout the country, even coming close to destroying the ancient city of Dubrovnik that had been a medieval power but was no longer of any strategic importance. Artillery barrages lobbed from the sea and over the crenulated walls created havoc and destruction out of sheer meanness.

Although he was long gone from the city, Kazic never forgave the Serbs. And because the Serbs had supported the Jews in the world war, he blamed them as well, notwithstanding the fact that Israel condemned the current Serbian excesses.

This stand endeared him to the Palestinians in Paterson. He stood with them on the rooftops on September 11, 2001 as smoke rose high in the sky from the mortally wounded World Trade Center and smiled as the Palestinians cheered and raised glasses of wine to toast the suicide attackers. He broke bread with them as they brought out charcoal burners to cook celebratory meals.

The following day when rumours of the celebrations began to surface, Kazic vehemently denied that they had ever taken place. He marched into the offices of the local daily newspaper and virtually screamed at the city editor that he had been in the Palestinian neighbourhood and saw no evidence of any celebrations. The newspaper, with a reputation for taking on only soft causes, backed down and printed repeated denials that the Palestinians had celebrated the demise of the Twin Towers and more than 2,000 souls.

The grateful Palestinians, who had virtually no political power, adopted Kazic as one of their own and followed his lead at the polls.

Kazic stood well over six feet tall and was as solid as a brick wall. His handshake was crushing and his deep, dark blue eyes could turn to ice and burn a hole through an opponent. He was respected by the hierarchy of the Democratic Party in Passaic County and was often in the company of major government leaders. When the governor was in the city for a function, Kazic would invariably be on the dais near him.

As Martin Kazic returned to his home this evening, he gave scant notice to the car parked several houses down the street from his residence and the good looking young man sitting behind the wheel. He climbed the steps and opened the old fashioned glass framed door, walking into a huge living room.

Less than an hour later he exited the house, climbed into his Cadillac Escalade and drove off. Kazic was wearing a tuxedo and he looked resplendent in the finery. He never saw the car with the young man still parked at the curb nearby.

It was nearly two a.m. when he returned from the political dinner, parked in the driveway, locked his car and walked back up the steps. He turned and looked down the street, but it was empty, quiet and dark. Kazic walked into the house and closed the door.

No sooner had he disappeared behind the door than a car turned the corner and parked a short distance up the block. The lights were off and the motor running as the young man stepped from the car carrying a package under his arm.

He walked quickly to the house and up the four steps to the porch and placed the package alongside the doorway where it would be seen by anyone entering or leaving.

The young man then climbed back behind the steering wheel and reached for the cellular phone on the dashboard. The numbers glowed dully in the dark as he punched in the ten digit code and listened as the phone rang at the other end.

"Yes?" came Martin Kazic's voice.

"Mr. Kazic, sir. This is Lt. Bennett at Police Headquarters. I'm sorry to bother you so late, but the Mayor asked us to drop a package off at your home. One of my men was just there and left it on your porch. He didn't want to knock on the door and disturb you at so late an hour, but I thought it must have been important and didn't want to leave it on the porch overnight."

"Thank you Lieutenant. I'll see to it immediately."

Kazic reached to his bedpost and took his robe, draping it over his shoulders. He stepped into slippers and started for the bedroom door.

"What is it? Is everything alright?" his wife asked in a sleepy voice.

"Yes! Yes!" he responded impatiently.

"Those fools at Police Headquarters were given something to deliver to me and they left it on the porch. I'm just going to go and get it."

Kazic descended the steps and walked across the living room to the front door. He flipped on the porch light and stepped outside. Alongside the door, to his left, he saw the box and picked it up.

Inside the car the young man watched. In his hand was a small device with a toggle switch. His thumb rested on the switch and just as Kazic made contact with the box, the young man flipped the lever.

The box erupted in a blinding flash and with such power that Kazic's hand was blown back into his face and then, along with his head, flew across the living room. The door frame splintered and began to burn.

Kazic's headless, handless body bounced back into the room and fell to the floor. His torso poured blood from raw edges where his head, hand and left leg had once been.

Across the street the man put the car in gear and slowly began to drive away. He had barely reached the corner when a police car raced up the block. As he drove, he again reached for his cell phone and dialed a number in New York.

"Make the telephone calls," he said, and then pressed the "end" button. He turned the corner and pulled onto the ramp for the Route 80 Interstate highway back to New York.

Almost simultaneously calls were made to Associated Press and several television stations. All calls were identical:

"This is Response, the Jewish Vengeance League. We are notifying you that we have executed three criminals today. The Nazi killer Frey in Paraguay, the Hamas Terrorist Fahd in Paris and Kazic, both Nazi and Hamas, in New Jersey. This is only the beginning. Those who have killed our people will themselves die. They are marked."

VII

RESPONSE

Dan Halevi sat chafing at his desk assignment at the Israeli Consulate to the United Nations, a post he held since his attempt to resign from the Mossad, watched the television images of the torn steel and bodies in France and the reports of the killings in Paraguay and New Jersey.

Ben Chaim had flatly refused to accept his resignation, telling Dan that he was too valuable to both the agency and the country to let him slip into retirement. The Minister finally reached a compromise with Halevi that sent him back to his roots in New York where he was able to come in from the cold side of operations. Dan chafed, but he finally gave in and took the assignment on the condition that he could pick his own staff.

For Amanda it was a godsend. They could finally spend some quality time together and she had the opportunity to see family and friends that life in Israel had precluded.

Their apartment, overlooking the FDR Drive in New York, afforded a view of the UN building just to the south. It was a high end accommodation, but Ben Chaim had pulled a few strings at the Finance Ministry and deflected any questions that arose.

Dan turned the television dial to another station to see if there were any further details about the killings and involuntarily jumped as a knock came at his door. He opened it, admitting a very tanned and healthy looking Hesh Whitman, who had been assigned as his deputy.

"Where the hell have you been?" Dan asked.

"Oh, I was just out walking and seeing the sights. I thought I'd leave you and Amanda alone for once," he smiled. "You don't get much time together and instead of taking advantage of it, you're still in the office"

"Have you seen any news reports?"

"No. Why? What's up?"

"Some outfit calling itself 'Response' is claiming credit for the killing of a couple of Nazis and a Hamas biggie. No one at the consulate has ever heard of this group."

"There are all kinds of crazies in this world looking for revenge," Hesh said quietly. "I'm tired and am going to my apartment and to bed. I'll see you in the morning. Tell Amanda I'll be over for some of her terrific coffee."

Dan closed the door behind Hesh, thinking that the younger man had come a long way since the terrible events at Eilat. He was hurting, but he seemed to have put it behind him to the extent that he could once again lead a normal life.

Sayyid Hassan Musaf el Rashid sat back in his study, sinking into the plush leather chair to the side of his desk. The warm desert sun had begun its slide below the towering palms bordering the walled compound. Behind them rose the tip of the Great Pyramid of Cheops at Giza. Here his sanctuary was complete, cut off from the outside world in a place of silence and comfort.

His reverie was interrupted as the desk telephone let out a shrill, piercing ring that seemed to echo off the thick plaster walls. He reached for the phone and cradled it to his ear.

"Yes?"

"This is Ali. We must meet."

"Come in an hour. The others are here now and they must not see you coming in."

The old man reached across the desk to hang the old fashioned French phone back into its cradle and then pushed the button on his intercom.

"Sayyid, please see to the comfort and quick departure of our friends and then there are details you must attend to in the city."

El Rashid stood in the window, hands clasped behind his back, watching as the line of Mercedes moved out along the circular driveway; past the flowing fountain and down the long, palm lined drive toward the huge main gate that assured only those invited or expected would pass into the private confines of the compound.

There was a guard shack just inside the gates, but unseen by any was the corner room of the house, occupied at all times by two men monitoring a closed circuit television view of the gate and every inch of the wall surrounding the compound. They wore powerful Glock .40 caliber side arms with 13-round law enforcement clips for extra firepower. In a rack on the wall were four loaded AK-47 fully automatic assault rifles.

As though that was not enough, also racked on the wall were two RPG (Rocket propelled grenade launchers) for any extreme eventuality.

Unknown to all who walked the interior of the compound with the exception of el Rashid and the men who manned the corner room, were machinegun emplacements that covered the gate in crossfire and others that were capable of gunning down anyone attempting to scale the wall or cross the lawn without authorization. A panel of switches on a sideboard that rose to the bottom of the sill at the window and in view of the television monitors, controlled all of the guns remotely, causing them to fire and sweep the area in a controlled side-to-side movement. Sensors imbedded in the ground provided a secondary warning of anything weighing more than a dog that might cross any section of the compound unannounced.

El Rashid enjoyed his security.

He stood, watching as the last of the cars exited and waited several minutes as an American made Hummer, the civilian version of the U.S. Army's Humvee, drove to the gate. The huge barriers swung slowly open and a steel panel that ran the width of the entrance, slowly lowered into the ground. Imbedded in the panel were two lines of steel spikes that would have shredded the tires of any unwanted vehicle.

The driver waited for the panel to go flush with the ground and then moving forward, entered the compound..

The distance from the gate to the house provided a secondary security link. It was an open ground that could become a killing field to any intruder on foot or in any vehicle short of a tank. And in the unlikely event of an armoured vehicle breaching security, the RPGs would be put into play.

El Rashid had been aware of its approach from the point that it had gone from the paved highway onto the dirt approach road. More sensors under the roadway had triggered an alarm and cameras monitored the approaching vehicle and its passengers.

In the passenger seat directly behind the chauffeur slouched a man with naturally dark skin made even darker by the ever-present sun. Strangely, it had not dried to the leathery consistency of most desert dwellers, but maintained a smooth complexion. He wore a white linen suit that made the contrast with his complexion even starker. The man was clean shaven except for the lush moustache covering his upper lip and dipping down over his yellowed teeth.

El Rashid went to personally open the front door for his visitor, a show of respect for the importance of the man. He forced a smile as his visitor walked into the air-conditioned foyer, a blast of the desert heat accompanying him.

"Ali, how good it is to see you," the old man said as he extended his hand in greeting.

"Salaam Aleichem. Are you well?" the visitor intoned, wiping his forehead with a handkerchief.

Ali held his white Panama hat in his hand and bowed slightly from the waist. It was a motion that, while showing respect, gave no indication of subordination.

El Rashid bent his head ever so slightly. Not low enough to show deference, but sufficient to let his visitor think he had been given a sign of respect.

Respect in Arabia was arguably more important than it was to Asians and even the slightest inkling of disrespect could bring terrible consequences.

"My dear Ali, so good of you to travel all this way for our meeting. I would have considered flying to Libya to see you, but it would have been dangerous for me to take a chance on being recognized."

"Here are the plans for our warrior goddess Sekhmet's cruise and the ship's itinerary. Another ship has been placed at your disposal with sufficient weapons aboard."

El Rashid smiled and pushed a snifter of brandy across the table for Ali. The two men raised their glasses in salute and sipped the liquid. The laws of Islam were meant for most, but not all of its adherents and a sip of brandy now and then was as good for the soul as was praying five times a day.

"My President is counting on greeting the heroes of our cause," Ali said.

"All in due course my dear Ali."

⸻∞⊱❃⊰∞⸻

The sun rose slowly over the ship's stern as it crashed through the huge swells of the North Atlantic, rays of light playing over the neatly stacked cargo containers piled on its deck, throwing long shadows toward the bow.

In the wheelhouse the captain perched in an elevated seat looking over the state of the art instrument panel. Behind him a seaman tugged at the joy stick that had replaced the traditional ship's wheel in the technological age, as the swells tossed the ship about, aided by a computer that helped to compensate for the buffeting.

Normally Captain Ahmed would be asleep at this time, but because of the precious cargo he carried, he had opted to stay on the bridge for an additional watch…or at least until the seas calmed.

Ahmed cast a nervous glance every time the bow dipped and spray came over the containers. He knew they were water tight and could even survive the sinking of his ship, but they contained the most precious treasures and history of Egypt and the responsibility entrusted to him by President Mubarak himself, weighed heavily on his mind.

His ship had been chosen for the task because it was perhaps the most modern container ship afloat. Most of the common functions were under the control of sophisticated computers, producing maximum fuel efficiency and the smoothest possible sailing.

But in waters such as this, nothing could replace the sure and experienced hands of a human. A computer could be programmed to respond to set situations, but it could never have the instincts of a man.

Capt. Ahmed pulled on his slicker and walked to the ladder leading to the galley. A quick cup of coffee and a bite to eat for breakfast would feel good. The treasures would be safe for the half hour it took him to have some nourishment. Normally he would have had a crewmember bring it to him, but his legs needed to be stretched.

He nodded to the mate who would stand watch until he returned, glanced at the blinking lights on the control console and, assured that all was functioning properly as he descended the ladder.

"Watch that nothing amiss happens to His Majesty," Ahmed cautioned the mate with a smile. "You know there was once a curse on the tomb that doomed anyone showing disrespect to the King."

Ahmed knew that in just a little more than 24-hours he would be at port in the United States and the treasures, making their second visit to the United States, would go by armed convoy to their first stop at the Museum of Modern Art at the eastern edge of Central Park.

His government was sending the artefacts to the United States as a goodwill gesture in thanks for the intelligence tip that saved it from takeover by Iranian trained revolutionaries.

Ahmed had just put his coffee cup down and was preparing to climb the ladder back to the bridge when his name boomed over the intercom.

"Captain, there is a trawler ahead flashing a distress signal," the mate's voice called. "Shall we send a launch?"

"Have you tried to make radio contact?"

"Yes Captain, we tried to reach them on all the normal channels, but got no response. Her mast must be down and radio out of order."

Ahmed climbed back onto the bridge, took the oversize binoculars and resting them on a pylon on the ledge, trained them on the smaller ship. Under ordinary circumstances he would have immediately ordered the launch into the water to rescue the nearby ship. But these were not ordinary circumstances and the cargo he was carrying was not an ordinary cargo. Ahmed was a very cautious man; he could not endanger his ship for any reason. If the artefacts were lost, his country's history would be gone with them.

The mate pointed to the superstructure of the bobbing ship and noted: "The antenna seems to be missing. It may have been knocked off in the storm last night. They must have really caught it much worse than we did."

He nodded to the mate standing at the davit and making ready to climb into the motorized launch hanging from it.

"Take a portable radio with you and let me know what the situation is and if they need medical assistance. Primarily I want to know if they can proceed on their own. Our engineer should also accompany you in the event their difficulty is simple mechanical trouble and can be repaired with some extra help. If the problem is beyond our capability, radio me and we will notify the American Coast Guard to send assistance."

Ahmed watched as the davit was swung out and the longboat lowered into the water. Although the seas had calmed a bit, they were still treacherous.

The huge swells had shrunk to rolling waves, but the threat of a surge was always present. The motion of the waves on the ship gave Ahmed a lulling feeling as he watched the rescue boat touch the water, cut loose and begin a slow progress toward the trawler.

He watched as the longboat rose and dipped on the swells, disappearing from view and then suddenly riding the crest as it made its way toward the stricken ship.

Ahmed wondered why there was no flash from the ship or other signal…only the international distress flag whipping in the breeze. He saw the longboat make fast to the trawler and his men climb the ladder to the deck. He lost sight of them as they were led into the wheelhouse and the hatch was closed behind them.

The squeaking of a block and tackle hanging freely and swinging back and forth with each roll of the ship caught his attention and he turned away from the trawler for a split second. When he looked back he could see his mate coming back down the ladder to the launch with three men from the other ship. They cast off and pointed the boat's bow toward Ahmed. Nothing seemed to be amiss, nothing unusual.

Within minutes with the help of a following sea, the launch was at his boarding ladder and one of the men from the trawler began to ascend, followed by Capt. Ahmed's mate. Then the second man began to board as the other crewmen fastened the longboat to the dangling lines.

The men from the crippled ship were dark and appeared to be Asian. Nothing about that raised any question as so many ships were crewed by Arab, Chinese, Philippino and Indonesian sailors.

What did strike Ahmed as curious was that their complexions were smooth and unlined with no trace of seafaring on them.

"That is odd," he thought to himself."

"Captain, I am most grateful to you and your crew for coming to our aid," said the taller of the three men. He wore the epaulets of a senior ship's officer with three gold braided stripes across them. We have had some serious problems and I would be most appreciative if you could extend me the courtesy of discussing them in the privacy of your cabin?"

Ahmed, curious about such a request for privacy, nodded in agreement and motioned for the officer to follow him.

"What problem involving the functioning of a ship could warrant a private discussion?" he thought to himself.

While the other man's gait on the deck appeared to be sure, there was something odd about this fellow that Ahmed could not put his finger upon. The skin was too smooth, too unlined, but beyond that all appeared to be normal.

Capt. Ahmed entered the hatch with his guest following close behind. Had he glanced over his shoulder he would have seen the trawler lower two outboard powered launches with five men in each.

He heard the hatch clang shut as the visitor followed him inside and then proceeded through the passageway to his cabin. He stopped at the entrance, extending his hand in a motion offering his guest the opportunity to enter first.

"The man smiled: "After you, Captain."

Ahmed stepped into the cabin and turned to talk to his guest. The man stood with his right hand extended, holding an automatic pistol with a silencer screwed into the muzzle.

Captain Ahmed started to say something, but was cut short as the slug ripped through his mouth and out the back of his head. He jerked backward and was hit with a second slug in his left eye.

The man dropped his hand behind his back and exited the cabin, heading back up to the wheelhouse. Walking through the hatch he pointed the gun at the helmsman and pulled the trigger twice. The sound suppressed automatic spit out two slugs with a slight popping sound that caught the Egyptian sailor in the face. He spun violently back and off the bulkhead, bouncing across the console.

He died with his arms snagged on the joy stick and toggle switches, moving back and forth with each motion of the ship in the ocean's swells.

"Tariq, what the hell is the matter with you? He should have been killed as soon as you walked in here with him," he barked at his companion.

"I was afraid to alert the rest of the crew. There was another man in here with us."

"Damn you. Why didn't you just shoot both of them? It will have to be done anyhow. They should have been killed on the spot. Now get him off the controls and take the wheel while I go to the ladder for the rest of the men."

He strode from the wheelhouse toward the railing just as the two longboats arrived and tied up to the landing platform that skimmed the water at the base of the ladder.

Ten men began to ascend, each carrying a duffle bag. They wore short slickers protecting them from the wave spray and rubberized pants that were almost chest high and held in place by suspenders.

With all ten on deck, he nodded to them and they withdrew compact Uzi submachine guns from under their slickers. With determination and not a word passing among them, they opened fire on the Egyptian crew.

One Egyptian dove from the upper deck and onto one of the attackers, managing to wrest the sub-machinegun from his hands. The crewman turned and opened fire against his attackers. Two of the men went down as bone and blood splattered through their yellow slickers.

Before the Egyptian could continue his counter attack, he was almost cut in half as one of the interlopers opened fire on him. He lurched toward the railing and tumbled overboard, landing on top of the outboard tethered to the ship's landing platform.

The attacker, a full six feet tall and towering over the rest of the yellow slickered assassins, let out a yell as a second Egyptian exploded from a hatch, knife in hand, heading for the back of a gunman. Before the attacker could move, the Egyptian plunged the blade deep into gunman's back. He went down with a scream as his gun clattered across the deck.

The Egyptian sailor dove across the deck on his stomach, reaching for the gun. As his fingers touched it, four holes opened across his back from the base of his skull to his waist. He jerked as blood began pouring out of his body and then died.

The tall man turned his weapon toward the ladder and cut down another of Ahmed's sailors. Looking across the deck, he saw none but his own men standing. The deck was awash in blood and bodies. The man with the knife in his back groaned and tried to get up as the tall man walked over to him, pointed the gun at his head and pulled the trigger. Blood and brains spattered over his boots as he lifted the muzzle away.

"Why Sayyid?" the man in the officer's uniform asked.

"We don't have the time or facilities to take care of him." The tall man responded. "That was the understanding before we began and that is how it must be. Now, all of you, search the ship and make sure they are all dead. The first thing I want confirmed is that the radio is under our control."

He nodded his head and the attackers moved out immediately to undertake their assigned tasks. Gunfire rang out from the radio room as the operator was dispatched, but no other Egyptians were found and confirmation was made that no distress signal had gone out. The radio operator was in a closed compartment and had not heard any of the commotion from the deck.

On deck Sayyid fired a flare, alerting those remaining on the trawler to come aside the container ship.

Sayyid looked out to see the trawler making fast to the container ship and he motioned to the man in the officer's uniform. The man nodded and instructed one of his sailors to move the deck boom normally used for on and offloading containers. The boom swung out over the trawler and men on deck hooked it into a large crate lashed to the deck.

The crate was cut loose and hoisted onto the deck of the container ship where it was secured in a space between the rows of containers and the wheelhouse superstructure.

With that accomplished, Sayyid walked to the radio room now under control of one of his men.

"Transmit," he ordered.

"The radio operator twisted the dials to the desired frequency.

"The throne is secure," he repeated three times and then closed the radio down.

While Sayyid was in the radio room those on the deck had cut the trawler loose and were watching as it slowly drifted away. It was bobbing up and down in the swells about a mile from the container ship when it suddenly lifted out of the water, a great ball of orange flame rising from amidships. The bow and stern of the trawler pointed down into the water as the beam of the ship rose and split in half. Within seconds it had disappeared beneath the waves leaving only some debris and an oil slick to prove that it had ever been there.

Sayyid turned to the man in the officer's uniform.

"Soong, this is where I want to go." He pointed to a spot on a chart he was holding.

Soong Kim studied the chart and nodded, then returned to the wheelhouse and gave directions to the man at the helm who keyed in the computer settings and let the joy stick go automatic. He then turned to other crewmen and ordered them to fasten weights to the bodies, slice open their stomachs and thro them overboard. That would ensure that no gases would ever bring them to the surface and would provide food for the fish.

The ship nosed gently to the west and, taking its cue from the softly buzzing computer, headed to New York.

In the walled compound outside of Giza the Old Man listened intently to the long-range radio receiver and nodded in appreciation as he heard the coded message. He smiled and then slowly limped to the veranda, a brandy in one hand and a cigar in the other. He sat in a chair by the poolside, raised his legs and slowly sipped the beverage.

Closing his eyes Old Sayyid was content.

The analyst sat at his desk playing tapes of satellite surveillance photos of the North Atlantic. Something on the screen had piqued his interest but he wasn't exactly sure what to make of it. He played the tapes forward and then in reverse when it hit him. In one frame there was a ship in the water. In the next there was a bright flash and in the following frame nothing but empty ocean.

He moved the surveillance tapes and continued to study them. The experienced man spotted a second ship, followed it and picked up the fact that both ships were in proximity to each other. They then separated and the smaller of the two suddenly disappeared in the bright flash of light.

The larger ship, apparently a container vessel, began moving off to the west without investigating the flash and disappearance of the other ship. Odd!

The rules of the sea demanded that any ship in proximity to any other in distress is required to lend all possible assistance. For any vessel to simply move off, oblivious to the mishap of another was most unusual. And to not broadcast a distress signal was even odder.

He zoomed in on the telephoto capability of his satellite image and could see that it was a container ship with is cargo piled high on deck. The identifying numerals atop the wheelhouse were obscured and he was unable to position the pictures to see the name or registration number on the bow or sides of the ship.

The analyst made quick written notes and copied the pictures to a disk. He moved quickly into the corridor from the small warren of an office he occupied and into a room filled with television monitors, covering three of the walls, giving it the impression of the sports oriented ESPN Zone restaurant monitoring baseball games across the country with a wall of television screens, all on view at the same time.

But these were no sports events. Closer inspection showed scenes of military bases, missile sites and government compounds from virtually every corner of the earth.

He walked into a glass enclosed office and laid his package on the desk.

The tall, slender black woman sitting in the office belied the appearance of a bureaucrat and was very stylishly dressed, her shoes and dark slacks fitting and fashionable for the biggest advertising firms in the country. Her hair was nicely styled, but cut short and utilitarian without the kinky appearance of many African-Americans.

The picture of a librarian or mid-level government functionary was misleading. Practiced in the art of smashing the governmental glass ceiling, she had the ability to cut an adversary down with a simple stare.

"I have no tolerance for bullshit," she was fond of saying. "Tell it to me straight and we'll deal with any problems from that point on."

Mary Sapphire had begun working for the Central Intelligence Agency close to twenty years ago as a secretary. Her quick mind and ability to cut to the chase soon moved her into a position as an intelligence analyst. She now oversaw the entire satellite intelligence gathering operation for the CIA at its headquarters in McLean, Virginia.

Most people refer to Langley as the location of the CIA. They are wrong. The collegiate-like campus of the headquarters is situated in McLean, a Langley suburb and only about eight miles from the center of power in downtown Washington.

The original building was designed in the mid-1950s by the same firm that designed the United Nations in New York. It was envisioned by then director Allen Dulles, brother of Secretary of State John Foster Dulles, as a college-like setting to exude an aura of tranquillity. It didn't fool many people.

The new building, joined to the western façade of the old structure, was designed and built about thirty years later and includes two six-story office towers connected by a four-story core area. It is steel and glass as opposed to the pre-cast concrete of the original building where the deep covert, or Black Box operations, are conducted. The million and a half square feet of space in the standing building was nearly doubled with the addition. The overall campus sits on some 258 acres of absolutely secure Virginia hillside.

Lest anyone think the CIA was nothing more than a gray entity, art work is abundant throughout the grounds and facility. A heroic statute of Nathan Hale, executed as a spy by the British in the American Revolution, stands between two trees. Inside there is a life-sized statue of Maj. Gen. William J. Donovan, known as "Wild Bill," head of the CIA's World War II predecessor, the Office of Strategic Services, the OSS.

And although there is no statue honouring her, the CIA took pride in the fact that cooking guru, Julia Child and her husband, Paul, OSS operatives in Asia during World War II were part of the "Clan."

There are also various bas reliefs, including one of Allen Dulles. In the main lobby of the original building, etched into the wall is the biblical verse that most defines the CIA's attitude toward its mission:

"And ye shall know the truth and the truth shall make you free."

Throughout the building original art, some purchased and some donated, lines corridor and office walls. Oil portraits of each director, including such famous faces as George H.W. Bush, decorate the walls of one corridor.

But the most moving of all is the Wall of Heroes, a display of stars, one for each CIA operative killed in the line of duty. Because of the covert operations, names can not generally be displayed. But for those whose names can be spoken publicly, an open book nearby makes note of who they were.

Mary Sapphire saw little of the beauty of the CIA complex. Her operation was located in the basement of the old office building, buried beneath tons of concrete and far from any prying eyes or counter-surveillance equipment.

Satellite dishes fed information directly to her monitors and the analysts deciphering it. More, her responsibilities included receiving transmissions from agents around the globe who communicated with headquarters by encoded satellite telephones or other covert methods.

In short, her bailiwick was the central heartbeat of the Central Intelligence Agency.

"I've gone over Coast Guard reports," the analyst told Sapphire, but there is nothing to indicate a Mayday from that region."

Sapphire took the printout of the explosion and the previous frame and put them both under a magnifying glass on a stand on her desk.

"What do you make of this?" she asked. "It certainly does appear as though one of these ships has gone down and the other is not coming to the rescue. Why wouldn't either one of them have broadcast for help? Look into this and see if you can come up with any ships that are overdue in port. And let's keep this on the active role."

She left the disk on her desk and nodded to the analyst, dismissing him. The man turned to the door and walked back to his area of operation, referred to by his colleagues as "The Dungeon."

Alone in her office, Mary Sapphire picked up an internal telephone, punched in a scrambler code, and listened as it gave its distinctive high-pitched tone.

"Send a recon plane to these coordinates and see if they can spot any wreckage or indication that a ship has gone down. There was also a container ship in that area and I want to know if we can identify it, its owners and what flag it flies. Please have this undertaken with all due speed."

"Yes M'am," came the respectful reply. I have a Goose in the air not far from there. I'll retask it and see what we can find out. I should be able to get back to you within a couple of hours."

"That will do, but please make sure it is not much longer than that."

Mary Sapphire replaced the phone on the cradle and turned to other business at hand.

XIII

CLANDESTINE OPERATION

"**H**ey Kid, Amanda and I are going to take in a show and then dinner tonight. Why don't you join us?"

Dan looked as casually dressed as Hesh had ever seen him. He was wearing a pair of blue Levi 501 jeans in a stretch material that never seemed to lose a crease. Over that he had on a light, short sleeve shirt with military style epaulettes on the shoulders.

"Never saw a tight ass like you go out in anything but a suit and tie. Thanks for the offer, but I think I'm just going to wander around the city for a couple of hours. You guys go ahead and enjoy yourselves. I'll talk to you later."

"OK, if you're sure. We don't mind having you along. We can pick up some cheap tickets to an off-Broadway show. There are a couple of comedies playing and we can use a good laugh and for five bucks apiece, you can't beat the price."

"Thanks Boss, but I'll pass. Maybe next time."

"We'll see you later. Don't forget that we're having lunch at the Delegates Dining Room at the UN tomorrow. The Consul-General wants us to brief him and go over some information before he goes into the general session. I'll meet you at the gate on First Avenue and we can go in together."

"No problem. I'll see you there."

Dan turned to Amanda and his eyes roamed over her very trim body. She was about five four in her stocking feet with blond-brown hair that stopped just short of her shoulders. She easily fit into the junior size dresses she favoured that accentuated her curves.

She walked across the apartment's living room and sat on Dan's lap.

"Hesh hasn't gotten over what happened on the beach, has he?"

"No, I'm afraid that will be with him for the rest of his life. He seems to be getting on, but then he slips back. I can't blame him. Not after what he went through and only a month after he was married."

Amanda stood and Dan rose with her, taking her hand in his as they walked toward the door. Their apartment was in a building just off the overlook to the Hudson River on East 58th Street, only blocks from both the United Nations and the Israel Consulate. It was convenient enough for him to walk to either place and he enjoyed doing so, even in bad weather.

Dan remembered the days before he emigrated when he would leave the house in the rain or snow and walk the Rockaway boardwalk, smelling the salt air and revelling in the solitude. Once the "Summer Trash," as the locals called seasonal visitors, left, it was rare for anyone to walk there. He could think, talk aloud to himself and vent his feelings to the seagulls congregating on the deserted beach.

Perhaps over the weekend he might go back for a visit although the area had gone rapidly down hill. Most of the summer residences had long since been demolished in a fit of urban renewal. Fire had taken care of the rest and the blocks coming off the beach looked like Berlin after the war. There had been a rebuilding spree and the peninsula was well on the way back to becoming one of the most prized locations in The City.

For right now, however, he and Amanda were going to enjoy an evening on the town, a show and dinner. And then…..?

Hesh's apartment was in the same building, but three floors below Dan and Amanda. He watched the main entrance from his window as they exited the building and walked west on East 58th Street toward Broadway. He gave them five minutes to put some distance between themselves and the building and then he walked out the door and to the elevator.

He was wearing a New York Yankee baseball cap pulled down over his eyes and a loose fitting sweat shirt outside of his pants. With sneakers on his feet he moved quietly, almost silently, down the hall to the elevator.

Hesh nodded to the other resident on the elevator as the doors opened on his floor, thankful for the almost total anonymity living in a New York apartment building gave its residents. Few knew their next door neighbours, much less anyone living on another floor.

He exited the building and turned left to First Avenue and headed north on the wide, traffic clogged street. At the corner of First Avenue and East 62nd Street he stopped and waited.

Within a minute a black Lincoln Town Car pulled up and Hesh slipped into the back seat. The door closed and the car melted into mid-day New York traffic. The car turned west to Second Avenue and then headed south to the Queensboro Bridge at East 59th Street. The normally heavy traffic was absent and the car moved quickly, crossing the span into Long Island City and swung south to the warehouse district.

The driver turned a corner and drove directly through the open overhead door of a building advertising itself as "The Biggest Self-Storage Facility in New York." Barely had the vehicle passed through the entrance than the doors slid closed.

If this was a storage facility, there was precious little stored here. The cavernous building, brightly lit by the overhead glass skylights, was totally empty. Anyone who called to inquire about renting storage space was politely informed that every bin was full and there was a long waiting list. They were graciously given the name and telephone number of other storage facilities in the general area.

No one ever questioned the response and most expressed gratitude for the information about other locations.

Hesh stood aside as the car made a U-turn and faced the exit with the motor running.

"Up here, my friend," came a voice, seemingly from the rafters.

Hesh looked up and saw a steel mesh floor surrounding the building where a second floor would have been. A ladder, much like a ship's ladder, led to the landing and as he climbed it, he could see office doors lining the second level. All were dark except for one at the head of the steps.

The man approached Hesh and grabbed him in a bear hug, almost squeezing the breath out of him. Hesh returned the affectionate gesture and greeted the man with "Shalom."

The man was just short of six feet tall and perhaps no more than 185 pounds. Even through the zippered jacket he wore and the Levi blue jeans, Hesh could see the rippling muscles of someone who worked out and took care of himself.

"Simeon," how are you?"

"I am well, my friend. And you?"

"Good, as well."

"I am glad to hear that. We have some work to do. Are you ready and available?"

"I will make the time and opportunity."

"Good."

Simeon turned and walked to the lighted office as Hesh followed a quick step behind. His pace was as sure as the aura he presented. The man was a leader. He knew it and the people he dealt with knew it.

Simeon had served in the Mossad and was one of its more effective agents. His specialty was tracking down those who planned suicide attacks against Israel and instituting a rendition with extreme prejudice, and he was a master of the task.

He fumed thinking of the reward given to the families of suicide bombers that encouraged them to glorify the sacrifice of their own children and to trivialize the deaths of Israeli children and civilians. Saddam Hussein had begun the practice of giving the families of Shaheeds, martyrs, $25,000 and a new home if the Israelis destroyed theirs. The practice was picked up by Libyan leader Muammar Kaddafi with his limitless bankroll of oil money. To a people who looked on life as a cheap commodity, the reward was more than welcome although it cost the life of a son, daughter, husband or father.

The Shaheed's reward was in heaven with seventy two virgins.

So long as there was no direct pain to the families of the suicide bombers and they were able to reap the rewards of the mass killings, there would be no incentive for them to dissuade the would-be Shaheed from a murderous journey.

Simeon's wife and three-year-old daughter were on a shopping trip in Jerusalem and were in a bus heading home when a young woman boarded the vehicle and sat down behind them. She dressed no differently than any of the other passengers, a mix of mostly Jews and a handful of Palestinians, heading to or from work or shopping. The only difference was the bulky clothing. Even her large bag fit in with the shoppers.

The bus made several more stops along the busy street and was about three-quarters full when the young woman stood and said:

"Allahu Akbar, God is great."

Simeon's wife gripped her daughter, fear crossing her face. She tried to stand and make a desperate dash for the exit door. She never had a chance.

Aside from the sudden knowledge that they were all gong to die, their deaths were so instantaneous, that there was no pain. The bus dissolved in a ball of flame, the metal fittings melted and the fabric seats turned to ash. The people were reduced to little more than singed bone and dust.

Simeon was out of the country on a mission and did not find out about the loss of his wife and daughter for almost a week. The rage that built inside of him exploded in a fury. Although his superiors insisted he take time off, Simeon refused. He had missed their funerals as, according to Jewish tradition, they were interred the next day. His next assignment came barely a week after his return.

He and his team tracked a Hamas unit to a safe house in Cape Town in South Africa. Since the presidency of Nelson Mandela, South Africa had become a friendly haven for those who fought Israel. While most of the world lionized Mandela, he voiced support for the Palestinians and disdain toward the Israelis.

South Africa was far safer than Syria, Jordan or Libya because of its distance from the region. And although Mandela was no longer in power, his acolytes still controlled the government and his affinity for the Palestinian cause. Enmity toward the Jewish state still held sway in spite of a sizeable Jewish population in the country.

Simeon booked a suite at the colonial-era Mount Nelson Hotel, a British favourite from years gone by. The long road leading to the hotel was lined with tall palm trees and as he stood on the balcony looking out, Simeon could imagine a horse drawn carriage with a uniformed British officer and his feathered tri-cornered hat, coming up the path. It would not have been a hospitable place for a Jew. Almost like today.

A female operative had checked in with him as his wife and both listed their nationality as Croatian, a ruse they could comfortably pull off. The rest of the team was at the high rise Heerengracht Hotel in the city center.

Behind the city, rimming its border, was the high, flat topped Table Mountain. A long cable car took visitors to the top to see the spectacular view across the city and southward towards the Cape of Good Hope. Often a heavy cloud layer would drape across the top of the mountain and hang over its sides. The locals fondly referred to it as "The tablecloth on Table Mountain."

Simeon was oblivious to all of this. His ability to focus on the task at hand to the virtual exclusion of anything else had become legendary. And on this trip he was focused on eliminating an external planning cell of Hamas. He knew that there were myriad guerrilla groups with as many names. But he was well aware that was all a sham and that virtually all of them came under the command of Hamas and that the variety of names was simply to confuse and obfuscate, making it appear as though the opposition was more widespread than it really was.

His advance party had tracked the cell to one of the black neighbourhoods surrounding the city center of Cape Town, where they assumed they were fully protected by the local authorities. This is where much of the planning for the recent spate of suicide bombings had taken place. And it was here that orders had been given to a young Palestinian girl to strap a bomb under her robes, board a bus in Jerusalem and blow it up.

Simeon's advance scout reported that the cell members were in attendance in the small, indistinct house on the outskirts of town. The plan was simple. They would walk up to the door and announce that they were from a local missionary group seeking to "Spread the Word." Evangelists were a common sight in these neighbourhoods and would not rouse suspicion.

While they held the occupants attention at the front door, the assault team would move to the back and in a coordinated move, would rush the occupants.

Under ordinary circumstances they would simply shoot the occupants and disappear into the city crowds. Simeon had decided on a different routine. He wanted a prisoner for interrogation. That made things a bit more difficult, but not impossible, especially for a group of whites. Their skin may have been dark from the desert sun, but there was no doubt they were Caucasian.

Simeon, his faux wife and another man, dressed in white shirts and black trousers, carrying bibles and pamphlets under their arms, made their way down the street, ultimately reaching their destination.

He knocked on the door and a very dark-skinned man answered.

"Hello brother. We have come to bring you salvation."

"I do not need your salvation. Please go away and bother someone else."

"Are you so pure that you do not need to hear the word of God?"

"My God is not yours."

"Please, just give me a minute of your time and let me show you something."

As the dark skinned man leaned forward, Simeon reached into the briefcase he was carrying and pulled an automatic pistol with a silencer screwed into the muzzle. Before the startled man could react, there was a hole in the middle of his forehead, between his eyes. Blood ran down his nose as he crumpled in a heap just inside the doorway.

Simeon's "wife" pushed a button in her hand and a buzzer sounded for the team at the rear of the house. Together they rushed in from front and back. The pop-pop of sound suppressed weapons sounded over and over again until all those who had been inside the house lay dead on the floor in ever spreading pools of blood.

All except one man, prone on the floor with Simeon's boot pressing down on his neck. The man, who had been a principle in sending young boys and girls into Israel to blow themselves up as martyrs and heroes of the revolution, lay on the floor in a pool of his own urine, excrement staining the seat of his pants as well.

Simeon reached down, grabbed him by the hair and pulled him to his feet. The man stared into Simeon's hard, cold eyes and he broke into sobs that welled up from his chest, tears streaking down his cheeks, dripping off his chin.

""You have a simple choice. You can tell me what I want to know or you can die."

"Jew pig! You can go to hell."

"I think you will be there long before me," Simeon responded as he putt he tip of the silencer behind the man's kneecap and pulled the trigger.

Bone and blood spurted across the room as the man went down in a heap, screaming in pain.

Simeon again reached for a handful of hair and pulled him to an upright position.

"How about the next knee? Or do you think it might be in your best interests to speak with me now?"

The man hesitated and Simeon blew his left knee apart.

"The next one goes into your balls," he said as he lowered the gun, pointing it at the man's crotch.

"Please. Let me live. I don't want to die. Whatever you want," he sobbed hysterically.

Simeon looked with disgust at the hero of the Islamic movement and said:

"I want a complete list of those in your cell, where they came from and who their living relatives are."

The man began to blather information so rapidly that his words almost ran together. Simeon placed a micro cassette tape recorder an inch from his mouth so as not to miss a thing.

Tears were running down his cheeks as he sobbed in pain. But he parted with all the information asked of him. He looked at Simeon, his eyes pleading for mercy.

"The bus in Jerusalem that you blew up…my wife and daughter were on board," he said as he slowly lifted the gun and fired a shot into the man's testicles. Pain ratcheted across his face, bile welling in his throat and stifling the scream trying to exit the man's mouth.

Simeon looked down at him and asked: "Oh, I'm sorry. Are you in a lot of pain? I'll take care of that."

He placed the muzzle of the gun against the man's eye.

"Without your balls, I don't think you'll be able to enjoy any of the seventy two virgins." With that he squeezed the trigger.

"We'll make sure that none of the people on the list has time to enjoy the $25,000 reward they are given when their children martyr themselves. New homes and all that money for sacrificing their children and permitting them to become murderers of innocents. There will be no peace for them."

Shortly after that the Palestinian Authority police began dealing with a rash of killings of civilians in the territories who had recently come into large sums of cash. They lived in new, nicely furnished homes in comparison to the others around them. But none lived to enjoy the newly found affluence; all of them had been shot, men, women and children. Pet dogs were found with bullet holes in their heads as well. None survived and the message was being delivered.

Simeon sat in his office reading a Palestinian newspaper; he turned to his assistant and commented:

"What a shame. None of them lived long enough to spend and enjoy their bounty. Now they know that none of them will be safe so long as our families are not. They will know what our "Response" will be."

Simeon returned to Jerusalem and immediately tendered his resignation to the Mossad. As a freelance he would be subject to no government oversight or restraint.

Simeon turned to Hesh and handed him a photograph and a file folder. "This is the next one."

Hesh took the papers, shook hands with Simeon and turned toward the office door.

"This is our response. They will feel our pain until they learn."

With that he descended the stair, got into the waiting Lincoln and headed back to Manhattan.

IX

THE KING...AGAIN

Dan turned the corner of East 42nd Street onto Second Avenue and headed toward the glass enclosed guard box in front of 800 Second Avenue, only a block from the United Nations. He paused and displayed his photo identification card indicating he was a press officer for the Israeli delegation to the world body.

The uniformed guard wearing a patch on his left shoulder that identified him as an employee of International Protection Systems, a private security firm, gave Dan's card a hard look and then pushed a button opening the very secure entrance to the Israeli consulate.

Although the consulate provided much of its own security, mostly unseen to the public, and the New York City Police Department offered its services, Israel also opted for a trained, professional private service to add another layer of protection for its diplomats and visitors.

The guards provided by IPS, brought the term "rent-a-cop" to a new and much higher level. The operatives, both uniformed and in civilian clothes, were trained in profiling, executive security, hand-to-hand combat, black belt rated in karate and were all expert marksmen. Their job was to spot trouble before it became a problem and to defuse potentially negative situations.

Dan, who normally held non-Mossad operatives with a degree of disdain and had no use for those he considered amateurs and mercenaries, had more than a modicum of respect for these people. He knew they could be counted on in a tight situation to react in an appropriate manner. They were not senior citizens working as bank guards who would disappear under the counter at the first sign of trouble.

He entered the building and took the elevator to his fourth floor office. Although the exterior of the building was totally non-descript, the inside was bright and cheery with pictures of the Holy Land decorating the walls and offices. There were, of course, the requisite photographs of Israeli government leaders and historical figures, but they took second place to depictions of the Western Wall, Masada and a grand painting of Moses descending with the tablets carrying the Ten Commandments.

If you looked closely at that work of art, you'd notice Moses' eyes following you as you moved about the entranceway. It was as though he was observing all who entered and protecting the building from harm.

And he was "following" you. Behind his eyes were surveillance cameras neatly hidden from view that took in every inch of the area they covered.

In his small but comfortable office, Dan began to peruse the day's intelligence reports. His job was to prepare the Consul General's Daily Briefing, the CGDB, report of any relevant items that might affect his job in representing the country at the United Nations.

Normally he listed terrorist attacks, bombings, numbers of innocents killed and the retaliatory strikes. Little came his way that could excite him or move him out of the lethargic state he had fallen into since the day of the attack on the Twin-Towers and the Pentagon.

Although Minister Ben Chaim refused his resignation and attempted to absolve him of any blame, the guilty feeling just wouldn't go away. He had been beating himself up for years for not recognizing what the terrorists were planning.

But even with that feeling bouncing around in his subconscious, the routine of examining the day's intelligence for five years numbed his brain. He had fallen into a routine of simply listing the obvious and letting it go at that.

Pushing the papers across his desk he noted an intelligence report of a satellite transmission reading: "The Throne is Secure. His Majesty is in Our Control."

The little hairs on the back of his neck stood stiffly at attention as a chill ran down his spine. This was almost déjà vu and the memories of the raid against the compound began to flood back. But the World Trade Center was gone.

"What's the meaning of almost the same verbiage?"

He didn't add up the verbiage last time until it was too late.

Dan pushed the papers aside and reached for the folder containing recent intelligence communiqués. Frantically he began searching through his files for the transcript of information he shared with the CIA coming out of Iraq and the combat region. He found the folder he had dubbed "Spyder Hole" and spread it out on his desk.

When Saddam Hussein was captured, he was found by American soldiers hiding in a hole in the ground. They dubbed it the "Spyder Hole," and had taken him in to custody. They found copies amounts of intelligence hidden with him and were able to take down several clandestine units. To Dan the term had come to mean anything filled with hidden intelligence.

Intelligence indicated that although the Israelis had bombed Saddam's fledgling nuclear facility before it could go on-line, research had continued at other locations, the Spyder Holes in Dan's folder.

Their exact coordinates were never determined and Dan assumed they had gone "underground" to hide from satellite surveillance.

There were several references in the intelligence with similar comments and all made a "Royal" connotation. They referred to "His Majesty," or "The King," all of which Dan had pushed into the recesses of his mind after 9-11.

Dan walked to the wall and pulled down a map of Iraq and began noting with pins approximate locations referred to in the intelligence. Even with intense study he couldn't picture a pattern that led to a conclusion.

"It's a gut feeling," he thought to himself. "I'm not going to miss it a second time."

Each of these locations had been vetted by both inspectors from the International Atomic Energy Commission and, after the invasion, by American troops and even the CIA.

The American intelligence agency had a lot to make up for after providing seriously erroneous information regarding the possession of Weapons of Mass Destruction (WMDs) by Saddam Hussein. That information had given President George W. Bush the "raison d'être" to launch an invasion and drag his friend, British Prime Minister Tony Blair into the fray. Bush jumped on anything that might appear to indicate Saddam had WMDs stockpiled. None were ever found.

The Mossad, British MI-6 and other foreign intelligence agencies had tried to warn the CIA and American government that if WMDs were the reason for the invasion, there was no reason to go. What they didn't know was that there was a political agenda that had nothing to do with WMDs.

Bush had come into office hell bent on ousting Saddam because the Iraqi leader had attempted to have the elder Bush, the former president, assassinated as revenge for the first Gulf War. That effort blew up in his face, but Bush the Younger, never forgot. Whatever the reason, he was going after Saddam.

But if Dan's sudden gut feeling was right, they were there, somewhere. But where?

He reached for the telephone and punched in the 757 area code for CIA headquarters and a private telephone number. The line rang directly on Matt Morton's desk and finally a recorded voice greeted Dan. He left a message asking Morton to call back as soon as possible, turned on his phone forward app and walked from his office.

The top floor of the consulate had a series of built-in antennae, hidden from view either from nearby buildings or from overhead satellite observation. But the powerful radios they serviced were capable of reaching any part of the world in an instant. They were used for both reception and transmission. Unknown even to most of the consulate staff, they were also capable of picking up and monitoring radio traffic by bouncing their signals off a series of satellites circling high above the earth.

Only the Mossad Station Chief and his executive staff were ever permitted entry. Inside the room two men sat, spinning dials and punching numbered buttons as they zeroed in on traffic of interest.

One of the men looked up at Dan's entry, smiled and greeted him: "Hello Chief."

Dan nodded in return and asked the operator if he had picked up any information relating to the travels of a royal anywhere in the world.

"We've had some stuff in the last day or so, but it doesn't make much sense and we can't connect it to anything we are aware of."

"Locate the originations for me please."

The operator brought a map up on a wall-sized screen, tickled the keys on his computer and two lighted circles came on, indicating a location in the North Atlantic and one near the pyramids at Giza.

As he stood puzzling at the map, the phone on his belt began to vibrate. He reached for it and pushed the talk button.

"Got your message, Dan. What's up?"

"We've had some very interesting traffic coming through and I think we should go over it. I'm afraid we might be facing a similar situation to the one we had five years ago. I don't want to miss it again."

"I'm driving up to New York tomorrow for a meeting at Federal Plaza. Can it wait until then?"

That'll work. How about meeting me at the Stage Deli for a late lunch and I'll let you know what we've got?"

"See you tomorrow."

Dan turned to the operator and told him to put together all the traffic they had on the incident and to see if they could track the route of the ship broadcasting from the North Atlantic.

"I'll be in my office. Please put this at the top of your priority list."

Dan walked slowly back to the elevator, head slightly bowed, his left hand rubbing his chin. So many things rattled through his mind that he could feel his head begin to pound.

"Why would they use the same code words again? Makes no sense. Imagination? Overreacting? Hell, I'd rather be wrong than be really wrong again."

The pictures of New York's World Trade Center going up in a giant ball of flame and crashing to earth in a cloud of dust that took weeks to drift away; the overwhelming smell that covered the city of humans whose miniscule remains being cremated in the fires that lingered for weeks after the attack were never out of his mind. To this day he felt that he had the information in hand and had he understood its meaning, could have saved all those thousands of people in the Trade Center, the Pentagon and the plane that crashed in Pennsylvania.

Within minutes of sitting back at his desk, he was on the intra-consulate phone to the operatives in the monitoring room.

"Have you got anything yet?"

"Boss, we're working on it. You've got to give us a little time."

"I don't know how much time we have. I want this moved along faster than anything you've ever done before. We could have a day. We could have a week. Or we might have only an hour. Just do it."

The intelligence analyst hung up the phone and a shiver went through his body. He had never seen the Station Chief act this way before. He was usually quiet and mild mannered and never overly demanding. This was a new side to him and the analyst wasn't about to test him.

"Let's get this done before we get our asses kicked back to Jerusalem," he said as they went to work.

Less than an hour later the man stood in front of Dan's desk. In his hand was a file folder with a red diagonal line that ran from corner to corner and the words "Utmost Secret" stamped on the line.

He held a chit for Dan to sign as having received the file. Israeli policy was to maintain a strict chain of possession. Any material rated this highly secret never passed from one hand to the other, even for a moment, without a signature. Bureaucratically annoying though it may have been, no such file ever went missing. Not when your ass was on the line.

Dan laid the file on his desk and motioned with his head for the analyst to leave and close the door behind him.

"What the hell…?"

Dan looked at satellite photos of an 853-foot long container ship, piled high with boxed cargo, moving away from a ball of flame that had only minutes earlier been a trawler, a deep sea fishing craft.

Sequential photos of both ships tracked their progress. Dan noted that the trawler had worked its way north from the Panama Canal and the container ship was traced to Portsmouth, England.

The angle of the Israeli satellite came in low over the horizon and had picked up the name of the container ship, the Cairo Pride, an Egyptian registered vessel. The cargo manifest listed a variety of commercial products and artefacts from the King Tut collection that had just completed a run at the British Museum in London following a month at the Louvre in Paris. It was now on its way to the Metropolitan Museum of Art in New York City.

"His Majesty? Am I over reacting? Are they only referring to the Tut artefacts or is it something else?"

Dan pushed the papers to the middle of the desk, tilted his chair slightly back and stared at a spot on the ceiling.

"Why didn't they report a ship in distress when the trawler blew up? What am I missing here?"

He called back up to the surveillance room and ordered that the container ship be kept under regular observation.

Dan went back to his computer and pulled up a web site posted by the Museum of Modern Art (MOMA) and listing its upcoming events. Sure enough, there was the King Tut exhibition, slated to go display in three weeks.

"Maybe I'm just paranoid. But maybe I'm not."

He reached for his telephone and put a call through to Matt Morton.

"Can you check with your people and see if they have any information on a trawler that may have gone down in the North Atlantic and a container ship named the Cairo Pride and registered to an Egyptian company?"

Morton copied the details of time and coordinates and handed them to an assistant with a gesture indicating the need for speed.

"What's going on Dan?"

"Hey, this could be just a nightmare of mine, but I simply have a gut feeling that something is very wrong. There's been radio traffic referring to royalty; almost the same as just before 9-11. Then our surveillance crews pick up satellite intel showing this trawler disappearing after a big fireball lights up the area and the container ship, which had been alongside of it, sailing away without issuing a May Day. Now that's what I call more than just the gut feeling of some nutty Mossad operative. There should have been a GPS ID broadcast from the container ship and possibly from the trawler as well. But nothing. Nada. No signal at all. There are precious few ships that don't have ID that we could pick up. That's more than strange."

"I don't know if I should hope you are right or wrong, but we had better look into it. I'll get back to you as soon as possible. Why don't you bring your information to our meeting tomorrow? The two of us can sit down and see if we can piece together any kind of pattern."

"See you then."

Dan waived off the security escort who had brought Morton from the consulate entrance to his office.

"Don't you guys trust anyone?"

"The last time we trusted someone, one of our cells was blown. And I don't mean just exposed."

Because of the need to examine documents, the meeting had been transferred from the public venue to the consulate. Food could come later.

Dan pushed a button and a large screen slowly lowered, covering the wall opposite his desk. The high definition LCD screen lit up and Dan slipped a disk into the tray on his computer terminal; he gently pushed the tray and it was drawn back into the machine.

He held a wireless mouse in his hand, clicked the buttons and watched as scenes of the North Atlantic came into sharp focus. The two operatives watched as the satellite view moved in, first on the trawler and then the Cairo Pride. The pictures were sharp and snapped about every five seconds, giving the movement the feeling of an old Charlie Chaplin movie.

Dan stopped the progression at the frame showing the two ships adjacent to each other. He brought the magnification zoom in, showing figures on the deck.

"Matt, look over there. It sure as hell looks as though there are some bodies lying on the deck."

Spreading out from one body they could clearly see what appeared to be a pool of blood. The high definition cameras in the satellite could bring even a blemish on someone's face into clear view.

The two men hunched over in their chairs, as though that sign of intent observation would enhance what they were seeing.

"Never ceases to amaze me how clear pictures snapped from a satellite in space are and how they can zero in on such small objects from so far away," Morton mumbled.

Dan pushed the button for progression and it became clear that there was trouble on board the container ship. They spotted bodies being dumped overboard and then the two ships separating. Suddenly the trawler was gone in a ball of fire and the container ship continued on its way.

Morton reached for his cell phone, punched in a series of numbers and waited as the phone at the other end rang.

"Sapphire? I want you to pull up anything you may have on the Cairo Pride."

He gave her the time frame and coordinates and waited as she fingered her computer console.

"Matt, we noticed this the other day, but couldn't find any report of a ship in distress."

What did you find out when you followed up?"

"We didn't follow up because there was no distress call," Sapphire commented.

"What the hell were you thinking? There's a fireball and a ship disappears, but you didn't think that was important enough to follow up on?"

"I'm sorry, but we were retasking our satellites to cover certain other actions and this didn't seem to be a priority. You wouldn't believe how many ships actually go down on a regular basis. We don't follow them unless we have reason to be suspicious about something. At the most, if we see trouble, we'll notify the Coast Guard"

"OK. Get suspicious. I want to know anything you can find out about the track of those two ships. And see if you can get me some information on the container ship; where it came from and where it is going. The last we heard it contained major historic artefacts and was headed for New York."

Matt turned to Dan:

"I think we better have a unit at the docks when the Cairo Pride comes in and give it a thorough going over. We'll have to find out where it is slated to dock. It could be Manhattan, Brooklyn or even in New Jersey."

"Call NYPD and see if they are giving an escort from the ship to MOMA. For a collection of that importance I can't believe they'll just hitch a tractor to it and drive off. I can't call One PP (Police Plaza) because it would look strange for a foreign government representative to do that. On the other hand, I don't think it would be a good idea to have the CIA making inquiries like that either. It'll raise too many eyebrows."

"I can handle that."

Matt turned the car onto the long pier jutting into the East River from the Brooklyn side. He was followed by two vans, each carrying eight passengers dressed in the uniforms of U.S. Customs & Immigration. The timing was perfect as the dock rats were just tying the ship to the heavy steel davits on the pier.

An empty tractor-trailer was standing to the side and a group of men dressed in suits were congregating at the point where the ship's ladder would drop.

Dan and Matt, dressed in Customs uniforms as well, walked over to the men and asked for identification. Each produced an ID card from MOMA and told the government agents they were there to escort a very valuable shipment of artefacts on loan to the museum back to the institution for preparation and display.

"I'm sorry, but you will have to wait a while," Matt told them. "We do a spot check on incoming ships that is very thorough and the Cairo Pride drew the lucky number."

"I insist on accompanying you when you check our containers," one of the suits demanded. "I will not take a chance on any damage to those artefacts."

"You will not accompany us. You will not board the ship and if you so much as take one step toward the vessel, I'll arrest you and impound the shipment."

"You can't do that. I represent a very important museum."

Matt motioned to one of the men who had emerged from the front van.

"Please escort these gentlemen outside the gate until we're finished. If they so much as make a move to resist, arrest all of them."

"Matt, how in heaven's name are we going to inspect hundreds of containers? It'll take forever."

"My quasi-Israeli friend, watch and you shall learn."

Matt motioned for the uniformed crew to board the ship and begin its search. A man who identified himself as Capt Ahmed demanded to know what the problem was.

"Routine inspection." He was told, and then firmly moved aside.

Each of the "Customs" agents wore a small box that hung from a strap around his neck. Attached to the box was a cable leading to a boom about five feet long. When a toggle was thrown forward, a slight sucking sound came from the tip of the boom. When it was thrown the other way, a light on the box slowly flashed.

"If there was anything on board with even the smallest amount of radiation, these will pick up the scent. We don't even have to open the containers. All we have to do is move the wands around the doors."

The agents moved across the ship, the wands covering each and every container on the deck. Others climbed into the below deck holds and examined the entire cargo.

"Nothing! There's got to be something," Dan mumbled.

One of the agents moved between two rows of containers on the deck, stopped to rest for a minute and let his wand drop to the deck. The light on his console began to flash more rapidly until it seemed to be a steady, but flickering light.

"That's a pretty strong scent," Matt noted. "Get the Captain over here."

Ismail looked at Dan and Matt, a nervous tick on his face.

"I have no idea why you claim there is a radioactive response here. We do not carry hazardous material. Our cargo is only commercial items and, of course, the museum shipment on this trip."

Dan looked at Morton, a quizzical expression on his face.

"What are we missing?" he asked

"Why don't we let the crew finish its inspection and see if they find anything?"

A half hour later the crew chief motioned to Morton to step aside.

"We've gone over every damn box on the deck. We've looked into every crate in the hold and there's nothing here. We are picking up traces of radioactivity, but they're coming from an empty space on the deck."

"OK, wrap it up, but I want the captain and the entire crew hauled into custody. Let's keep them for questioning about the trawler that blew up and find out what the hell that was all about."

Morton nodded to Dan and Hesh and the three men walked back to the dock and their car. Inside the vehicle he turned to the Israeli agents.

"I'll put a call through to Sapphire and she if her people picked up anything we can use. See what your people have. In the meantime I am going to have the captain and his entire crew taken into custody"

"It sure looks as though they met up with another small ship after the trawler went down. What are they doing, playing forward pass?"

Dan sat at the console in the safe room at the consulate, tickling the keys and bringing surveillance images up on the screen. They watched as the Cairo Pride pulled alongside another smaller craft and appeared to be offloading a crate. The two ships parted with the Cairo Pride heading toward New York and the second ship nosing its way south. Surveillance lost it as it sailed into the harbour in Charlotte.

The young man walked out of the car rental agency in Charlotte and toward a line of cars parked alongside a chain link fence. He stopped at space number 43 and put a key into the door of a silver Ford Explorer, a comfortable car, arguably the biggest selling SUV in America, with enough look-alikes that it would blend in on any highway.

He sat down and adjusted the seat and then the mirrors, started the engine and drove slowly through the gate and headed south toward the port in Charlotte.

Lined up at the pier were a dozen ships, most of them ocean-going freighters or container vessels. Toward the end of the line sat a small, intra-coastal freighter that hauled goods from Canadian ports southward along the United States' East Coast to Miami. The ship passed through no customs checks and the Drug Enforcement Agency had no interest in it because its manifest never included uninspected international shipments.

This made the small ship, of American registry, the perfect carrier for a variety of illicit goods earning more money for its owners than the shipments of fruits it carried north from Florida's orchards or south with manufactured goods from Canada.

Sayyid steered the Explorer to a spot near the small ship, parked and walked over to the base of the ladder. A crew member approached and they spoke quietly. The crewman motioned to another on the deck above and the man responded with a nod of his head.

Within minutes Sayyid watched as a wooden crate, held fast by steel straps, was hoist high above the deck. The boom swung out over the pier and began slowly lowering the crate. An enclosed 18-wheeler stood just below the crane, its rear doors open.

The crate was placed gingerly on a wooden pallet on the dock and stood for only a moment before a large fork lift approached and engaged the pallet. The cargo was lifted into the bay of the 18-wheeler and pushed to the middle of the storage area. Two men jumped on board, secured it to the floor, jumped back to the ground and closed the doors.

Sayyid walked to the rear of the truck, placed a massive tempered steel padlock on the doors and then a strip of metal through two loops in the door, a seal with a government marking on it indicating the container had been inspected. He handed a manifest to the driver, cautioned the man to follow all speed and traffic laws and walked back to his Explorer.

The big truck slowly lumbered off the pier and headed toward the State Route 17 for the hour-long drive to Interstate 95 and Miami. Behind him, just far enough back to avoid a tailgating problem, was Sayyid.

At the little town of Coosahatchee the big rig inched slowly around a cloverleaf and southward on the interstate, hugging the right lane and moving at a maximum speed of just under seventy miles an hour.

Sayyid sat back in the plush SUV's seat. Even though the seat was quite comfortable, he felt his nerves jangling just a bit. He wouldn't feel comfortable until the cargo was loaded and on its way.

The nearly 600 mile trip to Dodge Island in Miami was just too long and the possibility of any kind of mishap was always present. It was the unknown that bothered him. He knew that the Interstate, a long and tedious highway that reached from New England through Florida, was virtually straight and monotonous to drive. It would take about nine and a half hours to drive without taking any stops into consideration.

He wanted to arrive at the Dodge Island cruise ship terminal, just after dawn and hours before passengers began arriving to board the enormous pleasure ships docked there.

Sayyid timed the drive for about ten hours, taking into consideration an opportunity to gas the tractor-trailer, time for a pit stop and to grab something to eat.

The driver was not privy to his cargo, but he was used to taking "unusual" items from port of entry to various locations around the country. He had a great client list because the word was that he never asked any questions, picked up his load and always delivered it on time and without a hitch.

Most luxury cruise passengers are unaware that the ships they are relaxing on also have a major commercial business. The ships generally loaded up before passengers arrive or while they are touring various ports and islands. The cargo brings in a large portion of the cruise line's income and fills up otherwise unusable space in the belly of the huge ships.

The Celebrity Summit cruise ship was one of the newer ships afloat, rising from the waterline and seeming to touch the sky. While passengers boarded from hatches on the ships side, the bow was capable of lifting up on hinges to accept large cargo items. Other, smaller pieces were loaded through hatches below the passenger entries.

Since the luxury ship was heading north from ports in Mexico and the Caribbean toward Canada, there would be no customs inspection after departure from Miami. The ship had been gone over with the usual very casual inspection and passed as "clean."

Sayyid knew there would be no further check of anything on board. His cargo would be safe for its journey northward to the Port of New York. The ship would sail into the harbour under the Verrazano Bridge, past the Statue of Liberty and the Ellis Island complex. It would sit at the foot of West 46th Street, just north of the Aircraft Carrier Intrepid, the former warship, now a major tourist attraction on the west side of Mid-Town Manhattan.

"Or where Mid-Town Manhattan used to be," he thought, a slight grin creasing his mouth.

He would have time to contact the Associated Press, make his demands for the freedom of that damned blind sheik, Omar Abdel-Rahman, the mastermind of the 1993 bombing of the World Trade Center, and the fool, Zacharias Moussoaui, whom the American press had dubbed "The twentieth Hijacker" involved in the 9-11 victory.

As a final stab at the Americans, he would also demand the release of Sirhan Sirhan who had been in prison since June of 1968 for the killing of Sen. Robert Fitzgerald Kennedy. Each of the prisoners whose release he would demand had a special significance to the Americans and would deeply wound their national pride. He had added the names of Moussoaui and Sirhan without the knowledge of his mentor. The original plan had been to demand the release of the old sheik who was in ill health and would soon die. Another thing to rile fundamentalists against the Americans and the Jew Israelis.

Omar Abdul Rahman was a blind sheik, a mullah who preached at a mosque in Jersey City, New Jersey to a large Muslim population. His sermons were noted for their anti-American vitriol, always referring to America as "Satan America," and Americans as "The American Whores."

According to Rahman, all Americans were "infidels, and Mohammed, the prophet of Allah, God of the "peaceful" religion, had decreed that "All infidels must convert or be put to death."

The fact that he was on the State Department's "Watch List" was no hindrance at all. He was convicted in 1995 of Seditious Conspiracy for his cooperation with Al Qaeda and his part in planning the truck bombing of the World Trade Center..

Moussoaui was convicted in a Northern Virginia court in the spring of 2006 for withholding information that could have prevented the 9-11 attack and was sentenced to life in prison with no hope of parole. In addition, he was to serve his term in solitary, having no contact with other prisoners and only allowed out of his cell for one hour a day to exercise.

Rahman would be freed as a favour to Bin Laden. If he lived or died after that was of no importance. The cause could use another martyr and in jail he served no purpose. Moussoaui was another story. He had current information and there was always the danger he could be made to talk. Sirhan was a bonus.

Sayyid knew that the policy of the United States, like that of Israel, was to never bargain with terrorists and to never pay ransom in any form.

"But what would their attitude be faced with the annihilation of millions of people in New York City? We will find out."

Sayyid smiled with satisfaction as he watched, the crate rose on a pulley and moved through the hatch into the cargo area of the Celebrity Summit. He turned the car around and headed into the city for a leisurely breakfast before he returned to board the ship. The cruise along the Atlantic seaboard to New York would be pleasant and relaxing because, Allah knows, everything else would be hectic from that point on.

He placed a call to Cairo.

"His Majesty has been put to bed in his quarters. Please advise the court jester to do what must be done."

X

TRACKING THE DEVICE

"**D**an, it looks as though we have a major cluster fuck on our hands. I couldn't say anything before, but we have an agent working inside Iran trying to get the lowdown on the madman's nuclear capability. We know that what they were doing was fairly primitive and couldn't possibly be a threat for years to come."

That doesn't sound as though it still holds true. What's happening now?"

When our troops captured Saddam they picked up intelligence that has been held at an almost "Eyes Only" level because of its sensitivity. He was perhaps two steps away from creating a workable nuclear weapon. With the International Atomic Energy Commission inspectors breathing down his neck, he knew it would be only a matter of time before they found the device. He had to get rid of it and there was only one place in the world no one would ever suspect him of sending it to."

"OK, twenty questions is over. Where did it go?"

"The one place everyone thought would have no compunction about dropping it on Israel."

"Iran?"

"Yup! They hate each other, but they hate America more. They'll sign a devil's compact to destroy the United States."

"Then we go in and dismantle his facility."

"Not so fast. That could blow everything up in our faces. First, we've got to get an exact location of the device."

"Matt, you're mad. We're dealing with a lunatic." He handed Morton a file with a recent newspaper clip.

"Iranian President Mahmoud Amadinejad has renewed his attack on Israel, saying the Jewish state will be "annihilated". He said the existence of Israel was a threat to the Islamic world.

"Like it or not, the Zionist regime is a rotten, dried tree that will be eliminated by one storm and is heading toward annihilation," he said.

"Guess what he means by '…one storm…' He's got Saddam's bomb and will use it on us. Israel will never sit back. There's going to be a nuclear pre-emptive strike. Matt, the shit's going to really hit the fan."

"We've got more trouble than that. We thought there was only one bomb. We've traced one to the United States. If they are going to threaten Israel, that means there is at least one more and I'd venture to guess you can multiply that.

"This Ahmadinejad is a true nut case. He was one of those so-called 'students' who took over the embassy in Teheran and held the staff for more than a year. Our security chief had negotiated with them and the stand-off would have ended in a couple of hours until Ahmadinejad and his radicals took control. That was the end of it until Reagan came into office and they used the hostages to embarrass Jimmy Carter. Too bad Carter didn't have balls and Andrew Young was looking over his shoulder and pulling the strings.

"I'll tell you a funny story that never got out to the public. When Reagan sent Carter to Germany to greet the hostages after their release, all the TV crews were kept behind a fence and couldn't get too close to the hospital. They narrated Carter's approach and after he went into the building they heard cheering. The news hotshots, not having any damn idea of what was going on, reported that the 'former' hostages were giving the 'former' president a warm welcome.

"What really happened was that Carter entered the room, his head was bowed because he couldn't look them in the eye. One of the guys walked over to him, stuck his face in Carter's and called him a 'miserable son of a bitch.' That when the others started to cheer and what the TV crews heard and misunderstood."

"Well, we don't have either Carter or Andrew Young to screw things up this time, so we had better get both of our organizations off their collective asses and figure out what's going on. And we damn well better find out what happened to the device we lost track of."

"Dan, this is Kyle Norman, British SIS. His organization has been working with a North Korean defector and they've picked up some very interesting intelligence." Matt said, introducing the two agents.

The British Secret Intelligence Service (SIS), better known to the World as MI-6, one of the more efficient and covert government agencies in the Free World, is under the authority of a Director General (DG). Although it has oversight from two judges appointed by the Prime Minister, it is basically answerable only to the Foreign Secretary.

The Judicial Commissioners, Lord Brown of Eton Under Heywood, who is liaison for Intelligence Services and the Rt. Hon. Sir Swinton Thomas work with SIS on interception of intelligence.

"Watcha got, Kyle?" asked Matt. "Does James know you're here?"

The reference to "James" made Norman wince. MI-6 is the home of the fictional James Bond and Norman could have passed for the suave British agent. He was about six feet, one inch tall, dark haired and about one hundred eighty five pounds of solid muscle.

"If those at Legoland heard you making that reference, there would be hell to pay. We must absorb that crap from a self-amused press, but from someone at The Company?"

British operatives referred to SIS headquarters at 85 Albert Embankment, located on the bank of the Thames and bordered by railroad tracks, giving it some degree of isolation, as "Legoland." From the air the low-rise complex has a faint resemblance to Lego blocks.

While the CIA was known as "The Company," insiders called MI-6 "The Firm." To other British agencies it was known as "The Friends."

It was first established in 1909 as the Foreign Section of the Secret Service Bureau and was headed by Capt., Sir Mansfield Cumming, who had the habit of signing all correspondence and orders only with his initial "C," a practice followed by all of his successors since. That gave rise to the famous "M" as head of the service in the 007 movies.

"Is there really an "007" designation that gives operatives free range to kill?" Dan chimed in..

Norman would only offer a half smile in response to the question.

"I have a communiqué from Legoland that has raised serious concern for us. Information we received appears to indicate that there would be an assassination attempt on a monarch. We believed that was Her Majesty The Queen or one of the Royal household. We now believe it is not a direct threat on Her Majesty, but something that is quite more far reaching than that."

"That might go along with what we've been looking into here. Lay out what you have and let's see if we can put it all together."

"This feels like déjà vu all over again," Dan mumbled. "Let's not mess it up this time."

Muhktar al Hamadi walked down the long, winding steps, past the uniformed security guard and out the front entrance on the east side of the United Nations Building onto a sunlit First Avenue side of the world parliament. He could have taken an elevator to the basement delegates parking area, but then he would not have been seen by the television crews standing by the entrance.

He personally cared little for publicity, but his position as President Ahmadinejad's personal representative to the "Den of Evil," as he referred to the United Nations, demanded that he be as visible as possible.

Hamadi affected the dress favoured by Ahmadinejad, a sports jacket, slacks and open collared shirt. He much preferred the comfort of a robe and normally wore one at United Nations sessions. Today was an Ahmadinejad day.

As he stepped through the door, a microphone was thrust in his face, the CNN logo facing the camera.

"Mr. Ambassador, your president has threatened the use of atomic weapons against the United States and Israel unless all foreign troops are pulled out of the Middle East. Aren't you setting a standard that will be impossible for them to meet? And aren't you afraid this will create a nuclear conflict?"

"Satan's troops have no business on our soil. They are an affront to Allah and there will be destruction unless they leave. Israel? Why do you persist in calling Palestine Israel? There is no such country and the land is being occupied by a tribe that will be annihilated."

"Are you saying there is no diplomatic route that can be followed to avoid a conflict?"

"Avoid a conflict? The conflict already exists. War has been ongoing against the Troops of Allah and that can not be permitted to continue."

"Your president has threatened nuclear war. Is that still an option for you?"

"The occupiers of Palestine have a nuclear arsenal and you do not appear concerned by that."

"They have not threatened to use nuclear weapons unless the same is launched against them."

"The sand in their land will be fused into glass. They will all be destroyed in the fires of hell and all the infidels who remain in the Land of Allah will be destroyed."

"No chance for peace?"

"We do not negotiate with the devil."

Hamadi turned and walked away as the reporter was about to voice another question. He walked to the semi-circular driveway and his waiting car. The Lincoln Towne car was built on a super chassis and was reinforced with Teflon and bullet proof glass. The engine was souped up and could move the big vehicle at speeds in excess of 100 miles an hour. Although where in New York traffic they expected to go at that speed was questionable.

The vehicle could withstand almost any attack except a direct missile hit. Or a bomb.

Hamadi nodded to his driver who was holding the door open for him and slid into the back seat. The man closed the door, moved to the front compartment and sat behind the steering wheel. He turned the key and the engine kicked to life.

One of the security guards punched a button that opened the gate to the driveway and the car easily moved into the northbound First Avenue traffic. He was headed to the FDR Drive and out of the city. But first, just as those without diplomatic immunity, he had to contend with the normal traffic of Mid-Town Manhattan.

Hamadi bristled as he looked out the window at the hundreds of vehicles surrounding him; every day Americans in their personal cars, businessmen in taxis and a Hummer limo a few cars ahead of him. There was even a messenger on a Vespa-type scooter, his heavy sack draped over his right shoulder, weaving through traffic and making better time than any of the cars.

Even the scooter messenger couldn't seem to beat the traffic light and all the vehicles came to a stop as it turned red. The little two-wheeled scooter moved between the line of cars and up to the front by the intersection where Hamadi sat waiting for the light to change.

As he pulled up alongside the car, the messenger moved the heavy canvas bag off his shoulders and held it to his right side, between himself and Hamadi's car. As the light changed and traffic began to move, he placed it against the passenger door of the limo and a strong magnet gripped the reinforced steel.

The messenger pulled away in traffic and made a left turn onto East 49th Street. The limo continued, oblivious to the package stuck to the door and had gone barely fifty feet when the bag erupted into a ball of flame, crushing the door inward and slamming thousands of tiny metal shards into Hamadi's body.

The force of the explosion killed him instantly. The driver wasn't so lucky. He lay draped over the steering wheel, the back of his head open, exposing the grey mass of brains as his vital fluids drained from his body. He died slowly and painfully.

The telephone rang at Associated Press Offices in Rockefeller Center. The usually busy newsroom had hit a lull and the AP correspondents were sitting and relaxing.

Ned Josephs casually reached for the instrument and said: "Associated Press. How can I help you?"

"This is Response. We have delivered a blow against the Iranian Nazi at the United Nations. He has called for the destruction of Israel and Jews around the world. We have delivered the same justice to him. Anyone who wishes us harm will meet the same fate. We will no longer go willingly into the 'showers.' Never Again! Never Again!"

Before Josephs could say anything, the line went dead with only the sound of a disconnect buzz.

"I don't know what's going on, but we had better check the UN. Some guy who says he's from a group calling itself "Response," is claiming they attacked someone there."

The three intelligence agents were at the consulate going over surveillance reports when the door flew open and the press secretary blurted out:

"They've killed Hamadi. Blew his car up on First Avenue right down the street from the UN."

"Who?"

That bunch of renegades calling themselves "Response," is claiming credit. Their call to the press came too soon after the incident to be bullshit."

Dan looked at Matt and Kyle.

"That's it. It's hit the fan. There is no way that Ahmadinejad is going to sit back without retaliating for this one. Hamadi was his closest personal advisor and friend. They go back together before the takeover of the embassy. We had better figure out what and where they are planning their next move."

Early the next morning Dan was on board an El Al flight back to Jerusalem. He had coordinated with both Matt and Kyle and expected to be back in New York within only a few days. He needed speed on this trip and so chose the national airline.

"Not staying long enough for jet lag to set in," he mumbled to himself as he sat back in the seat. As a ranking official he had First Class privileges here as well and although he normally disdained luxury, these long flights took a lot out of you…especially when you had to be in top form for critical meetings.

XI

THE TAKEOUT

The Mossad car picked Dan up at the airport and rushed straight to headquarters. He had been on the secure satellite phone with Ben Chaim and said that he wanted back in an operational role.

"I was wondering what took you so long to realize that's where you belong," the Minister said.

"I'm ready. They won't fool me a second time."

His team waited for him in the secure conference room and Dan motioned for them to sit down and get to work.

"Brief me on what we've gotten. I want a full SITREP."

"Colonel, there is no doubt that the Iranians are involved in an effort to explode a nuclear weapon. But the intel we are receiving doesn't seem to indicate that they have a bomb or that they are the crux of the situation.

"We know that they have a facility that has been in operation since 1974 at Saghand that is extracting uranium for production of Yellowcake. They need that to progress to the next step and ultimately nuclear fission."

"OK, stop with the history lesson and let's get up to speed as to what is happening today. I don't think we have that much time to waste."

"Yes, sir. It appears from information obtained after Saddam Hussein was captured that his nuclear technology was spirited to Iran. That was the last place anyone would look for it because of their enmity for each other. But Saddam knew he was about to get hit with a shit storm and saw that as a way to cover himself. He was able to deny having any weapons of mass destruction and yet still hoped to have them within reach."

"So?"

"OK, we've traced them with the cooperation of the Iranian National Council of Resistance, the NCRI. They want to get rid of the mullahs as much as we do. Maybe even more so because it's their country. But they are able to place operatives in situations we could only dream about.

"Our contact in the NCRI tells us that Iran expects to be attacked and has moved up its schedule for producing a fissionable bomb. They are working at Lashkar Ab'ad, a uranium laser enrichment plant. They've told the International Atomic Energy Commission that they have dismantled the facility.

"But what they have really done is to keep it up to snuff with nuclear development and have dug in their heels. They have moved it underground into a lead-lined facility that is almost impossible to detect. But it's there."

"Another Spyder Hole," Dan mused.

"Have they reached the point of chain reaction yet?"

"We believe they are only a step or two away from it."

"OK, we go in. There's no choice but to take out this facility before they begin to mass produce bombs. If that happens, we're gone and so is a major part of the United States and Europe. They don't care if they inherit a wasteland as long as they kill all the infidels."

Dan pointed to his planning and logistics man.

"Get everything you have from all of our assets ASAP. We're going to have to go in by land. Let's move."

The crew dispersed to pull up satellite images of Lashkar Ab'ad and the surrounding area. They would not only have to get in without being spotted, but Dan's directive, seemingly impossible, tasked them to destroy the facility and make it look like an accident.

The operatives moved, but shook their heads collectively wondering how in heaven's name they were going to accomplish this. But Dan had always laughed and repeated one of his American sayings:

"The difficult we can accomplish immediately; the impossible will take a bit longer."

Unfortunately, they did not have a bit longer.

By noon the following day Dan had reassembled the team. He was taking a chance by not informing Morton or Norman of what he had planned. And Hesh would want to kill him again because he was still in New York.

He worried about Hesh. He still hadn't managed to put the terrible incident at Eilat behind him and he had developed an unmitigated hatred for all things Arab. That was understandable, but he was letting it overwhelm him and to a point that it was a distraction a Mossad agent could not afford.

"Colonel, we've got something here, but the risk is tremendous."

"The risk of not doing anything is even worse. If we don't stop them, the whole world is going to go up."

The logistics man laid out the plan for Dan and then sat back waiting for a sign of approval or disapproval.

Dan studied the schematics, logistics and time frame and looked up with a degree of satisfaction.

"The only thing we seem not to have is a guarantee that we'll be able to get out and get back here. Oh well, I guess there are no guarantees in life."

He turned to his group:

"Let's face it, this is far more dangerous than any operation we've ever undertaken before. We always expected to fire and be fired on. But we can't even bring in heavy weapons here because we don't want them to suspect we were involved. If they catch any one of us…if they kill even one of us, there's going to be a war. It would be the excuse Ahmadinejad needs to rile up the rest of the Muslim world to kill the Jews and the infidels.

He looked at the group of twenty men sitting in front of him.

"I will take no more than ten operatives this time. More than that, I will not assign anyone. This is strictly volunteer and there will be no negative against you if you opt out.

"Volunteers?"

Twenty hands shot into the air.

"Dan smiled, feigning surprise.

"I feel like Col. Travis must have felt at the Alamo when he drew the line in the sand with his sword and asked those who wanted to stay to cross over." The Texans knew it was certain death and yet all but one man crossed. The one who didn't cross over, a Frenchman who had come to the New World for adventure, had decided departure was better than death and he didn't need that kind of adventure.

There were no Frenchmen in the Mossad.

Dan pointed to ten of his men. He picked two explosive experts, a radio operator, a medic/electronics specialist/pilot, two auto mechanics, and four long-range marksmen.

In fact, all of his men were accomplished at most of what the others did. That was a tribute to his Green Beret training where all Special Forces operatives were crossed trained in at least one other specialty. Most could handle several different chores with a great deal of expertise and that was what he insured that his Mossad teams could do as well.

No matter how many might go down as casualties, there was always someone else who could do his job and finish the mission. And this mission had to be finished.

When he had the team assembled, Dan detailed the plan.

"I was going to go for a HALO (high altitude, low opening) jump, but that would leave us on the ground with too great a distance before we got to Lashkar Ab'ad. We'll go in on a Hercules, skim the floor, unload and get the plane the hell out of there. I don't think they would ever expect something like this.

"The exceptional danger comes in that we'll have to do this at night and flying just off the deck, we could hit almost anything. We've got dibs on two of the best pilots the IDF (Israeli Defence Forces) have to offer. The Hercules is easily big enough to carry everything we'll need."

He went over the remaining details of the operation and then ordered the men to bed.

"Get some sleep. We'll leave here just after midnight and arrive while they are asleep like all good Muslims should be at that time. We'll be far enough away from Lashkar Ab'ad so as not to raise any eyebrows and close enough to get there when we have to and minimize the danger. I'll see you all in a couple of hours."

Dan stepped into the cargo bay of the huge Hercules and the smell almost caught him off guard. He looked to the top of the ramp and was staring at two donkeys, strapped to the floor of the aircraft by a harness that ran over their shoulders. In front of the animals, strapped to the floor as well, were two, double-wheeled wooden carts. The carts didn't smell.

"We get on the ground I'm going to stick a pound of C-3 up their asses," mused the explosives man. May not stop the smell, but it'll spread it around a bit."

"Do that and you can carry the explosives and gasoline on your back," responded Dan.

The entire patrol was dressed in Bedouin robes, each of their heads covered with a kaffiya. The compact and rapid firing Uzi sub-machinguns were fastened to shoulder harnesses beneath the robes.

"We've got, literally, only seconds to get off this thing and move away. We can't let any of their security forces realize what's going on. Stay on your toes."

The boarding ramp ratcheted up and was secured in place, sealing off the bay as the giant engines roared to life. They could feel the gentle rumbling as the Hercules began its slow taxi to the head of the runway, turn and then pick up speed retracing its route as it rose smoothly into the night sky.

The flight would take them to the south and around to the Gulf of Oman. Then from there to the Bay of Khar Kumzar where it juts out and forces a curvature on the Iranian coast, looking much like the convex curve of South America and the concave reciprocal coast of Africa, giving rise to the legend of Atlantis.

On one side is the Oman Gulf and the other side of the point is the Persian Gulf bordered by Oman and the United Arab Emirates. With both Oman and the UAE non-combatants, security in that area was at a minimum. A low flying craft would raise little suspicion and if it did, it would be thought of as one of the myriad smugglers flying into the area. There was little fear of jets being scrambled to check them out because they would be afraid of offending local war lords.

The Hercules would land just inside the Iranian border off the Gulf of Oman and they would proceed overland from there. The second team would be waiting at the border with Turkmenistan for support and evacuation.

The Hercules hugged the coastline of Oman as it approached Khar Kumzar and dropped in altitude until it was barely skimming the water below. It passed the point of land that almost seemed as though it was a directional signal aiming at Iran and dropped even lower.

Dan marvelled that spray from the white caps below was not hitting the windshield of the huge cargo plane.

Overhead a red light came on and the team stood. They were now dressed in Bedouin robes, their heads covered by the chequered kaffiya of a northern tribe. Most had been so tanned by the hot sun of the Negev that they easily passed for desert tribesmen. And, in truth, that was part of the reason they had been handpicked for this mission. There were no blondes with blue eyes aboard.

Two of the team members pulled the donkeys into position facing the rear ramp and hitched them to the wooden tumbrels filled with straw and wrapped packages of goat cheese.

The pilot and co-pilot both wore night vision goggles giving them the appearance of one-horned gargoyles as they surveyed the landscape, tinted green by the night vision light permitting them to see the flat terrain of the desert floor.

The Hercules dropped from the night sky, its extra wide wheels, made especially for sand, touched down ever so lightly, leaving a wide track across the desert. No sooner had the wheels brushed the desert floor than the ramp began to drop, even before the plane had come to a full stop.

Dan grabbed the halter of the lead donkey and pulled it toward the ramp. The animal hesitated for a second and then followed his lead. The second animal and cart followed closely behind.

The aircraft was still moving as they gingerly made their way to the edge of the ramp as it dragged across the desert floor, hesitating only at the edge to wait for the craft to stop. The stop was but a brief hesitation, more like the time of a deep breath, but long enough for the team and the two carts to drop onto the sand before it increased the rev of its engines and lifted back into the night sky.

"Been here before," Dan thought, "But it's always like standing at the gates to hell. Dark. Unfriendly territory. No idea of who or what may be out there."

He turned to the team and silently motioned for them to move out as quickly as possible.

"We want to be as far away from this spot in the shortest amount of time so that if the plane came up on anyone's radar, we won't be connected to it. We're far enough away from Lashkar Ab'ad so that no one should make any connection after we send it up in smoke."

Dan knew from recon that there was a semi-paved road only about ten miles from the drop point. He wanted to get on that road for a short distance so that anyone following their tracks from the drop point would lose the trail. It would take them the better part of the night to cover the ground. They had packed enough water in goatskin containers and food to carry them through. There would be no stopping in villages for food or water and they had to jackass everything.

Although the entire team spoke the language fluently and knew enough about the country to pass the indigenous question test, he wanted to get done and get out as quickly as possible…with everyone on the team intact.

Dan jumped into the makeshift seat in front of the wagon, his medic alongside of him. Three others moved into the back and lay down on the hay. The second cart lined up the same way and the small caravan moved out across the hilly terrain toward Lashkar Ab'Ad. They hadn't been on the move ten minutes when all but the drovers were fast asleep.

As the sun began to rise over distant dunes the team switched places, a new driver for each cart. The goatskin water jugs sweated in the heat and kept the fluid inside cool to a reasonable temperature and quite drinkable. Food in small tins underneath the straw avoided the suns rays and was edible. Edible was a kind word because they couldn't eat anything other than what Persian peasants would dine on under these circumstances.

The donkeys plodded along as the sun slowly sank behind them and the hot day morphed into the night chill of the desert. They had robes to ward off the cold and brought them over their shoulders.

So far they had been lucky. A military caravan of trucks passed by without giving the carts a second glance. Other peasants in their own goat carts passed heading to market or home from the market. The team sighed with relief in the knowledge that they fit in and so far so good.

They stopped only to relieve themselves and to give the beasts of burden an opportunity to rest and drink. Those not driving rested. They knew that after the mission there would be little or no time to rest until they were safely out of the region. They had to exit not only Iran, but completely out of Muslim territory for safety. Regional and religious differences would be put aside if there was so much as a hint that Israelis... make that "Jews..." were undercover in the area.

And they had no illusions that any would give them succour.

Dan checked his GPS for their precise location and how far they had yet to go.

"We've got about three hours so get some rest. We'll start putting things together about an hour out. I'll let you know when."

If things continued this well they would be able to hit the facility at Lashkar Ab'Ad with more than enough darkness to cover their action and still get away in the pitch dark of the desert.

Dan could feel the chill finally starting to penetrate his robes. His teeth chattered and the cold was working on his kidneys.

"Maybe I should've been a lawyer," he smiled to himself. "No one likes you, but at least you stay warm."

He turned to the team members in the back of the cart and motioned for them to get ready, then waved to the following tumbrel, signalling for them to prepare. Each checked his Uzi and then began placing primers into the explosive backpacks they carried. The charges would be detonated remotely and batteries were placed into the small transmitters. They had been left without power as a safety precaution, but now they were set to go.

Also in the carts were packages of highly flammable gel that would melt, spreading fire throughout the facility, giving investigators the impression that a malfunction had caused both the explosion and ensuing fire. The heat of the fire should also melt any brass from the cartridges they left behind, helping to perpetuate the myth that an accident had taken place. They hoped.

If all went as planned, the Iranian investigators would have neither the expertise nor the will to do as thorough an inspection as would have happened in the West. Their resulting conclusion would be that a terrible mishap had taken place. This was critical to avoiding a major international incident.

"Hey, this isn't CSI." Dan thought

The last time Israel moved to stop nuclear advancement of its enemies was in the summer of 1981. Saddam had purchased an Osiris Class reactor from the French, allegedly for peaceful purposes. The French named the facility "Osirak," a combination of "Osiris" and Iraq." Saddam was soon well on the way to enriching material for bomb making purposes.

The Israelis felt that if they did not act immediately, the reactor would go on line and present a danger to their continued existence. A flight of F-16A fighters, escorted by F-15As, streaked over Iraq and bombed the facility, heavily damaging it.

Ironically, this was not the first attack on a nuclear facility. A year earlier the Iranians, holding the same fear as the Israelis, knew they could not permit their arch enemy. Saddam Hussein, to obtain a nuclear weapon. Also using fighter aircraft earlier provided by the United States, they flew a team of F-4 Phantom jets in on Sept. 30, 1980 to destroy the bomb making operation.

The facility at Lashkar Ab'Ad was ringed by dunes and surprisingly there was no security fence around the perimeter. There was a contingent of guards who were supposed to be mounting a constant patrol, but Dan knew from his informant that almost without exception, the guards slept through the night. No attack was ever expected this far into Iran and these guys weren't exactly Special Forces.

In fact, the troops guarding the nuclear facility were members of the Iranian Republican Guard, the best the country had to offer. They were far better trained than the average Iranian soldier but were no match for Dan's Green Beret background and the highly motivated Israeli Mossad agents.

The Republican Guards were at their best against student protestors, unarmed villagers, and old men and women who might defy the Will of Allah by failing to cover their faces or holding hands in public. Under those circumstances they were a terror force, but not necessarily a force to be reckoned with when they had to face trained opposition.

But they were there and they would have to be dealt with and in such a way that no suspicions would be raised.

The carts stopped at the base of the dunes and the team began to assemble. Dan held up a hypodermic syringe and plugged it into a rubber topped medicine container. The label noted that it was filled with Scopolamine.

"What a wonderful drug," he thought. "It could be used in proper amounts as a truth serum or to ease the pain of child birth."

But the syringes now being filled were to be used for a condition known as "twilight sleep." If handled properly, and the team didn't particularly care if it was proper or not, the person injected would fall asleep and awake in about an hour in a state of induced amnesia. Or, the fire and blast could awaken them, confirming the belief that they had simply fallen asleep on guard duty and they would be left to explain their actions.

The Republican Guard members might be able to talk their way out of punishment, but the most likely scenario would be that they would simply contend they were awake and on duty. That would reinforce the belief that there had been no incursion and the blast and fire were accidents.

The Republican Guard would be spared severe punishment and possible execution and the Mossad action would not be uncovered. It was a win-win situation.

There were three guard shacks around the compound; each should have had a Republican Guard member and a dog. But the fact was this was not always the case and the Guardsmen frequently skipped their posts.

The team all wearing night vision goggles (NVGs), split into three squads, each to handle one of the shacks. One member of each group carried a tranquilizer gun and would shoot a dart into the dog, should one be found.

Dan led one squad near the compound entrance, moving almost imperceptible inches at a time as they approached the shack, stopped and looked in the window.

No dog. That was a bonus.

Dan moved to the only door of the little wooden structure, one man poised to open the door and two others who would rush in, grab the guard and hold his arm out. A gloved hand would go over his mouth to squelch any sound.

They moved in one fluid motion, the door flying open, and pounced on the Republican Guard before his eyes were open. Dan thrust the needle into his arm at the inside elbow joint and slowly pushed the syringe plunger.

Slowly, as if in stop action photography, the man slid to the floor and within seconds he was sound asleep. He'd have some questions to answer later on, but would be able to tell his interrogators nothing.

The other two teams began moving to meet Dan at the entrance to the structure. They knew the interior of the building as if they had lived there…the power of having an inside man.

No need to worry about the surveillance cameras. If they did pick up anything, they would turn to ash in the fire. They were being recorded on an internal closed circuit video system that was fully contained within the walls of the Lashkar Ab'Ad facility.

Now there was no need for caution or secrecy. Anyone coming into view would be cut down by the fast firing Uzis. The weapon was so small and compact that the American Secret Service on the Presidential protection detail all carried them under their jackets. The guns easily fit into harnesses beneath a suit jacket, leaving little bulge. The gun had so little kick back that when fired, it rose only a fraction of an inch, thus giving its handler the opportunity to pour slugs out at a scathing rate of fire, yet group them close enough together that thirty rounds would leave only one big hole.

The ten men moved at a quick step through the corridor to the elevator that would carry them one hundred feet below the surface to the bombproof research and nuclear lab. One man remained in an alcove across from the elevator door as the rest of the team entered, pushed the button and began to descend.

The most nerve racking aspect was that they could not communicate by radio because signals could be picked up by a monitoring station and that would defeat the secrecy of the plan. Dan used hand signals to spread his team out. They now had to find the technicians and any other guards who might be in the facility.

But more importantly, they had to find any devices stored there, any nuclear material and, perhaps most important, any paper work that would detail the operation.

One man in a white smock sat at a console looking at lights flashing and glancing into a lab from the glassed-in wall of his office. He didn't turn when the opening door creaked slightly.

A single shot rang out and he jerked forward, a small hole in the back of his head and his forehead missing, now gushing blood and brains. One of the switches on the console hissed and sparked as the wet blood ran into it.

Dan could hear a low, rapid popping sound as others fired. It was a good sign that there were no normal sounding gunshots, indicating the occupants of the facility had not returned fire.

The team moved rapidly and with precision through the facility, some placing explosive charges, others planting a jelled accelerant. The rest scoured the facility looking for any nuclear weapons, fissionable grade material or documents relating to the work being done there.

Within ten minutes they had gathered in the office, the console still sparking and popping.

"Dan, there are no weapons here and nothing that could be considered a component for one. What's going on? Did we have a false alarm?"

"There's plenty of sign that this facility was used for putting the components together, but there's nothing here now. Let's collect all the paper work we can and evaluate it later. Saddam hid in a small Spyder hole. Let's see what this big Spyder hole has to reveal. Move and let's get out of here."

There was a feeling of dejection as the team members moved about the underground facility completing their job. There had to be no trace at all of an incursion. Paperwork was gathered and placed into canvas pouches and samples of the material in the lab were collected. The radiation meters showed there had been considerable nuclear activity in the facility, but nothing they could find.

"OK, let's move out. We'll set off the fireworks when we are about a mile out. We're heading north and we have a long way to go before we reach the border with Turkistan. Get rid of the robes, keep the kaffiya and we'll grab one of the trucks up above. Let's just make sure the tanks are filled and we have some extra fuel for the drive."

The men headed for the surface, now dressed as members of the Republican Guard and confident that no one, even regular army units, would dare to question any member of the elite force.

At the facility's motor pool they grabbed a canvas covered truck, checked the fuel gauge and loaded a dozen filled jerry cans of extra fuel into the back of the vehicle. Dan jumped into the shotgun seat as another slipped behind the wheel. The remaining team climbed into the rear of the truck, keeping the gasoline company.

Dan kept a close watch on the odometer and as it approached one mile from Lashkar Ab'Ad, he pulled the small transmitter from his pocket. The truck was running without lights to avoid detection and didn't even make a silhouette against the night sky…until Dan pushed the toggle.

For several seconds there was absolute quiet. The kind of quiet you can only find in the pitch darkness of a desert. The sun would be coming up in less than an hour and the early morning light would be accompanied by its own set of nerves.

Suddenly an early dawn lit the sky as a huge ball of flame expanded and rose skyward. The truck was bathed in light and the desert illuminated. Nocturnal animals scurried for their holes, upset by the sudden and unexpected dawn.

The ground trembled and the truck shook, but kept moving in a northward direction as the men in the rear shielded their eyes from the brightness of the blast. Even at this distance they could feel the heat.

At the site where the facility had stood there was now a huge crater. A Republican Guardsman, asleep in his guard shack atop a dune, jumped up, rubbing his eyes. The blast concussion tore the shack apart, leaving him standing in the sand. Then as the wind from the explosion tore past, it lifted him off his feet and carried him about one hundred yards before rudely depositing him back on the ground.

The man stood, trembling and not even noticing the wet stain growing from the crotch of his pants where he had soiled himself. He was blinded by the flash of light and could not see where he was going. He stepped forward and fell into the mass of concrete and steel that had only a short time before been the Iranian Lashkar Ab'Ad nuclear research center.

In Virginia Mary Sapphire, working late, looked up as the satellite monitor on her panel of flat screens showed a huge fireball reaching skyward in Iran. She called an assistant and ordered the man to zoom in on the site.

"What the heck is with this sudden rash of fireballs?" she thought.

By the time the CIA satellite came into focus, there was nothing left on the ground but a deep hole with dust and sand raining down. What the satellite did not see was an army truck on a road heading north and away from the facility.

Dan's team reached the Turkmenistan border without incident, crossed over at a desolate point and ditched their Republican Guard uniforms. They were met by a truck with the markings of an international oil cartel. The driver had work clothes for them, food and some cold drinks.

"Let's just get away from the border before we relax."

The man handed Dan a radio and he turned to an Iranian station. The broadcaster was reading news copy about the terrible toll taken at the explosion of an oil refining depot at Lashkar Ab'Ad. He noted that the probable cause of the explosion was inferior material and parts that had been supplied by infidels in Europe.

The announcer told his listeners that the government would seek compensation for the families of the oil workers who had died.

"That should give the real oil cartels a good reason for hiking gas prices again," smirked Tzvi Herzog, the master blaster. "This will have no affect on production, but what a reason to gouge more money for windfall profits."

An hour later they were aboard a private jet, again with oil company markings, and headed back to Jerusalem. They had to file a false flight plan and cross several Arab nations before they finally passed over Jordan and out to sea.

The small jet dipped low over the water, turned and headed back toward land and Israel. Dan picked up the microphone, punched in a frequency and then spoke a code word. The plane was instantly cleared for landing without worry of being shot down by the IDF jets constantly patrolling Israeli air space.

The canvas pouches, bursting with papers, were brought into the secure facility for analysis and a horde of personnel immediately went to work on them.

The following morning Dan returned for a briefing and left immediately to meet with the Reuven ben Chaim. The Defence Minister and several other key senior staff were also present as Dan walked in. Halevi stiffened and saluted as he saw the Prime Minister crossing the room toward him.

The PM extended his hand and grabbed Dan's shaking it with gusto.

"Colonel, you and your men have done an amazing job. But I am most grateful that you all returned safely." He motioned for Dan and the others to take seats at the conference table and slid into his own at the head.

After Dan detailed what they had uncovered, he was ordered by the Prime Minister to immediately share the information with the CIA and insure that the American President was made aware. He suggested MI6 be given a "heads up" as well.

Arrangements were made for an immediate departure to London so that he could catch the 4 p.m. Virgin Atlantic Airline flight to New York and then on to Washington. He looked forward to the comfort of a fully reclining seat and the privacy that the staggered seating and compartmentalized personal space gave him. He was flat out exhausted and this was the most civilized way of flying to London.

His El Al flight landed at Heathrow's Terminal 1 and since he had had little luggage, he moved swiftly into the terminal and transferred to Terminal 3 for the Virgin flight. Passing customs and immigration went quickly with the usual British business-like attitude. He carried no weapons with him. Even in checked luggage there was always the possibility of discovery. He could pick up what he needed from a consulate armourer and the weapon would be untraceable.

An hour later he was strapped into his seat and comfortable as the huge jet rumbled to the end of the runway, turned and raced into the sky.

As a passenger who had previously flown the airline, his likes and dislikes were already punched into the computer. The flight attendant brought a rum and coke with a twist of lime for him and handed him a menu with the current meal offerings. Dan made a choice, sat back sipping his drink and relaxed for the first time in days.

He demurred at the offer of a video player with a wide choice of movies and programs and instead opted for a night's sleep. He was due into JFK at 8:55 pm. He had crossed so many time zones in the past few days that time really had no meaning for him any more.

Dan savoured the relaxed meal, ordered another drink and then moved into the aisle to permit the flight attendant to convert his seat into a fully flat bed with sheet, cover and pillow. A real pillow, not the stuffed handkerchief size pillow used on most airlines. He took off his shoes and put on a pair of slippers that had been offered to him.

He pulled the covers up, put his head on the pillow and was out for what seemed to be only minutes when the flight attended gently touched his shoulder.

"Mr. Halevi, we will be landing in less than an hour. Would you like some coffee and perhaps something to eat?"

Dan sat up and shook the cobwebs from his head. He looked out of the window to see the fading light as night fell. He stepped aside again so that the attendant could return the bed into a seat and then he sank back into its comfort.

A tray was set in front of him with coffee and the light snack he had asked for.

Dan smiled as he thought of the term "light snack" as normally used in the airline industry. It would have meant some dry peanuts or a piece of stale bread with a thin slice of cheese. Instead he was eating gourmet food.

He could have used some more sleep, but he was refreshed and knew that he would have to hit the ground running.

He reached for the phone attached to his mini-compartment and dialed in Hesh's number.

"I'll be in soon and headed for my apartment. Tomorrow morning, seven am, I want to meet with you, Matt and Kyle. Please contact them now and tell them it is of utmost urgency."

"What's going on?"

"This isn't a secure line. Just do as I ask and we'll go over everything in the morning."

He clicked off the phone, sat back and sipped on his coffee.

The morning sun was slowly rising over the East River as Dan exited the elevator and walked out the front door of his building. The doorman held the door for him and asked if he'd like a taxi.

Dan politely declined and turned toward the consulate. Even walking he would be there before any of the others and would have ample time for preparation. Besides, it was a beautiful day and he wanted to enjoy it without thoughts of having to make a run for the border…any border.

It was a clean day. The air quality in New York was at its peak before the summer air inversions brought clouds of smog down on every living, breathing creature. When they lived in Queens, before emigrating, Amanda used to laugh and say she could always tell when he had gone into Manhattan because his shirt collars were dirty when he came home.

"If that was on my collars," he thought, "imagine what was in my lungs."

On a lanyard around his neck Dan carried a PNY Attaché, an eight gigabyte flash drive that could hold more memory than most computer hard drives. Dan had downloaded the information from the analysts in Jerusalem onto the drive that measured barely two inches long and less than a half inch wide. It would have taken a major sized steamer trunk to carry enough three and a half inch floppies with the same amount of information programmed into them.

"What a world."

Dan always marvelled at the advances in technology and how fast they came along. He considered himself almost brain dead when it came to scratching the surface of what a computer could do.

He remembered back some twenty years when Bob Rossi, a close friend and a top undercover agent for the Internal Revenue Service Criminal Investigations Division (IRS-CID) retired. One of his gifts was a credit card size calculator that cost about $50. Today they were free commercial giveaways. There was then no such thing as a flash drive.

And around his neck in the flash drive he carried information that could either cause or stop a nuclear war.

At the security checkpoint in front of the consulate Dan pinned his ID card onto his jacket pocket, the International Protection Systems guard glanced at it, studied his face to make sure who the bearer was, nodded and motioned for him to proceed.

Dan left word at reception that Matt Morton and Kyle Norman would be arriving soon for a meeting and to please notify him as soon as they arrived.

He had no sooner sat down at his desk than Hesh almost stormed into the office.

"Why was I left out of an operation again?"

"Hey my friend, calm down."

"Calm down my ass. Why am I being excluded?"

"You aren't being excluded from anything. But that doesn't mean that you are automatically a part of any operation that comes up. When your participation is required, you'll be included."

The angry confrontation was interrupted by the intercom buzzer.

"Mr. Halevi, your two guests have arrived."

"Please have them escorted to my private conference room and I will be right there.

"Now, do you want to be a part of this or are you going to keep on busting my balls over what you weren't invited to do? The choice is yours."

The firmness in Dan's voice was unmistakable. Hesh had stepped to the borderline of his boss' tolerance and, friendship aside, he was still the boss..

Dan fixed Hesh with a hard stare that set the younger man back on his heels. He was not used to so strong a reaction from his boss.

"We're friends, Hesh. But don't ever forget that I'm still your superior officer and I won't have any of my decisions or orders questioned. I receive orders from a higher authority as well and neither you nor I will question those orders. Understood?"

"I'm sorry. You're right and it won't happen again."

A chastened Hesh Whitman turned and walked out of the office toward the conference room, mumbling to himself: "If I can't be a part of taking these bastards down, I'll go my own way."

Dan closed the door to the secure conference room and took a seat at the head of the table facing Hesh, Matt Morton and Kyle Norman.

Morton sat, almost rigid, his face as beet red as a black man could show. The look on his face portended an explosion.

He look at Dan and, in a controlled fit of anger, said:

"What the hell did you people do? You went off on an adventure that could have set the whole world on fire and you didn't even coordinate with us? What the hell is the matter with you?"

"With us? When was the last time the CIA coordinated with the Mossad or asked our permission to mount any operation? We are an autonomous agency working for a sovereign government and we do not answer to the United States or anyone else outside of our own country. And frankly, the CIA has more leaks than a tenement faucet."

Morton stared in disbelief at Dan, his face contorting and twisting in rage. He stood at his seat, his hands balled into fists and resting on the conference table.

Kyle Norman reached over to Morton's shoulder and gently, but firmly forced him back into his seat. He attempted to sooth the situation and bring it back to some semblance of order. His crisp British accent cut through the heat.

"Let's go from this point and work as a team. I think what we are facing could be a terrible situation for all of us."

"Dan, Mary Sapphire's analysts spotted the explosion over Lashkar Ab'Ad and you suddenly call for an emergency session with us. Just tell me the link." Morton left no doubt by the tone of his voice as to how angry he was.

"Yes. There is a link and yes, that was our operation. To the best of my knowledge Ahmadinejad and his band of fanatical killers has no reason to suspect that it was an Israeli operation or that it was anything more than an accidental explosion caused by their own carelessness and ineptitude. We left no tracks for them to follow. But the results were worth the cost. Had they even suspected us, they would be threatening an apocalypse."

Dan took the little flash drive from around his neck and plugged it into the USB port of the conference room's computer. He slowly scrolled through pictures flashed on the wall-sized screen, of the Iranian nuclear facility, pointing out the research that had been going on there.

"Is that all? We knew they were working on the bomb at that facility."

"Matt, for once just listen."

Dan continued, detailing what had been gleaned from the papers taken in the raid.

"According to what we found there was at least one completed bomb in an experimental stage. That was shipped out. They had the components for another couple of bombs and the technology that had been obtained from Iraq.

"As bad as the news about one operational bomb may be, the information regarding the components and technology makes that pale in comparison. What the intel shows is that the components and technology have been shipped out to a third party nation.

"Have you traced its final destination?" came a clipped British accent.

"Yes. And that's the really bad news."

Dan clicked the mouse and a map came up on the screen detailing the Korean peninsula with a red circle around the town of Yongbyon, planted firmly in the heart of North Korea.

"This is one of two locations we are concerned with as I am sure your own intelligence has indicated. Yongbyon sits over a series of mines that have an estimated four thousand tons of exploitable uranium…and that's one hell of a head start on a nuclear program.

"The second facility is at Kum Changni, between Kusong and T'aech'on and is only about 50 miles north of Yongbyon. There is a facility at Sakchu, but that apparently is involved with chemical weapons and would be of interest in a later conversation."

Dan pulled up a CIA satellite surveillance photo of Yongbyon and pointed to an artificial island surrounded by a man-made lake. Surrounding both was a hi-tension wire capable of carrying three thousands volts.

"The region is isolated like a nuclear facility. Excavation at this site, of some four hundred thousand cubic meters of earth and rock could accommodate a two hundred megawatt-class graphite-moderated reactor. That's big trouble.

"These photos show the nuclear capability of this site. It should also be noted that the North Koreans maintain quite a sizeable military force around this facility. This is not Lashkar.

"In 1998 it was estimated that these facilities would give North Korea the ability to extract sufficient plutonium within five years to manufacture eight to ten nuclear weapons a year."

Dan now had their full attention.

"A five year period has come and gone. The participation of an elite group of engineers that includes Russian and Chinese, the installation of the electric wiring and the construction of a water-storage dam for the reactors prove beyond doubt that they are nuclear facilities.

"The question now is 'Do we permit a lunatic such as Kim Jong-Il to have a nuclear blackmail threat to hang over the rest of the world, or do we do something about it?"

"And they have the components Saddam was working on?"

"Kyle, that does seem to be the case. In the immediate future we have to track down the missing nuclear device and find out what they are targeting with it. And without too much delay after that, we have to neutralize Kim's nuclear threat. We have a little bit of work cut out for us."

About fifteen hundred miles to the south the Miami sun was reaching its noon zenith. It was warm and bright and there wasn't a cloud in the sky.

Sayyid sat in a coffee shop on busy Collins Avenue, the main north-south drag in Miami Beach. Although he felt a hint of nerves, on the surface he appeared calm and collected. He was clean shaven and his dark hair had been lightened with bleach ever so slightly.

He opened his wallet and glanced at the driver's license made out to Deepak Singh, an Indian national in the United States on a long-term work visa. He was a computer expert working for America-On-Line, the internet provider. While calls from most anywhere in the United States would be routed to New Delhi or Bombay for assistance, he was, according to his cover, here to coordinate those efforts.

Sayyid paid his tab at the counter, left a small but adequate tip for the waitress and walked to his rental car in the parking lot alongside the little building.

He was plain; he was ordinary. He would fit in anywhere in the United States without raising suspicions. He could fly on any American flag airliner and not worry about being unduly tabbed by the TSA for added security screening. He could even walk into a government building and not be stopped.

Sayyid drove across the causeway back into the City of Miami and headed toward the huge cruise piers at Dodge Island. He could see in the distance the stacks of oversized cruise ships in port. Most of them took up several dock spaces originally meant for smaller ships.

The newer cruise ships coming in to Miami would make the Titanic look like the Staten Island Ferry. They were huge affairs, towering eight to a dozen stories over the surface. It was as easy to get lost in the crowd here as in New York's Times Square on New Year's Eve.

And fading into the woodwork was exactly what Sayyid wanted. He would make no friends on board. He would have his meals at a single table on deck and would not be involved in any of the recreational activities. He would stand out to no one; no one would notice or remember him.

He pulled in to the auto rental agency, unloaded his suitcase and walked to the office to formally return the vehicle. He climbed aboard a shuttle and within minutes was at the foot of the great ship.

Sayyid walked through the gaping entryway and was caught off guard as a young girl in uniform snapped his picture.

He looked quizzically at her.

"A souvenir of the cruise," she smiled. "You can pick it up tomorrow at the display outside the dining room."

He nodded. This was an unexpected involvement but there was little he could do about it without raising questions. He walked into the ship's atrium and took the elevator to his deck, found his cabin and locked the door.

A half hour later he could feel a rumbling from deep inside the ship and then a gentle movement as it began to pull away from the pier and out to sea for its northward journey. Most of the passengers had embarked in New York City and were doing a round tripper to the Caribbean. Sayyid was going only one way.

His mentor had made all the arrangements for him and as soon as the ship had moved into deep water, the press would be notified of their demands to release Sheik Omar, Sirhan Sirhan and Zacharias Moussoaui. What the Old Man did not know was that Sayyid planned to detonate the bomb no matter what the infidels did. New York City would cease to exist and much of the surrounding area, reaching into New Jersey, would turn to cinders as well.

Moving the device from ship to ship covered his tracks and using the container ship with the King Tut artefacts afforded him the ability to skirt most security measures. No one would dare take a chance on causing damage to such ancient items.

XII

THE KOREAN CONNECTION

The private phone on Dan's desk rang; the shrill sound startling him. He reached for it and heard Amanda's voice at the other end.

"Dinner?"

"Geez, I'm sorry. I totally forgot we were having company. Please make my excuses to them. I'm going to be here for a while and am not really sure when I'll be home."

"Are we talking hours?"

"Babe, I don't know. This could be days or even longer."

"Dan, you just got back."

"I know. But this is really important. And I have no choice. It's a job that has to be done right now and can't be put off."

"What do you want me to do with the theater tickets we have for tomorrow night?"

"Give your mother a call and see if she's available. I'm not going to make it."

"I wish I had as much of your time as your job does," Amanda said, displaying an unusual loneliness and a bit of resentment tingeing her voice.

"I know and I am sorry. I wish we had more time together. Maybe at the end of this assignment we can take a couple of weeks. How about we plan to go to Park City for some of that Utah summer. We can do some hiking and a little mountain biking. We'll even spring for extra money, go first class and stay at the Stein Erikson Lodge. Never been there in warm weather and it'll be interesting to see a great ski resort in the summer."

"Dan, be careful." The concern in Amanda's voice was evident.

"I am the most careful person you've ever known. I'll be home just as soon as I can. I love you."

"I love you too. But please be careful."

Dan replaced the phone and sat back in his swivel chair. He smiled at the thought of a conversation involving friends, dinner and vacation plans when he was up to his eyeballs trying to save the world. He felt like Clark Kent in the City Room of the Daily Planet.

Only this time the bad guys had a load of Kryptonite and he had to stop them. One slip and "…we're on the way to becoming Planet of the Apes."

"Too bad I can't go into a telephone booth and change into a supersuit. Come to think of it, there are no more phone booths. I wonder what Superman does to change now?"

Dan picked up the copy of the British newspaper Kyle had given him with an article about the sentencing of Zacharias Moussoaui, the French Islamist who was known as "the 20th hijacker" after 9-11:

No lethal injection, no single blow of a sword: American justice triumphed

The Times, London

> *AS HE WAS led on Wednesday from the Virginia courtroom he has variously tormented and bemused for the past four years, Zacharias Moussoaui had a final taunt for his audience.*
>
> *"America: You lost. I won," he shouted in response to the jury's verdict that he should serve life in prison rather than the death penalty for his part in the September 11 plot that killed 3,000 people.*
>
> *It was an odd boast for a man who embraced death, who craved martyrdom, whose fantasies were filled with visions of burning infidels on earth and pliant virgins in heaven.*

But over the next 30 years or more Moussaoui will have time to reconsider his hasty judgment. Not just because life in the Florence Federal Correctional Complex in Colorado will be several virgins short of a good time for this eager jihadi; but because in fact America won something quite big this week in Alexandria. It won back something it has lost a little of in the past few years. It reminded a world that has grown a bit doubtful that the United States still represents the very highest ideals of humanity — freedom, fairness, compassion and above all, justice.

The prosecutors lost, for sure. They had assembled a case with a powerful narrative whose end-point was always intended to be a syringe and an unmarked grave for the anti-hero. But they never persuaded enough jurors that Moussoaui's guilt warranted the ultimate penalty.

Understandably, some of those bereaved family members of September 11 victims feel they lost as well; that the suffering that will haunt them to the ends of their lives should have been matched at least by the satisfaction of seeing an end to the life of the only man who has ever had to answer directly for his part in the infamy.

But justice was surely done this week and it should send a signal to the world that American's values are the right ones. This is not because, as some of America's critics believe, the death penalty is necessarily wrong and that this week's sentence somehow represents a rare moment of civilisation in American justice. You can oppose capital punishment — as I do — and yet not necessarily believe its existence makes America a fundamentally barbaric country.

Yesterday Moussaoui was back in court one last time for his formal sentencing. As I read the reports of his last, defiant shrieks, his condemnations of the judge, the jury and the 9/11 family members whose lives he helped to ruin five years ago, another image of another sort of justice came to mind — that of the last moments of Nick Berg, the young American contractor, beheaded in Iraq by Abu Musab al-Zarqawi, the al-Qaida terrorist and associate of Moussoaui's. Before his sentencing Berg was allowed no trial, no defence, no final observations, no condemnations, no compassionate consideration of extenuating circumstances. They just sawed his head off because he was an American and a Jew.

Consider the contrast: civilisation's enemies in Iraq, Afghanistan and elsewhere summarily and routinely execute innocent men and women — humanitarian workers, contractors, those who are deemed to have insulted Islam. America, confronted with the boastful confession of a man who conspired to kill thousands of its innocents, and who would, given the chance, willingly have liquidated every single American, chose to spare his life.

Zacharias Moussoaui's fate, and that of Nick Berg, reminds us that we should never forget whose side we are on.

"I guess there are some people who understand what we're up against. Too bad they are a quiet majority," Dan thought as he put the newspaper down.

Matt and Kyle had gone back to their own facilities to work. There was the skeleton of a plan, but not much more. The first priority was the nuclear device they had lost track of. They didn't know if the other components had been put together yet, but it didn't seem likely.

"One freakin' device in the hands of these religious madmen is too much. If we miss on this one there is no tomorrow," mumbled Dan, a touch of fear in his voice.

The three agents had spent hours developing a plan for satellite surveillance of North Korea and an effort to locate the missing device. They had determined there was no point wasting any effort over Iran because everything had apparently been shipped out.

They had all gone back to their surveillance experts. Each had authority from the highest civilian and military authorities in the United States, the United Kingdom and Israel to access any personnel or equipment they felt necessary. And each had fully used that authority.

Mary Sapphire had complained loudly to Matt Morton. She had so many priorities that dedicating the time and resources he demanded would put too much of a strain on her other activities.

"Mary, I'm sorry. I can't go into full details with you, but there is no choice. You will take whatever personnel that may be needed and you will retask the satellites over the coordinates I've given you. And as soon as you locate the information I am after, you will stop everything and get it to me. Understand?"

"I don't like it. We have on-going surveillances that will have to be stopped so that we can retask the birds and reassign personnel to monitor them."

"Ms. Sapphire, that's too bad. You've seen my authorization and authority. That ends the discussion. Now, please, go do it."

There was an icy edge to Morton's voice, a tone that Mary Sapphire had never heard before; but one that set her back on her heels. She decided not to challenge Matt and risk putting her ass in a blender.

Mary Sapphire sullenly walked from the office to break the news to her people that no one was going home and that they were facing a workload of enormous proportions.

Kyle Norman had been on the secure line with Legoland. His scrambled call was placed directly through to "C" and authority was given immediately to retask Britain's satellites. Personnel would be assigned and whatever other assets might be needed would be made available without delay.

And yes, MI-6 did have an "00" designation for a handful of agents. It wasn't "00" but nonetheless Kyle Norman and a chosen few did have executive authority to "terminate with extreme prejudice" any adversary who in their personal judgment was worthy of such action.

Kyle had only used that authority twice in his career and both times the subjects had been Islamic fundamentalists bent on causing death and destruction in London. He would use it again without hesitation if necessary.

The Mossad did not have a "License to kill" designation for its agents, but there was no question in the agency that should any of the operatives feel it a necessary option, it would happen. The government would either look the other way or would cover his tracks.

Although the CIA was forbidden by federal law from engaging in "assassinations," since the Jimmy Carter regime, there was an unspoken understanding. If an agent had to make an on the spot decision, the Company would back him unless it was egregiously wrong. In other words, as long as he hadn't fucked up too badly and wasted an innocent or someone who was very high profile, they would cover his ass.

Each agency had a "clean up crew" whose sole job it was to erase all indications that such an operation had taken place. They were able to sanitize a scene to a point where even the CSI investigators with their luminal and other blood detecting equipment would not find a trace of blood spatter or bone fragments.

This was all secondary now with the first priority assigned to locating the device. The Cairo Pride's captain had decided, after some unorthodox persuasion, that it was in his best interest for continued health and a long life, to cooperate. That was the nice thing about dealing with mercenaries. Once the money stopped, their loyalties faded. So long as it flowed, there was loyalty.

But all the Captain knew was that once the ship had the device, it moved away from the scene of the sinking trawler to a location off Cape Hatteras where the huge crate was transferred to another ship. He did overhear a discussion that appeared to indicate it would be transferred again, this time to a truck, for delivery somewhere in the south.

No amount of persuasion could induce him to part with any more information and Matt was convinced the man had spilled all he knew.

But at least they had a description of the ship that had taken the device and they could now attempt to track its movements. The operation moving the deadly cargo from ship to ship and location to location was brilliant. It made tracking almost impossible. And using a ship with the King Tut collection was brilliant as well because no one questioned the movement of such artefacts and it managed to throw another layer of cover onto the movement of the nuclear device.

Dan appreciated the way Matt felt, but it wasn't a rogue operation into Iran. It was sanctioned by the Israeli government and he didn't feel the need to inform Morton or ask permission to undertake it. And the results were well worth the risk he had taken.

The three had agreed that from this point on they would coordinate everything and every piece of information they gathered with the others. That was the only way they could track the nuclear device. Professional rivalries would have to be put aside…for the time being.

Morton hit pay dirt first. It wasn't hi-tech. Just good old fashioned police footwork. An asset had come in with a story about a mysterious cargo that had been off-loaded from a ship in Charlotte.

The informant was a member of a mosque in Miami and ostensibly an activist who had worked his way into the confidence of the mullah. Virtually every mosque and madrassa was a hotbed of anti-American activity. Unless, of course, the mosque was in London and then it was anti-British.

Because of the policies in both countries of full religious freedom, the mosques and schools, the madrassas, were sacrosanct cesspools of Islamic fervor and the teachings of hatred for all things non-Muslim. They were also safe havens for the storage of weapons for the coming jihad.

Matt's informant was Muslim and a devout follower of Islam. But he had become disenchanted with the hatred spewing forth under the cover of a strict interpretation of the Koran. He hated the fact that the word "Islam" had become synonymous with "terrorist" and he wanted to do something about it.

The informer couldn't speak out at the mosque because it would have cost him his life and probably the lives of his family members as well. He worked in the reservations department of a major cruise line and had been approached by his religious leader to provide assistance to "a person of great importance" from the homeland.

His assignment was to get four crates on board four different cruise ships without them being given undue attention and then to book passage for four people on the same ships, one on each.

He reported the activity to his FBI runner who, in a fit of good sense, passed the information along to the CIA. When the information reached Morton's desk it immediately set off an alarm.

"The ships are at sea in international waters," he told Dan. "If we send a team to board them, the press will pick up on it immediately and we're going to cause a panic. But we can't let it go for too long."

"It looks as though one of the ships will sail into Newport, Rhode Island for a one-day stop. From there it comes into New York Harbor on Saturday morning. It's an overnighter as it comes down the coast with an early morning arrival."

The remaining ships had varying itineraries. One sailed directly to New York while another headed for Boston. The fourth ship sailed to Maine and then on to New York.

The one common denominator was that all of them terminated in New York's busy harbour.

The buzzer on Dan's intercom went off and the disembodied voice on the speaker caught their immediate attention.

"I think you better turn the television to one of the networks and listen to what's going on."

Dan reached for the remote control, pushed two buttons and the flat panel lit up showing the ABC network anchor with a very serious look on his face reading from a bulletin sheet.

"This just in. We have word from Al Jazeera, the television network that frequently has contact with Al Qaeda. According to Al Jazeera, a threat has been made that nuclear devices will be set off in New York City and London unless the American government immediately releases Sheik Omar Abdul Rahman, Sirhan Sirhan and Zacharias Moussoaui.

"Sheik Rahman, the Blind Sheik, is serving a prison term for encouraging and helping to plan the 1993 bombing of the World Trade Center. Moussoaui is on appeal from a life sentence before a Federal court in Virginia where he was convicted for participation in the planning of the 9-11 attack on the WTC and the Pentagon that resulted in the deaths of more than 3,000 people. He has been referred to as the "Twentieth Hijacker.'

"Moussoaui was also charged with aiding in the attacks for not providing information that could have stopped the terrorist action. Sirhan Sirhan is serving life for the killing of Sen. Robert F. Kennedy. The President has called his entire cabinet and the Joint Chiefs of Staff into emergency session at the White House."

"Oh shit. Now we know what they are planning." Mumbled Morton.

Dan sat back, an ashen look on his face. He missed the signs in 2001 and never realized the ramifications of the current situation. Last time many people died. This time he had to stop it. He felt as though this was his assigned mission directly from God.

"We are truly caught between the proverbial Rock and a Hard Place," the CIA agent commented.

"OK Matt, the ball is primarily in your court. We have no authority to stop ships in American waters or in the international zone."

"My government will never agree to release these killers. If we do that, this will be only the first blackmail demand of this sort. Your government has had a similar policy and has never agreed to terrorist demands. There is no option. We find the bomb and destroy it."

"Let's throw a little more fuel on the fire," Dan interjected. "We know Saddam sent technology to Iran and then Iran passed it along to North Korea with the components for making at least a half dozen more bombs. What if there is a nuclear device on each of these ships? And what if they have been distributed to other locations? Man, we are facing a shit storm. We don't know if we have a couple of days or a couple of hours."

"OK Dan, Kyle, I'm in a stickier position. As limited as the CIA authority is within the borders of the United States, you two have no authority here whatsoever. If you are caught mounting an operation in this country, the bomb won't be the only thing about to go off. And especially if the press corps gets wind of this, everything will blow up in our faces.

"Dan, your case is a bit less complex. You've kept your American citizenship."

"I am always an American. I could never give that up even with my move to Israel."

"OK, I have the authority and am deputizing you as an agent of the CIA. There is no problem with you coordinating intelligence with any other agency outside of the United States. Hesh, you're here as a guest, but I understand you have papers that may indicate you are an American citizen as well. I don't want to question the authenticity of those papers and we'll simply assume they are legitimate."

"I do."

"OK, you'll be in the same category as Dan. Kyle, I'm not sure what the hell to do with you. I think it best if you work directly alongside of me. This way if anything goes wrong, I can at least try to mitigate the problem.

"What I am going to need is any intelligence that either of your governments may have gleaned with respect to the North Korean project. We need to know if they did actually assemble any more devices and are they capable of doing so in short order. Kim is a crazy man but he does keep somewhat of a grip on reality. I don't think he'll chance setting off a bomb because he knows that we will turn North Korea into a radioactive wasteland."

"But that doesn't mean he may not have done a forward pass with an assembled devise," Norman added.

"Let's assume that each of these ships has a bomb on board. We know the potential is there. We have four days before any of the ships are due to dock in New York. I don't think they would waste the opportunity on Newport. Boston is a possibility, but New York is the bigger target," Matt said.

"None of the ships will have to worry about customs inspection because they've already gone through that in Miami after returning from the islands. The rest of the itinerary is strictly domestic."

Dan turned to Kyle Norman.

"I don't think we can discount the possibility of a device being brought into the UK. The borders in Europe are about as porous as can be. You can drive from country to country without ever having to stop for a border checkpoint. With the ferry coming in from Calais to Dover and the Chunnel from France almost anything can be moved anywhere over there.

"Even train passengers coming from Paris or Brussels are supposed to go through a security check just like they would have at the airport. But in fact it is only a cursory inspection before they get on the train to cross the Channel. And since the train carries cars, trucks and buses, they could load a device and have it pass through without detection."

"I'll send a message to Legoland right away and put them on the alert. I do think that if a device is going to be brought into the UK, it will probably come on the train through the Chunnel. It will be virtually in the heart of London when it arrives and off-loading it is a quick matter. It could be by

Parliament or Buckingham Palace within a matter of minutes. My God, what are we facing here?"

"There's got to be a comprehensive plan somewhere. These bastards love paperwork almost as much as the Nazis did. They write everything down and put all their plans on paper. I'll put a call through to Jerusalem and get them on it immediately. Maybe one of our assets will be able to come up with something."

Mary Sapphire was contacted and given the GPS signature for each of the cruise ships, told to locate them and keep a minute-by-minute track of their whereabouts. She wasted no time retasking satellites to hone in on the signals each ship emitted.

With the advances in computer tracking technology every cruise ship and most freighters, container ships and oil tankers emitted a signal permitting precise tracking by satellite. Each ship had a unique signal, its "signature," that immediately identified it and brought its precise location up on a screen. Smaller ship such as the trawler normally did not carry such sophisticated technology.

Not only could the satellite locate the ship, but with proper tasking, its cameras could zoom in giving the observer almost an intimate look at what was happening on its decks.

Many Third World ships had not yet advanced to this stage, but it was an unwritten requirement that cruise ships and all those from developed nations carry the transmitting equipment. It guaranteed that never again would a ship go down and not be found by rescuers or searchers. There would be no more Titanics.

The phone in front of Dan's rang and he found Sapphire on the other end.

"Mr. Morton please."

Dan handed the phone over and watched Morton's face as he listened to Mary Sapphire.

"She's got a track on all four ships. Two are still pretty well out to sea and the other two will be in Newport and Boston by tomorrow morning. Both will be there the better part of the day to allow passengers sightseeing time and then they sail overnight for New York. They arrive here within an hour of each other.

"The other two will begin a circle and make a slow headway to New York. Both of them will arrive by late morning and early afternoon. Al Jazeera says the terrorists want Rahman, Sirhan and Moussoaui released by the day those ships are in port. All four are slated to board new passengers and be out of the harbour by six that evening."

"We've got to get aboard those ships well before they reach New York," Dan said, stating the obvious. "We'll have to bring detection equipment and go through the holds to inspect the cargo. We can cover what we're doing by making it look as though this is a DEA drug sweep. Bring in a couple of dogs and we can go through the entire ship without alerting anyone except those who might actually be packing contraband."

""The only problem we'll have is boarding the ships that have no port until New York. We've got to check them out before they come into the harbour. Dan, you and Hesh can handle the ship in Boston and I'll take care of the Newport cruiser. I'll have the Coasties board the two ships at sea. Frankly, it's not that unusual for a cutter to pull up alongside if they've gotten a tip. Makes it a lot easier than holding everyone on board after a ship docks. That's when the passengers start getting antsy and the press gets involved."

Matt pulled information on both Boston and Newport for them to examine. What they saw gave them cause to worry.

"Newport is the very heart of old American capitalism," Matt noted. "We've got all those mansions along one road and the yachts in the harbour."

"I can't see it," Dan countered. "There isn't enough of a concentration of population or business facilities for them to waste a nuclear device. It would cause damage, but not what they would want."

Dan pointed to the charts of New York and Boston.

"These are our two most logical targets. Boston is a major commercial center and a site of great historical importance to Americans. In the summer the tourist influx generates huge crowds and the financial district is right off the waterfront and near South Boston where any cruise ships would dock. I would be almost positive that the first target would be New York and the secondary in Boston. The critical question is how many devices do they have? The only thing they could lose without any national impact would be Fenway Park and the Red Sox."

"Great supposition coming from a Yankee fan, but we can't be 'almost positive.' One mistake on our part and millions of people are going to die."

"They've got us by the balls. We've got to put our best guess on the line because there is just too much to search for in the world. My bet is that they are going to go for New York and London. We know they have one device and components for others. With the time we have left we can't mount any operation into North Korea to determine how many other devices may have been assembled. That would start a war.

"The unfortunate fact of the matter is, I'm afraid, we are going to miss something and we may face a nuclear holocaust. I should've picked up on the signs in 2001 and realized they were going after the World Trade Center. I didn't and thousands died. I have a sinking feeling that the same thing is going to happen again and I don't know what we can do to prevent it.

"My feeling is that there may be more than the two devices we assume are on the way. Kyle is going to have a hell of a job on his hands trying to locate and intercept the device. We can assume it'll come in to either Southampton or Portsmouth. But it could also come right into the heart of London through the Chunnel. The best thing to do there is to examine every train at the French and Belgian end and to inspect every piece of cargo off-loaded at the ports and headed for London. That's massive.

"We are going to have to mobilize every possible asset and we can't be too delicate about it. The danger here is that if they get wind of the fact that we are on to them, they might just detonate the devices before we can find them even if it means taking out a smaller target. If that possibility comes to pass they could still destroy millions of lives with the initial blast and the radiation poisoning over the next couple of decades.

"Look what's happened in Japan after Hiroshima and Nagasaki. People are still suffering from radiation effects and those bombs were dropped in 1945. These bastards will have no concern or second thoughts about what they're doing. We've seen mothers send their sons and daughters out to become martyrs by blowing themselves up so that the families can collect the "Martyr's Reward" of $25,000 and new homes. They don't care about their own so why would they care about any of us?"

"Well, it looks as though that group calling itself 'Response' may have the right idea," Hesh chimed in. "They are taking out terrorists that normal means of justice can't touch. And it looks as though they are going after the families of the suicide bombers to teach them a lesson as well. We've got to drop the civilized attitude and fight fire with fire. That's the only thing these animals understand. They've got to know that if they hurt us, they are going to get hurt. And that if our women and children are going to die, so are theirs. Their mothers have got to understand that if they hope to collect the Martyr's Reward, they are going to die for their thirty pieces of silver and that no mercy is going to come their way."

Hesh sat back at the table. His face had gone beet red and the look of anger on his face surprised Dan and the others.

"That's not you talking, Hesh. I know what you've gone through. But there is something that differentiates us from them."

"Bullshit! They murdered Shoshanna without giving it a second thought. They shot that little girl on the beach and her mother the same as they killed my wife. And their families and friends hailed them as martyrs. What kind of martyr kills innocents like that? A soldier dying is just as traumatic to his family, but that is more understandable in conflict. But the killing of a woman on her honeymoon and a little child crying at her mother's body? None of them deserves to live and the sooner we understand that, the sooner we can come to grips with what we really have to do.

"We're sitting here talking about defusing a situation involving nuclear weapons that could destroy millions of people in the United States and England and you're going to stand there and tell me that we are different than they are? The only way we are going to defeat them is if we adopt their tactics. No life is sacred and no one will be spared. Fuck them. Fuck their mothers and fuck their fathers. Fuck their wives and children. Fuck them all into hell."

Dan sat back, shaken by the outburst. He knew Hesh was still hurting but he never expected it was so intense. And he never expected it to be manifested at a meeting of this sort. Hesh had never been anything but cool and fully professional.

But in the back of his mind Dan wondered if his young friend wasn't right to a great extent. Conventional methods certainly weren't working. The terrorists killed at will and they never stopped to worry about whether the victims would be children, hospitals, schools or families shopping in a village marketplace.

He knew that if any of their three countries adopted the terrorists' tactics, it would come out in a congressional or parliamentary hearing. And if not through the political process, some damn journalist would come across something, spill the beans and all the hand wringers would twist their hands in self-righteous agony, something that never happened when the Arab killers took their toll.

"We're fighting pure evil with civilized methods," he thought to himself. "I don't know…maybe he's right. I just can't stoop to the level of intentionally killing innocent people."

Hesh looked at those seated around the table:

"When these same animals began kidnapping people in Lebanon, they also killed several of the hostages. Terry Anderson and Joe Cicippio were the lucky ones, but how long were they held? Anderson was a prisoner for more than eight years. They finally made a misstep and grabbed three Russians off the street in Beirut.

"The Russians gave them an ultimatum, release our people or suffer the consequences. The terrorists not only ignored the Russians, but killed one of their hostages. Moscow sent in the Spetznatz, their Special Forces, and began killing the members of the known terrorist's families. Within days the other two hostages were freed and no Russian was ever at risk again. The families of the terrorists turned against them because they knew they were now at risk. How much more of an example do we need?"

Hesh sat back, his eyes brimming with tears, his fury somewhat spent, but the hurt and sadness piercing his heart.

Sayyid sat back on the sofa in his cabin and watched as the waves from the big ship's bow pushed out into the open ocean, forming rippled lines that moved off into infinity. The sun was low in the eastern sky and created a sharp yellow slash across the water that paced the ship's movement. It was idyllic, it was peaceful.

Sayyid pushed those thoughts from his mind as he thought ahead to what he had to do. He had sole responsibility for the action in the United States. But there were others involved.

Mahmoud was responsible for bringing the device into London through the tunnel from Paris. His truck would not be noticed in the Canary Wharf area during the business day because it was in the city's commercial district. Coordinating with Sayyid, he would set his device off at 9 am in London as Sayyid would do the same in New York at 2 pm so the blasts would be simultaneous.

Sayyid began programming his cell phone with the key numbers he would use to detonate the device in New York. What Mahmoud was not aware was that Sayyid had placed a receiver in the device headed for London that would be detonated by a call from his cell phone to make sure Mahmoud did not back out.

Sayyid would then dial the number of his own device and a second later the one that would destroy London would detonate. He would live because he would be making the calls from a remote location. That was critical because he was needed more to lead the fight than he was needed to be another silent martyr. Mahmoud was expendable, he was not. He preferred to enjoy the company of virgins…or non-virgins in this world rather than the next.

He sat back, dialed his satellite phone and heard Old Sayyid's voice at the other end.

"We are in position and ready to act."

"That is good, my son. We have notified the press agencies that we demand the releases of Sheik Omar, Sirhan and Moussoaui. Are you safe?

"I am sir. I have the devices programmed and will be in a safe location. It is only a matter of days now."

"My son, I have no problem with adding Sirhan to the list. But do not ever take such authority on your own without having the courtesy to discuss it with me first. I will not tolerate such insubordination. Is that clear? Is that understood?"

Sayyid lowered his head, although the act of submission could not be seen at the other end of the telephone call.

"Sir, I only did what I thought would make the strongest impact."

"I understand what you are saying, but hear me. This will not happen again."

Sayyid replaced the phone and switched on his laptop computer. He punched in HTTP://Azzam.com and waited for a second as the website loaded.

Azzam was the website of the Islamic Jihad and a conglomerate of terror groups who used it to publicize their acts and for communication with agents around the world. During World War II Allied intelligence communicated with partisans in occupied European countries via radio. By using radio programs, cryptic messages would be sent to inform groups of impending invasion plans, supply drops, orders for intelligence and to warn them that the Nazis were on to them.

Azzam served the same purpose for a variety of modern terror groups. It carried the coded messages and broadcast clips of bombings of Coalition forces. But most gruesome were the clips of the beheadings carried out by the cowards who covered their faces with ski masks, carried AK-47s and sharp swords.

There was little that could be done because their communications went from location to location and country to country. And, as a token from the hi-tech world, there were cyber cafes throughout the world, even in underdeveloped Third World nations and the mid-East. The mass of people had no money to feed and clothe themselves, but the terrorists were all equipped with laptops and wireless router links.

But more insidiously, the website was used for recruiting Muslims in Europe, the Pakistan region and even in the United States. The messages were propaganda-filled with a link for terrorist-wannabees to hook into and affiliate. They were looked at closely to weed out Western spies and used mostly as fodder for suicide bombings. Those who raised any suspicions were summarily killed.

It was a fantastic resource not only for the terror groups, but also for the lonely and disaffected who had little hope in life. Shoe bomber Richard Reid was a typical example.

The horrific Madrid train bombing was coordinated through Azzam with directions in how to assembly and detonate the devices conducted on Azzam's training link. The detonation method of choice is through the use of cell phones programmed to complete a connection when the appropriate number is dialed.

The website, and others like it, turned into a financial and tactical boon for the terror groups. No longer was there a need to transport operatives to training centers. That saved money that could be better used for killing people. It also lowered the possibility of detection since there was less movement of personnel. And most of all, it prevented retaliatory attacks from the United States and Israel against training camps following terrorist attacks.

Sayyid accessed the site, ticked on a tab and then typed a code that would allow him access to make a posting. This was a section of the site not open to idle chatter, as much of Azzam was. The cryptic comments here, if only NSA could decipher them, would open up a world of terrorist planning around the world.

"His Majesty's day has come," Sayyid keyed. "The curse of the thirty camels and the blessing of the ten virgins shall smite the infidel and all of his hosts. They shall perish as the Sodomites."

Sayyid's code was easy for those with the key, but made no sense to anyone else. He knew that not only were government watchdogs observing every line on the site, but also thousands of those, who like the multitudes monitoring the old ham radio frequencies, listened in as world wide eavesdroppers.

The eavesdroppers knew they were observing a passing of critical information, but try as they might, they had no better luck than the NSA, CIA, Mossad or the folks at Legoland. But the code was deceptively simple. So simple that you didn't even need a cryptograph to unscramble the message.

The first number was meaningless without a second number in the same or an immediately following sentence. The second number would be divided into the first and that would provide the time frame for an action. If there was no second number, there was no action planned and it served to throw a curveball at anyone who was attempting to decode the message.

"Sodom" was code for the particular action Sayyid was preparing and combined with the numerical code, prepped his team to be ready to execute in three days.

Sayyid knew that he could not be traced in time for any retaliation. Those communicating with him only had to move from one cyber café to another in order to access a speedy internet connection that would be untraceable.

He knew that once the nuclear devices were detonated there was little to no chance that the Americans would not retaliate. They would, in all probability, level Iran and turn the white desert sands to glass. The radioactive fallout would blanket the area and if the drift was as planned, would cover the land known as Israel.

But more than that, the retaliation from the infidels would so inflame the rest of the Arab world and would unite all of them against the United States and Britain, that the forces that once united Saladin against the Crusaders, would push them off the Arabian Peninsula and a great Islamic state could be proclaimed. The wrath of one billion Muslims could not be imagined.

What Hitler was unable to accomplish would be completed now. The accursed Jews would be placed in a ghetto in the United States, or what would be left of it. Their holy places would be destroyed. The churches and symbols of Christianity would, as well, be wiped from the face of the earth. Their Pope would be nailed to a cross as was their Saviour.

Their whore women, if they left Rome or the United States, would be required to wear veils with their heads fully covered and robes that touched their toes. If they didn't comply, they would be beaten. And if that didn't work, they would be killed.

"Allahu Akbar. God is great."

XIII

RETALIATION

"**Y**our Excellency, the American Secretary of State has demanded a meeting with you at his consulate."

"What do you mean he has 'demanded' a meeting? Who is he to make demands of the representative of the Democratic People's Republic of Korea?"

"Your Excellency, the Secretary has said that if you do not appear in his office, he will have you declared Persona non Grata and force you to leave the country within twenty four hours."

"The capitalist bastard. Have my car come around to the Delegate's Entrance and I will go. Inform them that I am on the way."

Byong Seong, Counsel General of the DPRK to the United Nations, stood and reached for his jacket. His narrow eyes glinted with an absolute fury as he walked through the corridor of the international debating society to the delegate's entrance. He motioned for his assistant to accompany him.

"What could the Secretary want so badly that he would risk provoking an international incident?" he asked Kim Tae Jon, his assistant.

The man simply shook his head, indicating a total lack of knowledge.

At the same moment a messenger from the U.S. Department of State was on his way to the Iranian Consulate delivering an almost identical message. The Iranian's back bristled more than the Korean's, but the message was delivered in such forceful terms that he decided it was more important to attend the meeting than to defy the American Secretary.

Within minutes Seong appeared at the entrance to the consulate and a uniformed IPS guard, the same trained cadre providing protection at the Israeli Consulate, in the company of two very large men in civilian clothes met him and escorted him inside. His bodyguard moved to the door in order to accompany Seong, but was physically blocked by one of the International Protective Systems trained men. Only Seong and his assistant were permitted entry.

The bodyguard's first reaction was to force his way in. That came to an abrupt halt as he was body slammed into the wall, grabbed by both arms and led into a room adjacent to the guard post. The civilian reached into the Korean's jacket and pulled his automatic from its holster.

He couldn't fight back; both of his arms had been pinned to his side and the large civilian growled in perfect Korean: "Move, resist and I will break your arms."

The bodyguard sat down, a look of total confusion on his face. Such actions were not only an affront to a representative of a United Nations ambassador, but were a clear violation of diplomatic immunity.

The civilian looked at him and spat words through his teeth:

"This isn't about illegal parking in New York. Please give me an excuse to do physical harm to you."

The Korean looked up, his face suddenly a mask of fear.

"Make one false move or resist and I'll send you back to Pyongyang in a box and have your family wear white for seven years."

The Korean sat back and closed his mouth.

In the American Ambassador's office Secretary of State Joseph McCrane stood behind an ornate desk as Seong entered.

McCrane had held the rank of full colonel, a "Bird Colonel" in Special Forces and commanded the 11th Special Forces Group in a previous life. He had a distinguished combat record in Korea and was determined that the young Green Berets in his charge would be ready for anything. He stood over six feet tall and was built as solid as a wall. He was former Marine who had seen the error of his ways and reenlisted in the Army. But his manner was never gruff. He was always firm, but projected an air of understanding and respect for and from those with whom he dealt.

His troops knew that he would go to the wall for them. But they also knew that he meant what he said and there was never any hesitancy to carry out his orders. He didn't negotiate; he led. He was from New Jersey and part of a politically powerful family; he knew privilege and he knew hard work. He preferred hard work.

The second civilian took Seong by the right arm and ushered him to a place about three feet from Secretary McCrane and then stepped back against the door, his arms folded. Both civilians bordered Kim, keeping him from any physical contact with Seong.

"What is the meaning of this?" Seong demanded. "I represent a sovereign nation and will not accept such treatment."

"You will shut your mouth and listen to what I have to say. If you speak one more word, I will have this very large gentleman shove your diplomatic immunity right up your ass."

Seong's mouth dropped open and he took a half step backward. The large civilian placed his hand in the middle of the Korean's back and shoved him forward.

His bodyguard moved to run interference but was stopped in his tracks by the Secretary's security team.

"Your government has been cooperating with terrorists based in Iran."

Seong started to say something, but only got as far as opening his mouth.

"I told you to shut up. I am not interested in hearing your bullshit lies. You can file all the diplomatic protests you want when I am through with you. But be aware, the fate of your country rests on what we have to say. If I do not get what I want, and get it immediately, your country will cease to exist within a matter of hours."

There was no translation from English to Korean. McCrane knew full well that Seong spoke perfect English.

Seong could feel his heart begin to pound, sweat broke out in his arm pits and his hands shook, more with fear than outrage.

"Your renegade country has been working with terrorists from Iraq and Iran. They have passed along to you both nuclear technology and the components for making nuclear weapons.

Seong opened his moth and started to speak.

"No! Don't you dare attempt to deny it."

"We have evidence that several nuclear devices have been assembled with warheads and then given to a terrorist organization. We know that at least one has been sent to the United States and another to Great Britain. We also know that they are going to be detonated within the next day or two.

"Understand what I am saying. Our entire missile system has been placed on Red Alert. The President has issued authorization for them to be fired. The switch will be pulled should a bomb go off, not only in the United States or Great Britain, but in Israel or any other allied country of ours for that matter.

"Should there be so much as a nuclear fart any where in the world, we will take that as an act of war against our country; an act of war participated in by your government and armed forces. That will trigger an automatic response from our missile system and one hundred nuclear tipped missiles will head toward Pyongyang and other major targets in North Korea. You will be a minister without portfolio because your country will no longer exist.

"Do you hear and understand me?"

Seong had slid down in his chair, the sweat now dripping on his shirt collar. His mouth was open and moving but no words were coming out. He looked as though he would pass out.

The American nodded to the civilian blocking the door and the man presented Seong a glass of water. He slowly sipped it and could feel plain water lodging in his throat. The American was mad. He was insane.

"Now Mr. Ambassador, this is what you are going to do. You are going back to your office and within one hour…no more…you will call my office here and will inform me of the precise location of all nuclear devices assembled in your godforsaken country.

"You will tell me the mission of each and who is in possession of the devices. Then you will open your borders for a team from this country to enter all of your nuclear facilities and destroy the components. If you will not do it, we will. If you do not comply within one hour; or if there is an attack any where, whether you are responsible or not, you will bear the brunt of the punishment. North Korea will exist only in history books.

"Now get the hell out of my building and do as you've been told. Remember…one hour…no more."

The Secretary sat down behind the desk and motioned for the civilian to escort Byong Seong and his assistant out of the building. They reached the entrance and Seong could see his bodyguard being almost dragged out of the room. The men were roughly escorted to the door and pushed out.

Seong, his voice, sounding as though it was cracking in fear, ordered his driver to take them immediately back to the consulate.

The Secretary of State turned to the civilian, who had just returned to the office.

"When that Iranian piece of shit comes in, I don't want him treated as nicely as Mr. Seong was. Let's truly put the fear of God into him. The time for diplomatic niceties is long since gone."

Ambassador Ahmadi came flying through the door and almost fell at the Secretary's feet. Before he could compose himself, the Secretary grabbed him by his shirt front. Ahmadi's security officer started to move and was immediately restrained.

"Your president Ahmadinejad has said that Israel and the United States will be eliminated. I am here to tell you that in one hour there will no longer be an Iran."

Ahmadi began screaming. He cursed the Secretary and the American president. He cursed the Israeli running dogs and all infidels.

"The options you propose are illegal," Ahmadi screamed. "We are legally entitled under the Nuclear Non-Proliferation Treaty to enrich uranium to provide fuel for civilian power. The use of a false pretext to threaten Iran is a violation of international law."

The Secretary reached over, grabbed his shirt and slapped him hard across the mouth. A trickle of blood began to drip from the corner of Ahmadi's mouth.

"This isn't a diplomatic discussion. This is to let you know that the President of the United States has authorized the use of nuclear weapons to destroy Iran. Please don't make the error of thinking this is an idle threat. The missiles have been armed and they are aimed. Not only will Teheran be burned in a nuclear holocaust, but your entire nation will be laid waste.

"This is not a show and this President isn't declaring 'Mission Accomplished.' Understand there will be no 'major combat operations' in Iran. We will simply push a button and finish the conflict before it begins."

The Secretary gave the Iranian the same one hour to provide the information as had been given to the North Korean.

After the Iranian was literally and physically dragged from his office, the Secretary of State sat back down behind the desk. He took a minute to compose himself and then pushed the automatic dial.

"Please put me through to the President."

"Dan, the president has given full authority for the two of you to operate in this country. The concern is that there may also be a device headed for some point in Israel. We can discount Jerusalem because they know if they blow that city, the rest of the Muslim world will come down on them. I think we have to focus on Tel Aviv."

"I've spoken with the PM and they're pretty sure they can handle anything that comes along in Israel itself. Right now the concern is with the United States and the UK. I'll guarantee that's where the detonation will take place. This isn't a matter of some nut case with a bomb strapped around his waist sneaking through a border patrol. The device is big enough to need a truck for transport. Those items will receive full scrutiny and if one is on its way to Tel Aviv, we'll spot it.

"I gotta tell you, I can't believe the Secretary took the attitude that he did and treated these guys in such a manner."

"Well, if you remember him from our Special Forces days, he was a hard-nosed old bastard then. He didn't take shit from any one. That's why the President named him as Secretary of State. This isn't a president who'll fly onto the deck of an aircraft carrier in full flight suit so he can pose for press pictures and then declare that it's the "end of major combat" while our troops are still getting killed daily. That was the same crap as MacArthur stopping a landing craft short of a South Pacific beach so that the newsreel cameras could take pictures of him wading ashore as though he was landing with the first assault wave.

"The President says he wants an end to terrorism and he means it. He knows full well what we're facing here and he knows that if he pussyfoots, millions of people are going to die. And he would rather it be their people dying than ours.

"Basically what he told them was that we know they were involved in the plan to assemble the nuclear devices and if they don't lead us to them and the people who are planning to set them off, we have missiles aimed at North Korea and Iran and will wipe both of them off the face of the earth.

"The President has given orders to the remote locations that if one nuclear device goes off in the United States, the UK, and Israel or anywhere else in our part of the world, the response is to be automatic. They do not need to wait for authorization from him to push the button. They already have it and that's the safeguard in case anything happens to him.

"There are so many remote missile silos and nuclear submarines that, as the Secretary put it, 'If there is so much as a nuclear fart,' Iran and North Korea will be less than fond memories. They got his message loud and clear and that should take care of even the hard cases like Ahmadinejad and Kim Il Jong.. The fanatics are another problem and that's what I'm afraid we are facing right now."

Ambassador Seong was the first to call.

"Mr. Secretary, I have spoken with President Kim and informed him of your ultimatum. He has directed me to inform you that as sovereign head of our nation he will not bow to ultimatums."

"Mr. Ambassador, please tell him to kiss his ass goodbye. I will report to the President and your country will no longer exist."

"Mr. McCrane, please give me a moment. President Kim will work with any legitimate request made by your government to ensure the safety of your nation."

"Mr. Seong. I have no time for bullshit or diplomatic niceties. You are couching your response in diplomatic terms to save face. I couldn't care less about your face or what happens to that insipid, mentally deficient bastard you call your president. I didn't just ask you for information. I directed you to provide me with certain details. Do you have them or not? Tell me now and let's cut the crap."

"Secretary McCrane, President Kim has ordered a search of our intelligence agencies to determine if we have what you are asking for. It will take time to determine this."

"Obviously you still do not comprehend what I am telling you. You have no time other than the one hour I allotted you when we spoke. The clock has almost run out and I still do not have what I want. If I do not have it within that time frame, there will be dire consequences for you, your president and your entire country. You only have a few minutes to stop the clock and I suggest you do so without delay."

McCrane slammed the phone onto its stand, sending shards of plastic across the room.

"What in the hell is the matter with that man? What part of 'nuclear destruction' does he not understand?" McCrane's top assistants stood in awe and backed away not wanting to incur his wrath.

Not ten minutes passed before the phone rang again and Seong's voice blared out from the speaker Secretary McCrane had switched on.

"Mr. Secretary, President Kim has authorized me to pass certain classified information along to you in the interest of international cooperation and the halt to terrorism.

"Cut the bullshit Seong and tell me what I want to know."

"Secretary McCrane, our intelligence agency has just today learned of a plot to possibly detonate a nuclear device in New York and one in London. We have learned that one device had been assembled in Iraq by its former regime and then obtained by militants.

"Mr. Secretary, the second device was assembled with components that were shipped to Iran from Iraq."

"Don't tell me things I already know Seong. I want to know who has the devices and where they are. And I want to know when they are scheduled to be detonated."

"Mr. Secretary, our Intelligence agency has learned today that the devices are in the hands of an off-shoot of Hamas. They will be used in an effort to free Sheik Omar, Sirhan and Zacharius Moussoaui."

Damn it man, don't you understand I don't have time for this crap. I know all of that; it's been all over the news. If you don't tell me…and tell me now…who has the devices and when and where they are going to be set off, so help me God, I'll push the launch button myself."

"Please, Mr. Secretary. Give me an opportunity to…"

"Listen Seong, there is no opportunity. I don't know if those devices are going to be exploded today, tomorrow or when. You've had your opportunity. Either I am told, and told now, the details of who has them and where they are, or I will terminate this conversation and your country along with it."

"Mr. Secretary…" Seong's voice had failed him. It came across the speakerphone in a high-pitched whine, almost pleading.

""Mr. Secretary…my President has authorized me to tell you that the devices were sent to my country by Iran. They came in components and were assembled at one of our nuclear facilities. There were only two devices assembled and both were given to the same party."

"And that party was?"

"Black Winter."

"My God, Seong. Your president truly is a lunatic. This is a man who issues a press release saying that he just learned how to play golf and shot 13 holes in one his first day out. He has no contact with reality."

"But Mr. Secretary…"

"OK, Seong, where are they now?"

"The device to be used in London is coming in on a lorry from the French side of the Channel Tunnel. It will be in a lorry with the legend 'Moselle's Farm Equipment.' The lorry is registered to a Belgian firm and will have Belgian license tags."

"What's the ETA?"

"The Estimated Time of Arrival two days hence. The lorry will come off the train after exiting the tunnel and will proceed to Canary Wharf."

"And the one headed for this country?"

"All we are aware of is that it travelled across the Atlantic Ocean by ship and was transferred several times to cloak its true purpose. It went from ships to a lorry and then back to a ship again for final transport to New York City."

"And when is this supposed to detonate?"

"I can only assume that since I was directed to leave the city in three days time that must be the time of detonation. My understanding is that the London device will go off within minutes of the New York device."

"Where is the New York bomb?"

"I do not know. Our dealings were with an old man whose identity I am not aware of.. His young protégé, named Sayyid, was in charge of the operation. All that I know is he planned to bring the devices into New York and London to demand the release of the three men I mentioned."

"Mr. Seong, you are not off the hook. We will find him. But if for any reason we fail to do so and either of those devices is detonated, we will take revenge on the DPRK."

"Mr. Secretary, my wife and grandchildren are in Pyongyang."

"My family is in New Jersey, within reach of an atomic cloud Mr. Seong. I don't give a damn about your family."

Dan's phone vibrated and he listened to the voice at the other end. He punched a button and brought up an image on the screen. Turning to Matt and Secretary McCrane, he showed them the image, a paper that had just been retrieved from an asset in Teheran, quoting a Revolutionary Guards commander, Gen. Mohammed Ebrahim Dehghani.

"We shall announce that wherever in Iran America does make any mischief, the first place we target will be Israel. We will definitely resist U.S. B-52 bombers. We scheduled military manoeuvres and war games to send a message. They were planned later in the year, but we have moved them up ahead of talks relating to our nuclear programs so that the Americans and their supporters will understand that we do not give in to their demands. We are entitled to our nuclear program and will not be bullied by them to abandon what is rightfully ours. Israel is not prepared to go to war against Iran, but we are prepared to destroy them. We were due to hold these manoeuvres forty days later, but because of timing, conditions and issues related to nuclear energy and upon the recommendation of Mr. Larijani (Ali Larijani, Iran's top nuclear negotiator) we moved up the schedule. They will understand we will not be stopped"

Dan turned to the others:

"Our Gen. Dov Halutz has said that the world has the military might to prevent Iran from developing nuclear weapons. If Iran does obtain nuclear capability, that will constitute a threat to Israel's existence.

"Understand that Dehghani was involved in the humiliation Iran heaped on the United States when it took over the embassy. He is as radical as they come and is ruthless."

Secretary McCrane spoke into the telephone to Seong.

"This is what you've created. You and that madman president of yours. I've got a good mind to push the button right now."

Seong paled.

"Mr. Secretary, please let me have the opportunity to put our intelligence service on this and determine their plans."

"It seems, Mr. Seong that we are rapidly running out of time. We have got to know precisely who has the devices and where they are going to be detonated."

"They have promised us the devices were to be used only as a means of obtaining the freedom of the three men from your custody. They are not to be detonated."

"First, you diplomatic idiot, they have already threatened to detonate them if we do not turn these murderers loose. And, second, I don't believe that they have no intention of setting them off. Why in the hell would they need functioning nuclear devices if their only intention was to use the threat as blackmail? Are you so foolish that this didn't occur to you?

"Understand this, Mr. Seong, and I am repeating myself; if a nuclear device goes off anywhere in the world, retaliation will be immediate, automatic and aimed at your country. And your family will be turned to dust.

"Now call me immediately with the information I need to put a stop to this madness."

"Gentlemen, I think he finally understands the gravity of this situation."

Minutes later the Iranian representative was ushered into the office.

"Gen. Dehghani and Mr. Larijani have issued a threat against Israel if any action is taken against your country."

"Mr. Secretary, I do not know what you are talking about."

"OK, I've had it with the bullshit. Your government is a bunch of outlaws who think they have a mission from God. Well, let me tell you this, you are on the verge of being totally obliterated from the face of the earth. And the damn part of it appears that you simply do not comprehend how serious I am. I am seconds away from giving the order to push the button and obliterate the entirety of Iran."

McCrane reached for the desk telephone and looked at the Iranian.

"Do you give me what I demanded or do I make the phone call?"

The Iranian hesitated and McCrane pushed the automatic dial button on the telephone.

"Hello, this is Secretary of State Joseph McCrane. I am speaking with the authority of the President of the United States. Are your missiles armed and activated?"

He pushed the speakerphone button and the voice of a military commander echoed across the room:

"Sir, we have received authorization from the President as previously determined and we are ready to launch."

"Roger that. You have two primary targets. What are they?"

"Sir, we are tasked to launch a total of fifty missiles, all nuclear ready. Twenty of them are to be directed at various targets in Iran and the remainder will strike targets in North Korea."

"How long after I give you the order will the targets be reached?"

"Mr. Secretary, the ETA for both target destinations is fifteen minutes for the initial strike. That strike will come from both land and sea based missiles. There will be a secondary strike that will impact on target fifteen minutes after the initial strike."

"Thank you Colonel. You are hereby authorized to prepare a launch against Iran. Launch time is five minutes from now. Please activate."

McCrane turned to the Iranian, now quaking in his seat.

"Mr. Ambassador, do you have any doubt that I will give the final order? If you do, you would be best served by dispelling it."

The man began to sob uncontrollably.

"I will give you the information you seek."

"You do that and get back to your General and President Ahmadinejad and inform them of the situation and that if they so much as make any aggressive move, the missiles will be launched. I'll give you another hour. If I don't have the information by that time, don't bother contacting me. And I would suggest that you find some other place to live because your homeland will not be there anymore."

Kyle Norman sat in the director's office in Legoland, the thin, sallow "C" behind the desk staring at him.

"Do you mean to tell me that there is a nuclear device headed into London through the Chunnel?"

"Precisely."

"And what information have we got in regard to this? I shall order an immediate evacuation of the city. I must tell the PM and have him advise Her Majesty to leave for Balmoral."

"Issuing an evac order would do little more than create mass panic and perhaps tip off the bomber. He would then go into hiding and make it just that much more difficult for us to apprehend him and stop the bomb. There would also be no way to clear the city as the traffic jam would be impossible to control"

"What do you propose Mr. Norman?"

"We have a description of the lorry carrying the device and have a decent idea of the route it will be taking. I suggest we locate it on the highway in France, shadow it through the Chunnel and set up an interception point whereby we may overpower the driver and take control of it."

"Why don't we simply have a stop put to it in France and avoid the danger here? There is more open land in France than there is here."

"Sir, my plan would be to avoid the consumption of time it would take to coordinate with the French. Their bureaucracy would delay and possibly create a deadly scenario. I would have our agents spotted along the highways leading to the Chunnel and once they have identified the lorry, follow it onto the train and into the UK.

"Once we are on our soil we can overpower the driver without complication, drive the lorry to a remote area and deactivate the device."

"Mr. Norman, please prepare as detailed a plan as soon as possible and I will authorize it. I will, however, advise the PM and recommend that Her Majesty take vacation at Balmoral."

Kyle took the elevator to the safe room where he was met by other members of his team. He laid the situation out for them and they drafted a plan whereby other agents would be brought in as spotters. The added agents would not be made aware of the gravity of the situation, but would only be told the lorry was carrying contraband.

Once it was on English soil, the takedown would be handled by his team and the lorry driven away from heavily populated areas. By nature of the island, there were no locations so remote as to be totally safe should the damn thing go off.

Kyle Norman knew that his plan and the actions of his team had to be foolproof because there wasn't an inch allowable for error.

With the added agents disbursed to France, Kyle moved ahead rapidly with plans to set up a roadblock on the route from the Chunnel into Canary Wharf in London. Such checkpoints were routine and shouldn't raise any questions. This one would ostensibly be looking for illegal immigrants and would not be searching any cargo. That should be enough to put anyone with ill intent at ease.

Secretary McCrane's phone rang and the voice of the Iranian representative came over the speaker.

"Mr. Secretary, I am pleased to inform you that my country has decided to cooperate with you in the interest of better relations."

"Mr. Ambassador, if you didn't cooperate, there would be no concern about future relations because you wouldn't have any.

"Please advise your president that once this situation is resolved, there will no longer be any toleration of your country possessing nuclear material of any kind."

"Sir, we planned to use it for peaceful purposes only. It would have been used for generating civilian power."

"Listen closely…no more nuclear power. You will use the bountiful oil under your sands and solar energy for all the power your country needs. This is not a discussion and not a negotiation. This is a directive from me to you. You can tell Mr. Ahmadinejad that he can announce that this is a decision reached by your government so that your people can save face. But if there is so much as enough radioactive material to light up the face of a watch in the dark, I will have your entire country lit up in one big, bright fireball."

The ambassador's voice rose several octaves as he detailed the plan to McCrane. The Secretary of State's face was a dark cloud as he listened.

"How the hell could any human being devise such a plan that would destroy literally millions of innocent people?"

He turned to Dan and Matt:

"The ball is in your court now. Get up to Boston, find that ship and disarm the bloody device. I have a meeting with the President."

XIV

THE DEVICE

Sayyid stood at the railing of the huge cruise liner and watched as the coastline of Cape Cod came into view. The ship was making a long, sweeping turn as it headed southward along the Massachusetts coastline on its way to Boston Harbor.

The sun was behind him now and some of the other passengers were beginning to stir as its rays crawled across the deck. On the huge megaships there was precious little open deck space unlike ships of only a few years ago where there were great, flat, open expanses for the guests to stroll or just take in some rays.

"Disgusting the way their females show themselves off,"

Sayyid had eyed the half-dozen bikini clad young women sitting around the pool. One wore a mini string bikini and another had on, but just barely, a thong that covered nothing in the back and a small area of shaven skin at the confluence of her legs. Her breasts were uncovered except for round circles of thread that almost made it to the edge of the aureole.

Near them were several men in bathing suits that nearly matched those of the females, especially the overweight man in the Speedo that just about let it all hang out.

He averted his eyes and looked toward the coastline.

"Allah has truly cursed these people. This is his will and their heathen ways will be ended."

Sayyid knew he was in range of the cell towers ashore and he opened his phone and dialed a number.

"This is Mr. Singh. We will be in port within the hour. Is the transportation ready?"

"Yes Mr. Singh. We have made arrangements for a truck and driver to meet your ship at the dock. He will have your merchandise off-loaded and placed aboard his truck for reshipment. Is there anything else you will need?"

"You have the cargo manifest that I sent your firm?"

"Yes sir. All the paper work is in order. Your cargo should be delivered by the end of today."

"No, please. Hold it for delivery tomorrow morning. I will pay extra for overnight storage. The drive is only about four hours and I would like to time its arrival for about 10 am when there will be someone available to receive the merchandise."

"That's not a problem. I'll have the driver return to our yard with the truck and then set out tomorrow morning at about six o'clock. That should put him at your loading dock at the time you require. I'll just charge your account for the additional fee."

"That'll be fine. Thank you for being so accommodating."

He next placed a call to his mentor. The phone rang in the old man's study as he walked with his slight limp to answer the call.

"Everything is in order at this end. I have checked with France and the truck with our cargo is on the way to the Channel Tunnel. It is timed to arrive at Canary Wharf before 2 p.m."

"The story has hit their television and newspapers and I understand there is a rush by civilians to evacuate several major American cities. The roads in London are crowded as well as the story broke there. I hope this will not affect the delivery of our cargo in either location. But to this point we have not had a response from the Americans. I am not sure they are taking us seriously."

"If they are not taking us seriously today, they will by tomorrow. I will call later."

Secretary of State McCrane's call to the president went through immediately. He didn't have to worry about going through the busy White House switchboard, having only to dial a number of the president's desk console that bypassed the busy operators.

"Mr. President, we've gotten most of what we wanted from the Koreans and the Iranians and I think we will be able to head them off."

"Joe, we can't 'think' that we'll head them off. If these crazy people are planning to blow up nuclear devices in our country and England, we've got to damn well make sure that we stop them."

"Sir, MI-6 has a pretty good heads-up on the device headed their way. They expect to tail it from France into London and will then take it down. They've got a good description of the 18-wheeler carrying the bomb. And they have sufficient operatives along every route to the Chunnel so that they will spot it."

"Good for them. What about us?"

"We've got it narrowed down to two ships heading into Boston Harbor and our men are already on board. They've managed to keep their presence quiet and I doubt if most of the crew or any of the passengers are aware that they are on board. Their cover is a story about looking for narcotics. That gave us the ability to bring a couple of dogs on board.

"The dogs are a cover. Our agents have meters that'll pick up even minute traces of radiation. It's a slow process but we expect to have it completed before the ship docks in Boston. We're almost positive that the real target is New York and what we want to do is disarm it and then let them take it to its final destination. We hope that'll lead us to their cell. What are we doing about Omar, Sirhan and Moussoaui?"

"Joe, you know there's no way we are going to release these men. If we do that now, no matter what the threat, it will only lead to more acts of the same kind. Our policy is now the same as it always has been. We simply do not negotiate with terrorists."

"Yes sir."

"OK Joe, get back to me when you have something a bit more concrete. I have a press conference set up in ten minutes. I'll respond to the terrorists at that point and they won't like what I have to say. I'm afraid it'll cause some panic in this country, but we have no real alternative. Good luck."

"Thank you sir. I'll call as soon as I have something definitive."

McCrane walked over to the bar in his office and poured himself a cup of coffee, turned back to his desk and switched the television on. The talking head announced that the president would be coming on momentarily with a major announcement. The Secretary of State waited patiently.

Within minutes the news anchor announced the president was on his way and a voice could be heard in the background: "Ladies and Gentlemen, The President of the United States."

A grim-faced president came walking through the corridor leading to the press room and mounted the dais.

Standing behind the podium with the circular seal of the presidency, he turned toward the bank of television cameras on a platform in the rear of the room, set up so that they had an unobstructed view over the heads of the journalists sitting in front of them.

"Good evening. I am afraid that I am in the position of announcing that we are facing the greatest terrorist threat this country has seen in its history. We have been given an ultimatum that we either release from custody Sheik Omar Abdel Rahman, Sirhan Sirhan and Zacharias Moussoaui or face the possibility of a nuclear device being detonated in a major city. The same threat has been made against our staunch ally, the United Kingdom.

"It has always been the policy of this country, as well as the policy in the UK, not to negotiate with terrorists. This policy is in place because we know that if we accede to their demands for any reason, it will only set off a rash of similar acts.

"We are therefore announcing that we will not free any of these men. They have been duly tried and convicted in American courts for acts that have cost the lives of many of our fellow Americans.

"We know which nations have cooperated with them and provided assistance in obtaining nuclear components. I am announcing now, and I do this only after long and serious consideration, that should any nuclear device be exploded on the soil of the United States or any of our allies, our nuclear missiles that are deployed in various bases throughout the world and on our submarines, will be launched at those countries.

"If one American is harmed or killed, their countries will be laid waste with such nuclear ferocity that they will be uninhabitable for a thousand years. Those countries know who they are and I do not need to name them at this moment. Their leadership has been placed on notice and I have given orders that the moment any nuclear device is detonated, our response will be instant and immediate annihilation.

"I trust this will not be necessary. I do not relish having to give such an order. But they must understand that they can not act in an uncivilized manner and not expect retribution with the most extreme prejudice.

"Thank you for your time. God bless America, its people and the nations allied with us and may God protect us all."

The president turned and walked off the dais to a cacophony of calls from the reporters present. They literally screamed questions at him and attempted to thrust microphones in his face. His stride never slowed and a phalanx of Secret Service agents and presidential aides closed in behind him, blocking the forward progress of the stunned journalists.

In the press room they began gathering in front of their own television cameras, telling their audiences again what they had just heard the president announce. Each attempted to do his or her own analysis, but most were simply too stunned by the ferocity of his statement to really add anything.

In his office Secretary of State McCrane reached to his desk for the television controls, picked it up and pushed the button that turned the set off. He sat back; his fingers entwined like a church steeple and closed his eyes.

"Now we're in for it and I hope Morton and his friends succeed. If they don't, this can of shit is liable to destroy the world."

Kyle Norman looked at the dispatch the security runner had just handed him.

"Package located. Messenger accompanied by company delivery personnel."

He breathed a sigh of relief knowing that his men had a confirmed sighting of the lorry and were now following it. He sent a condensed blast to Matt Morton and Dan Halevi and then turned to the task at hand.

A road block would be set up just after the egress from the mouth of the Chunnel and all vehicles would be stopped. His team, dressed as immigration officers, would inspect the papers of every driver, car and lorry, coming off the train. There would be no inspection of any vehicle's interior in order to avoid rousing concern.

Kyle rose from his chair, walked to the closet and took a lightweight yellow raid jacket from a hook. On the back of the garment was the inscription "HM Customs & Immigration." Each sleeve had three blue horizontal stripes indicating a superior officer. He pulled the rigid campaign hat over his head and down to precisely three fingers over his nose. Norman looked, for all intents and purposes, as the perfect government functionary.

He walked to the riverbank and the circular pad with a huge "H" painted in the center indicating it was a helicopter landing pad. The craft was waiting for him to board and its rotors created a mini-sandstorm as they whirled overhead; ripples formed in the water leading onto the Thames.

Kyle was unaware of any of this, his mind totally preoccupied with the task ahead. He bent his head low even though the overhead fan blades did not come anywhere near him. It was an involuntary movement done by almost every person boarding a helicopter to avoid decapitation; an unnecessary but uncontrolled movement.

He sat back in the co-pilot's seat, strapped himself into the safety harness and motioned for the pilot to proceed. The ungainly bird took flight, not rising straight up as most people assumed a helicopter takes off. It came about ten feet off the ground and in a straight line raced along the Thames, reaching an ever increasing altitude as it zipped over the water and gained altitude.

Kyle had always marveled at the beauty of Tower Bridge, the historic Tower of London just down the road from the river crossing and the classical architecture of the Westminster Palace containing the Houses of Parliament and Westminster Cathedral across the street. They went unnoticed by him today. He didn't notice the "London Eye," the huge Ferris Wheel" taking hundreds of visitors in one clip high over the city for amazing views. He never saw the boats slowly cruising the Thames with tourists absorbing the historic sites and eating lunch at the same time.

He sat staring straight ahead out of the glass bubble of the helicopter, his mind preoccupied by the mission and the consequences not only to the Kingdom, but to the entire world if either he or Dan and Matt failed. His had difficulty computing the devastation and he tried to push it into a recess of his mind as he had done with so many other operations. This time he was unable to do so.

The pilot's voice coming in over his headphones jolted him back from wherever it was that his mind had taken him. He was pointing to the ground and Kyle could see the mouth of the Chunnel and the railroad tracks leading into the huge tube. A short distance off he spotted the flashing lights of the roadblock set up by his men at the rail siding where cars and lorries would disembark from the specially built flat cars that carried them from France. Off to the west was a flat patch of land and the pilot headed directly for it.

The train was due to exit the channel crossing in less than half an hour and he wanted to make sure everything was in place and each man on the team knew precisely what his job would be.

Norman wasn't an imposing figure, standing just over six feet tall. He weighed in at about twelve stone, or the equivalent of 168 pounds, soaking wet. But his command presence was that of the proverbial eight hundred pound gorilla and no one ever hesitated to instantly obey his "requests." Norman never had to "ask" a second time.

He was quite fond of his team and they almost loved him. But there was none of the camaraderie that might be found amongst military combat commanders and their troops. He kept a simple arm's length from them when it came to anything social.

There were one or two incidents where he joined them for a pint at the pub after a particularly grueling mission, but aside from that, he was very much a private person. He was young enough to be from the modern school, but experienced enough to be old school in that leaders did not socialize with subordinates.

You simply didn't make personal friends with men you might be sending to their deaths. The psychological impact of losing a subordinate was bad enough that it didn't have to be exacerbated by losing friends.

He very much respected his men and did not think himself superior to them. But his training dictated that when he issued an order, "asked" one of them to put their lives at risk, it took on stronger meaning than if he was "one of the boys."

There was no question that his men would die for him or lay their lives on the line for anything he would ask them to do. They knew he would do no less for them, and had on more than one occasion.

He walked with a quick step to the blockade and was disturbed to see a look of concern on the face of his team leader.

"Sir, we've had a report from our man on the train that there is a serious complication."

"What's up now," Kyle asked, his voice betraying some testiness.

"It appears as though the lorry driver may be wearing a 'dead man' switch on his right hand."

"How the hell did the spotters in France not see that? If it was on the inside hand I could understand it, but not on the hand adjacent to the window. Damn! If we slip now the results will be utter disaster."

He called his team together and they began mapping out their new tactics to prevent any action on the driver's part. Minutes later they broke out of their huddle much like American football players and moved back to the gate they had erected at the off-ramp to the train's platform. Every car exiting the site would have to pass through their checkpoint.

Scant minutes later the train came running smoothly through the tunnel and pulled to its stopping point. Normally customs inspections were carried out at the point of entry so as to avoid great traffic backups on arrival.

One agent on a bullhorn moved along the line of the train announcing:

"Please have your passports and personal documents at hand. This is a spot check of identity papers."

As the vehicles rolled off they were each stopped and a cursory glance given to most of the drivers and passengers before they were waved on their way. Every third or fourth vehicle was stopped and the driver requested to exit. His papers were more thoroughly examined and a few incidental questions asked before they were permitted to reenter the vehicle and continue on.

Sitting in the cab of the lorry Mahmoud watched as the inspections drew closer. He relaxed as he watched drivers of passenger cars being asked to exit the vehicle and present their identity papers. He knew his papers were in order. After all, he was a French citizen of Moroccan heritage. That should raise no red flags because others of his background traversed the English Channel on a regular basis.

An involuntary shiver ran down his spine as he gripped the dead man's switch in his right hand, his elbow resting on the window. The switch would work within a hundred meters of the lorry and those being subjected to more thorough questioning were in the immediate vicinity of their cars and Lorries. If he suspected any danger, Mahmoud would simply open his fingers and the dead man's switch would transmit. He would become a martyr and bring thousands of infidels with him.

As one team member inspected the lorry directly ahead of Mahmoud, Kyle walked slowly to the suspect vehicle, his head bent slightly as though reading the papers on the clip board he carried.

"Good afternoon sir," may I ask your nationality and see your papers?"

"I am a French national born in Morocco and living in Lyon."

He reached inside the cab and deftly transferred the dead man's switch to his left hand so that he could hand the papers out the window to the inspector. He held his breath for a second until he had a firm grip on the device. If he slipped, the detonation would be almost instantaneous.

Kyle Norman peered at the identity papers and handed them back to Mahmoud.

"They do appear to be in order. Would you mind please exiting the vehicle?"

"Is there a problem, sir?"

"No problem sir, just a routine examination. I would like to ask you a few more questions."

Very unobtrusively several team members, their inspections of the forward vehicles completed, began moving toward Mahmoud's lorry as though they were headed for the next in line. They would pass within inches of Kyle and Mahmoud, but their movements were designed not to raise any suspicion.

As they drew abreast, one of the men whispered to Kyle and motioned with his head toward the vehicle they had just inspected.

"Are you sure?" Kyle asked.

"Yes I am," he responded, loud enough for Mahmoud to overhear. "I believe his papers are not in order and, in fact, may be forgeries."

The four team members closed as though they would be heading to the other vehicle. Kyle turned to Mahmoud:

"Please stand against your lorry. We may have a problem with the vehicle ahead of you and I do not want you to be in harm's way."

Mahmoud nodded and began to step back to his lorry. He got only half a step before the four men pounced on him, pinning his arms to his side. He tried to open his left hand but found both of his hands in an iron grip, held down by two of the agents.

"Do not attempt to open either one of your hands. If you do, I will cut them off at the wrist. Do you understand?" Norman hissed.

Mahmoud began to struggle violently. He would still be a martyr and take these dogs with him. His fingers strained against the grip holding them and it seemed for a split second, that he would be able to drop the 'dead man' switch.

He never saw the truncheon that came crashing down on his head from behind him. He saw stars, literally, as everything went black and he quickly slipped to the ground unconscious.

The two very large men holding his hands slid to the ground with him, each maintaining a virtual death grip on his fingers.

"It's in this hand," said the agent on the left side.

"Let's be absolutely positive before we relax on either hand," Norman ordered.

The agents slipped their fingers between Mahmoud's fingers and moved them around.

"I feel an object," said the man on the left.

"Nothing here," came the response from the right.

Ever so slowly Mahmoud's fingers were opened and replaced by one from the agent holding his hand. They couldn't permit the switch to move even a fraction of an inch out of contact or it could set off the bomb.

It took a full two minutes to make the transfer from one hand to the next. A second agent began pulling a strip from a roll of duct tape and placed it on the back of the switch. They slowly slid the switch to the edge of his palm, moving the tape onto it, while holding the trigger flush.

The agent finally brought the tape fully over the dead man's switch, wrapped tight to avoid any accidental release, then stood up holding it over his head.

"Let's not celebrate," Kyle commanded. "We've still got to get this infernal device out of this heavily populated area and disarm it. I want that switch placed in the armored vehicle and fully protected from any accident. We don't want it to release after all of this."

Mahmoud was handcuffed and dragged to a Black Maria transport lorry. He would be taken back to Legoland for a full and thorough interrogation. In the private interrogation room many of the niceties of normal criminal investigation would be put aside. They didn't use the rack or pull fingernails any more, but Mahmoud would definitely not be a happy camper. Modern chemicals usually provided a very beneficial result for the adept questioner and were more than a bit uncomfortable to those receiving the treatment.

The lorry rolled onto the highway and with a heavy police motorcycle escort, headed out to the countryside. There was a major Royal Air Force base about an hour from the Chunnel exit that would provide the open area and secrecy Kyle needed. At least if there was an accident, it would minimize the damage and casualties.

The Queen and her entourage had departed for Scotland and Balmoral Castle under the guise of spending a few days with her grandchildren. Her banner was already flying over the castle, signifying her presence.

So far the operation had been kept from the press. There was sufficient agitation after the reports of the demands for the release of the two terrorist leaders and Bobby Kennedy's assassin and the threats if they were not turned over. Blood pressure rose on the international level when the United States flatly refused to accede to the demands and the British PM went on television to support the Americans.

With the escort the trip took less than the expected hour and they rolled through the gates of the base to a remote location. A team of bomb squad members along with nuclear device experts were on hand to meet them.

"Just remember," Kyle cautioned, "this isn't a demolition. It is a deactivation. I don't want any mishaps. We simply can't afford them."

The men gingerly lowered the crate from the rear of the lorry with an oversize forklift and rolled it into an aircraft hanger. They went to work pulling the crate apart and exposing the devil's device.

"We have a problem," one of them warned Kyle. "There appears to be a remote receptor attached to the detonator."

"What, precisely, does that mean?"

"It is programmed to receive a remote radio signal that could set the detonation chain in motion."

"Would that be from the dead man's switch the driver was carrying?"

"No. That is a short range signal receptor. This appears to be set up for a long distance remote."

"Well then, I suggest you deactivate that without any further delay or we could all be turned into cinder."

The man gave Kyle a hard look and turned back to his mates standing near the device. One man operated a portable x-ray machine while another worked on it with a Phillips head screwdriver and a medical stethoscope.

Kyle stood nearby wanting to be in another place…any other place… but with his strong sense of duty and obligation, he knew he could not be any place else.

"We've got it," the technician announced.

"Got which?"

"We've got the receiver detonator. If anyone attempts to send a remote signal to detonate this device, it will simply make a clicking sound and we will know about it but it will not go off."

"That's brilliant. I'll have surveillance set up a trace program so that we might be able to locate the sender."

The man nodded and he and his crew returned to work on the device. They loosened all of the cover plates and gingerly placed them on the ground and then began a wire by wire examination of the bomb.

"It looks as though we may have lucked out," the chief technician announced. "At first blush I don't see any trick wires here. It appears to be a standard nuclear device with standard detonation switches. Unless there is anything unexpected, we should have it deactivated within about fifteen minutes."

Kyle turned to one of his team:

"Too easy. There must be a catch somewhere."

The words had hardly left his lips when the technician came off the low slung scaffolding over the device and walked to Kyle.

"And now for the rest of the story. There is a series of wires that connect the detonation activator to the actual detonator. The way they are set up, it appears as though the intent is to activate the chain reaction if the device is tampered with. I believe we have given ourselves some extra time by disconnecting the radio receiver, but it will take a while to dope out the schematic of this problem."

"Can you do it?"

"Given enough time, we can do anything. The question is, do we have the time and are there any other remote receptors we haven't found that could create havoc? We simply don't know. We can only go ahead and trace one wire at a time until we have a full understanding of this damned thing."

"I would suggest that you not let any grass grow under your feet in your efforts to accomplish that goal."

The technician turned and walked determinedly back to the bomb. Kyle couldn't hear what he was saying to the nuclear expert team, but he was sure it would motivate them to waste no time.

The technicians had brought protective gear but realistically decided that it would be futile and somewhat absurd to wear it. Should the bomb detonate, they would vaporize and no protective gear would do any good whatever.

Working without the bulky vest, gloves and head gear was actually a boon for them. They were more easily able to move and handle their tools. They also didn't have to worry about pushing through wires with thick gloves on their hands.

Kyle had given evacuation orders to all but the most critically necessary personnel. He knew that they would have to get one hell of a distance away to be safe and that didn't account for whatever distance the dirty nuclear fallout would travel. They were facing a disaster of monumental proportions and there was no way to protect the masses. A general evacuation order would create such chaos that more people would be killed in the rush to get the hell out of Dodge than if they were kept blissfully unaware of what was happening in their own back yards.

The lead tech followed wires, checked schematics he had brought and conferred with the men from the British Atomic Energy Ministry. They followed the lead wires and at one point Kyle could see them tense as the technician moved in with a small pair of wire cutters. He saw the man hesitate, snip the wire and then cringe as if waiting for the blast. It didn't come.

Within about forty five minutes the technician had severed a number of wires and he stood down.

"I do believe we have neutered the beast."

"Are you sure?"

"As sure as I can be. We've cut all the wires that lead to the detonator and I can not find any other way that it may be set off. I do find one problem, however."

"And that would be?"

"In spite of what appeared at first blush, I think it was far too simple a project. There were no real false leads, no dead lines and nothing that would have set the damn thing off if the wrong wire was cut. It was basically a straightforward wiring job."

"And what is the problem with that?"

"It has been my experience that when a terrorist goes about setting up a device for explosion, especially one of this nature, he inserts false leads and booby traps. None of that was present in this case."

"Was it a dummy device?"

"Oh no! It was real and would have taken this entire part of the country with it had it detonated."

"Perhaps they never expected us to take possession of it. Their plans seemed so elaborate, moving these devices from one carrier to another to bury the trail."

"Mr. Norman, I hope you are right. I just have a bad feeling about this."

Kyle looked at the demolition expert and directed him to remove all fissionable material from the device.

Matt turned to his associates:

"This blast just came in from Kyle Norman in London. They disarmed the device but one of the nuclear technicians has raised a question. He's suggesting that perhaps it was a mite too easy to disarm. Why would they do that?"

Dan sat back.

"A distraction? But what are they trying to distract us from? Let's worry about neutralizing the bomb headed for New York and then we can worry about the distraction. It might just be that they are trying to head us off from the device coming this way. I've got a feeling that the whole Rahman/Moussoaui/Sirhan thing is nothing but another distraction."

"How's that?"

"C'mon Matt, they know that neither your government nor mine is ever going to give in to any terrorist demands, especially for the freedom of convicted killers. That's always been our policy and yours as well. We all know that the second we give in, there are only going to be more.

"We all saw what happened during the Carter Administration with Andrew Young looking over the president's shoulder. Ahmadinejad and his 'student' militants took over the American embassy, the radicals made major strides in Africa and even the militants in the United States knew there would be no stopping them. Young was Carter's balls and his agenda was only to help the radicals.

"Look at what happened on a smaller level in New York when David Dinkins was mayor. He gave free rein to almost any anti-social militant group. When an Israeli citizen and rabbinical student, Yankel Rosenberg, was stabbed to death in Brooklyn, Dinkins held the police back from taking action. When those radicals began to picket a Korean grocer in Harlem, Dinkins permitted it to go on for more than a year by handcuffing the cops. The whole issue there was that the black militants didn't want a Korean on their turf.

"All of this comes under the same heading. It doesn't matter if the cause they are fighting for is right or wrong. The minute they begin issuing demands and the government backs down, it makes the next set of demands greater. They just up the ante.

"Let's negotiate. But let's do it from a peaceful platform without the worry of nuclear devices going off in our backyards. And let's not let a nut case like Ahmadinejad or al-Zarqawi frighten us off with their threats."

"Dan, that's one hell of a soap box you're on."

"OK, which part of it do you disagree with or don't understand."

Dan's face flushed with anger.

"I fought for the United States and laid my life on the line. I moved to Israel because I saw what was happening and how most of the rest of the world was content to sit back and condemn Israel every time one of these pieces of shit blew up a school or hospital, but say nothing about the terrorists. We wouldn't be here right now, facing a nuclear explosion if the world had the balls to stand up and be counted."

Dan stood and faced Matt, Hesh and Secretary of State Joseph McCrane.

"Let's get going and find the device and then we can debate politics."

They moved, sirens screeching, to the West Side heliport and from there to New Jersey and the small Teterboro Airport, used mostly by private prop craft and corporate jets and bypassing the constant traffic jams on the New Jersey Turnpike and the roads exiting the two trans-Hudson tunnels. Fifteen minutes later they were climbing aboard the twin-engine executive jet, sans any markings except for a tail registration number that, if tracked, would lead to a dummy corporation in New York.

Dan, Matt and Hesh buckled in as the craft revved its engines and swung out onto the tarmac. The pilot pushed the stick forward and the sleek plane raced down the runway, lifting into the air just short of busy Route 46 and over a line of factories. They banked to the southwest, climbing for altitude and then, over the more rural landscape of Morris County, did a reverse bank and headed northeast to Boston and Logan Airport.

A government car was waiting to take them to the Coast Guard Station in the harbor, where a cutter, engines running, and a heavily armed crew on board, was set to move out. No sooner did they climb aboard than the cutter cast off and, at near full throttle, pushed through the water out of the harbor, heading to the open sea. With good luck they would intercept the suspect cruise ship before nightfall and have a margin of time to inspect it. Three other crews had been dispatched to the other cruise ships, but this one appeared the most likely suspect.

Dan fingered the radiation detector and twisted its dials, checking the calibration and batteries to make sure it was in proper working order. The "sniffer" was highly sensitive and would pick up the scent of even minute amounts of radiation. If someone had a watch with a radium dial, it would spot that as well.

Dan had always loved the sea and salt water and at one time had considered enlisting in the Navy instead of the Army, but the lure of Special Forces was too great and after he received his commission as a second lieutenant, he immediately requested Green Beret training. He had always considered Army Special Forces to be the ultimate in training for a fighting man and the supreme honor in being accepted to the group.

He had nothing against the Navy SEALS, whom he considered on a par with Special Forces, but he was partial to the Army. He looked down his nose a bit at the Marines Recon units, considering them as more of a "me too" unit formed only because the Army and Navy had Special Forces and the Marines felt they couldn't be left out. Also, the SEALS did not accept Marines. He always laughed about Harry S Truman's comment when he called the Marines a "propaganda" outfit.

He sat in the Executive Officer's seat next to the wheelman; although calling a modern sailor a "wheelman" just showed his age. Today's wheel was a joystick and much of the controlling and navigation was under full computer control. Humans had truly taken second place to the machine.

The Wheelman had punched in the expected coordinates to intersect the cruise ship and switched on the automatic pilot, then sat back and simply watched a screen to make sure the cutter didn't drift off course or ram anything that might pop up in its path. The computer sensed any deviation and made instant course corrections as the speedy craft cut through the water, spewing white foam on either side of the gunnels. The radar arm spinning overhead would detect anything in their path, any object that might create difficulty and set the on a circuit around d it.

Dan could hear the metallic click of clips being inserted into automatic weapons, bolts sliding cartridges into the chambers and then safety slides being activated. The Coasties had pulled the salt plug out of the muzzle of the deck gun pointing out of the housing compartment of the Bofors 57 mm MK3 deck gun. The rapid firing weapon could easily handle other water craft, aircraft and even incoming missiles with ease. It made a great tool for use against modern day pirates, smugglers and terrorists.

They were prepared for anything.

Anything except a nuclear explosion.

All that had been said to the Coasties was that they were on a possible narco bust and they were looking for a drug kingpin who might be using the cruise ship as a means of smuggling cocaine into New York. They had been ordered to remain on the cutter and not make a show of force. The "DEA" agents they were ferrying would handle any search and seizure and arrests. They would only come in to play if there was a glitch and massive armed assistance was required.

They had their flak jackets and helmets lined up and ready. People who downplayed the danger faced by the Coast Guard knew little about what the branch of service was responsible for. Since World War II the Coast Guard had seen major combat against enemy forces and was involved in every fracas the United States found its way into; and that didn't take into consideration its activities on a regular basis fighting drug smuggling and terrorists trying to infiltrate their way into the country.

In peacetime it was responsible for rescue at sea in all weather. Many Coasties had given up their lives in such rescues, taken out by severe storms. They also were a major factor in guarding America's vast coastline from incursion by enemy craft, although that danger subsided considerably with the demise of the Soviet Union.

Today's Coast Guard was in the forefront of efforts at stopping or at least slowing, the importation of illegal drugs into the country. Their speedy craft and hardened servicemen had taken their toll on narcotics traffickers.

"This is all great in a firefight," Dan thought, "but it can't come into play in this case. God forbid it gets to a point of where shooting starts on a cruise ship. There'll be a lot of vacationers who won't make it back home.

Even at full throttle it would be several hours before they intersected the cruise ship and Dan sat back in the high backed chair and closed his eyes. The smell of salt air was pleasing and refreshing and almost lulled him off. But Dan was so keyed up that he kept peering out through the slits of half open eyes.

The cutter's captain brought Dan and Matt a sheaf of papers that had just been printed out, charts locating the precise coordinates of the cruise ship. They were making better headway than expected and would probably cut more than a half hour off the trip. They would be alongside the ship before dark and that would make things easier. Dan had been afraid that a night time boarding of the ship would unduly alarm the passengers. He knew that the sight of the cutter pulling alongside would do so.

Matt conferred with the captain and then the radio operator was called to the bridge. He confirmed that his equipment would be sufficient to block any radio signals from or to the ship and that included satellite phones. They were too far offshore for cell phones to grab a signal. The cruise ship would be cut off from all contact with the outside world.

The Coastie radioman sent a blast to the cruise ship, indicating they would be intersecting and to prepare for a routine inspection as part of the narcotic interdiction program. He asked that the captain please inform the passengers and to let them know what was going on so that they would be prepared. He also indicated that no passengers or their luggage would be subject to search. This would be aimed specifically at the cargo hold.

The presence of sniffer dogs would further enhance the story of a narcotic search and should put the vacationers at ease.

The cutter was literally plowing its way through the waves, the Eastern Seaboard passing quickly by. Slowly it nosed in a more easterly direction to intercept the huge ship that had left Boston Harbor several hours earlier.

It first appeared as a speck on the horizon and grew rapidly as the fast moving cutter approached. As it came within hailing distance Dan could see hundreds of passengers lined up along the railings on the ship's starboard side. The aft deck with the most open space was crowded and he could see faces at the porthole windows as those who couldn't find a spot on deck, ran to their cabins to watch the approach of the Coast Guard cutter.

A lower hatchway, used in port for loading supplies and cargo, had been opened and the great ship's captain stood in the gaping opening to greet the DEA officers he was expecting.

The cutter pulled alongside and was secured to the bigger vessel. Ordinarily a fixed ladder would be used for boarding, but the sea swells moving both ships up and down were preventing that. A boom was swung out from the cargo hold with a narrow platform secured to the ropes hanging from it. The platform would normally have been used for loading crates and sacks of flour and foodstuffs from a dock to the hold.

Today's cargo was a dozen men and four dogs. The agents were dressed in black BDU (Battle Dress Uniform) and flack jackets. On the back of each jacket was the inscription "DEA." They looked for all the world like a police SWAT team.

The dogs sported black bullet proof vests as well and the same DEA designation. The well-trained animals stayed close to the heels of their handlers as they walked off the platform and into the maw of the ship.

They conferred with the ship's captain, resplendent in his formal whites and the four braided stripes adorning his epaulets. He nodded and led the agents toward the hold.

Dan turned the radiation detector over to one of the agents as he, Matt and Hesh slipped away. Matt held the leash of one dog that had been trained not as a narcotics dog, but as an attack and guard dog. If this beast saw any hostile move toward his handler or the handler's companions, he would be on the attacker in a split second, his teeth sinking into the aggressor's forearm.

The captain handed Matt a manifest of the ship's passengers. The CIA agent scanned the list and then asked the captain to point the way toward the Lido Deck. The captain began to ask a question and was cut short by an icy glare from Dan.

The ship's officer nodded for the men to follow him and they walked to an elevator amidships. They entered and he pushed a button clearly marked for the "Lido Deck."

The freight elevator avoided the huge atrium amidships and the numerous elevators used by passengers, most of whom were still on the deck or at their portholes watching the ship and the armed men who had boarded them.

There was no panic or major concern except for a handful of the younger passengers. Several of them, quite nervous, made their way to the port side of the ship and when they thought no one was looking, threw a number of small packages overboard. Several opened as they drifted seaward and left a streaming cloud of white powder that eventually contacted the sea water and dissipated.

One of the young men, dressed in a floral pattern shirt open from his chin to his waist, turned to a female companion and said:

"That just cost me two thousand dollars."

"Well, it's better than being taken off the ship in handcuffs and spending time in prison."

"I never expected this to happen. I thought we'd use most of it up before we landed and since there's no customs check, who would have thought these goons would board us?"

The three intelligence agents bypassed the worried yuppies and made their way through the passageway on the Lido toward Cabin L-14. According to the manifest, that was where Mr. Singh was located.

They had motioned for the captain to remain at the head of the passageway and not follow them. At the cabin door Dan and Hesh stationed themselves on either side and Matt stepped up and knocked.

"Ship's steward, Mr. Singh," Matt sang out as he rapped on the door.

He stepped aside and waited. There was no response and he gently knocked on the door again. With nothing coming from within the cabin he inserted a master key the captain had provided. The door was pushed open and Dan and Hesh burst through the doorway and instantly moved to the left and right, getting out of the line of fire as quickly as possible.

Matt followed on their heels as they surveyed the comfortable unit. Aside from the shower and commode in an enclosed area, the cabin was one big open area. Clothes were hung from a rod to the side of a mirrored dressing table.

The bed was made; a suitcase sat on a folding rack and other indications that the room was occupied were about. The door to the shower was ajar and the space empty.

Matt stuck his head into the corridor and motioned for the captain to join them.

"Please have an announcement made requesting all passengers to return to their cabins immediately. Have the bars and all eating areas closed."

The captain keyed his walkie talkie and issued the order. Seconds later the ship's public address system blared the message in a polite but very commanding voice. Passengers queued up at the elevators and others walked the ornate staircases to the appropriate decks. Within a minute or two the Lido Deck was jammed with passengers moving to their cabins.

The agents had closed the cabin door and stood, Dan and Hesh on either side of the entryway and Matt directly inside, facing the doorway. As soon as Mr. Singh entered, he would be overpowered, handcuffed and held on board the cutter until the search uncovered the device he had shipped.

They waited. The voices and movement in the corridor began to subside and soon quieted entirely. There was no more movement and it was obvious that all passengers were safely ensconced in their cabins.

Matt looked at Dan and shrugged his shoulders.

"Well, my Israeli friend, I think we have a problem."

He radioed to the search crew and asked the supervisor to meet him in the Lido deck cabin.

"What's going on in the hold? Have you found anything?"

"No sir. We picked up a trace of radiation, but there was no signal strong enough to indicate there was a device still on board. The possibility is that it may have recently been here and subsequently removed. We can't tell."

Dan turned to Matt:

"Have the captain get us a manifest that shows everything that may have been off-loaded in Boston. We thought they were coming into New York by ship. Either we got the wrong ship or they changed the method of transportation."

The radiation traces led from the hatch into the hold and it was impossible to tell what was incoming and what had been removed. But that something had been there, and recently, was not in doubt. Where was it now and where was "Mr. Singh?" was the problem.

They examined the ship's manifest for both passengers and cargo. Nothing in the hold was registered to Singh and the passenger manifest listed Mr. Singh as a through passenger to New York.

"Matt, we've got to find him and even more importantly, we've got to find that crate. We can't let this happen again. I still have nightmares about those planes crashing into the Trade Center and the smell of what was burning inside is seared into my memory. Let's go over the manifest and see if we can track it and then go from there."

Within a half hour three suspect crates were pinpointed. One was on its way to Ludlow, Vermont, one to a warehouse in Boston and the third headed to New York's garment district and labeled as "fabric manufacturing equipment."

"I think we can pretty well dismiss the Ludlow package," Dan noted. "It's a great area, but the main attraction there is a ski resort. They aren't going to waste a village and ski resort, no matter how beautiful they may be. Boston is a possibility, but I don't see it as a primary target. The other thing is, why would they truck the crate to New York when the ship is headed there

"We don't have a choice but to check the Vermont and Boston crates out as well," Matt interjected. "But I agree with you that the most likely prime target is going to be New York and the garment district is just off the heart of midtown. Last time around they made a tactical error and launched the attack an hour too soon. Had they waited until rush hour was over before crashing the planes into the buildings, they would have destroyed ten thousand people. The WTC would have been filled with office workers instead of people still showing up from their commute. They won't let that happen again."

"Matt, there's no way that Manhattan can be evacuated. A truck parked in the garment area, the West 30s, will never be noticed. The place is a traffic jam nightmare during the day and trucks parked late at night, or even overnight are so common they won't raise any suspicion. We've got to pinpoint the right truck and do it quickly."

"I'll have the local FBI offices confirm Ludlow and Boston. I've already called for the helicopter and the three of us will head back to New York."

The road from Boston to New York was strangely wide open as Sayyid pushed down on the gas pedal of his rented Ford Explorer. He had picked the sports utility vehicle not for its comfort, but because it was one of the most popular cars on the road today. It's slightly off-silver color was a common choice and as long as he did nothing stupid, he wouldn't be stopped.

He had pulled onto the Massachusetts Turnpike headed south, just off Fenway Park, home of the Boston Red Sox. He looked at the pennants flying over the edge of the antiquated field and could hear the roar of the fans inside the park cheering their team.

"Americans and their stupid games," he thought silently. "It's too bad we can't drop an aircraft into their stadiums on a day such as this."

He knew of the rivalry between the Boston team and its hated competitor, the New York Yankees and he knew that despite their antipathy toward one another, either home field was filled to capacity when the teams played each other.

Sayyid looked toward the sky and dreamed of a plane, packed with explosives, bearing down on Fenway and destroying almost 34,000 fans.

"But only that many if they are playing the Yankees," he thought.

Sayyid had spent several years in the United States attending school and learning the ways of the enemy.

"To be effective against an enemy, you must know all there is to know about him. You must understand his ways and speak not only his language, but understand the nuances of his colloquialisms," he had been taught.

Sayyid still carried a slight accent, but his English was sufficiently American that he could walk into the Katz's Deli in New York and not raise suspicions; not that he was about to enter such a Jew enclave.

He looked at his watch and noted that he had almost three hours remaining on his drive.

He had booked a room at the Sofitel Hotel in New York City, at 45 West 44th Street, between Fifth and Sixth Avenues. It was conveniently located just outside the garment district and with a room on the top floor, a radio transmission signal would easily reach into the streets below. It was the perfect spot to trigger a detonation.

He had also booked a single room on the top floor of the Hilton Hotel in Hasbrouck Heights, New Jersey with a fantastic view of the Manhattan skyline.

Sayyid had made sure the car was gassed to the limit before leaving the rental agency. Driving toward the highway he spotted a grocery store offering "halal" food, the Muslim equivalent of "kosher," although you never wanted to say that to an Arab.

He parked at the curb and bought a pita pocket bread, beef wrapped in grape leaves, a small container of hummus and a piece of baklava and some Madjool dates for desert.

If he had to exist for a short time on enemy soil, he would at least be able to eat as though he were at home.

The highways between Boston and New York offered either no services or very limited ones. But they did provide picnic and rest areas for travelers to eat or stretch their legs. He planned to pull into one of these to relax, have lunch and then arrive in New York late in the day.

The Bell Ranger helicopter touched down at the helipad on the Hudson River, bucking about from the wind blowing in from the west and off the water. A car was inside the canvas covered hurricane fencing surrounding the heliport to avoid the problem of drivers on the remnants of the West Side Highway taking their eyes off the road to watch as aircraft came and went. New Yorkers may be the most jaded people in the world, but for some reason, the sight of a helicopter landing or taking off only a few feet from a major roadway always drew gawkers; and gawkers behind the wheel of a car were a danger.

The car pulled out of the gate and headed south to lower Manhattan and the Jacob K. Javits Federal Building. The building and the mid-town convention center had both been named for the late liberal Republican senator who had been laid waste by ALS, Lou Gehrig's Disease. Highly respected by both parties, Javits, a six-foot plus imposing individual ended his life unable to breathe even with the assistance of a respirator.

The agents gave no thought to the history of the name as they entered the building and elevatored to Matt Morton's office.

Boston's dock cargo policies had made life just a bit easier for them. To cut down on theft and pilferage they double checked every piece of cargo coming and going from the entire dock facility and entered the type of vehicle and license number.

They were able to have the truck registration traced while they were on the way to New York and by the time they arrived in the Federal Building, they knew where the vehicle was.

A surveillance team was sent to stake out the truck and report any activity or movement.

"Matt, I'm very concerned. Kyle suggested that the take down in London was too easy. He got the impression that the perps weren't concerned about whether or not they could protect the device. If they were planning on setting it off in London, why wasn't there more security? And why was it found and defused so easily?

"I think before we move in on this device, we've got to find the answers; but we can't wait because of the danger that it will be detonated and take out Mid Town and a couple of million people with it."

Reports in from London indicated that the bomb found by MI-6 was a low intensity device, a thousand times less powerful than those held by the United States or Russia.

"They didn't have sufficient fissionable material to forge a super bomb," Kyle had said in his dispatch. "The device we uncovered here would have taken much of central London with it, but the radiation and explosive power are far less than one might have anticipated."

"We can't assume the device in New York is of a similarly weak nature. But what the hell, even if it is of lesser destructive power, can you imagine what a nuclear bomb going off in the middle of New York City would do?"

"Dan, this is my city. I know you were born and raised here, but this is my city and I won't permit anything like that to happen."

"Matt, this is still my city and most of my family still lives here. And after what happened on 9-11 when we missed the signs, I have no intention of letting them blow up New York or any other city."

"You're right. OK, let's get down to some serious planning. We've got to interdict any effort to set it off and I really want to hang Mr. Singh's scalp on my belt."

Israeli scientists, in cooperation with the IDF and security forces, had developed a radio unit called "The Interrupter" that emitted signals that could block other radio transmissions. It had been used with a high degree of success in interfering with efforts by Hamas to set off bombs in Israel by remote radio control.

The radical Muslims had run into a severe shortage. Not of bombs or components, but of dedicated suicide bombers to carry their devices into restaurants and other places of public congregation of unarmed civilians and families.

The recent attacks by "Response" against the families of terror bombers had also taken its toll. Where the families once were publicly proud of a son or daughter who carried out a murderous attack against Israel, the United States or another infidel target, their celebrations had been tempered by the fact that they were now being targeted.

The families had looked forward to receiving the $25,000 award given to every successful bomber's family and the new homes made them the upper class of impoverished neighborhoods.

But what good did it do to have all of this money if retaliation blew up your brand new home? And what good was it when parents, siblings, spouses and children of bombers were also turning up dead?

The "reverse" terrorism of the new group in killing these families and wreaking death and destruction on ex-Nazis and the current terror leadership, had convinced the potential bombers, at the urging of their families, that being suicidal might not be in the best interest of all concerned.

This had little effect on the planting of remotely detonated bombs, roadside attacks with Improvised Explosive Devices (IEDs), and running around with ski masks and firing automatic weapons into the sky. The niceties of killing innocents rang hollow when the same tactics began to be used against them.

Dan had placed an order for a shipment of the Interrupters and they had been delivered to New York two days later, courtesy of El Al. They were delivered to the Javits Federal Building for safe keeping.

This was the rainy day they had been saving for.

Matt's agents under Hesh's supervision took the devices to the garment district along with the radiation sniffers and began a street by street sweep. There were hundreds of trucks lining the curb; some loading or unloading, taking advantage of the lack of Sunday Blue Laws in New York City. Scores of other trucks simply lined the curbs, waiting for the opening bell on Monday morning to begin their participation in the commerce of the area.

Within less than two hours the slow pace of the sweep paid off. A truck adjacent to the loading dock of a small clothing factory caused the sniffer to react. It wasn't a strong reaction, but there was a signature.

The suspect truck was parked just off Broadway. There was no driver, but there was also nothing outwardly suspicious about the vehicle.

What was once strictly the province of Jewish shop owners and skilled craftsmen designing, cutting and sewing both high fashion clothing and mass produced clothes for the department and specialty stores, was now a haven for illegal immigrants, primarily from Hispanic countries.

The last thing any of the cutting or showroom operators wanted was a problem with or scrutiny from the Federal government. They were only too happy to provide surveillance space requested by the government agents. They were assured that INS would not be present searching for illegal aliens who populated most of the workforce, but were concerned with drug trafficking.

The agents set up the radio sets and began transmitting on a predetermined frequency. The solid triangulated umbrella of the Israeli Interruptor radio waves "would-should-block" any effort to detonate the bomb by remote control. And if anyone showed up on the ground to attempt a manual explosion, the agents would be able to immediately pounce on him.

A transmission locator was also set up on the roof of one of the buildings overlooking the street where the truck was parked. With any good luck if there was a transmission designed to detonate the bomb in the truck, they would be able to locate it.

Two other transmission locators were in use, one atop the George Washington Bridge's West Tower reached by elevator and with a view clear of any obstacle to the site of Ground Zero. Another was placed atop the Federal building in Newark, New Jersey. Use of the three devices would triangulate the transmission and provide a precise location for its point of origin.

As a backup system, a GPS locater had also been put into service to hone in on any cell phone signal and would have the same capability as the triangulation, giving the agents the location within a few feet of where the phone was being placed in use.

They had it covered. They hoped!

Sayyid followed the signs onto Route 287 West and then headed south toward New York City. His cool demeanor was only slightly disturbed as he experienced a quick bout of nerves thinking of the coming day. What he was about to do would change not only America for the future, but would settle the issue of the so-called "State of Israel" once and for all.

He followed Broadway to his hotel and parked in a nearby garage. He had toyed with the idea of valet parking at the hotel, but decided to remain as anonymous as possible. Why take a chance and have more people remember him than was absolutely necessary.

The parking lot was one short block from the hotel and he yanked out the extension handle of his pull-along suitcase and started up the street. In the hotel he walked directly to the registration desk.

Sayyid wore a saffron turban in the manner of Sikh religionists. Although this made him stand out, it also gave him cover. That and the false beard and moustache he wore. To anyone who might ask, Mr. Singh was simply a representative from an Indian cloth manufacturer here in New York to sell his wares in the garment center.

He presented a VISA card in the name he was using and the desk clerk cleared it through the electronic swipe machine.

For a split second Sayyid almost stopped breathing as the clerk swiped it a second time and then waited with no response.

"This happens all the time, Mr. Singh. Just give it a minute and I'm sure it will be OK."

Sayyid was prepared to walk briskly out the front door if the card was challenged for any reason. But as he gripped the handle of the pull-along, the clerk smiled and turned toward the desk.

"Here's your card Mr. Singh. Sorry about that but these electronic confirmations sometimes go awry."

Sayyid thanked the man, took the envelope and his key card and headed for the elevator. At the floor he walked about halfway down the corridor to his room, inserted the key card and entered.

He looked about, thinking that it appeared quite comfortable, even though he was not going to use it.

Sayyid moved to the folding suitcase rack in the closet and brought it into the room, unfolded it and placed it by the window. Then he opened the suitcase and removed a package the size of a shoe box and placed it on the rack.

Opening the box he pulled a long wire from it and looked to open the window. The window frame was solid and inoperable. Most city hotels had windows not capable of opening for both security purposes and to save on heating and air conditioning costs. And after several instances when suicidal guests used the window as a launching pad, the hoteliers had had enough.

Unable to drop the wire antenna out of the window, he took a roll of duct tape that he had brought along for just such an emergency and taped the end of the wire to the top of the window. He then ran the wire around the edges of the glass, securing it with more tape.

The length of wire exposed would act as a sufficient receptor for a radio signal as well as an antenna for a transmission. He needed both.

Sayyid walked intro the ample bathroom and began to unwind the turban, followed by the beard and moustache. He folded the saffron material and placed it into his suitcase with the ball of hair, ensuring that no trace of DNA would be left behind. Then he unwrapped the small bar of hotel soap and washed his face to clear it of the adhesive used to hold the hair in place and prevent it from slipping at an inopportune moment.

He took off the beige jacket with the Nehru-like collar and tossed it in a heap on the bed, pulling a blue blazer out of the suitcase. He combed his hair with a part on the left and a slight wave over the forehead then looked at his image in the mirror and smiled with satisfaction.

No one would recognize Mr. Singh now.

He zipped the pull-along closed, took it by the handle and walked out of the room, placing the "Do Not Disturb door knob hanger on the outside of the door. This would guarantee that no one would enter for a good twenty four hours. After that it wouldn't matter because the room would no longer exist.

He moved down the corridor back to the elevator and pushed the button. When the door opened he hesitated for a second as a young couple, pushing a stroller with a small child seated in it, looked up at him. The young lady smiled and mumbled a greeting as Sayyid nodded his head in return.

He almost hoped they would check out and leave the area before tomorrow. Then he quickly pushed those thoughts out of his mind.

The door opened to the lobby and he stepped aside to permit the couple and baby to exit first. The husband voice a quiet "thank you" as his wife pushed the stroller into the lobby and they headed for the revolving door and the street.

Sayyid was close on their heels, pulling the suitcase behind him. He exited the hotel and turned right, walking for two blocks before hailing a taxi. Just in case of any errors he wanted to put some distance between himself and the hotel so there would be no tracing his next moves.

Hailing a cab in New York isn't for the faint of heart. Most accomplished New Yorkers will stand off the curb and in the street, daring the oncoming stream of traffic, with their right arm in the air, the universal New York signal for a vacant cab.

It still wasn't that easy. If a cab stopped anywhere in your vicinity, you had to be ready to rush for it and beat out anyone else in the need of public transportation. Two cabs later Sayyid had gotten the hang of it.

He looked up as a cab cut across the street from the lane on the far side, almost running a peddle-powered pedicel up on the sidewalk. The driver loosed a stream of invective that the cabbie didn't even bother to shrug off. He pulled to the side and almost ran over Sayyid's toes.

Sayyid grabbed for the door handle and yanked it open before anyone else was able to out maneuver him. He closed the door and settled into the well-worn seat.

"The Hilton Hotel in Hasbrouck Heights, New Jersey," he told the driver. "And go by the George Washington Bridge, preferably the upper level."

The compartment he sat in was a mini-armored car. The back of the driver's seat was reinforced with steel plate that could stop a small caliber slug. From the roof of the vehicle to the top of the seat back was a heavy duty reinforced plastic sheet with a slot in the bottom of the middle. A small tray opened through the hole to permit the passenger to pay his fare and for the cabbie to pass back any change.

Sayyid looked into the driver's compartment and saw a saffron turban on the man's head. As the driver turned, Sayyid laughed. The man had a beard and moustache and looked very much like the persona he had just left in the hotel room.

On an enclosed flat case on the rear of the seat was a driver's license, a picture of the driver and the name, Patel, Dahrmesh.

"This is an American?" he thought to himself.

During the drive north on the West Side Highway, Sayyid learned that the driver was indeed an American. He had been born in Miami to immigrant parents and moved to New York as a teenager. And he was indeed a Sikh.

Sayyid never ceased to be amazed at how much of a mongrel society America was. He was an Aryan and his people were all of pure blood.

"How," he wondered, "could a race of people so mixed ever have risen to the position of being the most powerful nation on earth?"

And, he thought, it would make it that much easier and more enjoyable to destroy them.

The ride to the New Jersey hotel took about forty five minutes with traffic moving. Sayyid sat back and looked through the taxi window and down the Hudson River at the New York skyline. He smiled to himself as he saw the hole in the sky where the World Trade Center towers had stood until September 11, 2001.

"The next crater will be even larger and the toll will be far more."

The taxi swung off the bridge and merged onto Route 80 West. The highway ran, uninterrupted from New York City to California and passed through some of the most beautiful scenery in America. But Sayyid could only envision it clogged with military traffic and emergency vehicles racing eastward to a smoking former metropolis.

Check-in at the "Heights Hilton" was swift and he rode the elevator to the top floor. His room was bright with the eastern light flooding in. He pulled the sheer curtains apart and looked to the east across the Hackensack Meadowlands.

The rising hills of the densely populated towns of Cliffside Park and Fairview rose from the lowlands but not high enough to obscure the full view of the entire Manhattan skyline from Washington Heights to the Battery.

He watched as a sleek corporate jet lifted skyward from nearby Teterboro Airport, banked and headed west to a business meeting, filled with a complement of company executives living the high life.

By this time tomorrow no planes would be flying over the United States or any where in the world. They would be sitting on the ground, security officials checking every passenger, every bag. But it wouldn't matter.

Inside the room he again moved the suitcase rack to the window and opened his pull-along. Sayyid removed another package and arranged the thin wire antenna by the window. Unlike the urban hotels, hostelries outside of major city centers often had windows that opened. This was no exception and he draped the wire over the sill and out of the window, hanging down the eastern façade of the building.

He was about fifteen miles as the crow flies from the Sofitel, an easy distance for his transmitter to reach, but sufficiently distant to keep him safe from any explosion and the fallout it would create; but that was not a concern.

Radiation would blanket Manhattan and drift over to Staten Island as well as parts of Brooklyn, but unless the prevailing winds were strongly blowing to the west, only the fringes of New Jersey along the river bank would be affected.

It was unfortunate that his Muslim brothers in Jersey City might just be in the path of the deadly debris, but those in the city of Paterson were far enough distant to be safe. The majority of those were Palestinians and could be counted on to give moral support once the wave swept over the infidels, just as they had done in the moments and days after the attack on the World Trade Center.

The brothers in New York's Queens County would be in the direct path of the fallout, but that was the price they would have to pay.

Sayyid set the timer on his transmitter sitting in the hotel room window. Its radio signal would easily reach the Sofitel, travel down the antenna placed in the window and trigger a signal from that transmitter to the truck parked in the street nearby.

This would be easy and he believed the Americans did not suspect a second nuclear device after the one in London had been uncovered. He had made it easy for them to track the London device and had it placed in such a location that they could easily capture the driver and defuse the bomb.

They would be complacent with the thought he had planted that there was only one device assembled from the components Saddam had sent to

Iran and later passed on to North Korea. There was no reason for anyone to suspect that there was, indeed, a second nuclear device.

Or a third one.

Sayyid smiled at the thought of the devastation tomorrow would bring. He kicked off his shoes and fluffed the pillow on the huge king sized bed and without pulling the covers down or taking off his suit, he lay down, closed his eyes and relaxed for what he expected would be the last time in weeks he would be able to do so.

Dan turned nervously to Matt:

"I know we have everything pretty well covered, but I've just got a real uneasy feeling about this. That damn truck has been standing there for too long. I think we should take it out and not chance anything."

"Not in broad daylight. We show up with a SWAT team here and with all the stories about nuclear threats, there'll be a panic. Not only that but the television crews'll be all over us and our mark, wherever he may be, will see the story and we will lose him."

"Matt, I think he's about outsmarted us almost every step of the way."

"Sorry my friend. He is not aware that we know there are two devices instead of just the one captured in London. That was just for show so that we would drop our guard. If Col. McCrane had taken any softer an approach with the Iranians and North Koreans, we would be sitting with out fingers up our asses and the bloody thing would blow up right under us.

"We'll wait until well after dark, when the streets in that area are fully cleared out and then we'll make our move. In the meantime the radio signals we've put up will block anything coming through. I understand there have been dozens of complaints from people in the area that they have no cell phone reception and can't tune radios or televisions sets. Our equipment is working just fine."

It was nearing dusk and as antsy as Dan and Matt seemed to be, Hesh was wound as tight as a drum. He paced the floor, walked to the window, backed away and then walked to the window again.

Dan tried to calm him.

"Hey, things are pretty well under control and we'll be making our move in a couple of hours. Why don't you try and get some rest while you can. Once we trace the detonation signal all hell is going to break loose and I'll need you at your best."

"I can't sit still and I hate the feeling of just sitting around here and doing nothing, waiting for this animal to make his move. I just think we should be doing something far more proactive."

"Well, that's just not going to happen. We have until about 3 am before we can do anything so just go into the other room and crap out for a while."

Hesh gave his mentor an icy glare and walked out of the room.

Matt turned to Dan:

"This kid is liable to screw things up if he acts in a precipitous manner. That could be bad for all of us and especially for me."

"I'll keep him under control. Don't worry about it."

Dan looked at the digital clock on the control unit under the television. It seemed frozen. Then a minute clicked on and then another. Time was relative. One minute to a man hanging by his neck on a rope from a tree was not the same minute for a man engaged in sex with a beautiful woman.

Dan Halevi was not having sex.

He watched out the window as the shadows lengthened and lights came on in some of the surrounding buildings. He knew that in another two hours there would be no one in the buildings besides cleaning crews and a handful of late working stragglers. The cleaning crews were mostly illegal aliens who were only interested in putting in their time and earning the few measly dollars they were paid. If they saw a SWAT team, they'd all hide for fear of deportation. The stragglers would be gone before the night wore on for too long and would not be a problem at three o'clock in the morning.

Dan checked the radio transmitter just to assure himself it was working. Then he ran a test on the tracking devices. Everything was in order as it had been the twenty or so times he had checked them this day.

He looked at the digital clock again and saw that the minutes had only advanced five numbers.

"This is going to be one damned long night."

In Hasbrouck Heights Sayyid looked at his watch:

"This is going to be a very long night," he thought.

He called room service and ordered a pot of coffee and salad to be sent to the room. Then he walked into the bathroom and filled the tub with smoking hot water. It would relax his muscles and serve to both soothe him and pass the time. Besides, by the time room service arrived, it would have cooled a bit.

Sayyid felt cut off. He was here alone and was not able to call his mentor. Even a scrambler call on a satellite telephone might raise suspicions and he simply didn't trust the hotel telephone.

He knew the CIA and the American National Security Agency had ticklers that would spot calls with suspicious key words. He had an idea of what some were, but couldn't chance accidentally keying a word that would alert the NSA or CIA.

He was totally on his own…for better or for worse.

Matt motioned to Dan and pointed to the clock. It was just after two thirty in the morning. There hadn't been a sound in the street for more than an hour and most of the lights in the surrounding buildings had gone out. The cleaning crews had moved on to other areas. They had an entire district to clean before the morning rush hour.

The stragglers were long since gone to their homes in the suburbs. Street sweeper machines had moved down the street, their wet trail of sweepings curled around the handful of trucks parked at the curb. Some of the trucks had sleeping compartments and their drivers were curled up inside waiting for the morning crews to arrive so they could unload the material for creating suits, dresses, blouses and shirts. Many of the illegals who were on the cleaning crews would do double duty and return as cutters and seamstresses for the day shift. It was the only way they could make enough money to send back to the families they had left behind in Mexico and other Latin countries.

The money sent back was an important part of their economies and, in fact, was Mexico's second biggest gross national product. To protect this flow of currency the workers had adopted the attitude of a turtle; they saw nothing and knew nothing. At least nothing that would get them noticed. If there was any problem, they simply retracted their heads and limbs and took on the appearance of a shell. No worry that any of them would report anything suspicious.

Dan walked to the other room and gently shook Hesh, who was finally fast asleep. He motioned to the young man to get his gear and get ready.

The Federal SWAT teams had circled the area with their big black trucks and several armored vehicles. The agents sat on bench-like seats lining either side of the trucks, awaiting their orders.

In a Ford Excursion with blind plates that could not be identified if anyone ran a vehicle check, was a bomb disposal crew. They knew that this device was unlike any they had ever worked on before. But they had detailed diagrams sent over the internet by Kyle Norman showing exactly what had been done to defuse the London nuclear bomb.

Theoretically that should make life a lot easier.

Theoretically!

This takedown would be a bit different. Even with the diagram and information there was no way they could chance working on a nuclear bomb in the center of Manhattan. They had considered moving it to the old Fort Tilden site at the eastern tip of the Rockaway peninsula, but even that was too close to highly populated areas if it detonated.

They toyed with the idea of moving it onto a barge and towing it out into the Atlantic. But the defusing was too delicate an operation to chance messing up because of an errant wave that might cause a slip while the technicians were working. They would need an isolated area with a barrier to stop the outward thrust of an explosion and mitigate the spread of radiation.

The only area that met such a criteria within a reasonable distance was in Highmount, New York in the heart of ski country. There were deep valleys surrounded by some of the highest mountains this side of Vermont. The normal drive of just over two hours could be cut short with a "lights and sirens" escort.

That, they decided, was the best option available. But first they had to take the truck and avoid an explosion.

The vans moved to the corners surrounding the parked truck. In the dark the black vehicles were difficult to spot, even with the overhead street lamps. The rear doors of the SWAT trucks silently opened and the black clad crews moved like shadows into the street. Hugging the side of the buildings they moved almost invisibly toward the suspect truck.

If this could be done quietly, their chances of not alerting the terrorists would be greatly enhanced. If they slipped, the bomb could be detonated taking all of them out and a large portion of New York City along with them. There were few residents in the garment district, one of the business centers in Gotham that was strictly for business. Should there be an explosion, the high buildings, forming an almost canyon effect, would contain much of a blast coming off the ground level; but not all of it.

Fortunately they didn't have aircraft capable of carrying a nuclear device and setting it off in the air over the city. Even with a low yield bomb the results would be disastrous.

Shadows carrying guns moved slowly to surround the truck. They had modulated the radio signals surrounding the street and they were unable to communicate with each other except through hand signals, a feat made even more difficult by the darkness and their black uniforms.

Each man carried a small red LED light strapped to the back of his right hand. A switch was wired in the crotch between the thumb and forefinger and could be pushed to light continuously or pressed to blink and signal the team. The tiny pin-sized red dots simply blended into the darkness.

The red light served the same function as a similar light did for airborne troops. It conditioned their eyes to the dark and because it was of very low intensity and could not be seen from any great distance.

They waited for three rapid red blinks, squinting their eyes as they looked through the oval shaped opening on the Balaclava hoods they wore. Little more than eyes were visible and the surrounding skin had been covered with black theatrical makeup. In the daylight they were a fearsome and scary apparition. At night they were like ghosts making their way through the deserted streets.

On their heads each man wore a night vision scope that would be pulled down over his eyes when the signal was given to advance. They each tensed slightly as three red flashes came from a position across from the truck.

The Federal SWAT team, most of whose members had come from the Army Special Forces and Navy SEALS, formed one of the most elite units in the world. They were the most highly trained and motivated individuals that could be called into service for action any where in the globe, at any time on a minutes' notice.

They had supersonic aircraft at their disposal, loaded with all the gear they would need for any incident and, in fact, had been called in surreptitiously, to assist in hostage situations in other countries. The other assignments calling for their expertise were not even discussed amongst other team members who had not participated in that particular action. Everything they did was on a "need to know" basis and if you were not involved, you didn't need to know.

On the surface they were a medical unit that could be activated in an instant to supplement ground forces at natural disasters and police or military actions. Even their wives could only suspect what the true nature of their jobs entailed. Some couldn't handle the pressures and frequent separations and divorce was a job hazard.

As the signal came, the men slipped the monocular night vision scopes over their eyes and the street took on a grainy, green hued look. But even the cracks in the sidewalk came clearly into view. Their automatic weapons had been charged beforehand so that the metallic click of bolts sliding rounds into the chamber would not give them away. They did not even click on the safety, simply operating the bolt and sliding a round into the chamber while they were still in the vans; a violation of all known safety procedures, but a life saver for them.

The team leader raised his right arm, forefinger pointed skyward and moved it in a circular motion over his head. Taking his cue, the unit began to encircle the truck and then, very slowly, moved in.

One of the vans had moved to the head of the street and on its roof, in a prone position, lay one team member. He didn't wear the night scope but had one mounted on the bolt action rifle tucked solidly into his right shoulder. His right eye was glued to the rubber cup at the back of the scope, the rifle trained on the windshield of the truck less than one hundred yards in front of him. His finger rested gently on the trigger ready to loose a shot.

He had been given a "red action" clearance with full authority to fire whenever he deemed it necessary. He didn't need to wait for an OK from any superior and would shoot the split second he saw anything that could be construed as a danger to his fellows.

The only safety procedure he followed was not to take in the trigger slack, letting his finger rest lightly on it instead. He peered through the scope, the inside of the truck's cab in clear focus. He could see any movement or danger and would instantly act accordingly.

With everyone in place, the team leader raised his right hand and pressed the switch, emitting a series of three flashes three times in succession. Then he put his hand down and waited.

Within seconds a New York City Police Department patrol car turned the corner and came up the street from behind the truck. It parked in front of the vehicle and two very large men in NYPD uniform stepped out of the car and approached either side of the cab.

The cop on the driver's side knocked on the window with his long, solid aluminum, four-battery Mag Light, the heavy flashlight preferred by most law enforcement personnel because of its ability to shine a strong light over great distances or to be used as a skull crushing weapon as well. It made one hell of a truncheon and brought grief to many who might otherwise have harmed a cop.

He tapped sharply on the window and waited for a response. None came and he tapped again. It would not be unusual for the police the check on trucks parked over night on the city's streets. As much as they might be looking for criminals, the cops often ensured that the drivers were OK.

Still there was no response and the uniformed officer tried the door handle. It was locked. He rapped on the glass one more time and then walked back to the patrol car to retrieve a Slim Jim bar.

The flat metal strip, known as a "Slim Jim" with notches cut into one end, was used by the police as well as car thieves. Slipped into the door of a vehicle between the glass and the siding, it would be used to hook the trip cable for the car's lock and permit entry into almost any vehicle.

The device took its name from the old fashioned crow bar used to pry doors open. It was known as a "jimmy" and the flat bar came to be called a "Slim Jim" because of its shape.

The sniper on top of the SWAT truck tightened his grip on the trigger, pulling all the slack in and only the less than two-pound hair trigger pull keeping the firing pin from connecting with the primer cap in the rear of the cartridge and sending the slug zipping through the barrel of the rifle.

The NYPD clad cop jiggled the Slim Jim around, felt it catch and pulled it up. There was an audible "click" as the lock pin atop the door came up. He stepped back, drew his Glock 40 and slowly opened the door.

Everyone was on high alert. If the driver showed himself, he would be pulled to the ground and his arms pinned to his sides as the "Breech Boys" jumped into the cab to make sure it was empty.

None of that was necessary. The word "clear" rang out and they moved to the rear of the truck, cutting the lock on the swinging doors and pulling them open. Mag lights shined into the body of the vehicle and illuminated a single crate lashed to the middle of the interior on the floor. The radiation meter told them they had found what they were looking for.

The team leader signaled and a second truck, identical to the one they had just entered, was driven down the block and parked behind the first.

One of the shadows moved to the rear of the first vehicle and another man to the front. Both had Phillips Head screw drivers and immediately set to work removing the license plates.

That done the truck with the device was moved forward and the decoy inserted precisely where the first truck had stood. The license plates were affixed to the front and rear of the decoy, leaving it for all to believe that it was the original vehicle.

Another member of the unit jumped behind the wheel, reached under the dashboard and cut several wires. He then reattached them, causing the engine to purr to life. He shifted into gear and drove it down the street. Several blocks away sat the siren and lights escort, a safe distance so that no observer of the original scene would connect the dots.

Lights flashing, they headed across town toward the West Side Highway and the New York Thruway Northbound.

Behind, at the scene, remained the sniper and a security crew. The radio interference was cancelled. Devices had been placed in the truck now moving to the highway to make sure an errant radio call or cell phone didn't set it off. That could ruin their whole day.

The convoy slipped onto the toll road and went into high gear hugging the left lane, the lights of the escort cars flashing red and blue and brightening the surrounding area. There were a total of twenty vehicles front and back, all carrying heavily armed police, federal agents and military, every man primed for action should it become necessary. The vehicles raced through Westchester County and across the long and low slung Tappan Zee Bridge into Rockland County.

Behind them the first rays of the oncoming day were beginning to peak over the horizon. Off to the south side of the highway the giant Palisades Center Mall greeted early arriving workers to prepare for the hordes of shoppers due in a couple of hours and on the southbound side of the highway commuters heading into New York City from their bedroom communities were still only a trickle.

Some gave a passing glance to the convoy with flashing lights heading northbound. It was not uncommon for such things to happen in this area and no one even wondered what might be going on. Such was the focus of New Yorkers on the way to work or in the evening, on the way home.

At Exit 19 the convoy swung off the highway, barely slowing down at the toll booths. New York State Troopers had been stationed at the exit to expedite their way and keep the pathway clear.

The trucks rounded the traffic circle to their left, swung right and cruised onto Route 28 West, not slowing at all. Most of the remaining thirty miles consisted of a road with one lane in each direction and only a couple of traffic signals. State Troopers were stationed at each intersection to avoid the possibility of an errant car jumping the light and causing an accident. The thought of such a happenstance was frightening.

The troopers had gone ahead as well to clear the road and give the convoy a clear path to the little village of Margaretville where it would turn off and head toward the even smaller enclave of Roxbury. There, in a small valley ringed by some of the highest peaks in the region and in open land was a government site where they would begin to work on disarming the damned device.

The area was known for its ski resorts such as Belleayre, one of the few government operations that proved government can do something right. The famed Baseball Hall of Fame in Cooperstown was about an hour distant by road and considerably less as the crow flies.

What even the residents of this very low key area were not aware of was the fact that a secluded and top secret government site was in their midst. Disguised as a private and exclusive golf club and country resort sitting between Margaretville and Roxbury, it provided the absolute seclusion needed for special training maneuvers. Because it sat in a pocket of the mountains, it now offered the protection for disarming the device and threatening the least possible casualties.

There was also a tunnel bored into the mountainside that would offer added cover and protection to contain any possible blast and the spread of radiation.

The convoy zipped past the sign for Belleayre Beach, still too early in the day for swimmers and picnickers to have arrived. Just down the road the sign for the ski area beckoned out of season hikers. Less than ten minutes further was the sign for what passed as Margaretville's "downtown" business district.

The convoy turned right at the traffic light, crossed the steel trestle bridge over the stream with the ostentatious name of "East Branch of the Delaware River," and turned right again at the only other traffic light in the region, bringing them onto Margaretville's main street with its still closed little boutique shops, antique stores and small restaurants.

It was only a matter of ninety seconds to pass through the business district and wind through to open fields. Within less than ten minutes the convoys reached the "country club" turn off.

The convoy slowed and began to snake up the roadway to the facility and then down into the sheltered valley and the mountain tunnel.

The New York Troopers were stopped at the gate and the vehicles continued on through with the Federal SWAT unit in escort. The captured truck drove straight on into the tunnel and a heavy blast door began to electronically seal it off. When it was fully closed it blended in perfectly with the surrounding scenery and no one would ever guess it was there.

At the entrance gate to the facility the State Troopers posted guards and would block off anyone who attempted to drive down the road. They were puzzled by what they had been involved in, but as one of the more professional police units in the country, they knew better than to ask. Especially in a post 9-11 world where things were not always as they seemed, they knew something big was going on, but they tried to not even guess as to what it was.

They all carried standard issue side arms, but had also been given automatic rifles and were instructed to make sure they all wore their Teflon vests. The vests they wore were not the ones in daily use under their uniform blouses, but rather the heavy duty flack jackets of the type generally used by military units in combat. These were only brought out by the State Police in serious riot circumstances.

The Troopers could look around and see there was little chance of a civil disturbance here in the peaceful countryside. But if they were told to wear the heavy duty gear, they wore it without question.

Three patrol cars were arrayed across the road and onto the shoulder to prevent anyone from passing or going off the asphalt to circumvent the blockade. Just behind the vehicles they had placed two tire stopper strips, expandable units made of spikes that would instantly flatten all four tires on any vehicle that attempted to get past them. The damaged tires would drop the car to its rims and would be enough to stop the vehicle.

The troopers had stationed themselves both in front of the blockade and behind it in the unlikely event anyone managed to get through. Their orders were to immediately fire upon anyone attempting to breach the blockade, no matter who or what the circumstances.

Even after 9-11 they had not been given such orders and they held their automatic rifles at the ready, with a round in the chamber for instant firing. Although the automatic rifles would pretty well cover any vehicle, two of the Troopers carried twelve gauge shotguns with shells loaded with buckshot that would take out the windshield of any vehicle and everyone in the front seat.

One of the officers carrying a shotgun had a fearsome weapon. It was called the "Streetsweeper" and had been placed in use by the former regime in South Africa as a means of controlling blacks who had the temerity to demand equal treatment and freedom from the oppressive apartheid laws that subjugated them.

The Streetsweeper had a round drum that carried a dozen twelve gauge shotgun shells that spit out as rapidly as the bearer could pull the trigger, sweeping the street of all and any opposition. The gun had long since been outlawed in the United States with the exception of law enforcement use.

This appeared to be a day where it could come in handy.

Inside the tunnel the technicians had been pouring over the diagrams sent by Kyle Norman before attempting to open the device. Radio interference waves surrounded the facility although there was little chance of such a signal penetrating the mountain and causing a detonation.

Two men looked at the diagram as another technician slowly began unscrewing the cover plates. He took one screw at a time out, moving as slowly and deliberately as he could. There was no need to hurry this and perhaps accidentally trigger the bomb.

He removed a large cover plate and picked up a pair of small wire cutters commonly used by electricians installing a light switch. He was a seasoned professional bomb squad member and despite his long exposure to infernal devices, his hands were sweating and even with the rubber handles of the pliers, he was afraid they might slip and drop into the maw of the bomb.

The technician griped the handles tightly and began tracing the wiring pattern as explained by those reading the diagrams. He hesitated for a second and then reached in and cut a blue wire leading from what appeared to be a radio receptor to a point deep inside the bomb.

The sharp edges of the pliers gripped the wire and he held steady for a second before squeezing the handles, cutting the wires. The two severed ends dropped into the opening and the technician froze as he heard an ominous ticking sound.

"I think we may have just fucked up."

He looked into the opening and could see red LED numerals in a descending count heading from what appeared to be five minutes to its zero point.

They frantically examined the detailed plans of the London bomb. "You did exactly what we were supposed to do," one of the men almost squealed. "What the hell went wrong?"

Dan turned to Matt:

"Kyle said it seemed deceptively easy. The bastards left it there for us to find and disarm. They knew we might locate the second bomb in New

York and they wired them differently. By cutting the same wire as they did in London, we've activated the timer's countdown.

"There's no point in evacuating," he said to Matt. "If this goes off there just isn't enough time for anyone to get far enough away."

One of the technicians began to tremble and Dan ordered him away from the bomb.

"We've only got a couple of minutes to figure this out and we can't take a chance on you messing things up. Please just step away. Now!"

Dan moved to the ladder at the base of the device and climbed the three steps and looked into the opening. He could see the numerals clicking their way toward zero.

He gingerly picked up the wires through the open hole and began fingering each one, tracing it from its origin to its connection point within the device. He reached his hand out for the wire cutters and impatiently wagged his fingers for someone to hand the tool to him.

There was barely ninety seconds remaining before it happened. Dan knew that he would feel nothing and neither would anyone else standing around him. It would be over in less than a flash and they would simply cease to exist; or for that matter, to have ever existed. They would be instantly vaporized and what little remained of their ash would be spread over the countryside.

Dan's thoughts were not on his own possible demise, but on Amanda, sitting back in New York and waiting for his return. What would she do without him and if this thing went off, what kind of world would she have to live in?

He knew that even with time ticking away he couldn't rush the process. To do so might just set it off. He had to do this by the numbers; step by step.

The technician had set the countdown in motion by cutting the blue wire as had been done in England with positive results. "Was it reversed and could it be the red wire? Or was it the black or white?"

He fingers reached deep into the bomb with his right hand. His left hand held a Mini-Mag light. He had twisted the front end cap of the little light and focused the beam so that it shone a concentrated light with which he was able to follow the lead wires.

He didn't like what he saw. There was a maze leading into a series of connectors, any one of which could terminate the countdown…or terminate him and everything around him. He had to make a choice and had to do it quickly or it simply would not matter.

Dan's fingers moved along the white wire to the connector point. Cutting the right wire would stop the flow of juice to the detonator and render it harmless. Cutting the wrong one would jump a spark and set it off.

Dan had worked both in the Green Berets and later with the Israeli IDF in defusing bombs set by the Iraqis in the first Gulf War and then throughout Israel on devices set by Islamic terrorists. He had a good working knowledge of what the innards of a bomb were and he had studied nuclear devices, but this was unlike any he had ever seen.

The blue wire had already been cut, leaving red, white and black wires. He studied the connectors and glanced at the LED countdown, noting there was less than thirty seconds before everything became a moot question

"OK, Halevi," he thought, "time to make a decision before it's made for you."

Normally the black line was a ground while other colors denoted hot wires leading in for varying purposes. But this time the black wire seemed to be connected directly into the device. With fifteen seconds to go, Dan made a hard choice.

He pushed the wire cutters into the opening, gripped the black wire and snapped. He involuntarily pulled his head into his neck like a turtle and waited for the flash that would prove he guessed wrong.

Nothing happened.

Dan slowly raised his eyes and looked toward the LED clock. It had stopped at the number one…one second left.

He climbed back down the three steps and sat on the bottom rung of the ladder, a cold chill coursing through his body.

"Dan, you did it," shouted Morton.

"Hesh ran over and slapped him on the back and then grabbed his shoulders and pulled him into a great bear hug.

"I thought we were over, done, finished. Boss, you are fantastic."

Dan turned to the technicians and ordered them to remove the signal receiver from the now harmless bomb.

"I don't want to take any chances that the receptor might still be able to activate this. Also, if and when a signal is sent through, we might just be able to trace it."

The three agents walked to the mouth of the tunnel, Dan holding the receiver. He turned it over to one of the men sitting on the rear bumper of the SWAT truck. The inside of the vehicle was loaded with electronic gear provided by the NSA and had the ability to track almost any message sent through the airwaves. By checking the frequency to which the receiver was tuned, they could almost immediately hone in on the spot from where it was transmitted.

"Let's see if we can catch this bastard now," Dan said.

The three men walked to a nearby building that looked like a clubhouse on an exclusive golf course. But then, that's what this facility was supposed to be.

They walked to the kitchen and found a hot pot of coffee. Dan poured a cup for each of them and they walked into the adjoining room and took seats in comfortable chairs set at a long table.

Within minutes a steward appeared and asked if he could bring some food. The men nodded and gave their requests and watched as the man exited the room.

"Don't worry about your conversation in this facility," Matt commented. "Every man here has been fully vetted and is either a CIA or NSA agent. Even the steward.

Sayyid was awake with the first rays of the morning sun as they came through the sheer white curtains that hung over the hotel room window. They let the light in and still afforded total privacy during the daylight, although there were no structures close enough of equal height to permit anyone to look into the room.

He turned the shower to a refreshing temperature, shed his peejays and stepped over the edge of the tub and under the stream of water. Sayyid closed his eyes as the warm liquid coursed over his head, down his neck and into his face. It felt good and relaxed his tense muscles.

The respite was brief and he walked back into the bedroom and dressed. Then from the pull-along he took a lap top computer, set it on the desk and keyed up the power. The sign-on screen appeared and he ran his fingers over the touch pad to access his internet provider.

Sayyid punched in his password and watched as the screen changed. Now on-line he clicked on an icon and brought up a somewhat pixilated picture from a video camera. He processed commands and the picture sharpened to show a truck sitting on a street in New York. He moved his finger across the touch pad and the picture zoomed in on the license plate.

Satisfied that the truck was still there and ready to go, Sayyid closed the flat computer and replaced it into his suitcase. He walked to the window and checked the transmitter, adjusted the time frame to show a nine thirty transmission time that would send a signal to the receiver in the truck. That gave him almost two hours to put as much distance between himself and danger as he could.

With the pull-along in tow, he headed out the door, pausing only long enough to place a "Do Not Disturb" sign on this door as he had in the New York hotel. The domestic staff would not even knock on the door until the next morning.

At the front desk he asked the clerk to summon a cab.

"Are you leaving us today, sir?"

"No. I'll be back late this afternoon following a business meeting. Have a good day."

He walked out the front door and waited for the car service to arrive. It was there in about five minutes and he entered the vehicle, directing the driver to take him to the East Air Terminal at Teterboro Airport.

The driver swung onto Route 17 South and drove to Route 46 East. Teterboro was only a few minutes down the road.

Security for private charter flights was virtually non-existent and Sayyid walked right on through the lobby of the charter service. The girl at the counter greeted him and as he identified himself, she pointed toward the runway and a small ten-seater jet waiting at the edge of the apron.

Sayyid walked to the plane and climbed the ladder into it. He looked about at the plush chairs and small galley. There was no need for any flight attendants and he had only chartered the plane and pilot for a flight to Dallas. The fuel tank held a sufficient amount for the trip and it had been topped off and ready to go before he arrived.

He asked the pilot if it would be all right for him to sit in the copilot's seat since a second pilot would not be on board and the pilot raised no objection.

Sayyid sat back, strapped into the harness, put on the headset connecting the pilot to the control tower and listened as instructions were radioed from the tower. The pilot taxied to the south end of the tarmac, turned northward and revved his engines waiting for takeoff confirmation. There were two aircraft ahead of them, waiting for the word to race down the arrow-straight ribbon of tarmac.

First a small, two-seater low wing private airplane got the nod and seemed to crawl ahead before finally gently and gracefully lifting off the ground and banking west. No sooner had that craft gone airborne than the second plane, a large, twenty-seat corporate jet taking some high ranking executives to an important meeting…or a golf game, rumbled down the runway and lifted off.

He could hear the crackle of the radio as the tower directed his pilot to the large painted insignia that seemed to be an "on-deck" circle waiting for the next batter in a baseball game.

The pilot held the stick firmly and revved the engines until he was given the "go" by the tower. He released the stick and pushed it forward causing the plane to race down the runway.

It slowly lifted off the ground and the wheels retracted. Just beyond the fence ran Route 46 and a field of factories across the roadway. The plane lifted higher and seemed to skim the factory as it went into a steep climb and banked first west and then south. They would follow this route for several hours before making a course adjustment to the southwest and Dallas.

There would be no concern about the FAA grounding all civilian aircraft today as there had been on 9-11. That incident was undertaken by the brave brothers in commercial aircraft. This action involved no aircraft other than the one he was flying in. The police would shut highways down, but there was no reason to suspect that they would close airports or ground flights. He was on his way and so would be the wake up call to the corrupted American civilization.

Sayyid would be far gone and out of harm's way, before the device detonated. And should there be a problem with the radio signal, he still held the ability to set it off using his cell phone. He relaxed knowing that the truck was still parked on the street only blocks from Times Square and in the heart of Manhattan.

Those idiots who mounted the attack against the World Trade Center, Pentagon and White House made strategic errors that he had avoided. His bomb would go off after the rush hour and would take out more than half the now occupied offices. His toll would mount to tens of thousands and possibly even millions.

He didn't need a force of operatives. All he needed was himself and his own brains. He was about to defeat the Americans. His next step would be to extinguish Israel.

The pilot angled his control stick for a small course correction and the plane took on a south by southwest heading. Sayyid could not listen to radio news broadcasts, but he waited for his satellite telephone to ring with a confirmation that the bomb had detonated. That message should be forthcoming in about an hour.

He glanced at his watch with a nervous look every few minutes and kept an eye on the big sweep second hand as it slowly made its way across the timepiece's face. The minute hand seemed to be locked in place and the hour marker never seemed to move.

As the small jet crossed over West Virginia the phone emitted a shrill beeping sound and Sayyid jumped. He reached to his attaché case, pulled the phone from it and keyed the talk button.

"The delivery has not been made."

"What happened?" he demanded.

"We do not know. The delivery vehicle is still in position and there is no visible problem. Perhaps the delivery system was faulty. We can not check it at this time."

"I will place a call and see if I can obtain the alternate delivery method that was put in place."

Sayyid ended the call and held the satellite phone in his lap as options coursed through his mind.

"What could have happened? Why didn't the radio signal trigger the detonator? If the truck was still in its place at the curb there was little chance that it had been discovered."

He had tested and retested the radio signal that would be sent from the hotel in New Jersey to the transmitter at the Hotel Sofitel in New York. That should have been sufficient to activate the detonator and explode the device.

Sayyid picked up the satellite phone and keyed in a number that would connect him directly to the detonator on the device. Once the connection was made, all he had to do was push any key on the telephone and the bomb would go off.

Dan was sitting in the lounge at the upstate New York facility, looking at the radio receiver. It was as sophisticated a piece of equipment as he had ever seen. This was not a device jury rigged by a small band of terrorists who were simply looking to make a name for themselves through such an attack.

He suddenly jumped and dropped the receiver as it made a clicking sound and then began to hum. It vibrated across the table much as a cell phone on silent vibrate might do.

Dan looked at it, quickly rose from his seat and raced to the door. He moved to where the technicians were still at the truck examining the bomb.

"Did you get that signal?" he shouted. "Someone is trying to key the device. Get him tracked and let's have a fix on his position."

One of the technicians punched his desk top computer and a map grid came up on the screen. A small dot of light flashed on and off as the man entered a tracking code.

"Where the hell is that thing?" Dan demanded.

"It looks as though it's in West Virginia. But something's wrong. It's moving from cell to cell more rapidly that he could possibly be traveling."

"Jeez, he's in an airplane. That's why it's moving so fast," Dan shouted. "Can we keep track of it and see where it's headed?"

The tech nodded his head affirmatively and locked in on the flashing dot on the map grid as it danced across the screen.

"We'll get him wherever he stops."

Sayyid sat back in the co-pilot's seat and waited for confirmation that he had triggered the bomb. The call never came.

A sullen look crossed his face and his mood became ill tempered. The pilot looked across the cockpit and decided that small talk would not be a wise thing to engage in at this point. He punched in a course correction as he had been directed to do and nosed the small jet toward Mexico City.

Sayyid pulled open the small air vent in the side window and dropped his cell phone into space. He would no longer need it and did not want it traced to him.

XV

THE LAST DEVICE

"**M**r. President, this is Secretary McCrane. Our unit has defused the situation. I believe it would be appropriate for you to make a public announcement that the prisoners will not be released and that the danger has been mitigated. Our unit is in hot pursuit of the perp and I'll keep you regularly updated."

"Thank you Mr. Secretary. I'll schedule a press conference immediately to put the public at ease. Please get me a detailed report about the results here and in London."

Within minutes the major networks had broken into programming, which had already been delayed by updates of the threat by Hamas and its terrorist allies to set off a bomb, and assured a nervous nation that all was well.

McCrane turned to Matt and Dan:

"It looks as though you guys did one hell of a job. We've got to finish it now and bring in whoever was responsible for this act. I want him put on trial for the entire world to see what happens when you screw with us. Whatever you need will be provided. I have the full authority of the president on this and he has spoken with your Prime Minister. Israel will back us to the hilt and is a full partner in this venture.

"Dan, as one old Green Beret to another, thanks for what you've done. No doubt in my mind that Israel's gain is our loss."

"Thank you Colonel, but please understand, I live in Israel now and serve her as my country, but I will always be an American. I love this country and always have. Nothing can ever change that."

McCrane shook hands with Matt, Dan and Hesh and reached over, his arm draping Dan's shoulders: The camaraderie and spirit of three Green Berets seemed to pass electrically from one to the other.

"You three and Kyle Norman have literally saved the world from a nuclear holocaust. It's too bad we can't let everyone know who you are and what you've done. But understand that we know and we appreciate."

McCrane turned and walked from the room. His burly bodyguard, stationed outside the door, followed in lockstep as they walked to the garage for the ride to the airport and then back to Washington. The feeling of relief in the air was palpable.

"Well I guess we can catch the afternoon plane back to Jerusalem. I'm looking forward to spending some down time with Amanda." Halevi bit his lip as he saw Hesh's face drop.

I envy you, Dan. I wish I could be doing the same with Shoshanna."

Hesh got up to leave, a look of utter and total sadness on his face. They had won this round, but he knew there would be more to come. Nothing changed the fact that she was dead; as dead as he felt inside. There was work still to be done and not all of it through the Mossad.

"Every last one of them will pay for what they did to her," he thought quietly to himself.

Sayyid walked into the cool air of the office and bowed at the waist to Sayyid-the-elder, seated behind his ornate desk."

"I have failed. It was my plan and it did not work, sir. I thought the decoy in London would throw them off the trail and the New York device would detonate. I knew they would never free Rahman, Sirhan or Moussoaui, but the blast would have sent our message to the Americans and to the world."

"My son, do not despair. What you planned may not have gone according to plan, but it was not a total failure. We have put the fear of Allah into the Americans and the British. They now know that even though they stopped both devices from detonating, we have the ability to circumvent their security and that the technology we used is as good as theirs.

"They know that another attack will come, but they do not know when, where or how. We must now plan another distraction and prepare for what our ultimate goal has been from the start."

The young man nodded and they both moved to a long table across the room with charts arrayed with details of Israel, Jerusalem and Tel Aviv.

"Thanks to our friends in Pyongyang we have not spent all of our ammunition. The surprise package we have saved for, as the Americans say, 'a rainy day' will give them a downpour. You will begin tomorrow to put the plan into action.

Sayyid nodded and left the office, returning to his quarters. His bedroom, although not spare, would have been luxurious in most Muslim households. The room was about twenty by twenty with a king-sized bed placed along the back wall. Others of his rank would have rooms easily three times the size with a bed filling most of it to accommodate the harem-like parade of women that passed through. Although Sayyid enjoyed his time with females, he was too focused to make it a regular ritual.

Sayyid was well built, the result of regular workouts and his training in the desert. He could run all day through the sand and was able to fill up with water like a camel at an oasis, and then go all day without a drink.

In a side room he had a treadmill, universal gym, recumbent bike and free weights, all of which were put to use on a regular basis. Tonight, however, he was tired and bypassed them in favor of a hot bath and a DVD played on his sixty four inch flat panel plasma television set. The large satellite dish set on the roof served both as a receiver for radio transmissions and to pick up television signals from Europe. He would never admit it, but he was a huge fan of the comedy Will and Grace and the popular CSI.

The fact that the portrayal of "Will" as a gay man shone in a positive light never seemed to bother his fundamentalist mindset. He did know, however, that were he to come across a gay man in real life he would have no hesitation in decapitating the "pervert."

A moveable wall panel with a picture of the Ayatollah Khomeini covering it, slid across the front of the television hiding the fact that so decadent an item was in his room. With a slight push of a button on his night table console, he could expose the television; fill the room with music from a Bose entertainment center that gave you the feeling of sitting in a concert hall, or tuned to the security cameras covering the entire compound.

Tonight was a Will and Grace night. He pushed the button, tuned the set and then lay back on the bed. He was asleep before the opening credits were run.

At about the same moment an El Al 747SP was pulling up to the gate at Ben Gurion Airport. Dan and Amanda, accompanied by Hesh, gathered their carry-on suitcases and deplaned then walked through the crew exit, circumventing the usual customs and immigration check that slowed down all arriving passengers. Dan inconspicuously flashed his credentials at the security officer manning the post and walked through as the young woman nodded to him.

They walked to the curb and Dan motioned to the drivers of two black Saabs who immediately got behind the wheels of their vehicles and pulled up to the three travelers.

Dan turned to Hesh:

"I think you can take the day off tomorrow. I've got to brief the ministers and then I'm going to head for the beach with Amanda and some down time as well. I'll update you later in the day."

Hesh gave Dan an exhausted look and a salute with the fore and middle finger of his right hand brushing his right eyebrow, the British version of the middle finger salute.. Hesh mumbled a "thank you" to the driver who was holding the door open for him and slid into the car. The door slammed shut and the driver pulled out into a heavy line of traffic.

Amanda moved next to Dan and slid her arm through his, escorting him to the open door of their car. She smiled at the driver and they got in. The driver placed their suitcases in the trunk and they sank, exhausted into the seat.

Amanda was less than thrilled when Dan dropped his suitcase off at home and pulled his car out of the garage.

"And where might you be going?"

"Sorry hon. I've got to get to the office and prepare for the meeting with the ministers."

She scowled back at him but it was a lost gesture as he pulled out of the garage and into the street. He shifted into gear and in his usual fast-paced manner, tore down the street.

"Good thing," she thought, "that there are no little kids on this block."

The sun was sinking over the mud colored walls of the city, casting long shadows on the surrounding structures and creating an eerie landscape as Dan stood next to a laser printer in his office impatiently waiting for the completed sheets of paper to exit the top of the machine.

Slowly the printer ground them out as Dan grabbed them individually. He quickly glanced over the report and then placed it in a file folder with the inscription "Utmost Secrecy" emblazoned on the front. He slipped the folder into a leather zippered portfolio and headed for the Ministerial Meeting Room across town.

Traffic was unusually light for this time of day in the middle of the week, almost as though it were a holiday. Still Dan zipped in and out of the lanes of cars ahead of him, ignoring the curses and frequent obscene gestures from other drivers as he headed to his meeting.

Learning how to drive in New York City was a terrific primer for keeping your cool in the face of drivers such as himself.

Dan arrived in the anteroom to the conference room and took a seat across from the door. The magazine selection on the low slung table in front of him was as poor as it had always been. If you were into articles about sanitizing and disposing of municipal waste or how to pave a highway, there was much to choose from. Dan couldn't give a damn about those subjects and always found his wait in that office to be strained and drawn out.

Today was different. The Prime Minister almost immediately interrupted the meeting upon learning Dan was waiting. He directed that all those below ministerial level were to leave the room.

Several of the aides and executive assistants hesitated and were greeted with an icy stare from the PM. With that motivation they immediately rose and walked quickly from the conference room.

The PM posted two exceptionally large uniformed military types outside the door with the admonition that no one was to enter unless Moses himself had returned and under no circumstances were they to be disturbed.

Dan looked around the table at the faces staring back at him. For the first time he felt uncomfortable surrounded by the host of politicians. The only thing that made it even slightly bearable was the fact that virtually every top Israeli leader had spent time in the military and there were no dilettantes amongst them.

The questions they asked cut to the core without any superfluous bullshit and they expected the same kind of response. There was no toleration for stupidity from this group.

Dan stood and addressed them, giving them a synopsis rundown of what had taken place in London and New York. He informed them that that the person who had set all of this in motion had unfortunately gotten away. They had tracked his plane into the southwestern portion of the United States and then lost it. He told the ministers that the signal was strong and tracking quite well, but that it ended abruptly as though someone had dropped it from the aircraft.

"So, Colonel, basically what you are saying is that you have no idea who this man is or where he may have gone?"

"Not basically, precisely. We were able to grab several of his subordinates, but they didn't even know who he was. They were hired guns and were not aware of the full scope of their mission. They were totally compartmentalized with each only made aware of his individual responsibilities. They were paid and could not care who was paying so long as they received their money up front."

"Do we have any idea who was behind this?"

"Yes sir. The American Secretary of State, Joseph McCrane, called the Iranian and North Korean United Nations representatives in and literally reamed their asses out."

Dan related the incident where the Iranian attempted a politically diplomatic protest and was rewarded by McCrane with a slap across his face.

The ministers stared back at Halevi, almost unable to comprehend so bold a move by any American politician.

"He actually slapped him?" asked the PM.

""Slap is hardly the word. He struck him across the face so hard the Iranian almost fell backward. There were finger marks imprinted on his cheek that probably won't go away for a month. But after that there was no doubt in the Iranian's mind that the Secretary meant business and would not put up with any crap.

"As a result of that we found out that Saddam had passed components for about a half dozen nuclear devices, along with the technical know how, to North Korea. President Kim had allied himself with the Iranians, apparently in hopes that the research they were able to pass along from Saddam would help his country assemble fissionable devices.

"Kim also saw the opportunity to use someone else as a scapegoat and cover his own ass. He figured that if the United States retaliated, they would hit Iran and not North Korea. Secretary McCrane convinced him that was the wrong conclusion.

"We know that at least two devices were assembled; the one disarmed in London and the one we found in New York. That would leave components for perhaps four more devices, but we can't confirm if any additional bombs have been assembled and I am afraid that North Korea is not a country in which we have any assets. Our chances of learning what they are doing are absolutely zero."

"What about Iran? We have assets in that country that we could press for information?"

"Sir, we are working on that avenue as we speak. I have had our office put as much pressure on our contacts in that country as possible. They have been informed that this issue is to take priority over anything else they may be working on."

"Colonel, I would like to thank you for a job well done, although there is still much more to do. The council and I held a brief discussion prior to your arrival and I am happy to inform you that we feel you and Capt. Whitman should be rewarded."

Dan started to speak and was cut short by the PM.

"Please, humor me. I am an old man and I enjoy the prerogative of speaking my mind without interference."

Dan smiled and nodded his head in understanding.

"I am pleased to inform you that you have been promoted to the rank of Tat Aluf, Brigadier General."

Dan stood dumbfounded as the PM handed him a small jewel box with the leaf and crossed sword emblem of his new rank. He reluctantly reached for the box, his voice stalling on exit from his mouth.

"I..."

"Gen Halevi, you do not need to say anything. It is our thanks that must go to you and former Captain, now Rav Seren, Major Whitman and the American and British agents who worked on this most challenging assignment with you. We will not be able to make a public presentation to either of you, but please be aware that both of you hold your new rank as of this morning."

The PM handed Dan another box with the stylized leaf, symbolic of the rank of major in the IDF. Although both men were in fact Mossad, their official designation was as training officers in the IDF, a cover that permitted them to move throughout the country and the world without raising suspicion.

"I am also pleased to award the "Order of Distinction" to both of you. Again, you may wear the ribbon but there will not be a public ceremony presenting the award. I will make a private presentation next week when we are scheduled to meet with the Ministers once again. Please arrange to have Maj. Whitman with you."

"Thank you sir, Ministers. I am most appreciative for this. I'm sure my wife will appreciate the extra shekels as well."

The ministers laughed out loud and stood to clap Dan on the back and clasp his hands in congratulations.

Dan presented a sharp military salute to the ministers, turned and walked out of the conference room. He wanted so desperately to just rest for a couple of days and not give any thought to enemy agents, bombs or intrigue of any sort.

He drove home with thoughts of a terrific night with Amanda. Walking into his house he took her gently by the arm and ushered her into the bedroom. They lay down n the bed and she turned to kiss him. Before her lips could reach his, Dan was fast asleep.

It was nearing dinner time of the following day when he finally stirred.

"You had me worried for a while," Amanda said. "You were so sound asleep I had to poke you every once in a while to make sure you were still breathing. I've never seen anyone out cold to such a degree as you were."

"Sorry about that. I had some great plans for last night. I assume it was last night?"

Amanda laughed and assured him that it had only been the night before when he had returned home. She suggested they go out for dinner and a drink to relax. He agreed without hesitation.

"Just give me a minute. I want to give Hesh a call and at least let him know that his salary has just been upped."

He dialed the phone and let it ring for several minutes before hanging up.

"I wonder where the hell he could be. He was as tired as I was and I just assumed he was going home to sleep it off."

"Perhaps he's gone for something to eat as well. That apartment can be a very lonely place when you're all alone."

He flipped the car keys to Amanda, indicating that she should drive because he was too tired to do so.

She turned the key in the ignition and the smooth engine purred to life as she shifted into gear and headed into the city and its wide choice of international restaurants.

She had suggested they go to a particular restaurant for some "good Jewish cooking," and Dan had agreed. He looked up as she pulled into a parking space at the Lotus Café Chinese Restaurant.

"I thought you said we were going for 'Jewish cooking?'"

"Go into any Jewish neighborhood in the world and you'll learn that this is Jewish cooking. Just don't eat the pork, shrimp or lobster."

The restaurant was situated in a small shopping center with more than ample parking. Amanda found a spot almost across from the entrance and, hand in hand, they walked in. They were seated at a booth about midway through the restaurant and had just ordered, Dan asking for his favorite Gen. Tzo's chicken.

Amanda looked at him and smiled:

"Maybe they should rename it 'Gen. Dan's Chicken.'"

"They would do that only if we were in a kosher deli."

The food was prompt and Dan had just picked up his set of chopsticks to eat when he felt a strong vibration on his belt. He reached down and opened the cell phone, speaking softly into it.

"OK. We're out to dinner. I'll be in just as soon as we finish and I drop my wife at home. No? OK, I'll be there."

She knew without any doubt that this would be perhaps the shortest dinner they had ever spent together.

Dan called the waiter and had the order wrapped, handing the man a generous tip to compensate for the meal they would not be having. They walked to the door and Amanda asked what had happened.

"I can't go into it, but it looks as though the job isn't finished. Drive home, they are sending a car for me."

"When will you be back?"

"God only knows."

Dan walked through the entryway of Mossad Headquarters holding up his new ID card. The guard, who knew him by sight, snapped to attention and saluted:

"Good day Tat Aluf. It's good to see you again sir."

Dan gave a half hearted return salute. The new rank was just fine but it made him feel a bit awkward knowing the deference that would be coming his way. It was amazing that as a colonel he still felt like one of the boys, but with the new General Staff rank, it seemed to divorce him from that camaraderie.

"It's like being single one day and married the next. It's an involuntary change."

He took the elevator to his office and buzzed for The Commander to let him know that Tat Aluf Halevi had arrived and was ready for a briefing.

Rav Aluf, Lt. Gen. Marcus greeted Dan warmly with both a handshake and a solid hug.

"Congratulations on the promotion. There is no more deserving individual than you. And I might add that Maj. Whitman was a fine choice as well."

Dan smiled and nodded polite thanks then asked what the emergency was.

"We have been analyzing the information recovered from our informants and linking it with other intelligence that has come in. Operatives have uncovered a series of Spyder Holes that apparently were intended to provide safe haven for Saddam or other high ranking Iraqis. Each location was filled with supplies for sustenance and was a treasure trove of confidential documents.

"It would seem the only hole in the ground that was sparse and uncomfortable was the one in which Saddam was captured. We believe he was caught off guard and otherwise would have been in another of these bunkers. The material that has been retrieved is most disturbing."

He showed Dan copies of documents forwarded by the CIA that indicated Saddam's nuclear program was far more advanced that had ever been believed. It showed that there had been one nuclear device already assembled, one close to completion and sufficient material to quickly put together the components for a third bomb. The remaining components were missing very little and a boost in the technological programs of either Iran or North Korea could quickly provide the missing links.

Dan's face took on a worried and wearied countenance.

"What now?"

"That's precisely what we don't know. The possibility is that there is yet another nuclear device. We don't know if that's correct and if it is where it might be. To complicate matters we suspect that the North Koreans are more deeply involved that we first thought. I've been in touch with the head of the CIA and we both believe that they gave up information too easily on the two devices you disarmed.

"We don't think they were involved in the actual placement of the bombs but we have no doubt that was undertaken by Black Winter. We do believe they may have helped to assemble the bombs and deliver them to Hamas.

"Since neither the United States nor Israel maintains even informal relations with North Korea nor we do not have any assets there, we are in a deep pile of crap."

The Director looked to Dan:

"I know that you and Maj. Whitman have been under unimaginable stress these past few weeks; and you did a great job, but I am afraid I've got to ask the two of you to pick up the case again. You both have the familiarity that would take another operative too long to get up to snuff. And, frankly, we just don't have the time."

"I understand. I'll give Hesh a call and we'll get in touch with CIA agent Matt Morton. I think we should also bring MI-6 into this and will request the assistance of Kyle Norman. They were both fully involved in the previous incidents and will not need much to bring them up to speed."

"Dan, you start with what you need from this end and I will personally contact the CIA director and "C" at Legoland to make the request formal. It'll carry more weight if it comes from me to their directors."

"I'll get on it immediately. It's a feeling of déjà vu, but in a real gut wrenching way."

XVI

KILLING FOR REVENGE

Hesh sat upright as his cell phone let out a sharp ringing sound.

"Maj. Whitman, this is a message from Gen. Halevi. Please report to the office with all due speed," the voice of the Mossad duty officer announced.

"What's up?"

"Sorry sir, I have no idea. I am simply passing the General's order on to you."

Hesh pushed the off button on his cell phone and then stopped.

"Maj. Whitman? Gen. Halevi? What the hell is that all about?"

He turned to the two men in the room with him:

"We'll have to finish these plans later. Please track our Saudi friend and let me know what his plans are. I'm due to return to New York in about two weeks and should be able to arrange a 'hot' reception for him. He lives in Manhattan and that will make the operation much easier. You can slip into the shadows and become invisible in a city that big. It's far more difficult in the suburbs as it was with the action in Paterson. Just get me as much information about his movements as you can and I will arrange a 'response' that will send the message we need to get out."

An hour later Hesh walked into Dan's office scowling.

"I guess we're right at square one again."

"It sure looks that way. I want you in New York to meet with Matt. See if there's anything you can dope out that might give us a clue. The Director is also contacting MI-6 and I want you in London first to brief Kyle. I don't think there's going to a problem in the U.K. For that matter I think the only two places they might try to detonate are the United States or Israel. Those are the only targets that would make any sense.

"You'll be my liaison with the CIA and with Secretary McCrane. But please don't slap anyone around the way he did. We don't need a diplomatic flap on top of everything else.

"I'll have the front office book you through to London on El Al and I'll give you a special treat and fly you back to the U.S. on Virgin so you can get some sleep and not have jet lag. It'll also cover your tracks more than if you arrive on our airline."

"My body doesn't know what the hell day or time it is. We've been running around so much I don't even know for sure where I am."

"Let's make sure we win this round and then we can all take a nice long vacation."

"Thanks Dan. I already had one at Eilat and I'm not sure if I can handle another one."

Hesh wasted no time returning to his office and picking up his secure telephone. He pushed the buttons and waited until the phone rang at the other end.

"I'll be leaving for New York sooner than expected. I have a flight to London this evening and then on to New York City. Please have the information we discussed earlier ready for me before my departure."

"We will have a messenger deliver the information to you at the airport. Please guard the confidential nature of the documents you will receive."

"Of course I'll guard them. What else would you expect that I would do?" he angrily responded.

Hesh grabbed his suit bag from a shelf in the closet and stuffed it with shirts, underwear and changes of mix and match jackets and trousers. He had a "ready to go" toilet kit with all the essentials set for a quick departure; and this qualified as just that. He had barely landed from the last mission and here he was, leaving again.

But that was just fine with him because it gave him the opportunity to remember Shoshanna and the people who had taken her from him.

He thought of the day he had first seen her and believed he fell in love with her at that moment. He had just returned from a mission with Dan and had been injured in a fall. The Hadassah Hospital was the preferred stop for military personnel who were not being treated at a military facility. The staff was about the best in a country that prided itself on having more Jewish doctors in one concentrated area than even the United States.

"The dream of every Jewish mother," he thought, "to have a son who's a doctor. What else would you find in Israel than all these Jewish doctors?"

He sat in the waiting room almost an hour before his name was called and then walked into the curtained cubicle in the emergency room. He was directed to remove his pants and don a hospital gown.

Minutes later the most beautiful woman he had ever seen walked through the opening in the curtain, just as he was stepping out of the trouser leg.

He jumped and held the pants up in a vain effort to conceal himself.

The young woman stood there, a stethoscope draped around her neck, and chuckled.

"Mr. Whitman, I'm Dr. Levine. Your chart shows that you are complaining about an injury to your knee. Can you tell me how it happened?"

"It was from a bad fall. It's filled with fluid and hurts like hell."

Dr. Levine ran her hands over his knee and Hesh began to respond in a very inappropriate way. But it was involuntary and he couldn't help it as his excitement rose.

"I think we'll need to x-ray this. There might be some cartilage damage and you might need arthroscopic surgery if that's the case."

Fortunately for Hesh the x-rays were negative and all he had was a severely bruised knee from his "fall" that he couldn't tell Dr. Levine, happened as he tripped while chasing a terrorist in Lebanon.

She prescribed pain killers for him and ice packs until the swelling went down, then took a long needle and aspirated the fluid to help reduce the swelling.

"Ice packs won't help the other swelling I have. I think she's the medicine that'll work on that," he thought.

Hesh was a bit more than surprised when she agreed to give him her home phone number and he wasted no time before using it. They had a dinner date for the following night and for almost every night after that, except when Hesh was out of town "working."

His cover was that of a government inspector who was frequently on the road to check that material requisitioned by the military was of the amount and quality that had been ordered. That gave him the opportunity to be away for frequent periods of time and to travel out of the country when necessary.

Luckily in the coming three months Hesh had been tied to the office and even though there were a number of late nights going over reports about terrorists, he was able to get away frequently enough to see Shoshanna. Feeling grew between them in a mutual fashion and it wasn't too long before the almost nightly dinner dates became over night dates and weekends together.

Not quite six months after their first date Hesh surprised her with a ring. There was no hesitation in her mind as she slipped it on her finger and grabbed him, planting a deep and passionate kiss on his mouth. They set the date for that June and planned a honeymoon in Paris. Hesh had been there but Shoshanna had never been out of the country.

Her family had come from what had been Lithuania after World War II. Her grandparents had somehow survived Hitler's Holocaust and met at a displaced persons camp after liberation. They were married while still in the camp and dreamed of starting a new life somewhere out of that hell hole.

Finally let out of the camp, they had no where to go. Their parents were all dead as were their siblings and aunts and uncles. Her mother had one cousin who survived and he had gone to Palestine and joined the Irgun, the Jewish guerillas locked in combat with both Arabs and the British

Although the British were amongst the saviors, their treatment of the Jews was only marginally better than they had come to expect in the Nazi camps. Out of the camps the Jews were considered to be two steps lower than the Irish for whom the Brits had nothing but disdain.

They wanted to get rid of the infernal Jews, but didn't want to release them from internment camps and most certainly didn't want to offend the Arabs who had designs on the small parcel of land the Jews hoped the United Nations would vote to give them for a homeland.

The Jews had taken to calling Palestine "Israel" and this antagonized the surrounding millions of Arabs. To alleviate the tension the Brits had forbidden any more Jews from entering the country. Somehow the Jews managed to evade all of the road blocks, air blocks and sea blocks and were streaming into the country infuriating the Grand Mufti of Jerusalem, the "religious" leader who had sided with Hitler against the allies during the recent war.

Jewish organizations primarily from America and the United Kingdom, to the consternation of British politicians, were in a major effort to smuggle new residents into the country. When they were captured, they would be brought back to camps such as the huge center on Cyprus.

But still they managed to get through. Shoshanna's grandparents had been taken in by a group seeking to resettle Jewish orphans. They were part of a shipload of refugees that had managed to evade the British blockade and made it into Palestine just under the wire before the United Nations voted for partition.

The vote created the State of Israel and caused the Arabs to launch an immediate attack. The British, pro Arab to the end, timed their withdrawal from strategic positions to coincide with the arrival of the Arab armies. The Brits left and the Arabs moved in, finding hoards of weapons and supplies the departing troops had "forgotten" to take with them.

The new Israeli government urged its Arab residents to stay and work with them. In response, the Grand Mufti issued a religious declaration, a fatwa, ordering them to leave so that the land could be cleansed of Jews.

Then, he said, they could return and reclaim the entire land instead of virtually all of it. This created the so-called "Palestinian refugee problem" that has vexed the world ever since.

Although never in history had there been a nation known as Palestine, with the people from that region mostly nomadic tribes, the people who had lived there were known for academic achievement that had surpassed most of the Arabs in the surrounding areas. Educators from the Palestine region populated many of the seats in universities throughout the world.

Their descendants, however, were considered by their Arab neighbors to be only slightly better than Jews. But they did serve a purpose...to keep an entire region afire.

It was to this that Shoshanna's grandparents arrived in Israel and migrated to a kibbutz, a communal settlement, near the Golan Heights on the border with Syria.

After formation of the State of Israel many of the Irgun fighters joined with the Hagannah, later to become the Israel Defense Force, or IDF, the only military establishment in the mid-East that accepted both Jews and Arabs. It was this to which her grandfather became a member and spent his career protecting Jews from another holocaust.

Her grandfather had become a Rav Aluf and wore the crossed sword and olive branch with two leaves marking him as a Lt. General, one of the highest ranking men in the IDF. He was more than happy to welcome Capt. Hesh Whitman into their family.

Fate intervened and a series of attacks on schools and a hospital by Hamas forced a change in their honeymoon plans. Paris was out and they would take some time off when they had the opportunity.

That opportunity came a month later and they were able to grab a couple of days at the beach at Eilat.

Hesh promised that only the Devil himself arriving on earth would interfere with their plans and they booked a hotel room and drove to Eilat. The drive was relaxing and pleasant and put them in very much of a honeymoon mood.

Hesh snapped out of his reverie. Thinking only made him depressed and when he was depressed all he wanted to do was take revenge on those who had so viciously destroyed his life. He called the office for a car and told them he would meet the driver downstairs.

His rank and organization gave him the special privilege of not having to arrive at the airport and queue up at the podium to confirm his flight status. He had one of the seats reserved for his organization on every El Al flight. The seats were held until boarding before they could be given away to standby passengers. The office had called ahead and the seat in the upper level of First Class was waiting for him.

The car pulled up at the entrance of Ben Gurion Airport and Hesh walked around to the trunk of the vehicle. His driver had already jumped from the car, run to the rear and was in the process of extricating the suitcase for Hesh.

A porter came by and began the security check process. Hesh inconspicuously flashed his ID and the porter immediately stamped the case and put it through to the loading dock. All other passengers were being matched up to their luggage and each bag given the most thorough examination that any airport in the world subjected any one to.

As Hesh passed through the terminal doors, a man exiting the building bumped into him, sliding an envelope under his arm. The pass was so quick and inconspicuous that no one would have noticed.

The man continued walking toward the curb and a waiting car and Hesh made his way into the terminal and the departure gate. The last passenger had already boarded and they were all strapped into their seats as Hesh walked through the hatch and up the spiral staircase to the 747 bubble.

The section wasn't full and he had an aisle seat to himself. He sat back, strapped himself in and motioned to the flight attendant that he would like a drink. A stiff drink.

Sayyid had arrived at the airport in Cairo well in advance of his flight time for the trip to Geneva. He had only an attaché case and one small suit bag and he opted to carry it on board. The flight was on time, giving him more than a three hour layover before his connecting flight to Pyongyang was due to leave.

Although he was wearing a kaffiyah at the airport in Cairo, he had folded it and placed it in his bag while in the air. There was no need to draw any attention to himself.

Sayyid was dressed as any business traveler would be, in a conservative blue pin-striped suit, subdued blue shirt and regimental tie. Looking around he could see that there were literally hundreds of people who could have been clones of his; most dressed in similar business uniforms and almost indistinguishable from each other.

Geneva was the best place in the world with the possible exception of Zurich for anyone to fade into the woodwork. Both were international cities and major banking centers. No one would take notice unless an individual made himself stand out in some fashion.

Sayyid had no intention of standing out.

His uncompromising hatred of everything Israeli was matched only by his desire to bring as much harm and damage as possible to the United States. If it were not for that country, Israel would have long ago ceased to exist. He knew that his mission in life was to ensure that was the ultimate fate of the Jews, even if he had to turn the entire country into a wasteland.

Palestine had been a barren land before the Jews took over and, he had to admit, they did an excellent job of turning the desert into an oasis. But if things went as he planned, the oasis would become barren of the Jews. If Palestinians had to die for this to become a reality, Allahu Akbar, God is great and that is the will of God.

Sacrifice is a small price to pay for the ultimate victory.

The plane began to rumble down the runway.

"It would all come together now and the misstep that took place in the United States with the device would be corrected," he thought. "The Jews will burn in hell."

Hesh was actually looking forward to the Virgin Atlantic flight, a strange reaction for him. Although he enjoyed flying, he never looked forward to the long flight. He found them boring and an awful waste of time. He felt that he was never productive just sitting in an airplane when he could be doing something more useful.

Kyle Norman was waiting for him and they retreated to a private lounge. The briefing was quick and perfunctory as they exchanged what little they knew and made plans to coordinate any necessary action.

Their meeting concluded, Kyle had a non-descript car operated by a non-descript driver take Hesh from the lounge to the proper terminal for the last leg of his trip. They shook hands with a firm grip, each knowing that they could be heading into historical times that could never be reported to history scholars.

The luxury and comfort presented on board a Virgin flight in Upper Class and the professionalism of the cabin staff almost made a trip from London to New York enjoyable. He looked at the other passengers and watched as many of them set up their laptops to make some use of the flight time.

The seat, laterally placed to provide more leg room and a bit more than a modicum of privacy and ample comfort, was perfect for Hesh's purpose of melting in to the crowd.

His meeting with Kyle Norman had gone well, but the two of them were both puzzled by the information that had come in. MI-6 had obtained similar intelligence about bomb components but the trail still led to a virtual dead end.

Most signs were pointing away from Iran and into North Korea and that created a problem. The country was one of the most repressive in the world and its dictator, Kim Jong-Il kept a tight rein on everything that took place within his borders. South Korea was busy attempting to open lines of communication with the North, but the efforts were painfully slow.

The one thing that Kim appeared to excel at was the ability to maintain secrecy and a cloak over the entire country that virtually prevented information from leaking out. This is what MI-6, the CIA and the Mossad would have to contend with. North Korea was known to be working in the nuclear field and desperately wanted its own bomb to make it a major player on the world stage.

Secretary of State McCrane had put a scare into them, but if they could circumvent him and avoid retaliation from the United States while crafting a nuclear bomb, they would succeed.

Hesh knew that the one possibility for obtaining information would be through assets in the radical Muslim world who might be working with the North Koreans.

He watched in fascination as the great aircraft banked over the giant marshland and bird sanctuary that surrounded John F. Kennedy International Airport. The plane drifted in a wide, slow circle over the Atlantic and came in low across the Rockaway Peninsula.

Hesh looked down trying to determine the location of the crash of American Airlines Flight 587 that went to ground on the peninsula just a month after the attack on the World Trade Center. The airplane exploded in the sky over Rockaway Beach on November 12, 2001 and came to ground in a residential neighborhood.

The "expert" pundits declared that it could not have been an accident coming on the heels of the 9-11 attack and amid reports that the terrorists would strike again on Veterans' Day. Many blamed al-Qaida without having a single shred of evidence. But it made these self-important talking heads appear to be experts with inside information.

Hesh had seen the confidential investigation reports and knew that the crash was nothing more than a horrible coincidence. And he knew that his fascination with attempting to locate the site was little more than a morbid fascination. Still he couldn't pull his eyes away.

The Virgin Atlantic jumbo jet dropped steadily, aiming at the runway on a long low approach over Jamaica Bay. Window passengers could see the small fleets of private boats zipping through the water while others sat anchored in an attempt to convince porgies and flounder to bite at the baited hooks dragging the muddy bottom.

The wheels barely touched the tarmac as the craft rolled to a smooth touchdown and raced to the end of the runway before reversing the engines and turning toward the arrivals building.

Hesh walked into the terminal and spotted Morton waiting for him, talking to an immigration officer. He smiled and waved for Hesh to join them.

Carrying his suit bag, Hesh walked across the crowded arrivals room and shook hands with Morton. Matt made the required introductions and motioned for Hesh to follow him through the exit accompanied by the uniformed immigration officer.

At the curb a Port of New York/New Jersey policeman stood guard alongside a new black Ford Crown Victoria, the most conspicuous undercover car used by most police agencies. The little antenna rising from the trunk served almost as a badge in case there was any doubt about the identity of those inside the vehicle.

The car was spacious and comfortable and had a powerful engine that could overtake virtually any other vehicle in an open road chase. In city traffic the suspension was stiff and produced a bumpy ride; but on the highway it handled like a dream.

Morton stayed in the left lane of the Van Wyck Expressway, tailgating any driver unfortunate enough to be in his way as he headed for the Grand Central Parkway and then the Long Island Expressway into Manhattan.

There never seemed to be a time of day or night when these roads were empty. They were in a perpetual state of "rush hour" traffic.

Morton's driving tactics could turn his passenger's hair a light shade of gray, but he did shave time off the ride.

On the way in they exchanged information and came to the conclusion that they really didn't know a heck of a lot about what was happening. They agreed that the key appeared to be in North Korea rather than the mid-East, but the mid-East connection was too strong to ignore.

The most likely scenario was a cabal of Hamas and the Communist government of Kim Jong-Il.

"But what the hell to do about it? That was the problem."

Byong Seong walked from the United Nations Building, across busy First Avenue, up Forty Sixth Street to Third Avenue. There were several boutique-style restaurants located along the stretch of New York roadway; most were quiet and patronized primarily by neighborhood residents and United Nations personnel. Few tourists ever found their way to the street and it afforded him the opportunity to get away from the frenetic pace of the World Body and all of its self-important little people.

He had been at the United Nations for more than five years serving his lord and master, Kim Jong-Il as Ambassador from the Democratic People's Republic of Korea to the United Nations. He had been in New York on a previous assignment as Chief of Protocol under Kim's father, the previous president for life, Kim-il Sung.

Byong had grown to enjoy his time in the United States although his movements were severely restricted by the Department of State to a radius of twenty five miles from the United Nations. He could visit New Jersey and the five boroughs of New York City. Pennsylvania and even Connecticut were out of the permissible zone and he had to go through a lengthy procedure to obtain permission if he wished to travel.

In the years he had been in the United States he had managed to move about the country on only two occasions and he knew that, both times, he was under surveillance by the FBI or other agents. The agents tailing him didn't even attempt to hide the fact that they were on his trail and it gave him an uneasy feeling.

It felt as though he were still in North Korea.

There was the time he had been invited to the home of an American journalist in New Jersey for dinner. The journalist had said he wanted Byong to see how a typical American family lived.

And he had to admit that from what he saw of the neighborhood, Americans lived fairly well. He saw the cars and satellite television dishes on the neat suburban homes. He saw children playing in the streets; streets that were clean and paved. In the home was a well stocked kitchen and a family that lived quite comfortably; and they were considered only middle class.

It was hard for him to reconcile what he had been brought up to believe and to consider the Americans as "corrupt dogs" when he came face-to-face with happy children who were not planted as a tableau for his benefit.

He stayed on espousing the party line to the World Body and hoping that someday he might be able to make a difference for his countrymen. He knew that Kim would have to be taken out of office, but there was no opposition party and no visible dissidents in North Korea.

Oh there were, but they were for the most part now all dead or in prison. For him to voice open opposition would only lead to the same reward. So he plugged on, hoping that things would change and that he would be a part of it.

As he rounded the corner his eyes involuntarily squinted from the strong rays of the afternoon sun. New York was hot and humid in the spring and summer, but it was still far better a place to be than North Korea.

Byong stepped off the curb to cross the avenue and paused as a panel truck slowed and blocked his way. He waited for it to move again and saw the side panel door slide open.

Before he had a chance to react, two men, hoods over their heads, jumped out and grabbed him. A third man came from the passenger's side door and pulled a pillow case over his head. They clapped handcuffs on his wrists, his hands behind his back, and violently threw him into the van.

Of the few passersby, fewer had actually witnessed what had just taken place and few of those reacted at all. One had the presence of mind to jot down the license plate number and a description of the truck. But, he suspected, as the police would later determine, the vehicle had been stolen.

Byong lay on the floor of the van in considerable discomfort. The streets of New York were in notorious disrepair and potholes were considered the city's emblem. Every time the wheels struck a hole, he bounced on the unpadded metal floor of the van, banging his head, jamming his arms. The pain was considerable and Byong frequently cried out.

The bumps smoothed out a bit and he could feel a steady vibration under the tires as though they were riding over a metal grid. In fact, the van was riding over the Queensboro Bridge, more commonly known as the "Fifty Ninth Street Bridge," on its way into the warehouse district of Long Island City, across the East River from Manhattan.

Then the bumping started again.

He felt the van stop and heard the sound of an overhead garage door grinding its way up and the van moving forward again. He had no sense of light or dark or even of smell. The sensual deprivation made his ride all the more terrifying.

Suddenly the door slid open with a violent sound as it hit the stops. He was jerked to his feet and pulled onto a concrete floor. Then he was dragged about ten feet, pulled to his feet and thrown onto a metal folding chair.

"Please! What do you want? I have diplomatic immunity. I demand to be released."

"You have no immunity here," came a voice from the other side of the pillow case. "We have some questions for you. You can spare yourself a lot of pain by cooperating with us."

"I have nothing for you." His voice was weak and affected a higher than normal pitch, testament to the fear that was creeping through him.

Byong reeled as something thudded into the side of his head and sent him crashing to the floor. Lights flashed in his head and the pain coursed through his entire body.

He was grabbed by both arms and placed back on the righted chair.

A low threatening voice chilled its way through him:

"I want to know the precise status of the nuclear weapons you have been assembling for Iran."

"I do not know what you are talking about."

A second wave of excruciating pain swept through him as he was slammed in the back of the head. This time he didn't fall to the floor, but was rocked forward and backward by the force of the blow.

"I'll ask one more time and then I will not be as gentle as I have been. What is the status of the nuclear weapons being assembled in North Korea?"

Trembling, Byong barely got the words out of his mouth:

"I do not know anything about nuclear weapons."

"My North Korean friend, to this point you have not seen our faces and can not identify us. If you continue to stonewall me, we will remove the pillow case from your head and you will see us. At that point the questioning will become even more intense and we will have no choice but to ensure that you do not leave here alive able to identify us."

Byong had served in the Army of the DPRK receiving treatment in basic training that bordered on what was happening now. His drill instructors were from a school that advocated the most brutal training methods; methods that almost harkened back to the days of the rack and the iron maiden. But for the first time in his life he felt total and abject fear.

"I can not tell you what I do not know. I do not want to be tortured, but I do not have the means to stop you."

He heard his captors quietly discussing his words. Although it was difficult for him to decipher what they were saying due to the fact they were speaking in such soft voices, it wasn't difficult to hear the anger in those voices; and the conversation was in a language he did not understand.

The men returned and he could feel something being attached to his finger tips. Suddenly a violent charge surged through his entire body, his eyeballs popping and his hair standing on end.

"Electricity is such a useful thing," the voice of his tormentor said. "It can be used for so many ordinary things and then you can find specific uses such as this. Do you have anything to tell me?"

Byong remained mute and then felt his belt being undone and the zipper on his pants pulled down. He was pressed against the back of the chair as someone pulled his pants off and then his underwear, draping them around his ankles.

He sat there, naked from the waist down, trembling on the metal chair.

Without warning an electric shock moved throughout the metal chair and into the bare skin of his body in contact with it. It seemed to last forever.

"Now my Korean friend, are you ready?"

Byong could barely move his head from side to side, signaling a negative response.

"OK. Your choice."

He winced in pain as he felt something being clipped to his testicles, the tip of his penis and the big toe on each foot.

"Mr. Ambassador, I feel it is my humane duty to give you one more opportunity to respond to the questions we have been asking you."

Byong was reaching the outer limits of his endurance and knew there was not much more that he could take. Yet he felt that he had to remain mute for as long as he could even though there was now a strong possibility that he would eventually give in.

This time the electricity didn't arrive with a full force jolt. He could feel the tingling in his toes and then into the connectors that had remained on his fingers. It began to increase in intensity and his body involuntarily jerked into wild spasms as the voltage increased.

His body was jumping about on the chair as though it was in a major epileptic fit when the full force of the electric current suddenly poured into his scrotum and penis. The scream he let out even caused his torturers to wince.

Then he was quiet, his head hanging down, his chin touching his chest.

The crackling of the electric still sounded through the huge room and the distinctive smell of human flesh burning permeated the air. It was a sickening smell that once you had experienced, you never forgot. Workers at Ground Zero, years later, could still feel the smell of the thousands of bodies burning in the flames of the giant towers, on their skin and clothes. It never went away.

One of the men shrugged his shoulders:

"He's dead. Now we'll have to dump the body and get the information somewhere else. I think before the word gets out about this kidnapping, we should grab the Iranian Ambassador. He might just have the answers."

The men loaded Byong's body into the back of the truck and one got behind the wheel. The room was big enough for him to circle the vehicle around and head for the overhead power doors and onto the busy Long Island City streets.

The others climbed into a passenger car, drove out the door and turned onto the main road leading to Northern Boulevard and then east toward Queens Boulevard and the Van Wyck Expressway. The van would be driven to the bird sanctuary off Crossbay Boulevard, between Howard Beach and Broad Channel, within sight of JFK Airport, on the long causeway connecting the two. It would be left in a road siding and could stand there for a day or two before being discovered. A second car followed the van and would bring the driver back.

Hesh Whitman stepped out of the sedan a block from his apartment and hurried around the corner to the entrance. He had to hurry or he would be late for his meeting with Matt Morton. The ever present sounds of police sirens on patrol cars racing through the city's streets pierced his ears. He much preferred the Israeli or European claxon that was loud enough to draw attention, but didn't wreck your ears and present the danger of tinnitus.

In the apartment he quickly changed from the blue jeans and tee-shirt he was wearing into a pair of slacks and sport jacket. He resisted the New York attitude of wearing a tie with almost any outfit and especially business attire. He chose a short sleeve shirt and left it open at the collar.

He opened the top drawer of his dresser to pull out a handkerchief and dropped a cotton version of a blue ski hat into the drawer.

He met Morton a half hour later at a small lower Manhattan restaurant, Villa Mosconi, just off Houston Street. He told the Maitre D' that he was looking for a "Mr. Matthews" and followed the imperious restaurateur through the noisy main section of the restaurant and a narrow passageway, past the kitchen on his left, and into a box-shaped back room.

Hesh looked around curiously. There was no rear door and the only way out was back through the narrow passageway and the main restaurant. He didn't like being boxed in, even if he was meeting with friends. Too many years in his job had taught him that you should always have two escape routes immediately at hand and at least one more for emergencies. This place offered only one.

Morton was sitting against the rear wall, his back to it, giving him a full view of anyone entering or leaving. He nodded to Hesh and with a wave of his hand, motioned for him to take a seat.

Hesh chose a seat next to Morton so that he too would have a commanding view of the entrance. At least he could cover his ass this way.

They ordered and passed very little small talk until after the main courses had been placed in front of them. Both ordered cocktails and sipped them in a relaxed manner before getting down to the business at hand.

"We had a major upheaval today," Morton noted. "The North Korean ambassador to the U.N. disappeared. I was hoping to have Secretary McCrane use some of his special brand of persuasion on him to see if we could find out anything about additional components."

"What do you mean he disappeared?"

"Just that. He's gone. No one seems to know where he is. His delegation hasn't filed a report because they just don't do that. But we have an asset inside their building who called and told us they were in a panic over the possibility that he may have defected. We know that Seong is not a big fan of Kim's, but he still toes the party line."

"Well, if he really has defected, your government will know soon enough. Where else is he going to go? Canada? Mexico? I don't think so. The United States would be his likely destination. And for that he has no choice but to contact your State Department."

"You can never tell. We do know that the North Koreans will come out screaming that he's been kidnapped by American agents if he doesn't show up soon. It would be great if he did defect, but I don't think so. He considers himself to be too much of a patriot."

"I guess we'll just have to sit this one out see what happens. We're going to have to come up with a solid plan to get information from them or from the Iranians. We still don't know exactly what they are planning?"

"Not exactly? We don't have a clue to their plans except for the sparse report we got that they may be planning to assemble another device. And we just can't let that happen. After finding the last nuclear bomb in New

York I don't know how much more pressure the people of this city can take."

"Hey, in Israel this is a daily happening with suicide bombers taking out our women and children in markets and nursery schools. And the threat of one of those renegade countries developing and dropping a nuclear bomb on us is something we've faced for years."

Hesh's voice took on an almost angry tone as he stared coldly at Matt.

"Look at what happened in the first Gulf War. Saddam sent those damn Russian SCUDS flying over Jordan to reach Israel. King Hussein then warned us that if we had the temerity to retaliate by flying over his little kingdom, he'd declare war on us. There's no place safe in Israel and my own wife was proof of that."

Hesh had flushed and his rising anger surprised Morton.

"Hey, hold it down. I never meant to denigrate what you have to go through. But after 9-11 this country and the New York area in particular, were in a state of shock. Compound that with a nuclear bomb planted in the garment district and we've got a pretty fragile population.

"I think we may be barking up the wrong tree with Korea and that the possibility is that the bomb has been assembled and moved out."

Matt pushed a newspaper article from the Associated Press across the table.

"This pretty well coincides with intelligence we recently obtained,"

"U.N. links highly enriched uranium to Iran's Military"

Associated Press

VIENNA, AUSTRIA---U.N. inspectors have found traces of highly enriched uranium on equipment from an Iranian research center linked to the military, diplomats have said. This is a revelation likely to strengthen U.S. arguments that Teheran wants to develop nuclear arms.

Initially they said the density of enrichment appeared to be close to or above the level needed for production of nuclear weapons. Subsequent information from the International Atomic Energy Commission contended it was not up to weapons grade, but considerably higher grade than that needed for energy production.

Sources indicated that the level of nuclear material appeared to be headed in the direction of weapons grade.

Iran has denied conducting an enrichment program for weapons grade material, contending it only wanted nuclear material to provide energy for itself. Iran has also denied conducting nuclear research at the site where the traces have come from, according to IAEA sources. The simple fact that such traces have been found on equipment coming from that site, raises great concern about the Iranian nuclear program.

The find also strengthens arguments that the fundamentalist government has hidden a program that creates fissionable material. The site's alignment with military programs also weakens Iran's contention that its nuclear program is essential for civilian uses.

Iran's President Ahmadinejad was defiant, accusing the United States of waging a 'propaganda campaign' against Iran.

'The people of Iran are not afraid of them,' he said.

Uranium enriched to between 3.5 percent and 5 percent is used to make fuel for reactors to generate electricity. It becomes useable for nuclear weapons when enriched to more than 90 percent.

Diplomats accredited to the IAEA noted that Tehran's enrichment program has progressed faster than agency expert's had expected. They also suggested that Iran has hidden research and development from IAEA inspectors.

"You knew about this?" Hesh demanded. "And just when where you going to share that information? After they dropped a bomb on Tel Aviv?"

"Slow down, Hesh. We just got confirmation of this information. We wanted to make sure of it before we started a panic."

"Bullshit, Matt. This is something that could threaten the safety and existence of my country and you people withheld critical information from us again. This isn't the first time that's happened and every time you do it, we are attacked. I'm starting to think that the old Irgun methods are the only way to go."

He stood and stormed out of the restaurant leaving a dumbfounded Matt Morton sitting alone at the table. Walking rapidly back to his apartment, Hesh could only think of the early Israeli guerilla force, the Irgun, that had circumvented diplomatic niceties and had a major hand in running the British out of Israel.

The Irgun, consisting mostly of former British soldiers of the Jewish Brigade, who had fought the Nazis and then made their way to Israel, had taken on the best the Brits had to throw at them, and won. They still smarted from the fact that while every other contingent of Commonwealth soldiers was permitted to fly its own colors, the British High Command refused permission for the Jews to fly the Star of David. Some defied the edict and others, winning the praise of British commanders by their bravery in combat, were given individual permission to do so.

Dislike of the Brits was palpable. So much so that after the Brits began their pullout from Palestine, assisting the Arabs as they left, the Irgun made no distinction and attacked the King's forces as well as the Arabs.

The Irgun had begun long before the pullout by blowing up Jerusalem's King George Hotel, home to the British military command. But in a startling maneuver, they warned the Brits of the coming attack, giving them time to escape.. Arrogant to the end, the King's commanders refused to heed the warnings and were blown apart in the crumbling hotel.

This was the spirit invoked by the modern "Response," credited, or blamed, for the killings of Arabs and former Nazis around the world. And the organization Hesh Whitman had become an integral part of to avenge the murder of his bride.

A worried look crossed Dan's face as he read the decoded dispatch Hesh had sent. He was as concerned with his assistant's lack of diplomacy in his reaction to Matt as he was with the confirmation that Iran had been enriching uranium. The question now was how many nuclear weapons were they capable of assembling and at what stage were they?

He sat, running the information through his mind and kept coming back to the report of the possibility of a third weapon having been assembled. Intelligence placed it at the feet of the North Koreans, but he had strong misgivings about that. Kim Jong-Il was a megalomaniac, but he wasn't as crazy as many Western reports made him out to be.

Dan knew the Korean dictator was ruthless with his own people, but he had never truly been much of a threat outside of the Korean Peninsula. He ranted and raved, he made threats, but he had never seriously exported any conflict. And above all he would do nothing that would bring ruin to his own firm control of the country and his continued existence as its head of government. He had no desire to become another Jean Clause Duvalier, Haiti's Baby Doc, living in exile in France.

No, Kim would remain at the helm of an ever more isolated North Korea and he would be content to do so.

The threat would more likely come from a religious fundamentalist of the Ahmadinejad variety; that, combined with the IAEA report were his prime concerns.

They had already taken out one major Iranian facility, but there were many more likely targets spread throughout the country. There was no way to destroy all of them.

"And what if a device was either assembled or capable of being assembled and where would it pose a threat?"

Dan's head began pounding as his blood pressure rose with each question, each thought for which he had no answer.

"How much time do we have?"

His own answer was the only one possible:

"We have no time left."

He pushed the buzzer on his desk and directed his secretary to send a coded message to Hesh ordering him home immediately. He would deal with Hesh's impulsive behavior when he got back. In the meantime he'd call Morton and mend some bridges. But he wouldn't let his former Green Beret buddy and CIA official off the hook too easily because, in spite of how he had handled it, Hesh was right. The CIA had no business withholding information of critical importance to Israel.

He'd make sure it didn't happen again.

Sayyid was in a foul mood. Both nuclear devices had been discovered and rendered useless before they could explode and his plan was a shambles. He had lost face with his mentor and with the men he expected to follow him. His triumphant entrance into Jerusalem as head of a Pan Arab nation, a modern Saladin, was beginning to fade into the desert sunset and he could not let that happen.

The remaining device had been flown from the research facility in North Korea to the remote base in Iran.

"Allah bless the Koreans for their assistance in providing the enriched fuel and the Russian scientists in assembling the components."

What German scientists had been to the nuclear and space programs of both the United States and the USSR following World War II, the Russians were to the development in Iraq and Iran. With the fall of the Soviet Union and Russia's economic downturn, the military use of nuclear power was downsized. Russia was no longer a super power and faced serious economic problems; its resources had to be channeled into commercial venues.

The scientists who had worked on military projects, especially those in the nuclear development field, found themselves out of work in their own country. But they were sought after by the North Koreans and the fundamentalist Arab nations. With petrodollars conveniently provided by the Western nations and their gas-guzzling ways, the pay they were able to offer was extraordinary and they could continue with the work they had done and it would be aimed at the same enemies, the capitalist nations and Israel.

Sayyid avoided meeting with Old Sayyid. He wanted to come with victory and not be patted on the head and told that everything would be alright. He wanted to be sitting on a triumphant chariot and not slinking through the desert. He would have what was rightfully his and no damn Jew was going to stop him.

He reached for his telephone and placed a call to Tehran.

"I will be there tomorrow. I want plans to proceed with no more delays. The longer it takes us to succeed, the more opportunity the bastards have to foil us and that will not be permitted to happen again."

He slammed the telephone on the receiver.

Dan was on a direct line to Matt Morton and the exchange between the two old friends was somewhat less than friendly.

"Listen to me, Hesh may have been out of line to act the way he did and he certainly shouldn't have walked out. But damn it, Matt, you had no right withholding this kind of information from us. We've been working together on this project and we've shared everything with you. The CIA has a lousy habit of hogging information and not sharing. How the hell can we work together if it's going to be a one-sided operation?"

"Dan, we hadn't confirmed any of it. The news leak caught us by surprise and shouldn't have gotten out. The information was unconfirmed and premature."

"So what? Perhaps our assets might have been able to add to what you had in hand. But if we are kept in the dark, there's no way we can combine information. And, let me tell you, if this happens again, we will work on our own and cut off the pipeline to the CIA. I will not let a lack of cooperation and information endanger this country."

Dan hung up the phone and buzzed his secretary, ordering him to be on the lookout for a coded flash from Matt Morton with the intelligence the CIA had obtained regarding the IAEA findings on the Iranian nuclear development.

He looked at his watch. Hesh should be over the Atlantic by this time, on his way home. No Virgin flight on this leg of the journey. Dan had authorized a flight on Continental in Business Class; a nice way to go, but certainly not the comfort of the British airline or El Al. But he needed him home on the first available flight.

"Next time he won't piss me off," Dan chuckled to himself.

As a general officer Dan would no longer normally lead raids into enemy territory. But as a general, he had the option of making his own assignments. Hesh had replaced him at the helm of the Strike Force and as soon as he landed, they would begin to formulate plans to uncover the location of the nuclear device and dismantle it, no matter what country it was in and no matter who it was aimed at.

And if Morton spoke nicely to him, he might advise the CIA of what was afoot.

But right now they had to find out precisely who had what and what they planned to do to whom. In his gut Dan knew where the next bomb would be headed; Israel. He just didn't know where it was coming from and the precise destination and timing. But he would find out and stop it. He wasn't going to let another Twin Towers happen on his watch, especially not in Israel. Once in a lifetime was more than enough for any human being to suffer.

"Never again!"

XVII

RING OF FIRE

Television news and newspapers trumpeted the story of the North Korean ambassador's body being found in a stolen van in a Queens marshland, a bird sanctuary. The CSI-types had gone over the vehicle with a fine tooth comb and had found no traces that would lead them in any direction. There were no fingerprints, no DNA and no biological traces. The vehicle had been sanitized to an extent the investigators never thought possible; and this led to suspicions about the possibility of a government agency being involved.

Reporters speculated that the vehicle had been handled by the intelligence agency of a government because of the thoroughness with which it had been sterilized. But while most only speculated, the North Korean's immediately blamed the United States. President Ahmadinejad, jumping into the contretemps, pointed his finger at Israel.

Few took him seriously. This was a national leader who contended the Holocaust was a myth propagated by Jews as a means of winning support from other nations. He was fond of quoting actor and movie producer Mel Gibson whose father was a Holocaust denier. When asked by a reporter if he too believed the Holocaust was a myth, Gibson replied: "My father wouldn't lie to me."

Ahmadinejad's contentions were in line with other Holocaust deniers, contending that most of the Jews in concentration camps died of typhoid and that perhaps only six thousand were exterminated. Gibson would have loved him.

Most world leaders had become accustomed to his anti-Israel ranting, but today, because of the recent near detonation of two nuclear bombs, they were less prone to dismiss his threats.

Ahmadinejad was threatening to "wipe Israel off the face of the earth" if any hostile move was made toward Iran or any Arab nation by the United States or any of its allies.

Secretary of State Joseph McCrane had asked the president to call a meeting of the entire Presidential Cabinet to address the issue. There was no hesitation in granting approval to move the American fleet through the Straits of Gibraltar and into the Mediterranean Sea. A second task force was dispatched through the Indian Ocean and into the Red Sea while a third force moved across the Indian Ocean, through the Arabian Sea, swinging around the Gulf of Oman and into the Persian Gulf.

American land and air force units were placed on high alert in Afghanistan, completing the ring of fire and totally encircling Iran. The world was on a "Red Alert" status.

Ahmadinejad didn't scale down his rhetoric. To the contrary, he upped the ante, threatening a wave of suicide bombers and declared that he had legions of Iranians and Arabs willing to lay their lives down against Israel and the Western devils.

"Mr. President," Secretary McCrane said, "our intelligence indicates that Ahmadinejad may have only a handful of suicide bombers, but they could do some serious damage if they get through. My concern is the lack of intelligence we have regarding the state of his nuclear development.

"The death of Ambassador Seong has left a gaping hole in our intelligence. He was our pipeline into North Korea and with him gone, that flow of information has been stopped dead in its tracks. Whoever group of vigilantes killed him is, they have put the rest of the world in grave danger."

The Secretary continued: "Our last dispatch from him informed us that three nuclear devices had been assembled. Two of them were dismantled by our Strike Forces: in London and New York. From his information the third device was still in North Korea, but he was sure it was going to be moved. Kim Jong-Il did not want to be the target of an American retaliation if we were hit and he felt he could conceal his cooperation with Ahmadinejad in assembling the components they obtained from Saddam.

"The Ambassador and I had put on a show for the Israelis because we didn't want them to be aware that he was our asset. It was simply too delicate a situation and his participation was on a "Need to Know" basis and they did not need to know. He was being run personally by a top ranking CIA agent, Matt Morton.

"Matt was one of my men in Special Forces and I hold him in the highest trust and regard. The main problem was the Mossad representative, Gen. Dan Halevi, also holds American citizenship and served under my command as well. Morton never confided in him, but Halevi was beginning to suspect that there was more than we were sharing.

"From intelligence we have been gathering I would make an educated guess that the third device will not be used against the United States. They simply no longer have the assets to get it here safely and then detonate it. The best guess is that they will head for either a European capital or, more likely, Israel.

"We are working with Gen. Halevi to try and trace the device and put a stop to these people once and for all. I am going to have to bring Gen. Halevi into our total confidence and share whatever intelligence we have with him. One more incident where he suspects we aren't leveling with him could be disastrous."

McCrane turned to the President and turned, waiting for a sign..

The President turned to McCrane and lowered his voice:

"You have my full authority to brief Gen. Halevi. Further, you are authorized by a Presidential Directive to take any action necessary."

"I will call the Israeli Prime Minister himself to insure that all lines of communications are open."

"I also direct Secretary McCrane to contact the North Koreans and assure them that we will do all in our power to resolve the case of Ambassador Seong. They are making threats, but I'm not concerned about an attack from that area. Unfortunately Seong was an asset that we could ill afford to lose."

McCrane turned to Morton:

"Matt, I don't have to tell you how serious this situation is. This would be worse than 9-11 and the fact is the world simply can not afford to let this attack happen. I want you to work out a plan with Dan and no matter what you need, no matter what the time, day or night, call me and I will make it happen."

"We can't just charge into Jordan or any other country in the hopes that we'll be able to find information about the device. Hesh, I want you to begin putting together an expanded unit for this job. I want not only our team, but there must be bomb experts and get some of our nuclear scientists. Bring them out to Hatzion and keep them locked down on the base. This way when the time comes we won't have to put out a call and wait for assets to be assembled. They'll all be right at hand.

"Minister Ben Chaim has given us the go for whatever action is needed. He's spoken directly with the PM and he's offered carte blanche. We have the same authority from the American President and will be working closely with Matt. I want a wing of fighter planes at the ready. The pilots are to be assigned to us for the duration.

"I want Sayaret Matkal (Israeli Special Forces) placed on the alert and brought into our compound. Tell them that Unit 101 has been reactivated."

Hesh and the other operational officers looked at Dan.

"Don't hesitate to do as I am asking you."

"General," Hesh asked, "this would make it virtually an all out invasion."

"Major, if we have to blast our way through every Arab nation, we will do it. They will not blow up that damn bomb."

The Sayaret Matkal was Israel's top Special Forces unit. Unit 101 was ostensibly disbanded after a retaliatory raid in which scores of unarmed enemy civilians were killed. Both were outgrowths of the original Special Forces units that were essentially copies of American Long Rang Reconnaissance Patrols (LRRP), known as "Lurps," who had gained fame in Vietnam.

Ariel "Arik" Sharon, the former PM had led Unit 101 on many of its raids. Ehud Barak, also a former PM had led Special Forces and the raid on the SABENA Belgian airliner held by terrorist groups. Called "Operation Isotope," it was the first successful raid to free hostages in such a situation and proved the worth of these highly trained units. Many of the current government leaders had served time in the elite units and were well versed in their capabilities

.Dan issued an order to arm the units with micro Uzis, a scaled down version of the rapid firing and highly accurate automatic weapon favored by the American Secret Service, especially those on Presidential protection duties.

The Uzi was reliable, rarely jammed and fired at an amazing thirty rounds per second with minimal muzzle climb. The gun could be fired with one hand, much like a pistol, and still held on target. It didn't move up as most other automatic weapons did when firing. That gave it extreme accuracy.

"This, in all probability is not going to be a hush hush operation. Once we get in there I want every damn terrorist involved in this operation to be face down and not breathing when we are done. They have got to know once and for all that Israel and the Free World will not tolerate such threats to security and peace. I want them all dead.

"Except for one or two," Dan smiled. "We'll use them for intelligence gathering."

Hesh, as Gen. Halevi's Executive Officer, was charged with preparing the base for the arrival of the Sayaret units and other segments of the strike force. He could assign mundane details, such as setting up living and eating quarters to a subordinate, but his position was needed to demand and get the cooperation of military commanders who traditionally balked at giving up any of their resources to anyone for anything.

As Hesh passed along the order to a Sayaret commander, the man refused to reassign his group. Hesh dialed his cell phone and handed it to the commander.

"Sir, this is Colonel Tzvi Rishon of the Sayaret Matkal. To whom am I speaking?"

Col. Rishon stiffened and kept repeating "Yes sir! Yes Sir!"

He turned to Hesh and indicated the order would be issued without delay and his unit would be on the move within the hour.

By morning what had a day before been an empty section of an airfield now was closed to all but essential personnel. A guard post was established at the gateway and curious onlookers were strongly discouraged from hanging around. Since the post was on a military reservation there was little danger of civilians wandering past and that lessened the chances of enemy intelligence uncovering what they were doing.

A Hercules transport landed and was guided to a spot in the middle of the runway and near the barracks where Unit 101 was preparing its gear. Within the hour a squadron of F16I Sufra (Storm) jets landed and took up a position in front of the Hercules facing the runway and set for a quick takeoff.

The Lockheed Martin F-16I was a combination long/short range fighter bomber with detachable fuel tanks that added 2,271 litres to the internal capacity, increasing mission range and endurance and reducing dependence on in-flight-refueling or the need to land to do so. This effectively increased its range by some 800 miles, giving it the ability to both fly missions and outlast enemy craft in combat situations. While the Bogeys would have to break off to refuel, the Sufra could chase them down.

The use of the "Conformal Fuel Tanks" (CFT) also freed up two wing stations, expanding the aircraft's air-to-surface weapons load. The F-16I had a dorsal compartment with mission avionics and chaff and flare dispensers that enabled it to conduct either pilot training or combat missions, thwarting both ground radar and incoming radar-directed missiles.

The two-seater jet fighter cost an estimated $45 million and expensive as that may sound, it was $39 million cheaper than the F-15 and was outfitted with space-age technologies such as internally mounted Forward Looking Infrared (FLIR) viewers and a cutting edge weapons system produced by Israel's own Lahav, a division of Israel Aircraft Industries. The Lahav technology allowed for simultaneous, multi-target air-to-air engagement and standoff and survivability capabilities. It has also been designated to use the new Python 5 imaging infrared-guided high agility air-to-air missile, another Israeli designed and produced weapon.

The forerunner of the Python 5, the Python 4, was acknowledged as the most advanced heat seeking missile in use. The new model is less prone to various anti-missile countermeasures.

Most of the troop and equipment movements were conducted under cover of darkness and by dawn the aircraft had been covered with camouflage tarps to afford some protection from satellite spying.

The concern was not so much Iranian or North Korean spy assets, but the Russians were still an unknown quantity. Although they had opened up considerable ties with the West since the fall of the Soviet Union, the current leadership was comprised of men who had made their bones in the KGB and were still very distrustful of the United States and any of its allies…and that pointed a major finger at Israel. Russia had courted the Arabs and consistently fought any sanctions against terrorist nations such as Iran. It opposed both Gulf wars and was known to have sent technology to the Arabs.

Russian satellites were a major concern, even under cover of darkness. The fear was that they would pick up the military buildup and forewarn Iran. But there was little choice; it had to be done and Israel had to be ready. The little nation had been gambling against overwhelming odds since 1948. Why change now?

Sayyid looked across the coffee table at the three dark skinned men sitting before him. All were dressed in cheap versions of Western suits and ties, rumpled by the oppressive humidity of the North Korean summer. The hotel in Pyongyang had no air-conditioning and the fan in the corner merely whipped up the hot, humid air.

"The components will leave Pyongyang tomorrow by charter jet. I want the lorry in Damascus to be at the airport on arrival and ready for an immediate departure. All arrangements have been made for customs and there will be no problem. As far as the Syrians know, this will be a cache of weapons for Black Winter and other Hamas supported groups. The government is in sympathy with us and will look the other way. However, we must load and depart without delay so that no questions are asked by any other parties.

"It is your responsibility to insure that there are no problems with the cargo and that everything is expedited as necessary. We will all travel together on the charter and once in Damascus you will continue on to the destination with the components and I will contact you at the appropriate time."

"Even the refugee camps are more comfortable than this," one of the men mumbled to Sayyid, commenting that this was a luxury hotel by North Korean standards.

"Please, do not speak ill of our friends," Sayyid replied, silently pointing to the ceiling. "They have been extremely good to us and we can not proceed without their indulgence."

Sayyid was fully aware that every hotel room in the so-called "tourist" quarter was bugged and monitored so long as there was any occupant in the accommodation. But there was no getting around it; his man was absolutely correct. North Korea had to be about the dreariest country in the world; it was varying shades of gray. Even the light was dark.

Many of the buildings reminded him of Croatia and other Eastern Bloc nations with architecture that was about as unimaginative as the human mind could create. Residential blocks looked the same…stultifyingly the same. There was no form to them and they were remarkable for their ability to blend into the horizon. "Communist chic," they were called.

On the way to Sunan, the airport masquerading as an international gateway, their car passed along the Daedong River bordering one side of Pyongyang and perhaps the only thing there with any natural beauty.

The city boasted wide, tree-lined, six-lane boulevards with a monumental lack of traffic. The green belt had parks adorned with gigantic statues of Kim's father, Kim-il Sung and were virtually devoid of human use.

The 18-mile ride to Sunan took only minutes. There was never a traffic jam to worry about. Tourism to the country was almost non-existent and the government prohibited individual travel, permitting only approved tour groups.

You could not choose your own hotel and your accommodations were assigned by the government. As Sayyid knew, there might be only a handful of guests in a hotel designed to accommodate more than a thousand people.

Tourists could not choose in which restaurant to eat and they could not determine an itinerary. They were herded around like sheep and only permitted to see what the government wanted seen.

Their government driver pulled into a space in front of the Sunan terminal, again with no worry about finding parking at the almost listless air center, the only means of international arrival or departure.

The airport seemed frozen in time and the Soviet-style terminal mimicked the architecture of the city. Sayyid had no worry about boarding his charter through the terminal. Who would be there to see him?

Sunan Terminal was no different than the parks and highways; it was almost empty with only a handful of North Korean functionaries moving about. But even with a virtually deserted terminal, Sayyid's trained eye was able to spot the security agents trying to blend into the walls and being starkly obvious because there was no one else around. They looked ridiculous in their long leather trench coats, as though they were refugees from a Humphrey Bogart World War II adventure movie with the Gestapo in similar dress.

There was a small duty free shop and Sayyid walked over out of curiosity to inspect it. It held little more than a handful of grossly overpriced liquor bottles. Sayyid gazed around the terminal and could find no evidence of any other passenger services. He simply wanted to take his bomb and be out of this depressing hole of a country as quickly as possible.

His original plan had been to fly through to Damascus and then via Iran Air to Teheran. But, as he quickly found out, even the Arabs didn't want to fly into North Korea. There was no passenger traffic and almost no goods; nothing to make the flight profitable.

He looked out the cloudy window to the runway approach to the terminal and saw that his aircraft was hooked to a boarding ladder and was awaiting passengers. The caterpillar tram with the boxes of his components was at the base of the conveyor belt and had already begun loading the crates.

His men stood on either side of the tram and belt, observing every box that was loaded. They had checked and double checked to insure that everything was on line. It would be a catastrophe if so much as one component went missing or was damaged.

He waited until the last crate ran off the belt and into the cargo hold and the hatch was bolted shut. One of his men looked up at the window and gave thumbs up signal. Sayyid waved his hand and walked to the ground level access door to the tarmac and across a short span to the ladder.

The cargo plane was not designed to carry passengers in comfort, but it did have a separate cabin for those who did fly the craft. The seats were hardly first or business class. In fact, they barely qualified as coach. The padding was thin and Sayyid could feel the rivets through the material. It would be a long, uncomfortable flight. But he would not be as uncomfortable as the Israelis were going to be.

He had just dozed off when he felt the charter plane banking for an approach to Damascus. The sun was setting and he could see the long shadows drifting across the tarmac below. Runway lights had come on and he could follow the advancing flashing of the red lights leading the plane to a smooth landing. The pilot reversed the thrusters and the plane slowed. Sayyid could feel his body straining against the seat belt until the pilot gently pushed the throttle forward and began to bring the craft around.

They were directed to a hangar at the far end of the airport and stopped as a tractor hooked up to the nose wheel and pulled the plane into the gaping entrance of the giant structure. Inside waiting for them was an eighteen wheeler truck and half a dozen ground crew.

Syrian military forces had taken up positions outside of the hanger's now closed door. There was a full platoon of heavily armed men and two half-track vehicles with swivel mounted fifty caliber machine guns. They were not told why they were there or what they were guarding. All they were aware of was that if there was a problem and it wasn't handled properly, they would answer to President al-Assad personally.

Bashir al-Assad had taken the reins when his father, Hafiz al-Assad, died on June 10, 2000. So tightly held was the government by Assad that parliament was called into immediate session to amend the constitution so that the then thirty-four year-old Bashir could assume the helm. The constitution required the president to be a minimum age of forty. But technicalities were never a problem for the Assad family.

Hafiz Assad was an implacable foe of Israel and only came into nominal peace talks in the 1990s. He had lost the Golan Heights to Israel in one of the failed Arab wars and wanted them back. The Israelis' main concern was the Syrian Army lobbing mortar and artillery into the lowlands killing many adult and children civilians.

Bashir had no military experience but held the rank of colonel as a result of a quickie stint in a military academy. In fact, his background was as an ophthalmologist…an eye doctor.

On the surface Bashir appeared to be a moderate and more inclined to the modern world than his father. In truth he was as ruthless, if not more so, suppressing dissent with a steel fist. He wanted revenge for the humiliation Israel had heaped on his father in earlier conflicts. In fact, in private he compared himself with American President George W. Bush who was believed to have invaded Iraq to avenge his father, President George H.W. Bush. Saddam had engineered assassination efforts to kill the elder Bush in return for the humiliation of the first Gulf War.

Sayyid had been working with al-Assad, but keeping the Syrian at arm's length so that he could assume a position of plausible deniability for any of the activities of the Black Winter faction. Assad offered whatever assistance and succor he could with the proviso that all aggressive activities must take place in a third nation.

The only nation Sayyid could trust and was far enough from prying eyes was the fundamentalist regime in Iran.

The threats made by Secretary of State Joseph McCrane had become somewhat bothersome. The Iranian government was seriously concerned with the possibility of retaliation from the Americans. But they were more concerned with a nuclear-armed Israel.

If Israel could be dealt with while they had reasonable deniability, the problem would be solved. President Ahmadinejad did not think the United States would actually launch a nuclear attack on his country if it could reasonably deny any knowledge or culpability in the destruction of Israel. There were simply too many militant factions out there for anyone to control and the blame could be laid to any one of them.

Sayyid had been promised help by Assad if he would move the components through Syria without detection. If there was a problem, the Syrian army would be forced to attack Sayyid and destroy the components. Ahmadinejad offered the use of his nuclear sites, but as well he demanded deniability. For all his bluster and threats and the persona of a seeming fundamentalist crazy, he was well aware that Secretary McCrane was not a man to be toyed with.

Inside the giant structure Sayyid personally saw to the unloading of the aircraft. The hold of the charter freight looked absurdly empty with only Sayyid's crates in the interior.

The crew moved a roller rack to the edge of the open hatch and Sayyid waved them off. He could not take a chance on the crates rolling down such a steep incline and possibly causing damage. He ordered the men to connect a belted motorized conveyor that would gently lower the equipment to the rear door of the lorry.

Progress was slow and Sayyid was beginning to grow impatient, but he knew that the care given each crate was essential and he checked his temper. Within a half hour the jet was unloaded and the crates transferred to the lorry.

One of the men who had been in Pyongyang with Sayyid climbed behind the wheel of the long truck. Another joined him in the passenger seat, carrying an AK-47 that rested across his lap.

Sayyid had made arrangements for four automobiles to travel with the eighteen-wheeler, two in the lead and two bringing up the rear. The four men in each vehicle were heavily armed with automatic weapons. Leading them to the border with Turkey would be two Syrian army vehicles.

They would have to travel north instead of cutting off long distances by driving directly to Arak because that would mean cutting across Iraq and praying that the Coalition Forces didn't spot them. It was a dangerous and unacceptable risk.

The route would take them to the Turkish border where they would cross at the village of Cizre, then heading eastward as quickly as possible, passing through the tiny towns of Sirnak and Hakkari until they could cross into Iran near Orumiyeh. From there the road would wind across the Zagros Mountains to Arak, a trip of about 350 miles as the crow flies. The distance would be tripled as the lorry drives. But Sayyid was determined to make the drive in one day. He couldn't afford to layover and risk either exposure or accident.

Sayyid thought that the circuitous route was necessary in order to avoid detection by the Western powers. By going directly to Iran from North Korea might have sent a red flag to the enemy's intelligence watchdogs.

The drive was strenuous, especially to the lorry driver as he negotiated steep mountain turns and switchbacks. He had to take care not to burn his brakes out on the down slopes and to moderate his speed on what passed for a straightaway, knowing that it could suddenly turn into a death defying hairpin turn.

The lorry carried several jerry cans of petrol to refuel both the cars and itself as the mountainous driving produced low mileage. There would be at least one refuel stop at which time they could eat and relieve themselves.

There were no gas stations or restaurants along the way and they had to pack their own food and water. With precious few exceptions the only vehicles they passed were antique buses and trucks and the occasional military vehicle. Most of what they saw were goat carts and mule pulled wagons. The Zagros was one of the most desolate and backward areas on the entire planet.

Darkness made the drive a near impossibility and slowed progress to a crawl. They could not chance a switchback unexpectedly coming up and the lorry driving over the edge into black space. The bomb wouldn't blow up, but the components would be useless after rolling down a mountainside.

The truck was running alongside Lake Orumiyeh on an almost straight run to Mahabad where it would turn westward to Rayat and then southward again. They would follow the Iraqi border, too close for comfort for Sayyid, to Saqqez and then swing down to Arak.

As they drove through Mahabad they were met by an armed escort of Revolutionary Guards who would escort them the rest of the way. They paused and placed Iranian military markings on all vehicles so as not to arouse any suspicion. By this time they were all wishing that the trip had ended.

Sayyid had placed a GPS on the dash of his Mercedes and kept a constant watch to make sure they didn't go off track. He knew that there were few roads other than goat tracks along the way, but this was his insurance; especially after the arrival of the Revolutionary Guards in whom he placed no trust at all.

"Fanatics do not think with any logic. Their only motivation is the idol they worship."

Sayyid knew they were drawing close as the road began to improve and he could breathe more easily. In the distance he could see the berm surrounding the facility at Arak and the guard post at the entryway through the sandy hills.

With the Guard escort they didn't slow down at the post and barreled through the gateway. The Guards pulled up at a bunker that seemed more appropriate to a munitions storage area than a major nuclear research facility and were approached by a senior officer.

"You will leave your vehicles here and my men will unload your cargo."

"That will not happen. You and your men will withdraw and we will take responsibility for unloading the lorry."

The Revolutionary Guard leader bristled and went nose-to-nose with Sayyid.

"I am in charge here and you will obey my orders."

Sayyid looked up to see the contingent of Guardsmen jumping from their vehicle and bringing their guns to bear on Sayyid's group. They too had exited their Mercedes' and brought their weapons to an aggressive stance.

Sayyid faced the commander:

"You tell your fanatics to put their weapons down and stand back. Then I suggest that you radio Teheran and speak with Jamshid Mossadegh."

The Guard commander's head snapped up at the mention of Mossadegh, the son of a former Prime Minister and now the force behind the fundamentalist dictators of the country. The former PM had a reputation throughout the world as a crazy man who ran around government buildings with his robes flying. His death was mourned by less than a few.

"I can not disturb him."

"If you do not disturb him and continue to impede what I must do, I think you will live to regret it. Only you will not have to worry about any regret for long."

The Guardsman lowered his weapon, a look of both puzzlement and creeping fear coming over his face.

"I'll not tell you again. Order your men to stand back while my people unload this cargo. You will provide perimeter security for us and you will not enter the facility unless I specifically give you permission."

The commander had clearly lost face in front of his own men and he began barking orders at them. They fell back and took up positions forming a perimeter around the entrance to the Arak facility.

Sayyid motioned to his men to quickly begin unloading their cargo. The lorry pulled up to a loading dock and the crates were rapidly moved from the vehicle to the platform. A forklift was brought around and each crate taken to a lift and brought into the bowels of the subterranean research facility.

The nuclear research laboratory was more than one hundred fifty feet below the surface and covered with twenty feet of reinforced concrete. It was impervious to bombs and could easily withstand the new Bunker Buster weapon developed by the Americans that could penetrate concrete. It was simply too deep and too protected. It might not withstand a direct hit from a nuclear bomb, but aside from that it was one of the more secure locations on earth.

As the last crate came off the lift, Sayyid turned to the Iranian technicians:

"This is now in your hands. We have no time to spare and the device must be ready without delay. Other plans are in the works and the timetable cannot be disrupted."

The technicians informed Sayyid that the device would be fully functional within two days.

He nodded approval and walked out of the laboratory. His men remained behind to keep check on the technicians so that the assembly went ahead without disruption.

"Seong was an American asset?" Dan said in a voice betraying total astonishment.

"He was about the most valuable asset we were running," said Matt Morton.

"Secretary McCrane sure as hell put on a good act, but not as good an act as Seong."

"The two of them had it down pat. But we are in a major hole right now because of the intelligence he was providing. The man really loved his country, but hated where Kim senior and junior had taken it. And I hate to say it, but it sure looks as though the ones who took him out were part of that radical Jewish group, Response."

"OK, let me see if we can fill in some of the gaps with our assets in Iran. We've had them working on this for a while now. Our belief is that they are not going to try and attack the United States again and that Israel is the most likely target."

"That's the same impression we get. We can't rely on that and take a chance so we are going to keep our security at a Code Red, but our focus will be on a location in Israel."

"Matt, in all honesty, the United States, as horrible as it would be, could withstand a nuclear blast. Israel would be destroyed. It's not even the property damage; our population is only a little more than six million souls. That's about what Hitler destroyed and we can't afford to lose that many people again. When they set off an IED in a marketplace and we lose twenty or thirty people that compares to a hell of a lot more percentage-wise in the United States. We must stop them before the bomb reaches Israel. Under no circumstances can we let it go off there."

"You're right and we will work closely on this. No secrets, everything will be an open book and we'll beat these guys."

Dan pressed the desk buzzer and directed his secretary to have Maj. Whitman come to the office.

"It looks as though we're in an intelligence hole. Response murdered Ambassador Seong and he was an American asset, a deep cover mole."

Hesh let out an audible gasp and Dan looked at him.

"Are you OK? What's the matter?"

"He was an asset? I had no idea."

"Neither did I, but the Americans were holding him close to the vest for obvious reasons. McCrane and Seong put on a beautiful act and had everyone fooled. If those damn radicals had left things alone, we might know where the bomb is and where it's going. Now we are going to have to fly blind and we have precious little time."

Hesh had visibly flushed and Dan again asked if he was OK?

"Yeah, I'm fine. Just a little surprised about Seong."

"That's what happens when vigilantes go into the field without benefit of intelligence or oversight. That happened in America with vigilantes lynching the wrong people and thinking they were meeting out justice. I want you personally to contact 'Aboud' and see if he can help. There isn't a hell of a lot of time and if we miss this one, it'll make 9-11 look like a fireworks display."

"I'll make contact immediately."

Hesh walked from the office thinking to himself:

"Shit! What the hell did we do? What a fuckup."

"Aboud" was one of the top clandestine assets being run by the Mossad. He was a Shia Muslim with a twist; he did not hate the West or the Jews, whom he considered to be "The People of the Book." But those beliefs were closely held because he knew that death would be the gift from his brethren if they were to find out.

Aboud had been part of the "student" takeover of the American embassy in Teheran when it was truly a student movement. They had negotiated with Al Zinski, the head of security for the embassy to demonstrate for a day and then leave. Then the politicians, both Iranian and American, got involved and it turned into a 440 day standoff until after Jimmy Carter left office.

After Shah Mohammed Reza Pahlevi was forced into exile and Ayatollah Khomeini took provisional control, a group of five Shia students plotted the embassy takeover. Among them were Ahmadinejad, the current Iranian energy minister Habibollah Bitaraf, Aboud and two others.

The Shia were strict fundamentalists who believed that when the Prophet Mohammed died, succession should have passed to his cousin/ son-in-law, Ali; while Sunnis hold the same religious beliefs, their idea for succession was that it should have passed from Mohammed to the most capable to be elected from his followers.

The Shia believe that a mullah is sinless by nature and his authority is more infallible than that of the Pope. They believe his authority comes directly from God and they are venerated as saints.

While Sunnis comprised about eighty percent of the entire Muslim population throughout the world, the Shia held a greater majority in countries such as Iran and Iraq where fundamentalism ran rampant.

Aboud, as an educated man, began to question the infallibility of any human being. He began to look at Ahmadinejad and how radical their movement had become and he grew disenchanted.

He was posted to Jerusalem on an intelligence gathering mission and was co-opted by a contact and arrested by the Mossad. His treatment was humane and he was never beaten for information. The comparisons began to gnaw at him and he questioned the motives of the suicide bombers and the actions of his friends, Ahmadinejad and Habibollah.

Mossad, sensing his pending turnaround, ameliorated his imprisonment even further with better food, cell accommodations and treatment.

Aboud made his final transition when one of his favorite jail guards failed to show up one day. When he questioned the other guards as to where the man was, Aboud was told that he had taken his wife and twin six-month old daughters shopping. They had stopped at a sidewalk café for lunch and were torn apart by a suicide bomber. He was told that there weren't sufficient body parts of the man's daughters to fill a casket.

He was shaken and began a long period of introspection, finally deciding that he had chosen the wrong path and that the student movement he had joined in the 1970s had strayed far from the path they had first chosen and instead of life becoming better for the people, it had deteriorated steadily over the years.

Aboud was a man of conscience and he could no longer abide the senseless fundamentalism of Ahmadinejad and Habibollah. He decided to accept the entreaties of the Israelis who had been so good to him. In this he saw a means toward peace throughout the entire region and the ability of his people to prosper as the Israelis had. If they could make the desert bloom without vast deposits of oil, Iran could make a better life for all its people.

An "escape" was arranged, Aboud made his way back to Iran and was accorded "hero" status and over the years rose in rank and prestige until he was a member of the Revolutionary Council, the ruling body of Iran..

As a Council member he had virtually free run of the country and could go where and when he pleased without worry. This provided the opportunity to observe military movements and troop numbers. As a council member he was privy to all political discussions and decisions… or so he thought.

His first "handler," Yehuda ben Moshe, had been killed on a mission into Syria and he was passed to Col. Dan Halevi. Dan worked to gain his trust and confidence and with Aboud's approval, brought Hesh into the clandestine operation.

Aboud had ultimate faith and confidence in these two men. He knew they would never betray his cover and felt he could trust them with his life. In fact, every time he was in contact with either of them, he was trusting them with his life and the lives of his wife, son and daughter.

Aboud's wife knew something was going on, but he never took her into his confidence. He felt that if she knew nothing, it would protect her and their son and daughter if anything went wrong. He knew in the back of his mind that was not true and they would all be executed.

The mullah's adhered to the principle that no virgin could be executed and took it upon themselves to make any virgin execution ready. Aboud knew what that would mean for his fourteen-year-old daughter.

But his sense of obligation to them took second place to his obligation to the people of his country living in grinding poverty. He had to help them better themselves and this was the means to achieve that.

Dead drops—the practice of leaving messages in a fixed location for pick up or delivery—were impossible because of the lack of Israeli operatives in Iran. Aboud had no choice but to use radio communication.

He had a mini-transmitter that was easily transported. His messages were coded, recorded and then condensed. When blast transmitted they were only on the airwaves for several seconds, not long enough for a radio direction finder to zone in on. In Israel the "blast" was received, diluted and decoded.

Before Hesh could initiate a transmission to Aboud a message from the Iranian came in to the surveillance center. It was quickly decoded and brought to Hesh.

"Dinner meeting tomorrow. Special dish of mushrooms on the menu."

Hesh grabbed the message from the radioman's hands and raced up the staircase taking two steps at a time. He burst into Dan's office and literally thrust the radiogram in his face.

"Do you realize what this means?"

Dan glanced at the paper and his mouth drew tightly into a straight line.

"Mushroom" was the code word for nuclear. The meaning of the blast was clear; the mushroom on the menu indicated that a nuclear device was about to be served. They had no time to waste.

Hesh's orders were to immediately infiltrate himself into Iran and make contact with Aboud. As dangerous as that was, it was an absolute necessity.

Dan turned to his organizational chart for the Sayaret Matkal and the other units he had requisitioned. The question now was whether to make it a full scale call up or keep it to a rapid deployment strike force.

He decided to keep the initial attack force to the limited team of well trained commandos he had assembled with a full assault group waiting in the wings for a quick deployment if necessary.

The logistics of this were almost overwhelming. There was no quick and easy way in and out of Iran, if that was where they would have to go. The shortest route would be over Jordan and then Iraq before entering Iranian airspace. The abject danger here was putting the Iranians on full alert before they could get close enough to be effective. They would totally lose the element of any surprise.

Dan knew the cooperation of the Americans was an absolute necessity, but the danger here, as it was in the first Gulf War, was that the Americans would be in a frazzle about upsetting other Arab nations. He would talk to Matt and if there was any hesitation on the part of the Americans, Israel would go it alone. If it didn't, it wouldn't be here tomorrow to worry about any consequences.

Hesh, as George Cohen, flew to Turkey and then vanished from the radar screen. In his place Abu Hazar made his way to the Iran Air gate and boarded a plane for Teheran. Less than a day later in the airport at Ankara, Abu Hazar landed and never left. However, George Cohen boarded a plane for Tel Aviv and shortly after he landed there, Maj. Hesh Whitman once again appeared.

His report to Dan brought information but no comfort. Aboud had learned of the activity at Arak and he had no doubt that the Israelis would move immediately to destroy the facility before the bomb could be assembled and moved.

Aboud's conditions for assisting were simple: no innocent civilians were to be harmed and the Holy City of Qom, only a few miles northeast of Arak, was to be spared.

Hesh had given him all the assurances he could, but was unable to preclude the possibility of civilian casualties. He reminded Aboud that even though there were no settlements abutting Arak, there were villages within the range of a nuclear explosion. Hesh assured him that all possible precautions would be taken and noted that Tehran, where Aboud's family lived, was well out of the danger zone.

Hesh's report to Dan was simple: if they moved without delay, they could destroy the bomb and the base at Arak before the device was moved. Once it was moved, it would head straight for Israel and even if it only made it to the border, the blast and fallout would be so devastating; the country might never recover.

Dan placed an immediate secure call to Matt Morton, summarizing as quickly as possible the information Hesh had brought back.

"Matt, we are going in to Arak and we will take out that facility. They've been brewing heavy water there and we all know that there's only one use for that. If they are putting this device together to use on us, you know that the U.S. won't be far behind as a target of opportunity."

"How the hell are you going to manage that?"

"With your cooperation and the participation of the United States Army Special Forces…you do remember them, don't you?"

"Just tell me what you need and I'll make it happen."

Sayyid was pleased with the progress on assembly of the device and called his mentor with the news. In four days it would be dispatched in a military vehicle that would change colors as it crossed borders. It would enter Israel through the West Bank, coming in on the direct road from Amman. With the scope of Israeli military movements in the area, it wouldn't be difficult to slip through and then move about with the Star of David on the bonnet of the troop/cargo lorry he would be driving.

He would cross from Iraq and follow the road past Al-Ruwayshid until it branched south. He would continue to Azraq 'Umari and then swing west to Amman and cross into the West Bank. From there it would be an easy ride straight on through to Tel Aviv on the Mediterranean Sea.

While Jerusalem would have been a better political target, it was politics that stopped him from aiming at that ancient city. There were too many sites holy to the Muslims and the backlash would have been counterproductive. The Israeli government would remain safe, but the main commercial center of the country would be destroyed.

Sayyid would issue an immediate warning that if his orders were not complied with, another bomb would be detonated in the city of Haifa. He didn't have another bomb yet, but there would be such panic that he doubted anyone would question such a minor detail.

Once the device was set in place in Tel Aviv, he would personally see to the timer and make sure to his own satisfaction that the bomb would not be discovered. He would then fly from Tel Aviv to London and await news of the horrific explosion.

Black Winter would become the preeminent organization and leader of the Arab world. And he would lead Black Winter.

"What the hell is that?"

Hesh's eyes opened wide as he looked into the crate that had just arrived from the American Special Forces Command in Iraq. I've never seen anything like this!"

"Matt came through for us and there's more to come. This is the Barrett fifty caliber long rang sniper rifle. The slug can tear through steel and concrete and will put the fear of God into those at the receiving end."

Dan held up the huge fifty caliber bullet and compared it to a .308 used in the AK-47 and the .224 most snipers chose. Both rounds were favored for their flat trajectory providing increased accuracy.

The fifty looked as though it would outweigh them by two pounds. The caliber was most commonly used in mounted machine guns and was generally seen in fighter aircraft and atop tanks and other armored fighting vehicles. Its ferocious recoil didn't lend itself to normal combat operations, although a recoil pad did mitigate it somewhat.

"If you fire this on automatic at its capacity of ten rounds in ten seconds you might want to make an appointment with your dentist because it'll shake your teeth loose. This round will travel at 2700 feet per second. The target will never know what hit him or where it came from. This won't wound; it'll destroy and can take out a target with considerable accuracy from more than a mile away. It's a fear maker because the target will never hear the shot fired."

From another crate Dan extracted a stainless steel revolver with a hardwood grip and seven-inch long barrel. He smiled as he handed it to Hesh.

The younger man hefted the gun and turned to Dan with a puzzled look on his face.

"Why are we using a revolver instead of automatic pistols?"

"This is no ordinary revolver. It's a .454 Casull and is the most powerful revolver made. It makes the forty-four magnum look like a toy. They comparison fired this against the .357 magnum and the .44 magnum into quarter-inch steel plate. The .357 dented it; the .40 made a big dent and the .454 punch a neat hole right through it. This isn't going to replace your Glock, but it sure will add punch. It'll do at closer range what the Barrett does from long distances"

Hesh looked at the cartridges, about the same diameter as the traditional .45, but considerably longer.

"If you put one of these in a standard .45 revolver, it'll blow it apart. This only carries five rounds in the cylinder so that it can be strengthened by an extra thick section between chambers. When this gun first came out the user had to tighten the screws after every few rounds. The recoil and vibration were so ferocious that it loosened everything. They've since fixed that.

"Oh, and I might add, it's accurate as hell. But don't try shooting it with one hand; it'll tear your nails off."

Dan called his team together and handed the rifles to the long range shooters. The Casulls were distributed to Hesh and two others while Dan kept one aside for himself to use.

Word had come in from Matt that the President had approved a transit of Iraq for the Israeli force under the condition that the Star of David was not visible on any uniform or equipment. A Special Forces Group would be added as a supplemental force for the assault but all soldiers were to go in without markings of any kind on their uniforms. All would wear black BDUs, (Battle Dress Uniforms) making them as anonymous as possible.

The Israeli Hercules would fly over Jordan without interference. Secretary of State McCrane had taken care of it personally, initiating a telephone call between the President and King Abdullah II and the King ordered military units away from the flight path and radar units there to be shut down for maintenance.

The Secretary had used his finely tuned "diplomatic" skill to help convince the King that it would be in the greater interests of Jordan to "look the other way" while certain specialized equipment was flown to Iraq.

Abdullah, who assumed the throne after the death of his father, King Hussein, knew that if either Israel or the United States wanted him to go into exile, it would not be a long time in coming. He was used to issuing blustering comments and threats, but taking little or no action. And he wasn't ready to go into exile in Paris, no matter how exciting that city might be.

Dan summoned up a second Hercules and beefed up his forces with a second Sayaret brigade. That combined with the American Green Berets should be more than enough. This was still slated as a basic "search and destroy" mission and not the start of an all out war. In fact, if they were successful, it would avoid an all out war.

Kyle Norman was alerted and requested the inclusion of an SAS observer team. The SAS (Special Air Services) was one of the most highly motivated spec ops units in the world and frequently provided specialized training for the Green Berets and other such groups.

Accommodating Norman Dan and Matt added an SAS squad and a unit of MI-6, making the covert operation truly international.

Aboud had provided blue prints of the Arak facility and Dan had them enlarged and displayed on the wall in the conference room. All commanders had been called in for a full briefing, signaling that the start of the operation was imminent.

As Dan entered the conference room the assembled officers jumped to attention. He still wasn't used to the deference given to general officers and he politely motioned for them to be seated.

He approached the American Green Beret colonel seated in the front row and extended his hand. The man stood and they shook hands, and then grabbed each other in a warm embrace.

"Good to see you again, General," said Special Forces Col. Chantland Wise.

"General, crap! How the hell are you Chan?"

"Couldn't be better Dan. Are we going to pull this off?"

"Chan, we have to. If we don't there'll be such hell to pay on a world-wide scope that no one will get away unhurt."

Dan and Chan Wise had both joined Special Forces as young lieutenants and had even served together under Joe McCrane. Each had the confidence in the other that only comes from a relationship forged under fire.

Wise wasn't happy that his unit was to be given a role less than responsibility for the forefront of the assault.

"Chan, McCrane has asked that we keep American troops off the initial assault."

"Well what the hell good are we if our capabilities aren't being used to their full extent? I'm sorry the Colonel feels that way, but I want my men to be full participants in this operation. This bomb may be aimed at Israel, but the next bombs will be headed for New York and Washington. We don't need another 9-11."

"OK, Chan. You and your men are in as full players. I'll handle the Colonel if there's a problem."

Dan pointed to the overlay map of the area with markings of different colors spotted around the Arak facility.

The nuclear plant was not actually in the city of Arak, but was several miles outside of the main populated area, although it was still technically within the municipal boundaries. The overlay covered that entire area and the hills and fields surrounding the plant.

"There are Armored Personnel Carriers in front of the main gate along with tanks guarding ingress and egress. I want the four Barretts placed in a line facing the main road and the front of the facility. These guns are long enough as it is, but I want muzzle sound suppressors on each of them.

"You will take out the guards on signal. Even if they are in their bunkers or the guard post, these guns are powerful enough to blast right through sandbags and the concrete walls of the guard house. They'll even penetrate the skin of the APCs (armoured personnel carriers).

"The guards will drop and no one will know where the shots are coming from."

He pointed to two of the snipers and said they would fire the Barretts on semi-automatic, emptying the ten-round magazines into the guard houses. The slugs would rip through the concrete walls and take out anyone standing or sitting in the small rooms.

"Make sure you cushion your cheeks and don't let them kick back into your teeth or you'll be eating baby food for the rest of your lives. They have suppressors, but there is so much kick that you can't contain all of it"

Dan spent the next hour going over the assignments and detailing the responsibility of each unit, almost down to the individual. He knew the commanders and had full confidence in them and their men. They would not be here otherwise. This was not the time or place to use untested troops or commanders you didn't know.

Gen Dan Halevi stood at attention and saluted the unit commanders arrayed in front of him: Green Berets, Sayaret Matkal and SAS.

"Gentlemen, this may sound very much like a cliché, but it isn't. The fate of the entire world depends on the success of our mission. If we fail, there might not be anything to come back to. I know you and your units are all highly motivated and the best troops of any forces in the world and that is precisely why you were chosen for this job.

"Please let your troops know that we leave in three hours. They are to take care of any personal matters in that time. I suggest they get all of their affairs in order. Letters may be written to loved ones and family to be mailed if they do not return. However, under no circumstance is anyone, and I mean anyone, permitted to make a phone call or have any communication with persons not in the secure area of this base.

"I suggest that you all grab something to eat and try to get some rest. I need all of you at peak performance. Thank you."

The commanders snapped to attention as Dan walked briskly from the room and joined his Mossad brigade. He could feel butterflies in his stomach as pictures of the Twin Towers scanned through his mind followed by mental pictures of a bustling Tel Aviv superimposed over the smoldering World Trade Center.

There was no option other than stopping the bomb. Anything else was unthinkable.

"The device is almost ready and the transport is here. We will be ready to move the day after tomorrow. The bomb should trigger uprisings throughout the Muslim world and an all out push into the occupied lands. We must make sure Black Winter is ready to take the helm."

"Sayyid, you have done well. Our operatives throughout the region will be preparing for the attack. Not only will they return the occupied territories to us, but the cowards who now hold power in the surrounding countries, those who have given in to Western dress and entertainment, will be pushed aside and buried. We will have a Pan-Muslim society throughout."

Sayyid pictured himself walking in to the great palaces of the Arabian world, not as an honored visitor, but as a potentate. He saw himself in residence with the proverbial seventy two virgins that the Shaheed were promised in paradise after blowing themselves up, surrounding him and pleasuring his every need; but he pictured them in this world and not the next.

His men in Tel Aviv would become Shaheed, martyrs, and he hoped they would find their virgins, but he had work to do on earth and could not leave yet.

"I will see to the execution of the plan and then will join you in Damascus so that we may watch the news reports and then begin the assault."

"Good, my son. The trigger for the action will be the first reports of an atomic explosion in Tel Aviv. We will have the world press at out beck and call from that point on. You will be the new, modern day Caliph of Muhammad."

Sayyid ended the call. He enjoyed the thought of ruling all of Arabia, possibly more than he enjoyed the thought of all those riches that would come with it and the seventy two virgins at his feet...while he was still alive to enjoy them.

The desert of the Central Negev is hot during the day and casts a chill at night that could freeze water or the blood in a man's veins. It was as dark as the far side of the moon and about as cheerless as its crater-ridden surface.

Anyone outside the gates of the compound would not have been aware of the movement inside except for the drone of vehicle engines. The troop movements created little noise as the international force of Spec Ops troops moved into position at the foot of the ramp leading into the Hercules. One of the great aircraft would hold the assault force and the skeleton-like desert dune buggies that could zip over dunes and through deep sand in a flash.

The second Hercules contained an APC and several more dune buggies. The heavier armor that had originally been considered was dropped at the last briefing. Dan had opted instead to go for the quick movement and lightening strike. Extracting the teams would be faster and easier if they didn't have heavy armor to lug around. It would also help in leaving no trace behind.

Dan stopped his preparations to take an urgent call from Matt Morton.

"Dan, we just got work that Ahmadinejad is going to Arak to hold a demonstration asserting Iran's right to nuclear power. He's still insisting that it's for peaceful purposes and will be used for energy."

"If that's the case why the hell are they working on heavy water capability? The plutonium by-product of what they are doing is weapons grade and the minute they have the ability to produce their own nuclear weapons, no one in the world is going to be safe. Are your politicians losing their balls?"

"Well, there is some hesitancy because of Ahmadinejad's presence…"

"Matt, we have passed the point of no return. The teams are loading into the Hercules' now and I will not give an order to stand down. I expect that the facilities we discussed will be available when we land in Iraq and that Jordan will be otherwise occupied when we fly over."

"Dan, I…"

"Matt, cut the crap. You know as well as I do exactly what's at stake here. If you waffle now, we're all dead. If Jimmy Carter hadn't listened to Andrew Young and pulled the carpet from under the Shah, we wouldn't be in this shitty position. If Bush 41 had listened to Schwarzkopf, he would have taken Iraq and this opposition wouldn't have had a decade to fester and foment trouble.

"Get back to whomever you have to and tell them that the operation is going forward and will not be stopped. I don't give a damn if Ahmadinejad is standing in the gateway when we get there. In fact, I would hope that he was standing there."

Dan abruptly ended the conversation and walked to his office door. Hesh was standing in the open doorway, a smile creasing his face.

"Matt tried to bug out on us?"

"Trying and doing are two different things. He tried and we are doing. Let's go."

The open Humvee pulled to a slow stop at the Hercules ramp and Dan and Hesh stepped to the tarmac, walking rapidly to the foot of the ramp.

Col. Chan Wise stood there waiting for them, dressed in full combat gear with a parachute strapped to his back. Normally he would have had a reserve chute hanging between his legs in front but with the low level jump planned for tonight, there was no need for a reserve. If the main didn't open he would become a streamer with no time to deploy a reserve. The jumper would hit the desert floor so hard there would be no need to dig a grave; the impact would do that. He offered Dan a smart salute and then brushed his hand across the General's face.

"OK, old buddy. You lead, we follow and may the devil take the hindmost."

Dan climbed aboard and saluted the assault team from the three nations and gave them a thumbs up. He smiled, sat down and strapped himself into the uncomfortable metal seat.

Both Hercules rumbled slowly to the head of the runway and sat, revving their engines. They would maintain total radio silence from this point until extraction. Any transmission could be picked up by a variety of radios from military to intelligence service to sophisticated amateur operators.

The pilots looked down the long strip of tarmac and saw a stationary red light. Both pilots went through pre-flight check lists and coordinated with co-pilots. Navigators in both craft signaled they had their coordinates punched in and were ready.

The lead pilot flashed his running lights and saw a response with the red light waving back and forth. He turned to the co-pilot and nodded, then gently pushed the throttle forward and sent the huge aircraft fleeing down the runway. The giant craft rose in the air and gently banked to the east heading toward the southern end of the Dead Sea. They would cross from there into Jordan, flying over the panhandle and into Iraq.

The flight plan was for a low level crossing, coming up in altitude only over the Jabal al Ashagif highlands. By keeping just above the tops of the dunes, they would avoid any errant radar and although the noise might attract some attention, it was dark enough that no one on the ground would see anything but silhouettes.

The two Hercules landed at the American base in Iraq and refueled. The teams remained on board and no one besides the refueling crew was permitted near the planes. Less than an hour later they were airborne, skipping over the dunes, practically blowing the sand around.

They had to maintain a reasonable altitude because the Hercules' were not as maneuverable as the F-16I Sufas and would not be able to avoid a sudden rise in the land mass. The fighters had departed before them and were waiting at a desert strip just on the Iraqi side of the border. They would not be placed into action unless they were needed to protect the transports; the less bang-bang, the better.

The Hercules' skidded slightly to the north so that they could enter Iranian airspace from the lower corner of Syria, allaying fears since the craft would be coming from an ostensibly friendly nation.

Shortly before 1 a.m. the red ready light came on in the cavernous bay of the airplane and the first teams to be deployed stood and readied themselves. They moved to the open maw of the rear ramp and prepared to jump.

Normally they would be doing a HALO (high altitude, low opening) bail out, but this jump was only a LALO, a low altitude, low opening jump. They would have to pull the rip cord as they exited the low flying aircraft, using as much care as possible to avoid being sucked into the slipstream and slammed back against the side of the Hercules.

The planes would bank sharply away from the drop zone and then circle around, giving the American Green Berets, SAS and Unit 101 an opportunity to set up a perimeter around the base. The four snipers with their deadly Barretts would position themselves at a thousand yards out and wait for the signal to open fire.

The others would then jump from an area outside the perimeter and would take the dune buggies with them. With any good luck all the equipment and men would land in one piece.

Strapped to a railing at the opening, the jumpmaster raised his right hand in a clenched fist. The unit lined up, waiting. The navigator's voice came over the headset worn by the jumpmaster and he pumped his fist up and down rapidly.

The jumpers moved quickly to the edge of the platform and, one after the other in rapid succession, made their way into the dark void.

Exiting from the rear of the plane instead of a side hatch permitted them to open chutes immediately without fear of fouling on a wing or engine. The bent rectangular canopy permitted far more control than the old umbrella parachutes that would land wherever the wind and current would take them.

Within minutes they were on the ground and moving rapidly to assume their positions. The snipers set themselves up in the shadows of the rising dunes and tuned in their night vision scopes. In the distance they could see green-tinted figures moving about. The scopes were adjusted for distance and they sat back, waiting for the signal to open the gates of hell.

The second string came down within a hundred yards of each other, each holding a dull red flashlight. The lights would register brightly for the Hercules pilots who were wearing night vision goggles, giving them both a base line that they must stay above to avoid a crash, and a straight line to fly through as they unloaded the dune buggies. To anyone on the ground without those goggles, the light would have been invisible beyond a few yards.

The remainder of the strike force exited the planes in the same manner as the first stick of jumpers and touched down in minutes. They moved to join their teams as the Hercules circled and prepared to drop the vehicles.

The two aircraft came in, one behind the other, in a straight line, passing through the two strips of red markers held by the team. Only feet off the ground the cargo crew activated drag chutes that opened immediately and pulled the buggies out of the rear of the Hercules. Mounted on wooden skids, they slid quickly out of the hatch and in seconds were on the ground.

The snipers were on alert. They could hear the muffled sounds of aircraft engines in the distance and assumed if they were able to, so were the targets. They peered through the night vision scopes but couldn't detect any unusual activity. Maybe God really was on their side.

Dan moved the buggies to a position encircling the front of the facility. His radioman turned up the signal on his transmitter, emitting radio waves that would cut out any transmissions from within the compound. No one would consider this unusual because it was a frequent occurrence in the desert and they would simply wait for conditions to change. That would give the strike force an ample window of opportunity without worry of reinforcements coming in like the cavalry.

They would have to take out the guards without raising an alarm or the elevator to the subterranean nuclear facility would be slammed shut and there was no other way to make entry.

The strike force sat, four men to a buggy, waiting for the signal that would begin their assault.

Dan had moved to a position overlooking the front gate. There was one man leaning against a gate post and a light coming through the window pane in the guard house. Inside he could see the silhouette of two men apparently seated at a table. Communicating with radio silence was a bitch, but he couldn't take a chance on being intercepted. And with the radio interference put up by his operator, it made no difference.

He moved from sniper position to sniper position, checking each man's observations. When he was satisfied that the only guards on the exterior perimeter where the three he had seen, he motioned that they were ready to go.

Dan ran in a low slung position to the center sniper and held up a cricket clicker, very similar to the device used by Allied paratroopers at the Normandy invasion to identify each other. He pressed it three times in rapid succession, waited a second and pressed it three more times.

The snipers now had authority to fire at will.

He watched as the first man took aim through the night vision scope and Dan again cautioned him about the rifle's vicious recoil. The man nodded and placed his face in a position where he could see through the scope and not loose his teeth at the same time.

Dan knew that all the snipers had experience with the rifle, but he was a Mother Hen and a Jewish Mother Hen at that. It was in his nature to make sure his people were as safe as possible and didn't do anything to hurt themselves.

The sniper peered through the scope, waiting, and then slowly began to squeeze the trigger. It was a long shot, almost a thousand yards. Once the guards were dispatched, the strike force would have to cover that ground in a flash and get inside the facility.

Then Dan saw the rifle jerk violently upward. He brought his night vision binoculars to his eyes and saw the man standing by the gate fly off his feet, high into the air and then slam down to the ground. He never moved again. Being hit by a fifty caliber slug left no doubt about your lack of a future.

The sound caused the men in the booth to stir and one of them came to the door. He had no sooner opened the door than the little structure ceased to exist. Some thirty rounds from the Barretts slammed through the concrete, glass and wood, reducing it to a pile of rubble. The two men inside would not need a burial.

"Time to go," he thought.

"Dan raised his hand with the muted signal light and could hear the sound of the well tuned engines of the dune buggies revving up. The vehicles were capable of traveling across the desert floor at high speed and they covered the ground from their hidden positions in the dunes to the front gate in no time flat.

He jumped into his buggy, stationed just behind the sniper's position and led the charge toward the open gate of the facility. The snipers moved back into the shadows, holding their positions should the need arise to take out any more of the Iranians.

So far, so good.

Advancing through the gate they could see the shattered arms and legs of the two men who had been inside the gatehouse. The third man lay about fifteen feet away on his stomach. There was no need to check his pulse; the fifty caliber slug had exited through what was the middle of his back and now was a gaping hole almost devoid of flesh and bone. He had bled out almost instantly and certainly felt nothing from the second that he was hit.

"CSI would call it 'instant exsanguination,'" he thought to himself.

Dan's professional eye took in the scene without emotion. He needed to evaluate and sympathy for the dead had no place here. He had developed a psyche that permitted him to take in a scene of death and destruction with a cold and calculating composure, able to make instant decisions without emotional involvement…most of the time.

The steel entry doors to the complex were laced with malleable C-4 and detonators set in place. His men backed off a safe distance and prepared to make a rush attack to maintain the element of surprise.

Dan nodded to Tzvi Herzog and the explosives expert pushed his finger toward the toggle when he crumpled and fell to the ground. Automatic fire began to erupt around them, the task force taking fire from three sides.

On the dunes the four snipers spotted the flashes of enemy gunfire and set their Barretts in semi-automatic mode. They peered through the night vision scopes and saw a platoon of Revolutionary Guardsmen moving to encircle the task force. They had come from a billet behind the entryway to the underground nuclear facility and were moving in for the kill.

"Sir," the man's voice, in a state of near panic, called to Sayyid. "Something has gone wrong."

He motioned for Sayyid to accompany him to a bank of monitors that were fed from television security cameras spotted around the compound. Sayyid could see the rubble that had been the guard house and another body on the ground nearby.

"Wake those lazy dogs in the billet and get them out there immediately. Radio Teheran that we are under attack and have them provide reinforcements immediately."

The man was back in an instant.

"I have sent out the guards to repel the attack, but can not raise Teheran. There is interference and the radio signal cannot get through."

"There's a military base on the other side of Arak. Get someone over there immediately and bring in support."

Sayyid stood watching the screen and could see several shadowy figures moving in toward the fence and crossing through the gate. He saw them dismount from what appeared to be toy vehicles, but knew this was no game. The monitor zoomed in on the soldiers, but he could find no markings on their uniforms and their faces were covered with camouflage makeup giving them the look of devils that were there to take all their souls to hell.

He ordered the blast doors closed and called for guards to take up positions around the entrance to the subterranean laboratory. The technicians had just completed their assembly of the device and all it needed was a timing mechanism attached to the detonator to be set.

Sayyid eyed the bomb and the detonator. He could play it safe and set it now or take a chance and wait. What where the odds of the infidels blasting their way through the secure doors and taking control of the facility? He simply wasn't sure.

There was time. If they appeared to be making headway, he could always set the timer. But he wasn't a Shaheed and had no desire to become one

Suddenly his world was rocked by a monstrous explosion and he fell to the ground. He looked up in horror as the nuclear device rolled back and forth on its base and then the struts collapsed with the bomb dropping several feet to the floor of the lab.

Sayyid's entire body tensed. He looked around and could see the technicians staring, looks of abject horror on their faces. He knew that it would only be seconds before the infidels came through the hole in the blast door that they somehow managed to mangle off its hinges.

He sprang to his feet and sprinted across the room to the bomb. The panel to the detonator was on the bottom of the device and he put all of his weight into attempting to roll it over. He could feel the strain as he pushed, but it didn't budge.

Sayyid called to the technicians, milling about in fear and confusion, to come over and help him. They stood, looking is disbelief, almost frozen to the ground. He could hear the firing of automatic weapons and knew that only seconds remained.

The Presumptive Leader of the Arab World let out a blood curdling scream, demanding that the technicians get over and assist him. Two of the men snapped out of their trance-like state and ran to his side.

They attached a chain to a hoist loop on what was now the top of the device and hooked it into a pulley system. One of the men pushed a button and, slowly, the bomb began to roll over.

Sayyid stood with his right arm raised and when the panel was on the side of the device, he closed his fist in signal to stop. The bomb kept turning and Sayyid loosed a string of obscenities that compared the man's mother to a camel that had sex with every goat in the oasis. The startled technician pushed the button again and the device stopped with the panel just above eye level.

Sayyid grabbed a small stool and a battery operated screw driver and climbed to reach the panel. The screws that had just been inserted earlier that day and had never been intended to be removed, were difficult, their heads stripped.

He stood in an awkward position because of the height of the panel, but had no time to readjust. Placing the screw driver in the head of one of the fasteners, he put his entire body weight against the tool and pushed as he pulled the trigger. One screw came loose. Then a second.

There were eight screws holding the cover in place, one in each corner and one in the middle of each side of the panel. Sayyid worked feverishly to loosen one side and the two adjacent side screws. He cursed the technicians who had sloppily placed them and then forced the screws, stripping the heads.

Slowly they began to loosen until he had removed five of the screws but he was unable to budge the remaining three. The more he tried, the more stripped the heads became until it was impossible to place the head of the screwdriver into the crossed slots.

He reached for a pry bar and began to force the end of the plate upwards, bending it in the middle. It would be tight, but if he could raise it far enough, he could get his hands into the opening and set the detonator.

The steel was tough and didn't give in easily, but he persisted and slowly the edge began to rise. His position was awkward and that added to the difficulty, but he pushed the pry bar with all that he could muster. Sayyid stopped and placed his hand in the opening. It was tight, just a bit too tight. He'd have to keep trying.

The gunshots were getting ever closer and the lab guards had taken positions behind steel tables and equipment scattered about the room. He could hear slugs pinging off the steel and ricocheting around the room.

"These damn camel screwing pieces of desert shit had better hold off the infidels," he thought.

Sayyid saw two of the guards fall to gunshots. He knew the infidels would not be able to use grenades to dislodge them because of the danger of setting off the nuclear device. How the hell did they learn of this laboratory and what was being done here? He cursed to the hundredth generation the family of whoever had provided the intelligence to these dogs.

Even though he knew that this was his final act, the human reaction to avoid pain was still strong and as he forced his fingers into the device, the sharp edges of the panel cut his hand. Sayyid withdrew bloody fingers and pried the panel once again. It was almost high enough. But not quite.

He forced the pry bar into the opening and pushed with everything he had. It began to move, a fraction of an inch at a time; slowly, ever so slowly until he had another inch of height.

Sayyid thrust his hand into the opening and felt his fingers touch the key pad of the detonator's timer. He could just see the numbers on the pad and he let his fingers push them. He had to hurry. The ricochets' were coming in greater numbers and he knew the wolves were at the gates.

Dan saw Chan Wise hit the dirt with bullets spraying all around him. The desert sand was being kicked up in scores of spurts as the Revolutionary Guard peppered the area, firing wildly. Then they began to fall.

The Barretts were taking a devastating toll on the Guards who had moved out of any cover in a headlong rush to overrun the invaders. They couldn't see where the shots were coming from, but they could see one after another of their fellow revolutionaries lifted in the air and then slammed back into the ground.

The Revolutionary Guard, the elite of the Iranian fighting forces, dropped their guns and ran for the cover of the desert darkness. The snipers picked them off one at a time.

Dan motioned to the unit to move out and enter the facility. He leapfrogged over the bodies on the ground before him, noticing that so far none of his force aside from Herzog had been hit.

He grabbed the toggle unit from the man's stiff fingers and motioned for everyone to hit the dirt. Then he pushed the switch and the entry doors buckled inward and shattered. The opening was wide enough to drive a truck through and the task force raced into the building.

The briefing they had received was a boon in familiarizing them with the layout and they knew exactly where to head. The first squad moved to the elevators and sent them down empty, listening to hear if any shots were fired when the doors opened. They then brought the cars back to the surface and filled it to capacity before dropping down again.

A second squad moved to the internal staircase and raced down, guns at the ready as they took the steps three at a time. One slip, one fall and they would pile up on each other.

Dan was with the second squad, Hesh and Chan with the elevator crew.

SAS Col. Sir Brian Kenworthy split his force, sending half to cover the entrance to the facility in the event any of the Revolutionary Guards made it through and the second half securing the teams heading for the subterranean lab.

Dan's unit made it to the lower level while the elevator was still making its slow progress down. They pulled the door to the staircase open and, alternating entry to clear the corridor, moved in.

"Remember, whatever you do, we're after a nuclear device. Be very careful about what you shoot at and under no circumstances are there to be any grenades thrown. I'd like all of us to get out of here.

He looked to the far end of the corridor where the elevator doors were situated and saw the muzzle of a gun peek around the corner. Dan waited until the rest of the weapon and the man holding it, rounded the corner and then fired a short burst.

The man straightened up and his body slammed into the wall behind him, then leaving a bloody line on the wall, slumped to the floor.

Dan could hear the pounding sound of boots running…in the opposite direction.

He swung around and raised his gun, an involuntary motion, as the elevator door opened and Hesh and Wise poured out into the corridor. Dan pulled a diagram from his breast pocket and motioned to the far end of the corridor and a steel blast door.

"That's where Aboud said the device would be assembled. He knew that they couldn't simply blow the door because of what was on the other side.

The auxiliary demo man pulled a pack from his bag of goodies and examined the door. He looked toward Dan who had a questioning look on his face.

"I can do this. We'll have to use an alternate method, but I figured that before we got here."

"OK, what do you want us to do?"

"General, get your men around the bend in the corridor and after the door is blown, come in fast. Make sure the men have sound suppressors in their ears."

Dan motioned to Hesh and Chan Wise to move to safety and take their men with them. He stayed with the demo man to provide cover and watched as the man placed a string of white detonation cord around the entire border of the blast door. He then motioned for Dan to get around the bend and followed him.

The man had dragged a detonator cord with him and connected it to a hand crank. The task force advance unit could hear a hissing sound and a sudden bright flash, but no loud explosion.

Dan and his demo moved back around the corner and he could see what appeared to be a melted line all the way around the steel door.

"What now? Do we try to batter this in?"

"No sir. That was just a preliminary. The door is steel reinforced. I could have blown it but we don't want that nuclear device going off accidentally. That melted part way through the steel. I'll place charges around three of the edges, the top and both sides, and will set them off. That should blow the door in with the bottom acting as a hinge so it doesn't go across the interior of the room. The first charge should have loosened it enough for this to work. If it doesn't, we'll have to take a chance and blow the thing off its hinges."

He placed charges along the edges of the door, just inside the burn channel and then inserted a detonator into each one. He connected a common cord to all charges and ran it back around the bend in the corridor.

"Get as far back as possible, cover your ears or you'll loose you eardrums. And close your eyes until after the blast. The light can temporarily blind you. It's also best if you go prone on the floor; this way you'll have less area of resistance to the blast wave that's going to rip through here."

The team members lay flat out on the corridor floor, hands outstretched in front of them with a tight grip on their weapons, ready for instant movement after the blast.

The demolition expert twisted the hand crank and for a split second there was absolute quiet. Then a deafening sound ripped through the corridor followed by a hurricane wind. Even through their closed eyelids they could see the sun bright flash as the charges detonated.

They never heard the clang as the steel door slammed into the concrete floor. It took them a second, even with their trained reflexes, to gather themselves and race for the opening where the door had been.

Dan flattened out against one side of the wall adjacent to the opening and Hesh and Chan on the other. Their team was lined up down the corridor.

Hesh was first through the opening and bounced back as a slug tore through the fleshy part of his left arm. He waved Dan off, stood and began firing into the room. Dan fired from the other side of the door creating a withering cross fire that sprayed bullets into the lab.

Dan could hear the bullets ricocheting off the lab walls and he hoped that a stray slug didn't set off the wrong thing. They had to push inside and he motioned to Hesh, Chan Wise and the team to make a quick entry.

Dan dove through the door, across the front and landed on the right hand side. He was followed by Hesh who took a dive to the left. Chan Wise and the team each followed in an alternating pattern.

He could see the device lying on the floor in the midst of a crumpled platform and a man on a ladder working on its side. Dan was concerned about firing at the man because a miss could penetrate the device. A shot to the man could go through him and into the bomb.

Dan slipped the selector switch on his gun to a semi-automatic mode so that he could get off only one round at a time; a lot safer that a spray of automatic fire.

He leaned against the leg of a steel table that had overturned and balanced his left elbow on his knee, pulling the stock of the gun into his right shoulder. Steadying the gun, he peered through the open metal sight atop the weapon and aimed it at the middle of the back of the man's head and slowly pressed the trigger.

The recoil was minimal and the slug tore through Sayyid's skull, bringing him instant status as a Shaheed. He bounced forward into the device and then fell backward, his hand stuck in the opening under the panel he had worked so hard to pry open. His body hung like a rag doll on the side of the bomb, twitching for a moment and then remained totally still.

There were a few more shots and the remainder of the Republican Guard in the laboratory joined Sayyid in Paradise.

Dan turned to Hesh and Chan:

"I hope there are enough virgins in Paradise to go around."

"I would assume there are a hell of a lot more there than on this earth," Wise smirked.

Hesh was already climbing the ladder and prying Sayyid's hand loose from under the panel. The corpse hit the ground with a dull thud.

"We have a problem," he said, his face pale.

"What?" Dan demanded.

"The device has been primed and is in countdown mode. And there isn't much time."

Hesh started to move down the ladder when a shot rang out and he clutched his chest. He looked down and saw a wet blotch beginning to spread across his black BDU. The black uniform didn't show red, but the pool of blood that leaked onto the floor did.

Hesh doubled over and tumbled down the ladder, falling in a heap alongside Sayyid.

Dan was at his side in two steps, pulling a gauze pad from his backpack and pressing it onto the wound.

One of the Green Berets whirled at the sound of the shot and put three slugs into the head and chest of the wounded Guard who had fired. He had been lying on the floor without moving and the team hadn't noticed that he was still breathing. With only a slight movement he managed to bring his gun up and get off the one shot that took Hesh down.

Looking at the placement of the wound and the profuse bleeding, Dan knew immediately that it was not good.

Hesh knew it as well.

Dan's radio suddenly buzzed and he placed it to his ear.

"General, the spotters have reported that a contingent of troops from the barracks on the other side of Arak is on its way to this site. It's a fairly large movement and there appears to be armor as well. I don't know if we'll be able to hold them off."

"OK guys, we've got to get the hell out of here. Let's take this bomb out of commission."

Hesh pushed himself up on an elbow and looked at Dan.

"Hey Boss, I'm not going anywhere," he wheezed.

What are you talking about?"

"Come on, we both know that this hole in my chest isn't giving me much time. Just get out of here and let me cover your ass." His voice was weak and strained.

"We don't leave anyone behind."

"Dan, you're not leaving me behind. I'm not going to be here for long and neither is this place. I'm going to see Shoshanna and that's what I want. Now please! Get the hell out of here before all of you disintegrate."

"I can't..."

"You can't do anything else. There's more to it as well. Ambassador Seong...I'm the one who killed him. I had no idea he was an asset and thought he was involved in putting this bomb action together. Dan, do it for me. Just get the men and go. Please. Put me in an upright position and give me my gun, then leave."

Dan looked at Chan Wise, his eyes moist.

"Dan, he's never going to make it. He's only got a little time left. I know how hard this sounds, but let him go the way he wants."

Dan Halevi leaned over and placed his hands under Hesh's arms, pulling him into a sitting position against the bomb. He handed him an Uzi and several long clips of ammunition.

Hesh lifted his lips to Dan and whispered in his ear.

Dan leaned over and kissed his friend on the forehead, lingering for a long second before standing up and walking rapidly to the blown door.

Tears trickled down Dan's checks and he waved Chan Wise off as the American officer started to say something to him. They raced up the stairs and out the front of the building. The dune buggies were revved and waiting for them.

Within minutes they were headed, full tilt, into the desert and the rendezvous point for the incoming Hercules.

While they were inside the building a team of the American Special Forces had ringed the location with explosives and as the racing Republican Guard units came tearing into the compound, they tripped wires, setting off explosions that ripped through their vehicles sending many more of them for a visit with the virgins.

Miles into the desert the dune buggies came to a stop at a plateau and the men moved in parallel lines to form a landing strip for the giant aircraft. They placed the flares in the ground and then mounted the buggies, waiting for the landing.

The first Hercules swooped in and landed, dragging its loading ramp in the sand. The first contingent drove the buggies into the still moving transport, jumped off and began to fasten them to the flooring as the plane increased speed, closed the ramp and took off into the burgeoning morning light.

The second Hercules swept up the remainder of the task force and followed its leader into the horizon. No trace that they had ever been there was left to be discovered. The raiders had come and gone, leaving nothing but small ripples in the desert sand.

Hesh gathered all his strength and raised himself to his feet. The explosive sounds of the battle that had raged in the room were gone and the quiet was almost deafening. Hand over hand he dragged himself to the top of the ladder and looked into the opening beneath the bloody panel. He could see the red LED numbers ticking down, but they had a long way to go.

He wasn't an expert, but as part of his cross-training he had opted for a course in bomb disposal and he recognized the type of detonator in the bomb.

As he examined the device, he could hear voices speaking in Farsi and boots pounding down the steps. He reached in to the opening, gripping two raw wires he had just cut and held them apart in his fingers.

Hesh smiled as the first of the Iranian reinforcements stormed into the room, not knowing what to expect. They looked around and took in the carnage of their comrades lying all over the floor in spreading pools of blood. They had seen the bodies on the desert floor and were ready for trouble.

His black BDUs set him apart from them and they raised their rifles, aiming at Hesh.

"On behalf of the State of Israel and Jews and men of good will around the world," he said in Farsi, "I would like to welcome you to the Gates of Paradise and the virgins that wait within."

The soldiers stopped, a look of curiosity crossing their faces, and then took aim at this odd creature standing in front of them. As they pulled the slack from the triggers, Hesh left his finger slip from between the raw wires and felt a slight tingle as electricity arced between the raw ends.

Hesh smiled and thoughts of Shoshanna brought him peace. He didn't need seventy two virgins. All he needed was his wife and he would soon be with her again.

The two Hercules had beaten a hasty retreat, again flying at very low altitude to avoid the radar. It would be only a short time before they would intersect with the fighter escort that was heading to meet them.

The morning sun was climbing in the east behind them as they raced toward the border with Iraq when suddenly bright daylight flooded the cockpit of the aircraft. They never heard the sound and didn't feel the fury of the shock waves that flowed out from Arak. They did see the huge mushroom shaped cloud growing ever larger behind them.

Everything around Arak ceased to exist at that moment. The desert sand fused into a sheet of glass; debris rained from the sky, the bright light faded away and the hurricane wind died down.

Then there was nothing but silence.

Dan hung his head and said nothing. The team knew better than to speak to him and he was left to his thoughts.

President Mahmoud Ahmadinejad held a dispatch in his hand from the American Secretary of State. On his desk were also dispatches from the British Prime Minister, the French President as well as the President of Russia and they all basically said the same thing.

"Your protestations of not seeking atomic weapons have been proven false with the disastrous nuclear accident in the city of Arak. It is unfortunate that so many of your citizens died in the explosion and that many others will die in the coming years from nuclear fallout.

"Be aware that the world community will not tolerate nuclear weapons in the hands of the Iranian government. You will accept, unconditionally, the placement of a United Nations monitor to work with the International Atomic Energy Commission. Should any further evidence be found of nuclear facilities or components in Iran, a multi-national force will occupy the country and take all necessary steps to rid it of such weapons. If this should come to pass, the multi-national force will arrest you and other government leaders and you will be placed on trial in The Hague as war criminals."

Ahmadinejad turned to his friend and confidant:

"How did this happen? The plans with North Korea had been so carefully put in place and then everything we have worked for fell apart. What shall we do Aboud?"

"I don't think there is much we can do except accept those demands," Aboud said and walked from the presidential office.

Dan lay on the couch, his head in Amanda's lap.

"I've made flight arrangements for us to The States. We're going to take a real vacation this time. We have a stopover in London for a couple of days and then into New York to see the family. Then, I have a surprise for you. We'll fly on to Miami and take the Celebrity Eclipse for a nice, slow cruise through the Caribbean. I blew the budget and booked a suite for us."

Dan's face moved from a relaxed smile to one of pensiveness.

"I think Hesh was happier than I've seen him since his wedding day. He knew what he was going to do and there was no way to stop him. I have a hole in my heart that's going to take a long time to heal."

"Dan, it was what he wanted and now he's at peace. Before we leave for the cruise, why don't we take a few days and go to the beach at Eilat and have a drink their in their memories. I think they'd like that."

She leaned over and kissed him on the mouth. He was sound asleep.

"Mr. Secretary General, I am pleased to present my credentials to you as the representative of the government of the Hashemite Kingdom of Jordan. It will be my pleasure to serve on the panel assigned to ensure that there will be no more nuclear threats from Iran. This is an essential step to achieving peace for our children in this turbulent world."

The Secretary General stood and extended his hand to the tall man, dressed in a suit, but wearing the traditional Arab kaffiya. His guest grasped the extended hand and smiled.

He then turned, heading for the door, his pronounced limp requiring a slow step. Sayyid Sayyid Musaf el Rashid Salim Hassan carried with him the portfolio presented by the Secretary General detailing the nuclear status of each nation in the world and the location of the facilities where weapons grade material was being produced. He smiled as he passed through the door.

Secretary of State Joseph McCrane sat back in his car as his driver identified himself to the uniformed Secret Service guard at the west gate of the White House. The guard stepped back into his blockhouse, punched a computer and then motioned for the driver to proceed.

The car crept up the circular driveway to the entrance of the Executive Mansion. Secretary McCrane's chauffeur jumped from the front seat and ran to the right side of the vehicle to hold the door open. The Marine at the white doors snapped to attention and smartly saluted.

McCrane was ushered immediately to the Oval Officer where the president and a small group of advisors waited. He extended his hand to the former Green Beret and clasped his shoulder.

"Joe," the President began in a low and serious voice, "I have been in contact with the Prime Ministers of both Israel and Great Britain after the Arak incident. There is no doubt in our collective minds that we have to be prepared should any such incident rise again. The multi-national unit of Special Forces and intelligence agencies has convinced us that there is a continuing need for such cooperation.

"We have decided to establish a quick response team consisting of Special Forces, the CIA, Mossad, Syaret Matkal, MI-6 and SAS working together on a regular basis to guard against this ever happening again. I am instructing the CIA that Supervisory Agent Matthew Morton will be our permanent representative and that Col. Chantland Wise will head our military contingent. The British will be represented by Kyle Norman and Col. Sir Brian Kenworthy of the SAS. The Israelis will be represented by Gen. Dan Halevi, whom I understand you know quite well. Those governments will designate members of the SAS and Sayaret Matkal to work with our Green Berets.

"As a Ghost Force their existence will never be made public and they will be able to move around the world as necessary using means that conventional forces, diplomats and governments could never participate in. The Ghost Force will be the first line of defense for democracy.

"I hope they are never needed, but they will always be there in the event they are. Please pass our commendations for a good job to all those involved. It's unfortunate that they cannot be commended publicly"

Secretary of State McCrane, his military demeanor always there, stiffened, saluted the President, shook hands with the others in the Oval Office, executed a smart "about face" and walked from the room, a tight smile creeping across his face.

With a weapon such as the Ghost Force, action could now be taken against terrorists without the glare of public knowledge. This would be more effective than several divisions of combat troops. A Ghost Force, moving with stealth and swiftness to take down those who would harm his country.

"I like it," McCrane smiled and returned the salute of the Marine guard as he exited the White House. It was a warm, clear and sunny day. It was a great day.

If you enjoyed reading "Spyder Hole," we are sure you'll want to look for Bob Nesoff's next Ghost Force novel, "Shaheed." Here's a sample of what to expect:

SHAHEED

BY BOB NESOFF

I

Samir shifted in his seat, trying to move his leaden arm from around the shoulders of his beautiful Arub. The flight from Paris was smooth but ever so long and he had his arm over her shoulders as she slept for more than an hour.

He knew of her beauty, something other men could not see behind the black hooded hijab she wore. The ankle-length covering gave only a hint of the shape beneath it; just enough to tease any men who might covet her. The scarf attached to the hood covered her face from her nose to her neck; appropriate dress for a devout woman, unlike the Western whores with their clingy blouses and short skirts that advertised what they had to offer.

Samir glanced lovingly over her to the window seat where seven-year-old Aludra sat looking out the small window at the little puffs of clouds and the passing landscape 38,000 feet below. She was transfixed by the wonder of it all and excited to be returning to Riyad and the friends she had not seen for so many months.

Samir Khoury had traveled with his family to Paris when his job posting of Deputy Chief of Mission for the Saudi Arabian government called for his expertise in dealing with the French

Paris Orly Airport was always busy and was a confluence of cultures with especially heavy traffic from the mid-East. Herds of passengers wearing robes, kaffiya scarf head coverings for men and hijabs for women tracked through the terminal, shops and lines to the boarding area.

The French would never entertain the thought of asking a Muslim woman to submit to a thorough search and when presented with official diplomatic credentials, gave proper deference, passing the bearer through the normal lines.

Samir knew all this and although he was a loyal subject of his country and king, he had been drawn in by a higher calling.

But his position in the diplomatic corps demanded that he remain in the background, not revealing his true emotions and most certainly not the people he was devoted to.

Kinship to King Abdullah would not save him from the headsman's sword if his secret life ever became known. Samir was cousin to Abdullah, the Keeper of the two Holy Mosques; Masjid al Haran in Mecca and Masjid al-Nabawi in Medina.

Belonging to the Saud family in Saudi Arabia was much like being a Mormon in Utah. If you need a job, there is always a place for you.

Samir reached over Arub's shoulders and scratched the covered head of Aludra. That he loved her was never questioned by anyone. He doted on the beautiful young girl and even in the midst of his official duties he never hesitated to bounce her on his lap should she wander into his office.

Aludra looked at Samir with a twinkle in her eyes and he pursed his lips in a kiss to her. She placed her fingers on her lips and blew a return kiss to Samir as she clutched her stuffed teddy bear that he had given her while she was still in a crib.

Aludra never moved without the "stuffie" and always had it either clutched in her hands or protected under her arm. It was her talisman, her good luck charm.

Samir extended his hand and motioned for her to give him the fuzzy toy. He was the only person she would trust with her teddy and she placed it in his hands.

For a moment Samir toyed with the animal, holding it by its arms and making it dance in the air. Aludra watched with amusement as her father entertained her.

As Samir watched and enjoyed the look of joy on the face of his little angel, his finger slipped beneath the seam on the back of the toy and probed through the stuffing inside the little animal. He felt something hard and then, gripping it in his fingers, moved until he found a button.

For a long second Samir hesitated. He leaned over and kissed Arub on the forehead and then rubbed Aludra's chin, blowing her another kiss. Then he pushed the button.

Thirty-eight thousand feet below, cutting through the waters of the Mediterranean Sea, the container vessel Asoku Maru, was running low in the water, shipping containers piled high on her deck.

The helmsman leisurely held the joy stick with one finger as he sat back in the command chair and relaxed.

The seas were calm; no clouds in the sky and the winds were a minimal four knots. The sun streaming in through the windshield warmed him and put him into a state of near hypnosis. It was a bit of a struggle to stay awake, but he knew that this far into the Mediterranean shipping lanes there were no other ships to be reckoned with. This would be an easy day.

He almost didn't see the bright flash from high in the sky in the distance ahead of his ship. Shadows suddenly played across the deck elongating the shapes of the cargo boxes piled five high and lashed to davits.

The helmsman watched in curiosity as the bright ball of flame erupted in the sky, the visual image reaching him long before the sound of the explosion vibrated through the bridge, gently rocking his ship and causing a ripple across the calm ocean.

From an altitude of 38,000 feet it would take at least ten minutes for debris to reach the surface of the water as it floated down, almost like dark confetti on New Year's Eve. And along with pieces of aluminum, luggage and jet fuel came much of what remained of the human cargo.

Isoroku saw pieces of debris begin splashing in the water in front and to the sides of his ship, small pieces raining onto the deck. He jumped to his feet and pressed his face toward the window shielding him from the elements, watching in amazed awe as bits and pieces of what seconds before had been a 747 jumbo jet crashed loudly onto the deck and drew geysers of water into the air.

Then, without warning, it came through the glass, slamming him in the face and breaking his neck. Isoroku fell to the deck of the bridge, gasping his last breath.

The First Mate had been on his way to the bridge when the explosion rocked the sky. He looked up and saw the huge aircraft disintegrate into a million pieces and begin to float down to the sea and his ship. He ran to the bridge and kicked the hatch open. Isoroku lay on the floor in a pool of blood. On his chest was the body of a little girl in a hijab, most of her head blown away.